PRINTHOUSE BOOKS PRESENTS:

(Paperbacks available at www.PrintHouseBooks.com)

To: YARD.
Thank for your support
God Bless
ANT BANK$
3-23-12

MADE: Sex, Drugs and Murder, The Recipe for Success.

FICTION, Inspired by True Events.......

An Organized Crime Novel.

ANTWAN "ANT" BANK$

PrintHouse Books, Atlanta, GA.

www.PrintHouseBooks.com

VIP INK Publishing Group, Incorporated

Cover art, designed by SK7

eBook. ISBN- 978-0-615-59125-4   Paperback. ISBN – 978-0-615-59946-5

Library of Congress Cataloging-in-Publication Data

ANTWAN "ANT" BANK$

MADE: Sex, Drugs and Murder, The Recipe for Success / ANTWAN "ANT" BANK$

1. Organized Crime Novel. 2. Crime Novel. 3. Las Vegas

4. Romance Novel 5. Crime Thriller 6.ANTWAN "ANT" BANK$

Printed in the United States of America

Dear Reader,

The journey you are about to embark on is about Andy Cooper; a military vet, turned hustler, turned Gangster, turned Crime Boss. His marriage is on the rocks; fresh out of the military, AC finds himself broke and lost with a Wife and three kids to feed. Trapped in Sin City and working any job he can get from day to day, to make ends meet. Hating the state of mind he's in right now, a really fucked up way to be! Gone are the days when Uncle Sam paid for housing, day care and groceries. Now, all own his own again, with no idea of where life is going to take him. One thing for sure, Andy "AC" Cooper no longer wanted to wear that Army uniform another day. Coop loved every minute of it and would not trade it for the world but the next chapter of his life was about to start. It just so happen that he landed in Las Vegas, one of the hardest cities to make it in, it is truly the land of the Hustler. What the outsiders don't know is that beneath the bright neon lights, the delicious buffets and luxurious casino's, lays a whole different world that would eventually suck him in.

We hope you enjoy the first novel by PrintHouse Books, Author; ANT BANK$. This is the first of many titles from the new versatile, innovative, prolific writer. So get comfortable, grab a cup of Joe, wine, cigarette, cigar, cognac, or whatever your heart desires and get lost, in this fresh new, invigorating tale of organized crime. The first of many, to come from PrintHouse Books, Atlanta, GA.

Dedicated to The Hustlers, Pimps and Gangsters. Keep it M.O.B.

ANT BANK$

MADE: Sex, Drugs and Murder, The Recipe for Success.

VIP INK Publishing Group, Incorporated.

Atlanta, GA.

Table of Contents.

Chapter 1, The Day his life Changed.

It's 1996 and the desert is hot, he finds himself single and staying at a condo in the center of town. Gina, his wife; parted ways after a long drawn out family fight over money, kids, and unemployment. Well that's another story all in itself, so let's get to this one. Down on his luck, in the gutter, constantly searching the Las Vegas Journal for any job that was available. One of the most adventurous ones was in door to door sales or multi-level marketing shall I say. AC attended this small seminar of about 25 people, a day he will never forget. This white kid; Matt, was giving a seminar and mentioned that he's looking for leaders, go-getters, you know, only motivated people. He went on to give this story of how he can make them independent, own their own business and make lots of money. Player was dressed in the finest attire, Italian leather shoes, Brooks Brothers Suit, crisp white shirt, nice tie and a wine face Rolex.

Looking at first impression, one could assume that he makes decent money, just from the way he's dressed and his overwhelming confidence. Then he says, today I'm gonna throw all the shit on the wall and whatever sticks is what I'm going to keep. OK, now you really have my attention, I'm ready to get to it! AC says to himself. Matt then proceeds to pull out these bottles of perfume. This is our merchandise, it cost $32.50 a bottle, the owner of the company is going to front you the merchandise and you pay for it after you sell it. At that moment the shit started falling off the wall, people were saying screw this, it's a scam and all kinds of negative comments. Coop on the other hand wanted to see where this would lead, after all, time was something he had plenty of, so he waited to see what was next. OK, now that all of the bullshit has cleared the room, let's get to business. Tonight, I want you to go home, tell your family, friends and relatives about this hot new product you are selling; they are renditions of all the popular fragrances. Remember the cost is 32.50 but all you have to bring me is $25.00 per bottle. You can keep everything above that or just sell it to them for $25.00 and just bring us the money, totally up to you.

The next day came, a few people had sold a good number of bottles, AC sold maybe 2 at $32.50, attempting to make some kind of profit. But what most interests him was the fact that Matt got $25.00 a bottle, it was 15 people in the room and they all started with 10 bottles a piece. Andy knew he had to get where Matt was, he wanted his spot! Sitting with a blank stare, he imagines doing this every week with new people! Money, money, money! So needless to say, he stuck to Matthews's ass like glue; Coop learned everything about him and the business. In a month and a half, he had his own corporate office, recruiting new people and making his own money. By this time, all he had to turn in was $12.50 a bottle, anything between 12.50 and 32.50 was all profit, how sweet it was.

They sold so much perfume in Las Vegas, the corporate office had repeat customers ordering by the case and the money was flowing in $1,000.00 to $2,000.00 a day, then like anything, it came to an end. The police got to know the staff by first name and told them to stop harassing people with perfume, I mean every time one of the staff tried to sell something they would stop them. Hell, they even barred the entire crew from the strip! So, there he was, stuck with an office that could no longer produce. Saying to himself after realizing the obvious. Damn, how am I going to tell Monica that she can no longer be my secretary! Just then, she walked in, he sat on the desk and asked her to come in his office. Hey Monica, could you come here a minute, we need to talk. OK, I'm coming. She walks in. We really took a big hit this quarter with very low sales and staff leaving. It doesn't look good baby, I'm afraid I have to leave all this behind and start all over. What do you mean by that AC? We have to close baby, we are all out of money and we can't move any product. Aww man, that's some bullshit! So, I want be seeing you again? Well not for a while baby, come here and let me kiss those juicy lips. She moved closer to him and leaned her forehead against his, then made their lips touch. Muah. Dang, my dick just got hard, kiss me again, um, I love those lips.

Yeah I know you do daddy. She reached down, unzipped his pants, pulled out his hard penis and proceeded to kiss it. Monica, your juicy lips feel so good on my dick, nice and warm with every stroke. Knowing that this would probably be the last time seeing Monica, he made her get on the desk and open her legs so he could lick that sweet pussy of hers, one last time. She was wearing a white summer linen dress that seem to bounce across her ass when she walked, whenever she wore it, she knew it turned him on. Monica leaned back against the desk, lifted up her dress, removed her panties, then laid back with her legs opened and placed a foot on each of AC's shoulders. Like a cat cleaning its coat, he begins licking the inside of her pussy and rubbing his tongue over that clit, it didn't take long for her erotic juices to start flowing.

Ohhh baby! Damn, I hope this isn't the last time we fuck. He stops, looks up at her and says. No, it want be baby, I just have to close this damn office and go get my hustle on. I'm sure your husband can make you happy until we hook back up. She looks at him with a long sad stare and her eyes begin to tear up. Hey, stop it; don't start crying, look, here's $2,000.00 to get you through the next week or so. But Daddy, I don't wanna leave you, Eric's a lame! He can't handle me like you can. I know baby, but it's that time, come here. He pulls her up off the desk and starts kissing her while his hands caress her bottom, massaging her butt in a slow circular motion as he pulled her closer to him. The friction between the two had given him another erection; slowly, he lifted up her dress and turned her ass around towards him. With his right hand, he took a condom from his back pocket, opened it with his mouth and placed it on his hard dick; grabbed her butt cheeks, spread them apart and stuck his 8-inch cock in her wet pussy. Ummmm. Oh daddy! Oh daddy! Dammit daddy! Hey baby, bite on the chair or something; you know there's people across the hall! Ummm. Fuck it daddy! Fuck it! What are they gonna do, put us out? Fuck it!

Ummmm-Ummmm. I'm going to miss this dick! He thrust forward, she push backward, then he thrust forward, she pushed backward, back and forth they went for the next 20 minutes until one of them surrendered. Oh shit! Oh shit! OHHHHH SHIT!!!! I'm cumming baby, oh-oh-oh, yes daddy! Ummmm. She stops and leans over the desk, its 6pm baby, the landlord should be here any minute, we have to go, put on your panties so we can lock up, hand me my belt off the desk. Damn, I'm gonna miss you MO. In a rush, he pulls up his pants and puts his belt back on. Come here baby; promise me you will be safe, you know how to reach me if you need me, right baby. She turns around, sits on the desk and begins to put on her panties. Wow, really, it's like that! So that's it motherfucker! One last screw and send me on my way huh! Look, I gave you some paper to hold you over for a week or so. But that's all I can do for now, I got to get back on my grind, be easy and stop trippin. You know I got love for you, I will find you when I get my shit together. Alright, I hear you nigga! She pulls her panties all the way up, jumps off the desk, hugs him and walks out of the office. Later MO, you know I want forget you, with that fat juicy ass! Oh, tell your husband I said what's up too! Ahhh, fuck you nigga, that shit aint funny! Your black ass better call me when you get shit poppin too! Come on, you know I got you! Yeah, umm, hmm! Bye AC! She exits into the hall way.

Chapter 2, The Epiphany.

The night is young and AC decides to scroll down Vegas Blvd, passing the casinos and wanting to be in the position of the guy sitting at the black jack table that was playing $5,000.00 a hand. His mind scrambled on ways to achieve that financial success; after all, he was walking in the city that started as a dream of mobster Benny Seagall, a paradise in the desert. But while walking down the sidewalk, he kept being bothered by these annoying Mexicans; they were relentlessly forcing these Adult booklets on everyone. Sex, Sex, and Sex! Beautiful Asian, Latin, Caucasian and African woman laced the covers of these booklets, with prices and direct phone numbers to call for a date. Coop was zoned in on the whole make up of this industry and how legal it was to promote here in Las Vegas. He then wondered how one could get behind the scenes and be the big dog collecting the money. The interest didn't lie in the desire to order sex or to even be a pimp, the shit he was looking at, was bigger than that. AC wanted to know the ins and outs, the infrastructure of the business. How the escort service worked, who got what cut and how did they hire the girls. Intrigued by the idea of the sex industry, he walked into Babes, a Topless club on the corner, a block from his office on the Strip and Charleston. He started to befriend some of the dancers by using the people skills learned during his days of door to door selling. AC asked the girls about the Strip and Escort industry, if they worked as escorts also, if so, what was it like and how much did they make?

One of the dancers went by Yum-Yum; she mentioned trying it for a while but preferred dancing and went on to say escorting was too risky, that it was illegal in the City of Las Vegas but legal in the county. So vice was always locking up girls and shutting down agencies in the city. The money was OK if you wanted to take that chance, but the agency usually got 30%-40% of what you made, in the clubs you pay a house fee and a small percentage on your VIP Dances, plus you can work a shift 5 days a week in a safe environment. What Yum-Yum expressed helped a little, but he wanted to take it a little bit further. Interested to know if the girls in these booklets were real or just models, he got a room at a nearby casino and called to get a date. Coop ordered a sexy 5'9" Latino, named Carmen, in the picture her hair was sandy blonde, shoulder length with brown eyes, juicy lips and 38-D breast; ones dick would get hard, just by looking at her. AC was so excited, if she showed up at the door right now; he would probably cum before she could get in and sit down. When he called the number, a raspy voice answered the phone. Hello, Angels Escorts, how can I help you? I would like to book a date with Carmen. OK Sir, where are you staying? Are you visiting and what's your name? He replied. I'm staying at the Casino, on the corner of Vegas Blvd. and Charleston, yes I am visiting, my name is Cooper and I'm in room 564. OK sir, it will be $500, she will be there in 45 minutes, thanks for choosing Angel's and enjoy your date.

Coops forehead was sweating like someone had just dashed his face with a bucket of water; his heart was beating so fast, he could feel it hitting his chest. He couldn't sit down and found himself pacing the room, back and forth from the window to the door, talking out loud. What will my mom and grandma think of me now? I just ordered a prostitute! He had to calm down or he would definitely scare Carmen when she got there. Pouring a drink while sitting on the couch, he decided to watch some TV to pass the time. Knock-Knock. Oh shit! I have to get it together, she's here, and I can't wait to see how she looks. He walked towards the door and glanced through the peep whole. What the Fuck! I know this is not Carmen, this Bitch is a crack head, if I ever seen one, maybe it's a mistake. So he asked. Yes, who is it? This is Carmen, your date. Bullshit! You don't look anything like that picture, I changed my mind, you can take your ass home! What! You owe me! I don't owe you shit! Get the hell on before I call hotel security, you crack head Bitch! The phone starts to ring. Ring-Ring-Ring. Hello! What's the problem Sir? You sent me a crack head! That's the problem! Well, I'm sorry you are not happy but there's a $150.00 agency fee that you have to pay for booking the girl. You can take that fee and shove it up your ass, with that girl! CLICK!

Sitting on the bed with his hands on his knees and shaking his head, he says to himself. This is too much; maybe I should go downstairs and play some cards or something. I really want to know more about this industry, it's getting late and that Carmen incident was unforgettable to say the least. First thing tomorrow I'm going through the classifieds to see if there's any jobs available in the Strip clubs, maybe I can be a bouncer or something, that would really put me on the inside of the sex business. He begin to really focus his energy on getting into the industry, it bothered him so much he couldn't sleep because it was on his mind so heavy. Where is that room key? I'm going to get some of that New York pizza and a cold beer from Louigi's. He could feel his stomach rumble while walking to the pizza parlor. Damn, I'm hungry! As he approaches the pizza parlor, the smell of fresh cheese and dough filled the air. Ahhhh, smells so good. Hello Sir, how can I help you? 2 slices of Italian sausage please and a cold beer. This is really going to hit the spot, maybe now I can sleep. He takes his order and go have a seat at the table. Excuse me! Yes? Is that pizza good? It's great, you should try it, here, have a slice of mine. Why thank you! You're welcome. I'm Sabrina by the way. Nice to meet you Sabrina, I'm Andy. Hello Andy.

Sabrina stood 5'8" with a model type body, olive skin that was smooth as cream and long silky black hair. Andy being the man that he was, wasn't about to let her get away, he proceeded to ask what kind of plans she had for later. What are you getting into later? Well, I was thinking about going to get a margarita, then some dancing on the rooftop at Club 74, it would be great if you came along. Is that an invitation Sabrina, are you meeting someone there, maybe some friends or were you just going alone? Actually, the idea just came up, I was just coming over to get a bite and ran into you Mr., and so would you like to join me or not Sir? Taking a long pause, he finally answered. Sure, we can go party baby, the first round is on me. No, I was thinking, more like the whole night would be on you, it will be worth your while, you sexy black man. Is that right, well, let's just see what happens Sabrina. The two get up from the table and leave the pizza joint. They acted as if they knew each other for years as they walked along side one another through the casino and out the door.

Chapter 3, The Club.

The line to enter the club was about two blocks long, they by passed the patrons and walked over to the doorman. Yo, my man, check this out. What's up bruh? I got $100 for you, if you let us enter through the V.I.P entrance. The bouncer lifted the velvet rope, stuck his other hand out for the money and let them through. Sweet! Here you go man! As Andy and Sabrina entered the club he started thinking, maybe this is not such a good idea. The club was full of attractive sexy women of all nationalities; he walked slowly through the crowd, gazing at the beautiful women. Sabrina grabbed his hand and led him to the V.I.P area. Then he noticed how gorgeous she actually was under the neon lights of Sin City, her Italian skin gleamed of blue neon as her shiny black hair sparkled, while the wind blew a few strands across her sexy moist lips. Will this section be fine baby? She said to Andy. Yeah, that's straight! We will take this one Sir! Please can you have the waitress bring us a bottle of Moet and two glasses? Sure thing Sir, will there be anything else? Yeah, some strawberries! No problem Sir, will get you all taken care of. Wow! Strawberries Baby! What do you have plan for me Daddy! Remember, it's on me baby, watch how I do my thing. OK Big Daddy, I see you.

A Kiss from a Rose by Seal played in the background. " There used to be a graying tower alone on the sea" "You became the light on the dark side of me" " Love remained a drug that's the high and not the pill" "But did you know that when it snows" " My eyes become larger and the light that you shine can be seen". Andy and Sabrina sat in the roof top V.I.P, enjoying each other's company sitting under the stars on this warm Vegas night. She reached over and lightly placed her left hand on his knee, then proceeded to move up to his inner thigh as she got closer to his dick, Andy made a remark. Don't start something you can't handle. Let me be the judge of that. OK Ms. Thing! Ummmm. You got a nice package there Sir, when was the last time you masturbated? Really, I can't believe you just asked me that, but to answer your question, maybe two weeks ago, I only do it if I really need to. Well, I'm doing it right now Andy. Are you a bad girl? Only when I need to be, and right now, I need to be. So tell me, do you eat pussy Sir? Damn, you get right to the point, don't you! That's the best way daddy, so do you? Yeah, only if it smells like water!

A voice interrupts their moment. Hello Sir! Here's your Moet and Strawberries. Thanks a lot, here's a little something for your trouble. As Andy took care of the waiter, Sabrina slid her hand up her dress to her pussy, pushing aside her silk panties; she stuck her index finger in her Vagina slowly so that it would be moist. Like water huh Daddy? Yep, like water baby. She removed her finger from under her dress and picked up her glass of Moet. When she drank from her glass she secretly sniffed her finger to see if it indeed smelled like water. She planned on letting him taste it and didn't want to be embarrassed once he licked her finger. Sabrina picked up a strawberry with her thumb and wet index finger, then proceeded to feed it to Andy. Ohhh thank you, that's delicious baby. She stuck her wet finger in his mouth while feeding him the strawberry. Andy licked her finger then continued sucking it in one long slow motion. So tell me, how did my pussy taste baby? Well that taste like strawberries and if your pussy taste anything like that, I would eat it all night, then again in the morning. Oh really, in the morning too? That's nice to know, I will definitely be holding you to that. She reached over and picked up his glass from the table. Here, give me your glass so I can pour you another drink.

The club was now packed to capacity, standing room only. Bottles of Moet, Cristal and Dom were flowing at every table in VIP. Girls were dancing on the bars and guys were taking body shots off of double D breast in every corner. Tupac's Bonnie and Clyde filled the airwaves, this calm Vegas Night had come to life. "All I need in this life of sin, Is me and my Girlfriend" " Ride with me to the very end, just me and my Girlfriend". Yeah that's the shit right there baby! Oh, you like that Daddy? Damn right! Me and my Girlfriend! AC and Sabrina sat on the couch rocking and boppin to the music while sipping on Moet, when a familiar voice screamed out. Yo, what's up A! AC stood up to see who called him. Hey what's up Jerm! What's crackin man; I haven't seen your ass in a bunch of Sundays. Come on over here and join us playboy. He lifts the velvet rope to let them in. Where the hell you been my nigga? Man, I've been chillin bro., I got this A&R Job in L.A. Oh, and this is my lady, Tammy. Tammy this is my homie, Andy.

What's up Tammy, nice to meet you. This is my friend Sabrina, Sabrina this is Jerm and Tammy. What yall sippin on pimpin? Oh man, this is just some Moet. Cool! I'm going to order another bottle, so we can keep this party jumpin. Sabrina had taken her shoes off and stood up on the white leather couch, she grabbed Tammy by the hand and pulled her up too. Sabrina called Andy over to her and started French kissing him and whispering sweet nothings between every kiss. I'm having a wonderful time baby, I can get use to you black man, I like your energy, your sexy chocolate ass and that smooth baldhead. I'm glad you're having fun baby, now come here and let a nigga get a slow dance. Down low by R Kelly was controlling the atmosphere; couples had invaded the dance floor to get their grind on. " Listen girl, you want me but he needs you" " Yet you tellin me that everything is cool" " Tryin to convince me baby to do as you say" "Just go along and see things your way". Andy turned around, grabbed Brina by the waist and lifted her off the couch. She was blushing so hard her cheeks turned cherry red. Wow baby, you trying to show your strength? No baby, just getting this first dance. The two had only just met a few hours ago and the chemistry was astronomical. Holding her gently by the waist, he gazed at her and thought, man I can't wait to get this sexy ass motherfucker back to my place. I'm going to have to pull out the satin sheets and pillows for this one. Look at her flat stomach, long black hair, nice lips and juicy tits, those got to be a 38 D or something, she even has some ass too. Yep! This one is a keeper! Hey Andy, what's wrong, you just going to stare at me or say something?

He looks at her with a smirk and says. You have the most gorgeous smile Sabrina and softest lips. Why thank you! So what comes after the club? Well I was thinking, maybe we can walk the strip and spend some more time getting to know each other, we really don't know anything about one another. OK, that sounds like a plan, where do you live, do you stay on the Strip? Yeah, I have a Condo about a mile from here, how about you? Well, I stay with my parents out in the Valley, it's just me, my Mom and Dad, that house is way too big for just them two. Are you ready to get out of here baby? Yeah Daddy, let's keep this night moving. Hey Jerm, I'm out pimpin, it was good to see you again man, stay in touch, I will give you a call the next time I come to L.A.. Nice to meet you Tammy, take care of my boy. Nice to meet you guys too Andy, see you later Sabrina. Alright Coop, be easy playboy! Andy and Sabrina walked out of the club and met the sun as it came up over the horizon across the Nevada desert. The neon lights had dimmed; the traffic had seemed to come to a standstill as crowds of people filled the streets and casinos after a long night of partying.

While the two were standing on the corner, waiting to cross the Blvd., A deep Latin voice spoke out. Well, well, if it isn't AC! What are you selling now, Mr. Andy Cooper? What, you traded in your perfume for women, are you trying to be a pimp AC? Damn! Detective Espinoza, do you ever take a day off? I will take off when you take off Mr. Cooper. Yeah, Yeah, whatever, let's go baby, this damn cop gets on my nerves, he's always in my shit. Coop grabs her hand and they ran across the street to the restaurant. We're going right here, to the Pepper Mill baby, to get some breakfast. That's fine Daddy, I love the Mimosa's there and the ambiance is so romantic. They enter the building. Hello guys, welcome to the Pepper Mill, will it be a party of two? Yes Mam! Alright, what's your last name Sir? Oh it's Cooper! OK, it will be a 15 minute wait. OK, thank you.

The couple sat down and joined the other patrons that were waiting to be seated. While waiting, AC noticed Sabrina had pulled out a roll of cash wrapped in a rubber band. Damn baby! Who did you rob? Nobody silly, this is all me, I made this last night at work. What kind of work you do? Slang crack, coke, weed, what? Well I'm an entertainer. Oh yeah, like whom do you entertain? Whoever pays to see me baby! OK Sabrina, let me have it, you can tell me, are you an escort or something? I should of known, man how did I miss it! No baby, I'm not an escort but I am in the Adult Entertainment industry. Doing what baby? Exotic Dancer baby! Oh a Stripper, hmm, that's interesting, where do you work? Over on Industrial at Dolls, I took off tonight, needed a break; it's been 12 days straight now without a day off. So how long have you been dancing?

Sliding his hands in his pockets while leaning against the wall, he looked her up and down then thought to himself. Damn, I bet I can make about 5 g's off her in a week, hell she's already in the game; I just need to learn a little more about her and be patient. Got to wait for that right moment but the first step is getting a position at this club she works at. Man, if I can get 3 more like her, that's like 20 g's a week, yep I'm definitely getting in to the sex industry. Hey did you hear me? Oh! What were you saying baby? I was saying, I worked off and on for about 6 years, I went to school and got my Business Degree but I came back to dancing because I missed that fucking money! You're not upset are you? Nah I'm cool, actually, I was looking to get in to that business myself, I have been thinking about it a lot lately. Oh really and what do you plan on doing baby, dancing too? Don't tell me you want to be a Chip and Dale's dancer? Hell to the Nah girl, more like Security, DJ or Manager, something like that.

Are you sure Daddy, this business is not for everyone. 100% sure of it, why you ask? I can put in a word for you at my job and see if there's anything open. But can you handle seeing me dancing and flirting with other guys, while I'm half-naked? Shit, I'm about my money, plus, you know who the fuck you going home with. Why you know it's you Big Daddy. Cooper, party of two! Yes, that's us, let's go eat baby, dang I'm hungry. You better save room for desert Daddy, I got something for you. Oh yeah, what's that? Hold your horses, there's no need to rush, I can assure you, I'm not going anywhere Daddy. Just know that I got you, OK Daddy. Alright, say no more. Here you go guys. The waiter stops and shows them to their seats then pops a cold bottle of Moet and placed it beside the pitcher of OJ. He pulls two champagne flutes from his cart and proceeded to make two Mimosas'. Ooh, that looks great! She picks up a glass. Here, taste this Daddy! Yeah, it doesn't taste too bad baby. See, I told you! Sabrina, I have a question. What is it? Since you are in the business and all, tell me what made you get in to it, why you came back and how much money can you make a night?

Well, I was bored working at my Fathers restaurant and wanted to try something different. Me and some of my girlfriends actually use to hang out at Dolls every weekend during football season, the wings were great and the drinks were cheap! Being there so much I made friends with several dancers and we all started to hang out. One thing led to another and I decided to participate in amateur night at the club, I will never forget that night. I was so nervous after I signed up, my legs were shaking like crazy, then my girlfriend was like; Sabrina you got to meet Jose' for this one! I was like, who? Jose' Girl! Tequila! Oh! Right! Bring him on baby! So after 4 rounds of Jose' and a few cold Corona's, Daddy I was in full gear! The song I danced to was Tupac's; It's all about you! I don't know or remember what happened on stage but I made $800 in tips that night; ones, fives, tens and some twenties was on stage. Needless to say, I was hooked after that one time. Wow, I bet you had fun that night baby; so how soon after that did you start working on a regular? Ha-ha. I started the following week; my first night was crazy, naked Bitches everywhere with a bunch of attitudes. The girls I met when I was a customer there, kind of showed me the ropes.

It's unbelievable what goes on in those clubs. What do you mean? Well, some dancers do dates and others just dance. What do you mean; do dates? I mean they make appointments to go on paid dates with customers after the club. Oh! You mean they be selling that ass. Yep! Some girls get like $1000 off those tricks but the standard is $500 for a date, then you have the club tricks that come in the club and trick off all their money on hoes. It's really an addiction just like drugs and alcohol; dudes are addicted to bitches just the same. So when the girls go on dates, do the Club Owner get a cut? Hell no! Sometimes they have an idea about who is tricking, but most the time they don't. I bet the owner is some old fat pervert that has cameras in the dressing room and shit, spying on you guys when you're naked.

Ha-Ha-Ha. Your too funny AC, well no, the owners are Vinny and Bobby. Vinny and Bobby, sounds like two Mafia cats, know what I'm saying over here! AC says jokingly in a mocked Italian voice. Yes, they are AC and don't make fun of my people Mr. They are what, Italian or Mafia? Both! So you work for the fucking Mob, are you crazy? No, I'm Italian remember. Yeah but Damn! I never met any real mobsters before. Let's just say that's a good thing Daddy. So you actually think that your Bosses will hire a brother to work for them? It's not like that with them, it's about the money and if you can do the job. I can do any job, that's not a problem but I don't wanna be watching my back, I might fuck up one day. Don't wanna be chopped up and thrown in an alley on Industrial, in garbage bags and shit! Calm down Daddy, you're taking it too far; I will speak with them tomorrow and see what happens.

While sipping on his mimosa, AC couldn't help but to think about all the mob movies he's seen. Damn, this is some real mafia shit, I don't know if I should stick with this chick or not. What the fuck am I getting myself in to here, Vinny and Bobby might have a back room with a table saw, aluminum bats, acid and all kinds of shit. Hell, they can cut my ass up, dissolve me and make a nigga disappear from this motherfucker. Do I really want this shit, this bad? Daddy! Daddy! She taps AC on the hand then says in a sexy voice. I'm ready to go to your place, we've been here too long plus there is nothing to worry about anyway. Vinny's girlfriend is black! Come on, let's kick rocks, you have a lot to tell me about this business and that club you work at. They get up and head for the exit. Sabrina stops and pulls three $50 bills from here bank roll and leave them on the table, AC turns to here as they leave the restaurant. No shit, your Boss has a black girlfriend, really!

Chapter 4, My Place.

Sabrina and AC left the restaurant all over each other like they were on some ecstasy or some shit. Yo! Yo! AC yelled out to stop the limo. The black stretch Navigator slowed down and stopped by the curb. Hey man, thanks for stopping! No problem Sir, where's the destination? Oh! Take us to the Towers man, on Flamingo and the Blvd. As they entered the limo, he looked over at her. Brina you a sexy bitch, come here and let me kiss those satin lips of yours. He grabbed her by the waist, sat her on his lap, stuck his hand up her dress and removed her thong. Hmm. You don't need these anymore baby. AC! Give me my thong, what are you doing Daddy, you silly, but I like it. I see! AC had felt how wet Sabrina's pussy was as she straddled his thigh. Damn! I'm hard as a steel pipe baby. That's the way I like it Daddy, nice hard and long. OK people, this is your stop, The Towers. Damn, that was quick, thank you kind Sir, here's a 50 for your time. Why thank you Mr., have a great day. Oh I will brother, I will.

Exiting the Limo, you could see the white and lavender 85-story glass building that captured your eye like a huge Caribbean island. Waterfalls and Palm trees greeted you at the entrance as Benz's, Bentleys, Porsche, Jags and Rovers, populated the parking lot. Hey man! How was your night, looking good I see. Shit! It's all good Manny, anything interesting went down at the Towers tonight? Not really, who is the lady you got on your arm player? Excuse me Mam; do you have any idea what you're getting yourself into? Aw Manny, don't start that shit today. Just playing Mam, I'm Manny the Condo Concierge. Nice to meet you Manny, I'm Sabrina. It's nice to meet you also Sabrina. Hey Manny, you got some of that chronic on deck? AC, why ask a question you already know the answer to? That's what's crackin pimpin, send me up an O. Man, you might as well get it now, I'm not coming to knock on your dang door so you can tell me you busy. OK bruh, give it here, you got them blunts too right! Of course man, come on, you think I'm gone bring a bong to work? Here you go man; you guys have a great day.

He reaches under his desk; pulls out a small rolled up white towel and handed it to him along with two cigars. Daddy, you never told me you smoke. Well, we kind of just met like 8 hours ago or some shit like that but I smoke, do you smoke, because I smoke! Do you smoke? AC said jokingly. Boy, give me that blunt so I can show you how to roll. Damn! Baby, that's what the fuck I'm talking about, a sexy ass broad that smokes trees too. We bout to be Fuuuucccckkkkkeeedddd up!!!!

The elevator door opens. Catch that baby; we're going to the 44th floor. So this is where you live Daddy, not bad. You have great taste, this is a very expensive place, I thought you were unemployed Mr.? Well I am but that just happened recently. OK I hear you, come here Daddy; you turn me on every time I look at you. Sabrina started to rub gently across AC's dick; the elevator had only reached the 29th floor, on the way to the 44th, when she pulled it out. Wow, this is the life, are you serious baby? You gonna give me head right now, yeah this is gonna be a great ass night. Oh shit, lawd have mercy on me! Girl where in the hell did you learn to do that? AC grabbed

14

Sabrina by her long black hair as she was on both knees with his Johnson down her throat. Oh yeah, um, hmm, oh yeah, that's it baby, you are the best! The elevator had reached the 39th floor when he stood Sabrina up and turned her back to him, kissing on her neck as he finger fucked her wet pussy from behind. AC took his free hand and grabbed the condom out of his back pocket, ripped it open with his teeth and proceeded to slide the magnum on with one hand, while finger fucking her with the other.

The elevator was at the 41st floor when he bent Sabrina over and slid his dick in her wet vagina. Oh Daddy! Oh Daddy! Oh, Dammit Daddy! Ding! The doors slid open and they fell through the elevator doors to the floor. Sabrina had fallen to her stomach and AC was on top from behind, he lifted her to her knees and she went into the doggie style position. Ruff! Ruff! Ruff! What the Fuck! Daddy stop, some ones coming and they got a big ass dog! So what baby, it's too good to stop now, I bet this want be the first time they seen someone fucking. But, but, but we're in the God Dang hallway Daddy! Oh Shit! Oh shit! I'm cumin Daddy! Come on Baby! Come on! Get that nut! My God! You people should be ashamed of yourselves!

Shut up lady and get on the Damn elevator. Ahhh! Ahhhh! AAAAh! Oooohhhhhhhh! yeeessssssss. Thank you Daddy, damn, that dick is good. Glad you like it baby, I got some more for you after we smoke this blunt if you're not all tired and shit, that was just a quickie. Ha-ha-ha. Whatever! How much you want to bet that Manny's going to be calling in a second, you know that ladies telling as soon as she gets down to the lobby. Ha-ha! Daddy, you're in trouble. Whatever, Manny knows what's up, that's the least of my worries. I'm thinking about your naked ass, walking around my place cooking me breakfast and shit. Look, my partner is still standing up; I think he likes you bay, come here girl. She stands up and waits for him to open the door.

Really, AC, can you open the door already, I'm holding an ounce of weed in one hand and my thong in the other! Sorry baby, I had to pull my pants up. He runs over to unlock the door. OK, here we go, welcome to my castle. Can I get you something to drink; I have some Water, Bud light, OJ, Milk, anything? No, just a face cloth and the bathroom is all I need right now, where do you want this weed? Just put it on the table baby. Sabrina puts down the weed and goes to the bathroom. Damn Daddy, you sure you have enough cologne? It's like perfume depot up in this fucker! He yells out. I like to smell good, is that a crime! No, I like a good smelling man, where's the soap daddy? Look in the shower on the soap rack and I have some new bars under the sink. Thanks! She undresses, turns on the shower and jumps in, then yells out to AC. Are you gonna get that chronic ready for me, I want to roll up one of those blunts. Yeah it's on the table. Cool, do you have some of that Outkast daddy? I love to listen to Dre and Big Boi spit, while I'm high. Hell Yeah, got that Atliens, elevators and shit, them cats be spitting those crazy ass lyrics.

10 minutes had passed, Sabrina steps out of the shower soaking wet from head to toe. Can you bring me a towel please? Sure, one sec! He goes over to the hall closet and gets a towel, walks in the bathroom; she's standing there wet and naked. Here you go, you want me to dry your back off for you? Please, if you don't mind. She turns her back to him; he takes the towel and starts to dry her off. So you said that some of the girls at your job go on dates with the customers, have you ever dated a customer? Hell no! I'm not a prostitute. Just asking, don't want you to hit me with that surprise question when we wake up, like ah excuse me, can I get my $500 now? Ha-Ha. What the fuck ever, you got jokes now huh, you wasn't laughing when I was sucking your dick an hour ago. Hell nah, more like having spasms and shit, the mouth service is marvelous baby; you can be my head doctor anytime. Yeah, Yeah, don't try and be nice now. She takes the towel and dries the rest of her body, wraps it around her and walks in the kitchen. She picks the blunt up off the table, looks down at the weed, picks it up and starts rolling the blunt. Look at this; you need to tell your boy Manny we don't want stems and shit! How am I supposed to roll a good blunt with this bullshit! Girl stop tripping, that weed is free, so deal with it. Oh in that case, tell playa I said thank you. Ha-ha-ha! They both laugh. Can't complain about free shit, damn you got the hook up!

Free weed, that's what's up, is this fat enough for you Daddy? She finishes rolling and shows it to him. Yep, now go ahead and light that shit, I'm ready to get high so I can hit that juicy pussy of yours some more!

Sabrina lit the blunt and took 2 long pulls off before she passed it to him. Here you go, do you smoke everyday daddy? He takes a pull off the blunt then replied. Naw, I really smoke to wind down on the weekends mostly, don't use it when I have to work because I have to stay focused. Nothing will get done if I'm high all the time; know what I mean bay? Yeah I do but I have to get high every damn day Daddy! Really! Yep, there's no way I can put up with them girls and the customers at my job any other way. AC walked across the room and opened the balcony doors to a view overlooking the Vegas strip; you could hear the sound of the city as it awakens to take on another day. Horns blew constantly as traffic began to back up, the city buses had forced gridlock at every intersection along the strip; bus stops were filled to capacity with people waiting on the first stop of the day.

AC turns around, walks over to his couch and picked up a T-shirt he left lying there overnight. Here, put this shirt on bay and come out on the balcony with me. Oh, grab that Moet out of the fridge and 2 glasses from the rack too; I'll be outside waiting on you. The heat from the desert had reached its normal daily temperature of 105 degrees at 7:30 AM; the Sun was beaming through the open door, heating everything in its path. He stood there on the balcony in his gym shorts smoking on a blunt while absorbing the hot sun that only a true Las Vegan could appreciate. He reached for Sabrina's hand as she stepped on to the balcony. Look at it baby, Sin City! The town that your ancestors built, how does that make you feel? Reaching for the blunt and staring him in his eyes, she replied. Sometime it makes me feel really good, knowing that my people created this oasis in the desert this unbelievable array of buildings, great food and beautiful skyline. Then sometimes I feel embarrassed when people talk about the negative side of things, like the killings, prostitution and everything else that we brought here.

I understand why you feel that way baby but that was the past and things are better for everyone now. She took a long pull off the blunt, inhaled, exhaled and passed it back to him. This shit is the bomb daddy! Damn, I'm higher than a motherfucker right now, look at my arm; I'm getting a motherfucking tan out here. Yeah, you are getting a little red baby. Plus, looking at you in them shorts right now is really making me horny as hell daddy. Oh yeah. Hell yeah! Here, hit this one more time. AC holds the blunt to her mouth and she takes another pull, Sabrina lied down on the patio chair that was sitting against the balcony rail. She pulled AC over towards her by his shorts. He leaned against the scorching hot rail that was blistering from the hot Vegas sun; the fact that it was burning the fuck out of him didn't seem to matter. She started stroking his Johnson with her right hand and rubbing her pussy with the other.

AC picked up the bottle of Moet and proceeded to drink while his penis got harder and harder with every stroke. Sabrina's pussy started sparkling in the sunlight as she held her legs open and back arched, sensual moans of pleasure began to escape her body. Sabrina rose to the sitting position, pulled his penis closer to her lips and slid it in her mouth. He grabbed the hot rail and released a strong growl of simultaneous pleasure and pain. Grrrrrrrrrrrrrrrr. He had enough, the pain of the heated rail was too unbearable, but her head was so amazing, he felt the favor must be returned. AC flipped her over into the doggy style position, her legs spread wide apart with a slight dip in her back. She raised her ass in the air and her but cheeks begin to spread apart, all he could see was that beautiful wet sparkling vagina. Grabbing her cheeks, one hand on each, he went in to feast on the ultimate prize. He licked that pussy like a pop sickle that was melting from the hot Vegas heat, he couldn't get enough, the sounds of slurping and popping seem to play its own tune; the all mighty tongue had found the womb. She began to jerk; pull and wiggle as his lips touched hers and that tongue massaged her clit. She had begun to reach her plateau when AC stood up and stuck his cock in that wet throbbing pussy. One stroke after another, she trembled, her legs begun to shake, she stood up and grabbed the balcony rail and screams of pain filled the air as she tried to escape. But he was not stopping or letting go, he bent her over some more while fucking her and stuck his thumb

16

in her asshole. Then the heavens opened up, she bust so big, it was like a water faucet had been turned on full go. All you could hear was, Oh God! Oh God! Oh God! Oh God! Ooooooooohhhhh, ooooooohhhh, SHIT! Damn baby, that was amazing! You got that knock out, put a bitch to sleep dick! Whew! God Damn!

Chapter 5, The Business.

Ring-Ring-Ring. Hello front desk, how may I help you? Good morning, this is AC. Oh, hello Mr. Cooper, what can I do for you? Could you have the valet bring my bike up please, I will be down in 15 minutes. Sure, which one shall we bring out the 1500 or the Harley? Hmmmm, I will ride the 1500 today not in a cruising mood. No problem sir, see you in a few. Sabrina, are you up yet? Sabrina! Sabrina! Shit! Sabrina! Fuck! Hey Sabrina! Fuck, wake up! Her body laid under the covers at the edge of the California King Size bed, after calling her several times he began to panic. Damn, what in the hell is going on with this chick? Fuck, I hope she's not dead. AC moved over to the bed and stood over her, then with a push on the shoulder, he shook her a little. Still no answer, in a swift motion he pulled away the covers and heard her giggle. What the fuck! You Bitch! Sabrina started laughing so hard, she started to cry and grab her stomach. Ha-ha-ha-ha-ha-ha. Oh God! Ha-ha-ha. What, did you think I was dead daddy? Man you crazy; don't do that shit again. Next time I will throw some cold water on your ass, you crazy Bitch! Sabrina! Oh

Yeah -Yeah, you were scared as hell though, wasn't you baby? I'm done talking about it! Hurry up and get dressed, we have to go. I don't have to work until 9 tonight and it's like 11am. So what! I have to go and that means you are leaving too; so let's go joker. Besides you need to change and call your people, set me up with that meet later. OK give me a minute, I'll be ready. Sabrina gets up to find her things. If you're hungry you can grab a bagel on the way down from the lobby. Damn! They have breakfast downstairs every morning like that? Yep, every morning baby, we live well in the Towers. So are you going to call me a taxi? No, I can give you a ride, I have time. Thanks daddy, I'm ready to go when you are. Cool, let's be out then sexy. I had fun last night at the hotel and the club, but here, it was fantastic! Yeah I did too; we must do it again soon. Like tonight? Yeah, I'll hit that ass tonight if you want me to! Don't try that play dead shit again or I promise I will wet your ass up!

They made it downstairs; she headed to the breakfast bar as AC went outside. Good Morning Mr. Cooper, here's your bike Sir. Thanks David, what's the forecast for today? High's in the 100's and around 90's tonight. Damn! That's hot! I know Sir; the heat is going to be ridiculous. No, I was talking about that fine ass redbone on that green 1500 ninja over there. Who the fuck is that? Oh that's Ashley Marciano Sir. Damn, does she live here also; I've never seen her around before. She just recently moved in from L.A, two days ago. Cool, I will run in to her later, right David? He looks at David and winks his eye. Sure, I will let Manny know tonight Sir, I'm positive he will handle it for you. Thanks David, could you go get that chick in the white dress from the breakfast bar, tell her I'm ready to go. Sure thing Mr. Cooper! Sabrina had glanced in AC's direction with a bagel in her right hand and an OJ in the other. David started walking towards her, delivered the message; she simply blew AC a kiss and winked her right eye. He yelled out. Come on knucklehead, let's go, don't try and eat all the food up! She placed the bagels in a bag then stuffed them in her purse, Sabrina slowly walked towards him sipping on her OJ. Don't rush beauty daddy, where's my helmet? I'm not riding without one. Just get on, I got it right here. The smell of hot tar filled the air in the Towers parking lot; waves of heat emitted from the driveway and created a blur when you looked towards the ground. You could fry an egg or boil a pot of water on the pavement it was so hot, surprisingly no one's tires had melted to the lot.

A loud screeching sound along with a white cloud of smoke polluted the air as AC and Sabrina spin off onto the Vegas Strip. It was 15 after the hour and the Volcano show had just begun at the Mirage, tourist and cars alike had stopped in their tracks to see the attraction, all Blvd. traffic came to a halt for the next 15-20 minutes. AC stopped his bike and looked around for a way out. Man this is some bullshit; it's too hot to be sitting in traffic with a damn helmet on today. Daddy, let's just pull over and cut through the casino lot. Good idea baby, we can go through the back way. My car is at the club. What club? The one I work at Daddy; Dolls off industrial. Oh that's right, Doll's, don't think I have ever been there though but I do know where it is. So what time are you going in today? I'm scheduled to go in at 9pm. What time are you coming to speak with Vinny and Bobby? Maybe around 9:30! They maneuver through traffic and cut through the Treasure Island lot to get on Industrial Boulevard where there was no traffic. They rode about 5 minutes up indie, passing all cars along the way and ran 3 red lights while going 85 MPH. A pink and blue building dawn the horizon; AC pointed at the club. Isn't that it baby? Yeah, over on the left; right across from that warehouse. As they approached the club she noticed a familiar face over by her car in the parking lot. Ahh Fuck! What's wrong Sabrina? I don't feel like this bullshit today. What? Man, that fool ass ex of mine is sitting on my car; here we go with the drama, early in the damn morning!

What guy are you talking about? He looked over the lot. Oh, that guy with the Starz hockey jersey on? Yep, that's him, sorry ass Pharaoh! What kind of name is Pharaoh? Dude Egyptian or some shit! Naw his fool ass thinks he's a God or something, but he's a punk ass bitch that likes to beat women. Oh is that right! Well don't worry; I got your back baby. Daddy, that fool keeps his heat! I'm good baby, I can handle myself, don't you worry, and here let me pull over so you can get in your car. AC rides over by her car and stops the bike. Hey Bitch! Her ex jumps down off the car and looks at her. Where the fuck you been all night? I was calling you, all damn night! None of your Damn business boy! I aint your girl no more! Get away from me! Who is this ninja riding nigga you with? That's your new boyfriend bitch! Hey bruh, you can chill with all the Bitches and shit, it's not necessary. Oh yeah and you gone do something about it! Mark ass nigga! Pharaoh in a rage had begun to walk furiously towards AC; he was 6'2", black as tar, had long dreads down to his back and smelled like straight Chronic, he had to weigh a good 265 pounds solid.

AC stood to his feet, got off his bike and flipped up the seat. Pharaoh what are you doing, he has nothing to do with this. Don't start any trouble! Oh yeah, this mark ass nigga is going to get dealt with today! He continued towards AC with full speed, as he approached, he grabbed Coop by the shirt in a jerk motion. Then all of a sudden a sissy like moan spoke out. Please bruh, don't do it. I'm high and was upset; please forgive me! Fuck you nigga! You're not so hard now with this gun to your head, hah bruh? Pharaoh falls to his knees. I tell you what Mr. Pharaoh, I will make a deal with you, see, I have 1 bullet in this 357 and if it's meant for you, then you a dead ass nigga, if not, then I guess I'll let you walk free. So on the count of three; I'm going to pull the trigger, so say your prayers nigga! The way I see it, if you're a good person, God will bless you, if not, well, the Devil will be glad to have your ass. One! Please, Please Man! Please! Two! Oh God Help me! Please God! Please! Three! Pow! He pulled the trigger.

The blood from his head splattered all over the concrete and on Sabrina's car window. Oh my God Daddy! You killed him! Oh shit, let's get the fuck out of here! Let's go! Hey, what the fuck is going on over there? A loud Italian voice shouted out! Sabrina is that you! What in the Hell is going on? Oh my God, Vinny he's dead. Who is dead? Pharaoh is! Well that piece of shit deserves to die. What happened? He was talking shit to me, my friend AC approached him about it and all hell broke loose! Who the Fuck is AC? That's me Sir. Well what are you going to do about this dead bastard on my property? Shit, put his ass in the dumpster, I don't care. Are you fucking kidding me! How am I supposed to explain this to the cops! I'm not taking the wrap for your mess; I tell you what we're going to do. First I have to call my brother Bobby, let him know what happened, get him down here as soon as possible. In the meantime go get cleaned up and out of those bloody clothes, give me that gun too, we need to destroy all evidence. Sabrina take your car to the car wash on Tropicana, tell them I said to give you the special, come right back here when you are done. Vinny pulled his car keys out of his pocket and handed them to Andy. Here, go get that cadi, park it over here in front of the body so no one can see it from the street. I swear, it's always something at this damn place. He go gets the Cadi, parks it sideways so that it would block the view from the road. Good, now come with me!

Vinny took Coop in the club, sat him in his office, then opened the closet behind the office door and gave him one of the security uniforms, black cargo pants and shirt. OK brother, we have a serious situation here; you should understand that I'm doing you a favor and in my world this means you now owe me a favor my friend. Yeah I know Vinny and I do appreciate it. I'm sure you do, but we don't need any heat around this money maker, so time isn't on your side my friend. You will have to repay this favor. Tell me, what are you good at, how are you planning on repaying us? I'm good with organizing things, talking to people and I can handle my own. No shit! I see you can handle your own! I would love to work here at the club for you guys. Doing what? Fucking all the dancers, we don't need your big dick ass in here getting the bitches all crazy and shit.

Vinny's brother had just walked in the room. Hey bro, what's going on? Oh what's up Bobby, I was just going to call you. This here is AC. How you doing man? I'm Bobby nice to meet you. Well sit down bro.; I have something to tell you. What is it now, always something with you! Oh no! Not me! Our new friend over here did you a favor today. Really, what may that be? You remember Sabrina's crazy ass ex, Pharaoh! Yeah, that punk ass woman beater! Well Mr. Bro. man here blew his brains all over our back parking lot about an hour ago. Get the fuck out of here! You're kidding right! Hell no, the body is still out there. What the fuck! Why didn't you clean it up asshole! Waiting on you bro.! Vinny, sometimes I swear! How stupid can you be? Call Silvio and tell him to come clean up that piece of shit. He's up front re stocking the bar, hurry! Go tell him to put the body in the back room, bring the butcher knives and that bag of lye from the closet. Make your new friend cut that Fucker up, then put him in the waste barrel for pick up this Wednesday, don't forget to pour the lye on his stinking ass before you seal the barrel. Just what I need, another reason for the pigs to come sniffing around this joint! Go with him AC, we clean up our mess around here, you understand? Yes Sir!

Good, when you guys are done come sit down so we can figure out what we're going to do about this situation. Just in case you didn't figure it out already, you're with us for life now buddy or you can join Pharaoh. Hell, at least you already got one stripe for killing that piece of shit, once you get rid of his ass that will be your second stripe. The third one, I'm not so sure, we don't take kindly to strangers. I'm sure we can use a person like you around here though, I just don't know where yet. Where the fuck is Sabrina? Oh Vinny sent her to the car wash on Trop. When she gets back, tell her to come see me, I will be in the kitchen making some lunch and burn those bloody clothes when you're done with that job. Did my brother give you something to put on already? Yes he did. Good, where's the gun? I gave it to your brother. OK cool, get to work; see you in a few, hope you aint scared of blood, because there's going to be a lot of it. Trust me; I've seen my share during Desert Shield. Oh, so you're a military vet? Yes Sir, 555 division attached to the 82nd Airborne, Hard core! Well fuck, that's even better, we got ourselves a real life soldier over here.

Chapter 6, The Understudy.

So Bobby, what position are you going to give our new friend? I'm not sure Vin, he can be a great asset to us, we just need to see where he fits best. Yeah I agree, let's just train him on all the positions. How do we handle that Vin? I would start him behind the bar first as a bartender. Are you serious, can he even mix a drink? Debbie can teach him; really it can't be that hard to mix a damn drink! The back door opens and Sabrina walks in. Hey Bobby! Hey Sabrina, what kind of shit have you got us in today? I'm sorry, I fucked up but Pharaoh was waiting by my car when we got here this morning. Yeah -Yeah, don't go in to all that bull, he already told me everything. Go home and get some rest, take the night off. Oh thank you! Where's AC? He's busy cleaning up your mess right now; I will tell him to call you when he's done. Thank you! See you guys tomorrow at 6. Alright sweetie and don't tell anyone you seen that piece of shit ex of yours either. Who are you talking about Sir? Yeah that's the idea sweetie.

Vinny! Go get the security tape out of the camera room. Oh shit the tape, I forgot all about it brother. Don't you want to watch it first Bobby? Didn't you watch it knucklehead? Nope, going to do that now, can you bring me a beer? Oh I'm your servant now little brother! Man come on, give me a break. Damn I just asked for a beer. Yeah I got you, quit crying like a bitch. Vinny sat at the large oak marble finished desk, kicked up his feet and rewound the tape to 4 hours back. Hey squirt! Here's your draft; did you see it yet? Just rewinding now; OK here we go. There's punk ass Pharaoh walking to her car now. Damn, this asshole is trying to break in through the back window. No success at that attempt; look there's AC and Sabrina pulling up now. Wow, was she upset, she damn near fell off the bike trying to get at that punk. OK here it is, he's charging AC now! Bro.! Look, your friend straight put the gun to that punk ass fuckers head, no hesitation. Man is Pharaoh about to piss himself? He got that punk down on his knees. Damn! Damn! He did him right there, just like she said. I would say he is most definitely a natural Bobby, smart and cold hearted! Yeah, we can use him, put that tape somewhere safe, you never know when we might need it, good ass collateral! That Motherfucker is ours for life now, he's never walking away from this shit.

Silvio and AC come in the office wearing bloody aprons and rubber gloves. Hey Bobby, we're all done with the body. Good! That dude was a sorry ass motherfucker and I hate sorry MF's! Sit down AC. His hands started to shake and knees started to knock at the request to sit, nervously taking a seat beside the oak marble desk, he noticed his 357 lying on the top shelf by the Hennessy. My little Brother and I were discussing your immediate future here with us. Do you have any skills behind the bar? Well, I can make the normal crown and coke, rum and coke, gin and OJ, you know the regular. OK this is the plan, for the first 3 months we will train you to bartend. Debbie our bar manager will get you started with some hands on training tomorrow, she's a looker man, so don't go try to stick your anaconda in her and shit. There is enough pussy around here for all of us, leave that one to the customers. OK Bobby, will do. Go home and get some rest, relax, smoke a blunt or whatever you do. Oh and call Sabrina, she asked about you. Guess I will see you later Vinny. You better change those clothes first, there's a shower right behind the office. Right, thanks man! Sure thing AC, don't go killing people for free no more, Mr. Daz Dillinger, that could of been a $25,000 hit you egg head. Ha-ha. Vinny laughs at him. As long as no fool try and cross me, there want be any problems. Get out of here hero! Yeah I'm going, see you guys tomorrow then. Yeah alright, go home already! Brother you believe this guy? He's going to be a nut case, one of those PTSD soldiers, watch what I tell you!

He entered the lot, started walking towards his bike and the crime scene. Damn! I got blood on my rims and my dang seat. Reaching in to his back pocket for his bandanna, AC kneeled down to wipe off his rims. He scrubbed the spokes rigorously to remove the dry blood from the chrome, while looking down at his chrome wheels he caught a reflection of a camera mounted on the corner of the building. What the fuck! These grease balls have me on tape!

He whispered softly under his breath, not to be too obvious. He mounted his 1500, started it up, and sped off as if nothing was wrong and thinking to himself. Man I really fucked up today, last night was awesome, got some new pussy, great weed, now this shit! Vinny and Bobby have me in a fucking corner; I aint even going out like that, them fools have to go. Fuck that! AC aint gonna be nobody's bitch. Time to get the homies together! This nigga aint going to the pen! The more he thought about it, the more upset he got. He hit the clutch and took his speed from 70 MPH to 115 MPH as the white lines begin to blur on the street and he sliced in and out of traffic making his way back to the Towers.

Night falls and Sin City is alive again, its 6:30pm, the air is humid and temperatures reached 95 degrees. He turns on to Desert Inn drive going towards the strip, up over the Vegas Skyline he could see the construction workers breaking down for the day as they try to complete the Stratosphere Tower at the North end of the strip. AC makes a right on to Las Vegas Blvd. into the night traffic of cruisers who ride the Blvd. every weekend to show off their 16 switches and candy painted rides. Asians, Mexicans, Brothers and White Boys try to show off each other with pancakes, side to side action and loud ass sound systems. AC slows up to a snail's pace as he passes through the mayhem and hears a voice call out to him. Hey what's up Coop! He sees a familiar face in the crowd. Hey what's good Manny, I'm on the way to the Towers. What are you doing out here, are you off tonight? No, I'm coming in later on bro.; I'm just fucking around a little bit before I go in. Damn the girls are looking good! Look at them, their out tonight home boy, ooh yeah!

Manny grabs a lady by the arm as she passes by. Hey Baby! What's up with you? Nothing! She pulls away from him and keeps walking. Ha-Ha-Ha. AC laughs. You crazy man, I'll see you later when you get to work; oh, I need to holler at you too, call me when you get in. OK Coop, hey be careful, don't hit the ladies with your bike bro.! Vroom-Vroom-Vroom. He burns out and a huge white cloud of smoke fills the air. Manny stands there shaking his head at him as the gravel starts to pop in the air from the spinning back tire. He takes off, weaves in and out of the moving car show and tourist traffic and makes it up the block to the Towers in one piece, parks his bike up front near the valet. How was your day Mr. Cooper? David I don't even want to think about it, to tell you the truth, I wish I stayed in today. I just seen Manny on the strip cruising a few minutes ago, he got you working 12 hours tonight I see. Yeah, it's my turn to pull 12; was he driving the 64? No he had the El Camino, candy black with 100 spokes. El Camino! I haven't seen that one. Looks like he's holding out on you Dave! It's all good; I got something I'm working on. Oh yeah! What you got white boy? You'll see in a few weeks during the Rebel car show. OK then, we'll see. AC turns around and head in the building, hey park this for me will you? No problem, will you be coming back out tonight? Nope, I'm in for tonight, got a long day tomorrow. OK Mr. Cooper, have a good evening.

Chapter 7, Rain.

Walking through the lobby of the Towers slower than he had before, he noticed the bellhop had pulled out a tub of umbrellas and the valet's had put on their raincoats and rubber boots. It was obvious that the staff was preparing for one of Las Vegas dirty little secrets. The rain was an enemy of the city, one may think that those in the desert would love rain once in a while; the truth of it was that the city had one of the worst drainage systems in the U.S. Hell, anytime it rained 2 inches or more the streets would flood for hours on end. Watching the staff prepare for what seemed like a disaster, AC noticed the chef's in the restaurant waving him over. Hey Coop, what's up man? Come here! He waves back and heads over. Chef, how are you this evening? I'm great; here try some samples of tonight's special, its New Zealand rack of lamb. AC reached on the platter, picked up a sample and popped it in his mouth. Wow! This is spectacular, the rich flavor and juices are making my mouth crave for more. Damn, this is seasoned well, can you send an order up to my Condo with a bottle of Pinot! Of course! Thanks Chef! Sure thing AC, we will have it to you in an hour. Thank you.

Making his way to the elevator, you could see that there was a since of relief on his face, saying to himself. Damn, I'm glad it's going to rain, now I know for sure that blood want be in that parking lot tomorrow when I go to the club. Hell, I wish it were that easy to make Vinny and his brother disappear! Stepping into the elevator all alone, looking at himself in the gold doors, he noticed that the hair on his head was growing back. AC rubbed his head and felt for new growth to see if he needed to shave tonight or the next day. Damn! I just shaved the other day! Now I have to again tonight! Ding! The elevator had reached his floor, walking out of the elevator he looked up and there she was. Hey Daddy! Sabrina! What are you doing here baby? Daddy, I couldn't go home after all that bullshit today! Well, how long have you been sitting out here? Maybe an hour or so! An hour! I'm fine; it gave me time to think. Yeah I bet! Today didn't go anything like I planned either, it just goes to show you that you can't change fate, what will be, will be. I know Daddy, I'm sorry for getting you into this mess. No need to apologize, let's just get on with our lives, forget that shit ever happened! I don't want to speak about it again! OK daddy!

He unlocks the door, they go in. Are you hungry, I ordered this good ass lamb a few minutes ago, I can call down and have them add another plate. Sure daddy, can I get some wine too? I'm already ahead of you babe, ordered some pinot too. Cool, well go take a shower daddy, get fresh so I can cuddle with you on this rainy day. Give me a minute, I'm gonna shave first then take that shower. There's a 20 sack in my pants pocket, get it and roll two blunts for us while I'm doing this. OK, where's the cd's, do you have any Too Short? Bitch! Sabrina shouts out. Girl what you know about Too Short? Bitch! Ha-Ha. Just Kidding, yeah I have that one "Getting It" with E40, Banks, D Shot, Dangerous Crew on it, look over by that Jodeci CD. He stood there looking in the bathroom mirror preparing to shave his head then pulled out the clippers to tape up his goatee. Buzz! Buzz! Buzz! As he's trimming, he says to her. Hey baby, you know you owe me right? What are you talking about daddy? I just solved one of your biggest problems, you gone say what am I talking about. Oh daddy stop playing, you know I got you. OK, I'm just saying though, a brother went all out, know what I mean? All Clint Eastwood, Dirty Harry and shit! Ha-ha-ha. That fool was like, please bro., please bro., don't kill me! That punk ass motherfucker had it coming baby, know what I'm saying.

I do, you can always count on me being there for you through thick and thin daddy. Through thick and thin baby, hope you mean that. Yep, no bullshit daddy, I'm forever in your debt, can I open the curtains? Sure go ahead. She walks over to the large picture window overlooking the strip and slid the curtains back. Wow! Look at all this rain, it's really coming down. I hate to be out there in that shit, you know all the streets are flooded; these fools can't drive in the rain out here. The rain drops were coming down seem like 40 MPH and sounded like balls of ice hitting the window, bouncing off the patio like golf balls on a driving range. Hey can you hand me a clean towel out of the linen closet, put that Cd on already too, what are you waiting on? He said out loud while shampooing his head, then proceeded to take his shower. While reaching to get his other rag, Sabrina stuck her head in. What are you doing daddy? Washing my ass girl, what does it look like? You want me to do it for you? Nah I got it, thanks for the towel though, but you can wash my back for me. OK turn around, let me get it. She washed his back slowly up and down as she began to sing the Too Short song that was playing in the background.

"You should be getting it. Everything you dream off" "You should be getting it." OK Too Short, hand me that towel so I can dry off. I got you daddy, come here let me handle this. Hand me the phone while you're doing that. Sabrina gives him the cordless phone off the bathroom counter. Here you go daddy. Thanks. He called room service. Ring-Ring. Hello, how may we assist you Mr. Cooper? Yes, could you add another order of lamb to my previous order and a second glass please? Sure thing Mr. Cooper, is there anything else you need? No that's it. Damn Daddy, you got some blood behind your ear, on your neck too. Well get it off baby. He gives her a face towel off the rack over the toilet. Here wet this rag with some hot water and soap; get that stinking shit off me! OK, OK, I got you! Chill out! She scrubs behind his ear and on his neck. He turned around looked in the mirror, checked the rest of his body for blood. Thank you baby, did you get it all? No, I forgot one spot. Where is it? I didn't see anything. Come here, let me get it.

OK where's the blunt? Its right here daddy, relax I got you, let me light it for you. She picks up the lighter and blunt off the counter, lights it, hands it to him. AC took a pull off the blunt and walked in the den to sit on the couch. Sabrina followed him, kneeled down on the floor between his legs and began to play with his penis. Once it got up, she spat on the head, massaged it with her hand, then started to lick the tip. Then ever so slowly she began to swallow his dick as if it were a pop sickle. He took a long toke off the blunt then responded in a low voice after exhaling the chronic smoke. Shit, I love that baby, you don't ever have to stop, this is the best feeling in the world. Slurp, Slurp, Slurp, she went on and on. Damn! Girl slow down, I'm not going anywhere, take your time, go back to that slow action. He took another pull off the blunt. Yeah that's it mommy, yeah that's it, suck that dick baby, suck that dick! Oh baby! Oh baby! I'm cumming! Oh Shit! Aaaahhhh, yeah that's that shit right there baby, hell yeah. Damn, that was quick as hell though; we've been fucking so damn much, my dick is sore. AC rubs his penis and looks down at her. I need to take a break from your sexy nympho ass. Man, what the hell ever! You the nympho daddy! Ha-ha! He laughs. Damn right, your ass is too baby, don't front. Sabrina stands up, sits on the couch beside him. But did you like it?

Hell yeah, I loved it, when you doing it again? Whenever you want daddy! Oh really, well, we can do that shit tomorrow, my ass need to rest up, here hit some of this chronic. He sticks the blunt in her mouth, she takes a pull. Dang, where's the food; A brother is starving. Ring-Ring. Baby hand me that phone please. Ring-Ring. She gets the cordless off the end table. Here you go daddy. Ring-Ring. Hello! Yo what's up nigga, this Jerm. Hey what's crackin pippin, you back in L.A yet? Yeah I just got some Laker tickets court side for next Saturday; I know you want one nigga. Hell Yeah fool, how many you got? I got 4 fool, you bringing Sabrina? I might, but keep two for me anyway. I might bring this other skirt from Riverside. Oh yeah that hot Latino mommy, what's her name? Ahhh. Constance right! Yeah that's it, with her fine ass. OK that's what's up Coop, just let me know what day you heading down, I got the bomb ass crib in the Valley, you can crash there when you get here. Alright Jerm, don't get in no damn trouble before I get to L.A fool. Alright cuz, get at me. Click! He hangs up the phone. Knock-knock. Room service! Hey baby get that, it's the food. Damn! I'm hungry as a motherfucker. Sabrina opens the door. Ummm-Ummm. That smells great! Baby, leave him a tip for me, my wallets in the room. She heads to the bedroom to get the cash. Would you like me to pour the wine Sir? Sure go ahead playa. Here you go Sir. Thank you Mr. Cooper, will there be anything else? No we cool man. OK, thank you for the tip, you guys have a great evening. Yeah you do the same, tell Manny to give me a buzz when he gets in. No problem sir, will do. The server collects his tip and heads back downstairs.

Chapter 8, The Deal.

The rain had only lasted a few hours and dried up quickly from this Vegas heat. Now the sun was setting over the hot Mojave Desert; Red, Blue, Green and Yellow neon lights illuminate the skyline. Just across the street you can see the water do its amazing dance as spectators watch with amusement. The temperature dropped a few degrees to 89 but the wind still felt like it was 110 blowing across your face. Amongst the crowd below you could see the ladies of the night in their 6 inch heels walking the strip amidst the tourist, making every effort to blend in; one could easily miss them if they didn't know the body language. The 1 second gaze into the eye, the lift of the eyebrow, the tossing of the hips. She would hunt you down like a Lion hunts his prey; beware, these Las Vegas streets after sundown has a life of its own.

These ladies don't flag down cars like hookers in the point, they attract their prey with animal like instincts, lure them in for the kill. Tourist scatter across the cross walks as several cars make their way through the traffic and turn into the towers. Amongst them is a black el Camino on 100 spokes, it pulls up to the curb and drops the back bumper; out steps this 6'1" , well groomed Latino male with black shoulder length hair; dressed in a dark Green suit with a gold nameplate over the right chest, which read Emanuel. Hey what's up Dave! Hey Manny, that car is clean as hell bro.! When did you paint it? Last week bro.! Looks good, did you wax it? Nah, got it done over at herbs on Maryland parkway. Damn! They did a kick ass job. I know bro., that's the only place I take my whips to. So what's going on at The Towers today, anything new I need to know about? Not really man, that new tenant Ashley got in earlier today; AC seen her and was like who the fuck is that? Ha-ha. Yeah that fools a Ho, what's he talking about? Wants you to call him, wants you to put a word in with Ashley too.

I saw him earlier, is he in now? Yeah but Sabrina's with him; they were gone all day until a few hours ago, been upstairs ever since. Damn what's wrong with that fool, he's usually in the streets this time of night. I don't know bro., but I'm out of here. What you in a rush for Dave, you got a big date tonight? Well some college buddies and I got this bachelor party planned for my boy at OG's around 10pm. OK, that's going to be crazy, have fun bro., see you tomorrow. Alright Manny, don't forget to call your boy. I want, catch you later man. He makes his way to the Towers entrance to start his shift, while checking with the Valet's to make sure they were ready for this busy night; he felt a tug on his arm from behind as he entered the building.

Excuse Me! Excuse Me! Sir! Sir! Yes how can I help you Mam? I just moved here from L.A, I wanted to know where I could get some good seafood from this time of night? Well let's see, do you want to order or do a buffet? What do you mean buffet? No one has a seafood buffet! Actually we have several in Vegas Mam. Oh Really! Yes Really! Crab legs, shrimp the works! We also have the crab shack where you can place an order. Which do you prefer? Let's do the buffet Emanuel. OK, no problem and you can call me Manny; I didn't catch your name Mam. Oh! I'm Ashley Marciano, nice to meet you Manny. Likewise Ashley, like wise. Do you need directions or will you be using our Limo service tonight? You know what; I think I will take the Towers Limo Manny. OK, what time will you be ready to leave? An hour will be fine, kind Sir. OK, see you then Ashley, oh there might be some other guest going along also, hope that's not a problem Ms. Marciano. No it's fine; I'm looking forward to meeting some new friends. Alright then, see you in an hour. Thanks a lot! She smiles at him and heads back to her place.

As Manny was walking over to his desk, he stepped in a puddle of water over by the wet umbrellas that were placed in the basket from earlier today. Damn it! Who left these out! Someone can fall, break their neck or hurt their back or something! He turns around and shouts at the clerk. Could you call maintenance to take care of this! Sure thing Manny! The lobby had begun to come to life, the bar lounge band was setting up to perform later tonight, cigar smoke and the aroma of hot grilled steaks filled the air. The valets were running to park cars every 10 minutes as patrons pulled up one after another to the Towers; trying to get seats to enjoy the live band and great food. Manny heard a loud noise and noticed a couple fighting. After taking a closer look, he saw a flashy dressed Pimp arguing back and forth with his Ho. He stood 6'5" with bronze skin wearing a baby blue suit, with matching Stacey Adams, Bamboo Cane, CK Shades and long black silky hair that seem to match his black tie that over laid a white shirt. She was only 5'2" looking like a midget standing next to him, your average blonde with 34DD's, Baby blue dress, clear 6" stiletto's with track star legs, which probably came from walking the strip every day.

Manny ran towards the entrance to stop them from coming in, but before he could get there they started going at it again. Get the fuck away from me! Get away from me, you Bastard! Smack! What did you say Bitch! Smack! Who the fuck are you raising your voice at! Smack! Dumb ass Bitch! Smack! Oh Shit! Sir! Excuse me! Sir! Manny sprinted towards the couple. What the fuck are you doing man? You can't be beating on her like that, especially not here! Smack! Fuck that Bitch! Smack! Now what! I'll smack her stinking ass again. Get your ass in the car Bitch! Smack! You stankin ass bitch, can't even get my damn steak now, fucking with your stupid ass. Get in the damn car! Smack! We leaving man, this Bitch fucking with my money, Pretty Tony don't play that shit pimpin, I'm leaving your establishment player! Manny grabs him by the arm. Get the fuck away from me! He snatches his arm away and walks off. Bitch I needs my money! Smack! I said go get in the car Bitch! Hey man, just get yo pimping ass out of my lobby. Damn! Vegas and these mother fucking pimps! Where is Metro when you need them! Damn! He walks behind the couple as they exit the Towers. Pretty Tony starts the car and pulls off yelling at the top of his voice. Bitch I'm going to beat your ass when we get home! Damn you a dumb ass bitch! Manny shakes his head at the situation, turns around and walks back inside.

Finally taking a seat at his desk, he dials AC's number. Ring-Ring-Ring. Hello! Wake up fool! Who is this? This yo Daddy! Ah shit, what's up Manny? You said you needed to holler at me. Oh yeah, no doubt. I will be down in a few; could you order me a bottle of Moet from the lounge? Alright got you playa, see you in a bit. AC gets up from the couch. Hey baby I will be back in a minute, I'm going downstairs to speak with Manny about something. OK sexy, I want some of that dick when you come back. Oh really? Yep really! Are you going to give me some? You motherfucking right I am! Get that pussy wet and ready for me; play with it a little bit so I can lick them fingers again too. She looks up at him, blushes and smiles. OK, daddy.

Manny was one of the few people that really knew AC, the two have history together from their days together in the Army. They were all in the same unit back in Desert Shield, he talked about Vegas so much that AC and 6 other members from their unit all eventually ended up here in Sin City. After slipping on his Jordan sweat suit and shoes, he made his way to the elevator. Ding! The elevator stopped at his floor, he could smell the scent of CK1 in the air, the door opened, there stood this 5'6" redbone beauty with a smile bright as the snow, her lips where juicy and looked soft to the touch, feet where perfect, no rough skin or corns, well-manicured nails, hands smooth as silk with the French tip finish. Her breast was sitting up perky like a firm C cup, oh lord the Ass was so round and perfect, it made him clinch his stomach to form a six pack when he seen it; the reflex he got whenever he encountered a sexy woman, like a dog in heat, the anticipation begin to take over his body. He knew he had to somehow have Ms. Marciano, from the first time she rolled up on that 1500. AC enters the elevator. Excuse me, how are you this evening lovely lady? I'm doing great and yourself? Well I was a little under the weather but seeing you has brightened up my day. Wow! I'm glad I could brighten your day. I'm AC by the way and you are? Hi I'm Ashley, just moved in. Welcome to The Towers Ashley, where are you headed? Manny told me about a seafood buffet that was great; I decided to go try it. Where are you off to Sir? I'm actually going to speak with Manny about something. Oh yeah, that's too funny! You should join me, if you don't have plans. Maybe I will Ashley, thanks for the offer.

The elevator reaches the lobby floor. Ding! She and AC step out together laughing, walking side by side, they approach the front entrance. Oh, I see you guys met! Yeah Manny, your friend seems like a very nice gentlemen. OK, yeah whatever Ashley, I hear you. I'm glad you guys like each other, will you be joining her for the buffet tonight AC? I'm going to have to pass man, I have to get some rest, got a big day tomorrow, but we can do it another time Ashley, if that's OK with you. Sure no problem, you get some rest so you can be ready tomorrow. OK

Ms., you enjoy your seafood, see you next time. She smiles at them both and heads out to the limo. So what's up bro? What you need to holler at me about? Let's talk over by the cigar room Manny, did you get that Moet? Yeah it's on the table, on ice. Cool, you want a glass? Nah, I have a long work night ahead of me. Oh no doubt, I understand. The two have a seat in the Cigar lounge.

Do you know a guy name Pharaoh? Yeah, I know this fool with dreds, real dark brother. He thinks he's God or some shit. Yeah that's him; well I met him this morning when I took Sabrina to pick her car up from work. Fool ass dude bro., isn't he? Yeah he tried that bad boy shit with me and I laid him down right there in the parking lot. Hell no bro.! You bullshiting right! Nah, Manny that fools gone, let's just say I got a job at Dolls now working for Vinny and Bobby. That shit took place in their parking lot, so now I'm in debt to those crazy ass mafia motherfuckers. Yeah that family is pretty loose in the head. Man, you need to be careful. No shit, Dick Tracy! So check this out, I need another piece, a 357 or 38 revolver! OK, that's no problem, I got you on that. I'm gone need to team up all the homies so they can be ready to ride when the time comes. What! You want me to call Looney, Big Will, Duck and all those fools. Hell yeah! This here is serious bruh! I aint going out like no mark! Those fools got me working at the club to pay them back for cleaning up that murder, I owe them now! They're going to hold that shit over my head forever! So I need to put a plan in action where I can be the one in control, I know my homies will ride with me. You aint said nothing but a word brother! We got you; I will call them fools tonight.

No Manny, go see them cats, don't use no phones and shit. I will hit you up when I get off work tomorrow; we can meet at the spot in North Las Vegas by the swap meet then. Cool, I will make that happen, here take this chronic, you need this shit more than I do! It's straight from Texas, got it off my connect 3 hours ago, the bomb ass smoke! He hands the chronic to him. Aright Manny, I'm out, talk to you later bro... Yeah, be easy playa. AC stands up, shakes Manny's hand. Oh check with Dave in the morning, he will have that package for you. Cool brother, I appreciate that, don't forget to get with the homies. I got you. Coop takes the champagne, walks back towards the elevator, drinking the Moet from the bottle. He slides the bag of chronic in to his right pocket and noticed two ladies dressed in black fitted dresses and black stilettos with silver heels, sitting on the couch beside the elevator as he walked by. Then there it was again, the scent of Ck1. AC couldn't resist, he had to converse with them. Hello ladies, what are you guys getting in to, looking all sexy and shit. One of the ladies stood 5'8" with long blonde hair, pink lipstick, white Gucci shades, a flat stomach, long chisel legs and some nice size C breast.

The other stood 5' 6" pretty brown skin, long pretty smile, brown Louis shades trimmed in gold with her black silky hair pulled back in a ponytail, which complemented her gorgeous hourglass frame and naturally manicured nails. Well handsome, our girlfriend just moved in from L.A, we decided to drop by and surprise her, but she wasn't in. So we were over here waiting for you and your friend Emanuel to get done talking, I seen him slip you that chronic and we want some. Ha-ha! Really, you're kidding me right. Nope, can we smoke with you handsome, we need to get high! I would, but I have company up at my place and there's nowhere to smoke down here. OK, listen daddy, let's start over, my name is Lisa and this gorgeous sister right here is my friend Jewel. What's your name handsome? My name is AC baby. Hello AC, nice to meet you, would you care to join us for a drink or share that Moet? She says with a devilish grin. You know what Lisa, sure what the hell, you only live once right. Yes! That's the spirit baby!

I tell you what, let's go to my place and make it a party. You guys can meet Sabrina; we can order some room service and smoke this chronic. Hopefully your friend will be back before the party is over, she can join us too. Now see, that sounds like fun daddy, let's go play handsome. Ooh, can you get Emanuel to come too? I don't know Lisa; I will call him when we get to the room, maybe he can sneak away for a bit. Ooh that will be awesome, I'm ready to party baby! Lisa shouts. Viva Las Vegas! Then turns to her friend and say. Jewel did you bring your baby daddy's cd? What! Girl you know I got that Tupac! Everywhere I go, I see the same hooooeees! Um-um-um-um-um-um-

um-um-um. I see the same hooeees! It's like candy! Ha-Ha. Girl, yo ass is crazy. What! West Side baby, the best side, you know what it is Lisa. Yeah, yo ass is crazy, that's what it is.

Whatever girl, you love me tho. Of course I do baby, you know you my bitch, fuck them other hoes. Oh see why I got to be a Hoe! Ha-Ha! Just playing girl! I'm ready to get high, what floor you stay on man. 44 baby. Damn! Your ass is up there, we were talking about getting high smoking, not going to the top of the Stratosphere playa, Damn! Ha-Ha. Yall some fools, we almost there though, by the way, what floor does your friend stay on? Man we don't know, we just called her phone and the voice mail came on twice, that bitch in the street somewhere. Oh OK, what's her name? My girl name is Ashley. No shit! I just met a chic from L.A name Ashley Marciano. Yep that's her yellow ass, so you know her? Where the hell she at? She just left, right before I seen you guys; she went to a seafood buffet. What! That greedy bitch always eating and don't gain no weight! Yeah she stays on the next floor, 45. Damn man, yall crazy for staying so far up here. What if the elevators break or some shit, that's a lot of steps poppy! Jewel don't be wishing no bad luck, yo ass will be walking too, because yo ass is right here with us. Shhhh, you shitting me, nigga I will be camping out on the couch until that shit is fixed, fuck what you talking about!

Ding! The door opens. Dang it's about time, which way poppy? To the left Jewel, it's the third door on the right. The three exit the elevator and walk down to his place. Oh snap! This shit says Mr. Cooper, on a gold doorplate! Wow! No room numbers and shit, they got name plates, Damn! AC approached the Mahogany wood finished door nervously, not sure of what was going to happen once the door open, after all he was accompanied by two bad bitches and Sabrina was inside. He dug into his right pocket to get the keys and Jewel smacked him on the ass. Ooh! You got nice buns poppy! Man you crazy as hell, but I like that though, come here and let me smack you on the ass. No-No-No, your girl might get upset, I don't want to beat a Bitch down tonight. Finally he opened the door; the scent of marijuana filled the air.

The Royal Blue plush carpet complimented the cocaine white leather sectional and love seat, white shear curtains draped the large picture window as it seem to effortlessly frame the Las Vegas skyline of dancing lights. In the far right corner of the front room sat a 12 man Jacuzzi, accompanied by a matching 5 foot bar, equipped with the latest wines and champagne. The Kitchen had black heated marble tiles, stainless steel refrigerator, stove and other appliances. The 4 foot by 6 foot island with a black marble top was centered in the middle of the kitchen which held all the party favors. A half bottle of Jose Cuervo, Alize, Grey Goose, 3 bottles of St. Ides, Hennessy and 3 ounces of weed sat on the counter. Oh Shit! Lisa look at all this chronic! Girl we about to be high up in here baby! Damn AC, you the motherfucking man, this is how you living poppy? I like it, where is that lady of yours? He shouts out for her. Sabrina, come here, we've got company! Sabrina! Sabrina! She comes out of the room. Hey Daddy, what's up? I want you to meet somebody. Hi. Sabrina speaks. These are my home girls Lisa and Jewel, this is Sabrina guys. So Brina, you gone smoke with us or what? AC told me he had that fire ass shit, I know you hit it already, is it that good girl? Yes girl, that smoke is like that! Some of that Doe Doe ass weed, have you laughing at everything girl.

Stop playing Brina; are you for real, that doe doe? That Doe Doe! Then where's the bong at player? Hold on J, you know I don't leave home without Phil. Pull his ass out then Lisa, light that shit up. Hold up baby, let me get him right, got to get that ice water, know what I'm saying. Yeah, yeah, hurry your ass up. I got this; you just put that 2pac on, mix up some of that thug passion. Hey Bre Bre, bring me that Henn dog and Alize bay, let's get this party rolling. Damn, where did AC go, let's start that Jacuzzi up too! Standing in his bedroom, leaning against the window, he reaches in his dresser drawer and pulls out a purple bag, then slowly pours a shot of Crown Royal in the glass he kept by the phone. After taking the shot to the head, he clears his throat and dials the front desk. Ring-Ring-Ring. Hello Towers! Yo, when is your break man, this chick wants you to come up and party with us. Shit, it's whenever bro., oh hold on AC, I got another call; Hello Towers! What's up fool! Who is this? Who you think it is

Nigga! What! I got yo nigga! Man quit bullshiting, it's Duck! Oh man, what's up fool, shit, I got AC on the other line, where you at? On the way there, I'm going to pick up Will and Looney now. Alright cool, I will tell AC. OK man, see you in a few homie. Hello. Yeah! Man that was Duck's crazy ass, they on the way here. No shit, well hit me back when they get here. Bro., you might as well come on downstairs now so we can talk in the conference room, might as well get that meeting out of the way. Hell, I got a date with my lady tomorrow anyway. OK, just give me about 20 minutes, got to see what these crazy hoes are doing. Cool, later then.

AC walked into the front room, he begins to sweat as the heat from the Jacuzzi and the outside Vegas air combined to create what felt like a 250 degree Sauna. All three ladies were butt ass naked, sitting in the Jacuzzi, passing the bong and sipping on what look like thug passion. His eyes had stretched wide as golf balls, his dick had stood to attention, all three ladies were in the Jacuzzi butt ass naked. Hey ladies, we got a party going now in this motherfucker, sssssshit let me hit that Chronic right there! He walked towards the Jacuzzi to get the bong, took a long toke. Jewel and Sabrina, pulled the drawstring on his sweat pants, Lisa pulled them down from the back. He took another toke off the bong, leaned towards Sabrina and Jewel. Lisa begin stroking his 8 inch cock until it was rock hard, she grabbed Jewel by the pony tail with her right hand, while holding his rod with her left, she stuck his cock in Jewels mouth, controlling her head by pushing and pulling on her ponytail. Sabrina moved to the back of Jewel and began to massage her pussy as Jewel's ass came out of the water while slobbing on AC's dick. Sabrina then began slurping on Jewel's pussy like she was a dog sopping water. Slurp-slurp-slurp-slurp. Ooh-mommy. Yesss-mommy. Hmmmm. She moaned as Sabrina slurped on that pussy some more. Damn baby, you eating the fuck out of that pussy, aint you bitch. Hell yeah she is poppy, now shut up and fuck her mouth.

Ring-Ring-Ring-Ring. What the fuck! Ring-Ring. Dammit, I have to get that. Ring-Ring. He runs to get the cordless phone off the couch. Hello! Yo man, where your ass at? Come on, we waiting on you fool. Damn! Manny, you can fuck up a wet dream! Damn! I'm coming, shit! Shit! Ladies enjoy yourselves; I have to go downstairs, real quick. Damn! I hate to leave all this pussy! Damn! Where are my pants?

AC slipped on his pants and headed towards the door, shaking his head in disbelief. OK, let's get it together. He said to himself. The last time all the crew met up was last Christmas at the Lexar party when Big Will got them all kicked out. Will was a Samoan who stood 6'7" and weighed 365 lbs., with hands as big as Shaq's shoe. Let's just say, you don't want to see him angry, a big giant with chino braids was no friendly sight. He threw 2 guys through the shopping mall windows at the casino just for jumping the buffet line. Looney was a sharp shooting lunatic that got kicked out of the Army, just so he could leave when everybody else did, he only had 6 months left, but instead of waiting it out, this dumb ass shoots his redneck squad leader in the ass during a road march just so he could leave with the crew. Surprisingly, they didn't put his black ass in jail. He got released with a honorable and diagnosed with PTSD, but he still could shoot a fly off a horse's ass 2 miles away. Duck got his name because the entire time during the war, he didn't shoot one bullet. What he did do, was set claymore mines and throw grenades all over the damn place during Desert Shield. This guy would be holding a conversation then all of a sudden, he would say, in 2 minutes we need to Duck. Hell, no one even knew he set a bomb or threw a grenade half the time. To make matters worse, you could barely understand his English because of his Arabian accent. To us, Duck always sounded like Doug.

AC exited the Condo and walked down to the elevator. Ding! The door opens; an old lady is standing there. Hey Ms. Harvey, how are you today? I am great young man and you? Busy day Ms. Harvey! Busy day! Well busy is good, I always say; better to be doing something then nothing at all. Yeah I guess you're right. The elevator had reached the 38th floor. Well this is my stop young man, have a great day and remember busy is good. OK Ms. Harvey, take care. The elevator had seemed to pick up speed as it went down. Then all of a sudden it stopped on the 5th floor, the gym level. The doors opened but there was no one there. Hmm that's odd, why is the gym so empty? He said to himself. The door closes and proceeds down to the lobby. Ding! The doors open, he walks out. Hey man, there's that knucklehead right there! Hey Coop! How the hell have you been man?

AC walks over to the guys and daps all of them up. Looney on the real, other than all the damn bad luck lately, I was doing pretty good up until today! Yeah, homie was just telling us the situation; pussy can get you in to some strange shit brother, got to be careful with these skirts man. Yeah I hear you Will but that's neither here or there, what's done is done. You always find them crazy ass bitches Cooper, with all the drama, I believe you like that shit! Man shut the hell up Duck! Where is Denna and Nina? We're going to need them for this deal. Shit, I told them what was up, but they was already on Lake Mead earlier, jet skiing, they said they would come by my place later to get updated. Denna and Nina were the last 2 of the seven that completed their Desert Shield combat squad. Their roles was Intel, they could infiltrate any camp or terrorist cell. Those two sexy Puerto Rican chica's got the job done; any man would fall to his knees amongst their beauty and aura. Let's just say you had to be one tough motherfucker to not get caught up when they paid you a visit.

Make sure you have a sit down with them tonight at your place Will? Yeah I got you, don't worry. Alright let's plan out this deal, which conference room are we using Manny? The Presidential, it has the most seats plus I already have a box of Cuban Cigars and a bottle of Martel set up for us. Cool that's what's up! Just like old times, there's no better way to plan out a strategic plan then to be smoking on a Cuban and sipping on some Martel. As the guys entered the Presidential you could smell the scent of fresh new carpet, the fibers formed to your feet as you walked across it, you could see the money green color shade from light to dark with every step. A 12 foot Mahogany finished table captivated your attention as it conquered the center of the room. 10 tall Mahogany leather back chairs complemented the gold molding that trimmed the Grey marble walls and the doorway. A Gold and Platinum Chandelier hung over the center of the table right above the trey of Crystal tumblers and Platinum bucket of ice. The five gentlemen pulled out their chairs and took a seat at the table, Looney picked up the bottle of Martel, asked everyone to bless the bottle by tapping it on the bottom before they opened it. Will took a cigar, passed the box to the right, Manny set up 5 glasses with 2 cubes each, Looney cracked open the bottle of Martel and poured everyone a glass. Duck pulled out his lighter, lit his cigar and passed the lighter to the right. Everyone was now ready to make a toast. AC stood at the end of the table and said. Today we take a drink to the next deal and a smoke to its completion. So here's to always finishing what we start, may this journey be just exciting as the last. Then they all said simultaneously. Death before dishonor!

Gentlemen have a seat; let's get this thing under way. I'm sure Manny told you guys that I'm in debt to the Delgato Family, Vinny and Bobby that owns Dolls over on industrial Ave. Hey; you know those are the same cats that owns the Adult Dvd store on Tropicana, plus Angel's Escorts. Duck are you serious, these guys own all that shit? Yep, my side chic use to work cashier at the DVD joint and her buddy drives for Angels 4 nights a week. This is going to be a big lick guys, it's probably going to take longer than I thought. So what are we going to do then, a smash and grab type mission or strategic? Will, I think the strategic path is going to work best; we can't leave any loose ends. You remember Dupree over off Boulder? Yeah Looney! You talking about that cat with the 45 right? Yeah that fool. What about him? He runs meth to like 3 of the strip clubs uptown, Dolls is one of them maybe we can talk to him and see what he knows about Vinny and his brother. Hell, they have to know he's pushing meth in their spot, maybe they are in on it too, who knows. These cats are about money on every angle Looney, they have to know! I will go see him tonight, see what info. I can get. Cool Looney, do that and let us know. So what's the overall plan brother?

Will, this is something that we need to take over, first we must determine what businesses they run and infiltrate them. We are definitely going to need Denna and Nina on this job, can't handle this one as a hit, got to be a straight take over. What we know for sure is that they own Dolls, LV Adult store, Angel's Escorts and possibly in on the meth trade. As of right now our primary targets are Vinny, Bobby and Sabrina, all of them have my nuts in their hands! Who the fuck is Sabrina? Oh, the damn chick that got me in to this shit in the first place. Where is she? Let's do her first! Hold up Duck; let's plan this thing out all the way to the end. I'm safe for now, we just need to know all the players involved first. Looney can you call Dupree now; we can't really afford to wait on that Intel. Give me a minute, let me find his number. So is the Delgato Family a Vegas outfit, Chicago, New York, what? I'm sure their Vegas, Manny knew of them growing up in Sin city. Then what's the status Manny? Duck turns to him and ask. Their two gangsta ass wops who made their stripes by mostly pulling hits for the old mafia back in the day. When Vegas went corporate and kick the mob out, they kind of took over the streets and prostitution rackets back then and parlayed that shit into what it is today. So we're dealing with some real street motherfuckers then! Exactly! These aint no pussies we dealing with! That's cool, we aint no pussies either bro! Damn right! Death before Dishonor my man, Death before Dishonor, let's get to business.

Looney! Did you find the number? Yeah hold on, calling him now. He goes over to the phone by the door and dials the number. Ring-Ring-Ring. Hello, this yo boy! What's Crackin? What up Pree, this Looney. Oh what's good fool? Need some info. on some club niggas? Fo sho, who you talkin? Vinny and Bobby over on industrial! Oh them good people, what you need? Looking to see if they are in the game, I got some chica's over there, wanted them to push some shit for me. Oh bro. that shit want work; hell that's my connect you dig. Oh my bad pimp, didn't know. Nah it's all good homie, you my people, but as far as them cats, they good on that product, new shit every week you dig. Alright Pree, good looking out, see you when I see you pimp. Later cat!

Yo, my man said those cats in the game too, on top of everything else. Damn! This is going to be the Jackpot move, we have to do this shit right, this is how it's going down. We move in on the club first, that's the starting point. Big Will, you need to be ready in a week or so to stop by the club and ask for a job; we can't let them know we know each other though. Looney you are going to play the new dealer, talk to your boy Pree and get him to put you on. Duck you the point man, going to need your eyes on the outside for the escort service, we have to get the twins in there somehow, all angles of their operation must be covered. I will start gathering Intel. My first night, the next morning I will call you guys and put the next move in action. How long are we going to run this mission AC? I really want to end it in December Duck, but let's see what we're dealing with first brother. Tell me this Coop; is it three marks or two? Definitely 3 but the 2 brothers are the main priority, Sabrina not so fast. Yeah I hear you bruh, that pussy must be good nigga. What! The head is amazing and pussy like Niagara Falls baby, got to keep that for a while yah dig! Man you crazy; just don't get your ass caught up fool, over no skirt! I'm good Looney; never have to worry about that. If you say so brother; if you say so!

CHAPTER 9, 44TH Floor.

The Presidential now filled with cigar smoke, empty glasses and ash trays, no longer had its upscale mystique but more of a restaurant feel after a Vegas lunch hour rush. Manny reached for the phone to call the front desk to come handle the mess they had made. Ring-Ring. Hello front desk. Hi Chrissy, this is Manny, could you please send someone to clean this conference room please, it's the Presidential. Okay, will take care of it right now. Thanks Chrissy. No problem sir. Fellas I have to get back to work, what are you guys doing when you leave here? Shit, I'm taking my black ass back upstairs; I have 3 butt naked bitches in my Jacuzzi with some smoke and drink, yah dig! What! Looks like we going with AC. Manny, hold it down bruh. Damn! Coop my nigga, always can count on your ass to have them skirts on point. Whatever Looney, bring some more smoke; I know them chics probably halfway through my stash by now.

The guys walked out jokingly, laughing amongst each other. Duck for some reason had separated himself from the group; he started walking towards the check in desk in a slow but curious manner. Hey! Duck where the fuck you going man? He ignored the guys and kept going. There standing at the end of the checkout counter was a pretty dark skinned 5'9", petite female, with the Halle Berry cut and Pamela Anderson breast that seemed to pop open the top 2 buttons of her blouse. She wore black heels covered by black business slacks and a Louis Vuitton belt that seem to perfectly help keep her white silk blouse tucked and aligned properly in her slacks. The silver name plate she wore over her left breast read, Megan; Human Resources. Hello Gorgeous, how are you doing today? Why I am fine Sir, thanks for asking. Hi my name is Dubai, but my friends call me Duck, I see you are Megan. Yes that's me. Do you work here Megan? No Duck I don't! I actually work at Caesar's; I just got off and came over here to speak to my girlfriend. Oh that's nice of you, so what are you doing when you leave here? Going home I guess, it's too damn hot out, to go anywhere. Well, me and my friends are having a party on the 44th floor, you should come. The guys were walking in the middle of the lobby talking about Duck's sneaky ass when he called them over. Hey fellas, come over here, meet my friend Megan. The fellas make their way over to the counter.

Hey what's up Megan! Hi fellas. Megan this is Will, AC, Looney and Manny. Nice to meet you fellas, how are you Manny? I'm great Megan, I see you met Duck. Damn man, you already know her! Don't tell me yall hooked up, no bruh, calm down, we cool, she's just a friend of one of my Coworkers. Oh cool. So fellas, I will catch up with you guys in a few, you need me to bring some more drink or something to the condo? Yeah get some more Goose. Dubai your friends seem cool, how long have you known each other? Ahh. About 6 or 7 years; so are you going to take me up on my offer? We have a Jacuzzi upstairs too. Well I don't usually go out with strangers on the first day I meet them but since you are friends with Manny, I guess you're cool. He smiles and grabs her hand. Yeah great decision; let's stop by the shop on the way up and get that Goose. What do you drink Megan? I prefer Martel or Hennessy. Really! Well I'm sure we have one of those if not both already. Hey AC! Hey AC! A voice yelled across the lobby. He looks around to see where it was coming from. What's up Ashley, how was the seafood? It was fantastic! What are you guys up to? Well these are my boys, Will, Looney and that's Duck over there. We are headed to my place for a get together, well a party. Hey fellas, how's it going? Better every minute I am at the Towers! Shut up Will, yo crazy ass. You joining us Ashley, you might as well, your friends Lisa and Jewel are already up there. Shut up! No shit! How do you know them? They were here waiting on you, somehow convinced me to let them come up to my place and party. Yeah those are my bitches, smooth and sexy as hell. Yeah you got that shit right. Well you can count me in too. Let's go party! Great, come on. He wraps his arm around her shoulders and escorts her with the crowd.

The night was young and perfect for a Sin city style party, the weed; Alcohol, Sexy people and a laid out Condo at the Towers made it the right place at the right time. Who could turn down, getting high, drunk and having all the sex you want in a Jacuzzi, a plush condo, with a deck overlooking the Vegas strip. This was going to be a night to remember. AC slid his arm down to Ashley's waste as they walked with the others. Duck and Megan stood at the counter of the Shopette waiting on their Goose. The boyz and Ashley had stopped in the lobby to wait on them. Yo Duck! Will yelled out. Grab some Dutch Masters player. Alright, I got you bruh. Cool, I'm rolling this chronic up, fuck that bong tonight, know what I'm saying, we about to get high as a motherfucker. You smoke trees Ashley? Boy that's my medicine, I got to hit that at least once a day. See Looney, this is a down ass Bitch, fine as a motherfucker and she smoke trees too. It's on tonight nigga and don't be crackin them whack ass jokes later either. We all know how your ass get when you get high, think you Eddie Murphy and shit, with them boring ass jokes. Aww shut up Will; you know my shit be funny nigga. Nah fool, we laugh because they stupid and we be high as hell. Yeah ok, AC don't my shit be funny? Man I know you're not asking me about them lame ass jokes you be telling, try to tell some when we are sober and not high, see if they funny then. Man whatever, you knuckle heads just hating on me. We love you bruh, that's why we keep it real, let's go catch the elevator, Duck's coming now.

As the doors open to the elevator, you could hear the voice of the cities Dj over the speakers. What's happening all my beautiful Las Vegans; welcome to Sin City all you out of Towner's. This is The G Man broadcasting over your radio. It's time to get the party started here in the City of lights, playground to the High Rollers, Hustlers, Players and Pimps. Up next is another bomb ass hit from That Death Row camp and The Dogg Pound, this one right here is called Respect! " I know you bobbing your head cause I can see you" "I know you bobbing your head cause I can see you" " I know you bobbing your head cause I can see you" " I know you bobbing your head cause I can see you" "You can't see me back up in that ass once again with some of that nigga Daz shit, beating up on your ear drums with some of that G Funk, some of that Gangsta Funk, some of that Ghetto Funk" " Call it what you want just don't forget the G" The Motherfucking Dogg Pound in the house" Yeah that's the shit right there boy, that nigga Kurupt be spitting them crazy flows. Man hell yeah, Death Row baby, killing the game with that gangsta shit. Oh shit, get it Ashley, move that ass baby, get this party started.

The crowd cheered her own as she gangster walked to the beat. Man that's my jam! West side the best side baby! What you a gangsta Ashley? I be getting my C walk on. Yeah whatever, your pretty ass aint no G. Awww don't be hating Will, I got that G Funk baby. Ha-ha-ha. Yeah OK. Man, you know who be getting his walk on, that nigga Dub C fool, skip, skip! Hell yeah, he be putting in work with that shit. Duck, do they be Gangsta walking where you from? Kiss my ass Will! Ha-ha-ha. Come on Duck, I'm just fucking with you. Did yall see that New York, New York video? Oh hell yeah! I saw that joint on the box the other day. That shit was crazy! Snoop kicking over buildings and shit! Damn fools; ordering that video like 20 times back to back!

They need to cut all that East Coast, West Coast shit out, that's what I think! I'm from Brooklyn and that was fucked up what Snoop did, you know all that shit is going to lead to somebody getting shot and shit! Well I'm sorry to hear you from NY Megan but it's just entertainment baby, them fools just selling records, aint nobody gone get shot over no damn video. Yeah I hope you right Duck, but them streets aint no joke. Ding! The door opens to the 44th floor. Oh what the Fuck! Damn what in the Hell is going on up here AC! Looney said in an erratic voice. Just in front of the elevators in the hallway, there was Jewel and Lisa sitting naked, tied up at their ankles and wrist, with duct tape over their mouths. The energy amongst the group had changed from party to panic in a matter of seconds. Damn who did this? Are you guys OK? Lisa had rolled her eyes towards the Condo to signal that someone was inside. Where's Sabrina? Is she in there? Jewel shook her head to say yes. OK you guys be cool, we got you, shh, don't say anything. Will said to Lisa and Jewel as he untied them and removed the tape from their mouths. Ashley you and Megan stay here with the girls, while we go check this out. OK Duck we got them, please go see what the fuck is going on!

Looney moved slowly against the wall as he made his way to the doorway of AC's condo. He took a peep through the cracked door and seen a brother with dreds, standing about 6'5", who begin kneeling down over Sabrina with a gun in his right hand. Bitch now you are going to tell me where the fuck my brother is, your sorry ass done got him in some shit! I told his ass to stay the fuck away from you and your bullshit! I don't know where Pharaoh is Monk! I swear! Quit lying Bitch, word on the street, you got him knocked off. No! No! Monk please, I don't know where he is, I swear! Will, Duck and AC had come up behind Looney against the wall, waiting for the cue to move in. He signal to the group with one finger, dropped it and signal again. This was the sign for one shot, one kill. Will reached behind his back, pulled out the gloc, attached the silencer he kept clipped to it then passed it to Duck who gave it to Looney. The guys moved away from the wall so that Looney could get down in a comfortable position. Shhhh-Shhhh. They told the girls not to make a sound. Now bitch, this is my last time asking you! Where the fuck is my brother? I don't know, I haven't seen him in like a week. Stop lying Sabrina or I'm going to shoot you in your fucking eye! No please, please, No don't! Please don't kill me! Fuck you Bitch!

Monk stood up and cocked his gun. Click! Then held it to her right eye. This is your last chance trick, where the fuck is Pharaoh? Then zoot! Zoot! Two quick shots let off, Monk big frame fell to the ground, one shot to the back of his head, another pierced the center of his back, the guys rushed in to make sure he was dead and to see if

Sabrina was OK. Oh my God AC! Baby I don't know how he found me, he just rushed in, held us at gun point and I was so scared baby! It's OK, it's all good now baby, does this motherfucker have any other brothers we need to be worried about? No, all I knew about was Monk. OK, OK, come on have a seat on the couch. He picked her up and walked her over to the sofa. AC what the fuck are we going to do with the body? Sabrina be quiet, let us handle this! Looney call Manny, tell him to come up here, get those girls in here too. Damn! This has been a fucked up day! Yo bruh, that bitch is bad news man, two bodies in less than 48 hours! I'm telling you Coop, this shit aint cool at all. Will, shut up man, let's just get this business taking care of, did yall call Manny yet?

Ring-Ring-Ring. Hello, thank you for calling the Towers, how may I help you? Yo bro. this is Looney, we got a major situation homie. What are you talking about L? There has been a 187 in Coops Condo. Man what the hell do you mean, a 187! You guys were supposed to be having a party with some bitches! Just get your ass up here ASAP! Damn! You fools; I swear man, OK, I'm on the way up. Shaking his head, he hung up the phone; while getting up to put on his jacket, a soft voice sounded out his name. Hey Manny baby, how you been poppy? He could smell the scent of Dolce Gabanna; he turned to see who it was. Standing there like a model out of Vogue magazine was this stunning 5'10" Latino beauty with a stunning coke bottle shape, wearing a sexy red body suit and black and red Louis Vuitton heels; every head in the lobby turned in her direction. She reached for him and gave him a great big hug, kissed him on the cheek. Hey Denna, how are you baby? Where's Nina? That chica's getting a martini, she's coming, so where are the fellas? Will told me we we're meeting today. We did earlier; I'm actually going to AC's to meet them now. Hey Manny Mann! Wow, hey Nina, you cut your hair! Yes! Yes! You like poppy? Yeah it looks good on you. Muah! She kissed him on the cheek. Damn you're working those jeans too! Ahhh, got to show off this body poppy! Nina stops to pose and turn as if she were doing a photo shoot. Ms. Nina is here baby! You guys are crazy, let's go up to AC's, I will fill you in.

This fool done drop two bodies in a day; fucking with this new bitch he got. What? Stop playing poppy; is it all good, do we need to get our gats? Nah, Loon said they took care of it but we have a really big job planned, this incident that just happened upstairs will only make matters worse, I'm sure. Wait a sec. girls, I left my keys on the desk. As he turned around to get his keys he noticed a police car pulling up the driveway, at that very moment he knew the situation changed. Everything seemed to move in slow motion as if he was outside of his body watching it all happen; the car pulled closer, panic begin to set in. Hey! Hey! Nina, quick hold that elevator and press 44! Damn ladies, we have to act fast, po po just pulled up. Wow! Are you serious? This is bad poppy, really bad! Nah, we will fix this baby, I already have an idea in the works. Nina once we get there, I want you to get all the girls, take them to the Spa and Jacuzzi area. Denna, there will be a house keeping closet at the end of the hall by the ice machine, get the big white laundry cart, bring it to the Condo along with a stack of towels and sheets. Roger that Manny! We don't have much time, so move fast!

Ding! The door opens to the 44th Floor, Manny and the girls approach the Condo to see a 6'5" corps laying in the front room. Hey Looney! Yeah Amigo what's up? Get AC's bed sheets, let's wrap this body up, Denna, hurry go get that cart, girl's you guys go with Nina. Duck, grab some towels and bleach, wipe this blood off the table and kitchen floor. 10-4 Manny! AC we need to talk bro! The two of them walk outside on the balcony. We have a really bad situation here, we need to figure out how we are going to fix it ASAP, the police was pulling up when I left my desk a few minutes ago. So tell me, do we have to cancel this Bitch that has raised your body count in the last 48 hours? No man, the way I see it, she's in deeper than we are at this point, plus we are going to need her to pull off this long hustle, we can use this as insurance. Insurance! Nigga you pussy whip, you done bumped your damn head, fool she didn't kill anybody, her hands are clean. If she decides to sing, we shit up the creek without a paddle! Trust me bro, she doesn't think like that, in her head, she feels she owes us a favor. OK AC, you better be right bro.; so did any of your neighbors catch wind of this incident? No one came out in the hallway or to the Condo, I think we all clear.

Hey poppy! Here's the towels and sheets, what's next? The guys walk back inside. Alright team let's make this fool disappear; Big Will go pull your truck around back by the laundry room. We are going to drop the body down the laundry chute after we wrap it, then put him in the back of the Tahoe and go burry his ass. What! Why I got to put the motherfucker in my shit! Man stop crying, you big baby. What the fuck ever Coop! Besides, where the hell are we going to bury him? Fool; all that damn desert out there! Take your pick! Ha! Very funny! Denna hand me those sheets, Manny we got it from here, go handle that cop downstairs, don't need his ass up here! At the time it all seemed so surreal, like it was a movie being filmed and everyone was playing a part, but this wasn't a movie, there was no directors, camera's or actors. This was the real deal, dead bodies, blood, guns, drugs, sex and alcohol; real life for this hard core bunch of US Veterans turn Gangsters.

Chapter 10, Chaos.

Denna, AC and Duck wrapped the body and placed it in the laundry cart. Denna mentions. Hey guys, this shit is not going to fit down the damn laundry chute, are you fucking kidding? Yeah, I agree with you on that one baby. Hmmmm, well maybe we can use the service elevator, take it down that way. What! Then someone might see us on the way down. Yeah, I was thinking the same thing Duck. Let's just add some more sheets on top of him and it will look like laundry, but I can't go with you guys, the tenants know me. You two can just get a few housekeeping jackets from the laundry closet and no one will ever suspect anything. Yeah let's do that, get this nigga out of here ASAP! Denna and Duck pushed the overloaded squeaky cart towards the hallway, AC checked to make sure the coast was clear. Alright guys we good! Come on, Hurry up! Hurry up! As they entered the hallway, AC ran to the laundry closet to get two housekeeping jackets. Here guys put these on.

The service elevator was at the end of the hall; which looked like it was a mile away. Damn, you could have gotten a bigger size Coop! Man shut your ass up, put on the damn jacket. Ha-ha-ha. What you laughing at Denna! Aint shit funny! Man put it on and come on before someone comes out. Excuse me! Excuse me! House Keeping! Can you bring us some clean towels? A ladies voice shouted out from behind. Sure Mam, give us a few minutes, we'll take care of you. Thank you and some soap too. Okay Mam. See, that's what the fuck I'm talking about! Hurry up; we're almost to the elevator. The gold doors to the service elevator appeared larger as they approached. OK guys, once on make sure you push the LL button, it will take you down to the dock area, Will should be back there with the Tahoe by then, tell him to pull around front, and I will meet him there. We got it AC; don't forget about the girls and Nina.

Damn! I did forget too baby, going to get them now, I will see you two in a few. The doors close, he turns away headed towards his place, he pauses for a moment, rubs his head with both hands, then tilts his head back, rubs his face; and then leans against the wall. It had all seemed to finally hit him at that moment, the fact that his life as he knew it had changed all because of a piece of ass. He could hear his mentor's voice in his head. Son, as a man you must learn to think with the head on your neck, not the one attached to your dick. It was too late for that now, the damage was done. He lifted himself up and went to lock his doors, while reaching in his pocket to pull out his keys, he looked up and there she was. Hello, excuse me Sir, can you help me? Yes Mam, how may I assist you?

Well I'm looking for my boyfriend, he came up here about an hour or so ago, I was waiting on him in the car; he promised that it wouldn't take long. What's his name? Monk! No, I don't know him. How does he look? He's about 6'4", dark skinned with dreds; he was looking for his brother Pharaoh. Sorry babe, I haven't seen anyone even close to that description around here are you sure this is the right floor? I think he said 44, I'm not sure. Well sorry I couldn't help you, I have to be going now, but good luck, hope you find him maybe you should check another floor. OK, thanks for your time. No problem! He said then quickly made his way to the elevator to escape the awkward situation.

The elevator doors open, the radio is playing Guy's; let's Chill. "From the first time I saw your face, girl you know I had to have you" " I wanted to wrap you in my warm embrace" "visions of your lovely face" "All this love is for you " " Whatever you want I will do" " You're the only one I want in my life.. For you I'll make that sacrifice" "Let's Chill, Let's settle down, that's what I want to do" Ding! The door opens to the pool area, the girls were sitting at the bar, sipping on margarita's as if they were on a vacation. Hey Nina, saddle up baby, time to get moving. OK girls, get your things and let's roll, Ashley are you guys OK? Yes AC, we're good, did you get this mess cleaned up. Yep! Yep is all you have to say? Yep! So you almost got my friends smoked, all you have to say is Yep! Look Bitch! Yall ain't get hurt, so just shut up; leave it alone before someone does. Oh is that a threat nigga! No it's a promise, play with it!

Fuck You AC! Nina get rid of that skirt, before she gets hurt. OK Ashley, come on baby let it go, no one is at fault, we are all are in a bad mood because of this shit. So why don't you and your girls go to your place, I will come holler at you guys later. That's cool Nina, I'm just saying, he could have been more considerate, know what I'm saying? Yeah I do, but that's my bro, he's always been that way. Alright, bye girl and fuck you AC, your bald ass head! Kick rocks Bitch! Sabrina, bring your ass over here. Yeah daddy, what's up? What's up! Your gig is about to be up if you don't come clean. This bitch came looking for Monk, said she was his girl and shit. Do you know her? I don't know, Monk always had a different chic with him whenever I seen him. Damn, aint that a bitch! Well she's still here looking for him, I left her upstairs a few minutes ago, if we run into her and she recognizes you, we have problems! No I take that back, you will have problems; I'm not smoking another fool over your bad luck ass! You will be pulling the trigger this time Bitch! OK daddy, calm down, I didn't plan none of this shit! Shut up; get your janky ass on the damn elevator. He pushes her in the back. Come on Nina, what the hell you waiting on? Hey don't yell at me poppy, I will kick you in the damn neck with these pumps! Just come on Nina, your crazy ass. I'm coming, I'm coming. The door closes, there's dead silence. Meanwhile Manny and the Vegas police are having a discussion downstairs.

Well officer I really didn't pay attention to what the two were arguing about, my main objective was to get them the hell out of my lobby; he smacked the shit out of her though! Do you remember what she was wearing? Not really, I want to say a blue dress to match her pimp's suite, if I'm not mistaking. Can you take a look at these pictures; tell me if you see her in any of them. He looks over the album of pictures and spots the lady in question. Yes that's her right there officer. Thanks, I was afraid you were going to say that. He then pulls out a few more pictures of the woman lying dead in an alley. Here she is now; we found her a few hours ago. Damn! That's fucked up! Do you know her pimp? No, can't say that I do, never saw him around the strip before. Do you remember anything about him? He was a brother, stood maybe 6'3", light skinned complexion and drove a silver Benz, I think it was. Did you get his name? Nope, afraid not! So you think he killed her? As of right now, he's our prime suspect. Well if I hear anything, I will let you know officer. Sorry I couldn't be of any more assistance. Well actually, where is your control room for your security cameras? That's on the 10th floor, just take the elevator up and go to room 1007. Thanks Manny, have a good evening. You do the same Sir.

The lobby elevator opens, out steps AC, Nina and Sabrina. I will be so glad when this day is over and I can get some damn sleep. Sabrina, take your bad luck tail home tonight! Ha-ha-ha. Boy leave that girl alone, it's not her fault she pussy whipped your ass! Shut up girl before you make my baby mad. Shit girl, that fool been mad about 5 hours ago at your bad luck ass. See Nina, you aint right. I'm just saying chica, I think I'm going to buy your butt a rabbits foot for some good luck, your behind needs it. Man both you guys are tripping, come on lets go meet Will up front. Bro., I'm serious, get that bitch two rabbit feet; put one in each pocket. No wait, put one in each ear, so when bad lucks coming, it will see them mother fuckers and go the other way. Ha-ha. Whatever, shut up Nina. Hey guys, there's Manny. What's up Amigo? Just spoke to one time, he was asking about that Hoe and Pimp that came in earlier. They found that skirt dead a few blocks away, a few hours ago. Damn, pimping killed his bitch; she must not have been meeting the quota. Shut up Coop, you crazy as hell. So what happened with that situation upstairs? Going to meet Will up front in a minute, we have to give our friend a lift out near Area 51; I remember seeing a new development going up out that way. That's even better, we can put his ass in the foundation of one of those Mansions before they poor the concrete.

Where is he already, they should have been up here by now. Look there they are right there! Why in the hell is he pushing the truck? Manny, AC and Nina run out doors to meet them. Girl what happened! Why are the guys pushing your ass around in this truck? Sis the damn battery died, the jumper cables are in Looney's car, we wasn't going to leave our dead friend and the truck in the back while he came and got the cables. Man, yall some dumb asses, girl you and Will could of stayed with the truck while Looney came and got his car.

Loon; go get the damn car, jump this truck already. I want you guys to take our friend out to that new development by Area 51 and bury him under some concrete of one of those new foundations. That's a great idea, because I really wasn't trying to dig no damn grave! Me either Will, plus I got a date later and I'm not getting dirty because AC's ass is pussy whipped. Damn bro., everybody says you are whipped fool! Fool shut up, at least I'm getting pussy, you got spider webs on your balls, it's been so long. OK guys, seriously go take care of this, I'm going to call it a night, I have to work at the club tomorrow, I will call you guys after and let you know when to put our plan in motion. Alright man, we will let you know how it went tomorrow. Sabrina, do you need a ride? No I drove but thanks, see you guys later. OK baby, I guess I will see you at work tomorrow then. Yes Sir, you will. Muah! Good night baby. She kissed him on the cheek.

The night was alive once again in Sin City; neon lights danced across the Mojave Desert, 95 degree winds blew across the strip and felt like someone had just opened an oven door. The lobby at the Towers began to empty around midnight as patrons headed out towards the strip, the 3rd shift staff had just checked in. Manny approached AC and gave him a pound. Goodnight Coop, get some sleep bro., smoke some of that chronic before you crash, it will definitely help you sleep well through the night and calm your nerves. Alright amigo, you be safe out there with them young chicas tonight, don't do anything I wouldn't do. Hey Coop, you know how it's going down pimping, I got that new chronic too; oh want you let me get those two magnums out of your wallet; I'm sure you have more at your place! He reached into his wallet and gave him the condoms he always kept on hand. Later bro., don't let Sophie catch you, she will slice your ass up! Yeah thanks man, you had to say that didn't you! Ha-ha-ha. AC laughs as he headed towards the elevators and ran into Monk's girlfriend again. Hey there lady, did you ever find your boyfriend? No, I looked all over this place. Well good luck, I hope you find him; did you go next door to Paradise and see if he was over there getting a table dance or something? He smirked as he said it. I tell you what, here's my number, if you ever get tired of his ass, call me, I will take you out and show you how a real man treats a woman. Aww, that's so sweet, but Monk doesn't like me talking to other men if he's not around. OK I respect that, but my offer still stands and good luck finding him OK.

The elevator doors open and the radio is playing the quite storm. "The quite storm, soft and warm' "The Quiet storm.... "This is your night time Dj, Shelly shell and all you lovers get ready to go on a ride with the Queen of the night. Next up is an oldie but goodie, here's Rolls Royce with I'm going down. "Time on my hands, since you've been away boy" " I aint got no plans, no, no, no, no, no, and the sound of the rain, against my window pain, is slowly, slowly driving me insane. Boy!" "I'm going down; cause you aint around, baby! My whole worlds upside down" 35th floor, 36th floor, 37th floor, 38th floor, Ding! A gentleman enters the elevator. Hey Scott! When did you get back in town man? Just got in last night AC; I was just coming to your place to give you back your Dogg Pound CD, thanks for letting me borrow it. No problem man, anytime. Man, this music right here nigga, Rolls Royce! That's when motherfuckers were making that love music, most shit is all gangsta now, except for a few groups. Yeah you right about that. 39th floor, 40th floor, 41st floor, 42nd floor, Ding! Well AC, I will get at you later playboy and thanks again. OK man, take it easy. The door closes. 43rd floor, Ding! Hey mister, I was just looking for you! Oh yeah, what do your yellow ass want? Don't be so cruel. Well, you were the one talking shit earlier like you was miss bad ass. I know, but I was angry, I came to apologize. I'm Sorry AC, do you accept my apology? Yeah I guess I can. Are you going out tonight? No Ashley, not tonight, it's been a long day and I'm going to get me some much needed sleep. 44th floor, Ding! Well can I come in and have a drink? Please, I promise I will have one drink and leave so you can get your sleep. OK just one!

Two hours had passed; Ashley was on her 3rd cocktail. So is Sabrina your girlfriend? No, we're just fucking, no strings attached. Oh, so if I wanted to suck your dick right now, would you let me? Would I let you? What do you think? I don't know, that's why I'm asking. I tell you what, put your head down here, and let me pull it out for you, so you can get busy! They both were sitting on the couch, AC laid back with his dick in one hand and a blunt in the other. Taking a pull off the sticky; he said in a low voice with his lungs full of chronic. Come here; let me see what those pretty lips feel like. He exhaled and blew the smoke in her face. She kneeled down before him in front of the couch, grabbed his penis with her right hand and started to slowly suck on it; she sucked and looked up at him with her pretty brown eyes to see his reaction. Aww baby, damn that shit feels so good right now. He starts rubbing her head and running his fingers through her hair. SSSSSSHHHHHhhhh, SSSshhhhhhh baby, damn. Suck that dick baby, Suck it! Oh shit baby! Baby! Baby! Stop baby! Baby stop! I have to pee! Stop bay! No! Why! I don't want to stop! But I have to pee!! Hmm-Hmm, you like that daddy?

 Hell yeah but I have to pee. Stop! Like that daddy! Like that! He stood up to get away, she wouldn't let go, and she gripped both his ass cheeks to keep him still. Ashley will you stop! No, No, No, it taste so good baby, I don't want to stop. Fuck it then baby, do your thing. AC sat back down on the couch; she continued to suck on his hard Johnson. Ohhhh, Ohhh, Ohhhh shit! You motherfucker! You pissed in my mouth! She spits it out on the carpet. Ewww! You nasty ass! He smirks and shakes his head. I told you to stop. Fuck You AC! You could have told me. Girl you crazy! I was trying to tell you for the last 6 minutes, so how did it taste? Ha-ha-ha. Bye, I'm leaving! I can't believe you! I'm sorry but hey, I was saying stop, you just kept on going, like that energizer bunny. BYE! The door slams. Bammmm!

He walks in the kitchen and turns on the radio. Hello out there, all my people in lovers land, the time is right, the incents are burning and here's some Jodeci to get you in the mood. "Every time I close my eyes, I wake up feeling so horny" "I can't get you out of my mind. Sexing you be all I see" Reaching in the lower cabinet where the pots and pans are located, he pulls out the big skillet, a small pot and a lid. Then places the small pot on the back left eye of the stove and the skillet on the right front. Yeah I'm about to get my eat on, up in this mother! I'm glad all those fools are gone; I don't have to share this here 5 star dish. Damn, where did I put my bud? Oh there she go! Coop picks up the weed, places it on the counter by the rolling papers and ash tray and yells out. Every freakin day and every freakin night, I want to freak you baby, your body so freakin tight! Yeah aye, yeah aye. Yeah that's that shit right here nigga. AC gets a cup of rice from the container on the counter by the stove. Puts it in the small pot, adds two cups of water then turns the back left eye on high to bring the rice to a boil. While the rice was heating up, he pulled out a rolling paper and began to line it with chronic, rolls a tight joint and sits it on the kitchen table.

 The rice had come to a boil, he placed the lid on the pot, turned it down to a simmer; then reached in the fridge for the onions, green peppers and peeled divine shrimp. He took the olive oil from the cabinet over the stove, poured enough oil in the pan so that it covered the bottom, turned the eye on low so that the oil could heat slowly. He slid the cutting board over near the stove so that he could cut the peppers and onions before they went in the pan. While walking over to the pantry to get the seasoning, he spots a black duffle bag under the kitchen table. Damn, I wonder who left their bag; I bet it's one of Ashley's friends from earlier. He said out loud. The pan began to sizzle and he added the veggies to the hot oil, rinsed off the shrimp and seasoned them as he placed them in the glass bowl. 4 minutes had passed and it was time to add the shrimp. The aroma of the food filled the air as it slowly simmered in the pan as the veggies sauté, the shrimp cooked to a bright red. AC turned the eye down to a simmer and spoke out loud. OK now it's time to hit this spliff, get my mind right for tomorrow. He lit the joint, leaned against the counter and looks down at the duffle bag. Hmm, let's see what's in this damn bag. He slides it from under the table, unzips it, then yells out. Holy Shit! You got to be fucking kidding me! Where in the hell did all this money come from? It has to be at least 2 million dollars in here, man it turned out to be a damn good day! He takes another pull off the joint then paced back and forth in the kitchen for the next few minutes. Fuck I'm hungry! He says out loud. Coop fixed himself a plate of rice covered with the shrimp and veggies then opened a cold beer. Damn this is too good, a nice dinner, cold beer, some Mary Jane and a bag of money. It's going to be sweet dreams tonight! Hell yeah, a nigga rich now baby! He finished eating, rolled another joint and headed to bed.

Meanwhile upstairs on the 45th floor, the girls are talking things through. Hey Ashley what's wrong girl? You look pissed as hell! Jewel this nigga AC is so damn nasty! What do you mean girl, Nasty? I was giving his ass head and he fucking pissed in my mouth! Wow! Are you serious; that's so gross, I wouldn't tell anybody else that shit bitch. Ha-ha. Did you swallow? Fuck you Jewel! I'm just saying, girlfriend that's something you might not want to repeat, A dude pissing in your mouth. Well, did you get the bag at least? Hell no, I was too busy getting my butt out of there after that damn episode. Ashley, you have to get that money bitch! Yeah I know. So what's the next move then? We will get it tomorrow morning, but you coming with me this time. That's cool, just don't try and include me in you guy's kinky sex circle. Girl shut up! Do you think he knows about us though? No, not yet anyway, besides what's he going to do, tell the police. Yeah you have a point there; we rob banks, but these fools be straight 187 niggas. Hell, the worst thing that can happen is he will want to keep it, but we have some cold shit on him and his crew, so there's plenty room to negotiate. Damn girl, you got it all figured out don't you? Yep, Bitch you know how we pretty gangsters do it. All day baby, we in it to win it! Where's Lisa's ass at? Oh, she went to bed about an hour ago, drunk as hell. She killed a whole bottle of Jose' when we got back here, poor baby was scared as hell.

Yeah that was some cold ass shit that went down. What did they do with the body? I have no idea, I just know AC's place was clean when I got there and the duffle bag was still under the kitchen table. What about Megan? She's friends with Manny, I'm sure he took care of that situation. OK that's a relief, that bitch seemed like a square, a fucking L7. I didn't think so, she seemed cool to me. Well anyway, I'm headed to bed girl; I will talk with you tomorrow. OK that's what's up. Good night Ashley. Good Night Jewel. Oh J, don't forget we have to case a bank in Bakersfield tomorrow, our ride will be here at noon. OK Ashe; got you, Good night girl.

CHAPTER 11, Club Dolls.

It's 11:30am and all neon lights are off, cleaning crews are hard at work, the city seems asleep again, one could hear the bus engines and cars roar as they drive along the strip. The not so lucky patrons; sit on the sidewalk benches in disarray because they just lost their life savings. Ladies of the night stand out like a rose blooming from the concrete as they stand there in 6 inch heels and party dresses waiting for the next cab to take them home after a long nights work. Lying there in a deep sleep, he starts to toss and turn as the 105 degree sun rays beams through his room window and starts to heat up the side of his face. Ring-Ring-Ring-Ring. Yeah hello! Hello Mr. Cooper, this is your wake up call, would you be having breakfast or should I say brunch today? Yeah, let me get some home fries with a T-bone, medium well, some A-1 sauce and a cold Bud; make that draft. Will they be anything else for you Sir? Yes, can you pull out the Land Rover for me, have it washed and waxed, I will be heading out at 2pm today. Sure Mr. Cooper, we got you covered. Thanks man. No problem Sir.

He picks up the remote and turns on the radio. Well it's official people; Iron Mike Tyson is scheduled to fight Seldon on September 7th at the MGM. This is going to be another title fight, so get your tickets ASAP; Sin City is going to be crazy that night! Hell yeah, that's what I'm talking about baby. Shit! I got to call Jerm so he can get some comp tickets for this joint. He picks up the phone and dials the number. Ring-Ring.Yo this Jerm, what's crackin? What's up playboy? This is AC. Aye, what's up fool? Man Tyson got a fight on September 7th, here in LV, want you see if your label can get some front row seats, I know its gone cost a grip through the box office. Cool, I will call Stan as soon as we hang up, give me a few minutes, I will call you right back. OK cool, that's a bet. Jerm calls Stan from his office on speaker phone.

Ring-Ring-Ring-Ring-Ring-Ring. Hey J, what's poppin? What up Stan, everything is smooth on my end; do you have a minute to talk? Yeah brother, what's up? Tyson is scheduled to fight at the MGM on September 7th, do we have any connects with his camp? Hell yeah, my sister's home girl boyfriend is his sparring partner in Vegas. Man stop that bullshit that sounds like some straight bull. Jerm, I'm serious fool! Yeah prove it! Man I got the tickets already, soon as old boy gets them. How many can you get? Probably like six. Good because I aint spending no g's on no damn Tyson tickets, the damn fight gone be over in the 1st round any damn way. You know that fool be knocking niggas straight the fuck out. Like that! Yep you aint lying bro, straight like that; so don't worry, we covered. Cool, that's what's up pimpin. He hangs up the speaker phone and calls Coop back. Ring-Ring. Hello! Coop! Yeah what's the word? We good bruh! Cool, thanks fam. Yeah no problem, so you coming down for the Laker game Saturday or what G? Hells yeah fool, have some bitches on deck. Man I thought you was bringing ol girl from Riverside. What girl? Constance fool! Oh damn, I need to call that chica, I forgot all about her ass. Alright J, get at you in a few days homie. Later fool, the game is at 5pm I think, get here early. Yeah man, I got you.

Knock-Knock-Knock. Room service! He opens the door. Yall fast as hell today I see, Mr. Mack must be in the kitchen; just put it on the table for me. Thanks, I don't have any change right now but I will take care of you later, alright lil g. Yes Sir, no problem. Looking through the balcony doors, he could see the sun glaring off the Luxor mirrors. Damn it's hot than a mother for it to be April, shit the summer aint even here yet! It's going to be a hot one this year. While sitting down to eat his steak and potatoes he noticed his pager going off. Man what does Looney ass want this time of day, that fool gone have to wait, I'm about to eat first, I'll call his ass later. Ummm, mm this smells good. Beep-Beep-Beep-Beep. Man this knucklehead paging me again! Let me calls this dude. Ring-Ring-Ring-Ring. What's up Loon? Yo Coop, we took care of that situation last night. That's what's up, everything cool then? Yep! Alright pimp, get at me later. OK bruh, be easy. Knock-Knock. Who is it? Ashley! He opens door. Hey Ash what's crackin? The girls left my bag here yesterday. What bag baby? It was under the kitchen table, a black bag. I didn't see one; you can look around if you want. He was just finishing up his breakfast when she came in, he gets up from the table. I'm going to jump in the shower real quick, lock the door behind you if I'm not out when you leave. She searches the front room and didn't find it; there was nothing under the kitchen table or anywhere in the front room. Nothing that resembled it was in the bedroom or closet. Man this nigga done hid my shit! I know his punk ass found my money. Hey AC! Yeah, did you get it? Reaching in her purse to get the Nine. Nah, I didn't find it.

She walks in the bathroom, pulls back the shower curtain, sticks the gun to his nose. What the fuck you doing Bitch! Look fool, this right here aint what you want, I will smoke your black ass and keep it moving about my paper! So where the fuck is it! Oh you gangster huh! You gangster! Do what you gone do then Bitch! Smoke me! Go ahead! I aint scared to die Bitch! Pull the damn trigger! ` Yeah, just like I thought! You Pussy like that stinking ass cunt between your legs! Get the fuck out of my way. He snatches the Nine and pushes her to the floor. Don't you ever in your life step to me again like that! You ain't no G! Hell yeah, I got all your ends and you aint getting shit back for that episode you just pulled. I'm sorry AC. Don't apologize hoe! You should have pulled the trigger! Get the fuck out of my crib before I smoke your ass and here take your damn gun too! He drops the clip and shoves the gun in her chest. No heart having Skank! Bye! Get the fuck out of here! Ashley almost tripped when he kicked her in the ass as she headed for the door.

Dang I need to call the club! I don't even know what the uniform is, can't believe this hoe just tried me! He walks over to the phone and dials the number. Ring-Ring-Ring. Hello, thanks for calling Dolls. Hey can I speak to Vinny or Bobby? Sorry their not in yet, this is Debbie, maybe I can help you? Yeah my name is AC; I am starting today and wanted to know what I need to wear. Oh hi AC, Bobby told me about you; well, you should wear black slacks, black shoes and a white button down shirt. Cool thanks Debbie; I will see you in a few. He hangs up the phone, walks over to the closet. Hmm. Where are those slacks? I know I sent them to the cleaners the other day, oh yeah I put them in the other room. Coop walked to the guest room closet to get his shirt and slacks. A voice comes over the radio. Listen up all you Dogg Pound fans, the pound will be performing live tonight at The Drink, so crease up those dickies, pull out the k-swiss, the chucks and prepare for the hot box, you already know it's 420 tonight baby, so until then go get your tickets and I will see you G's tonight in the Hot box.

Here's a little something to get your mind right. " When I met you last night baby, before you opened up your gap" " I had respect for you lady, now I take it all back" " Because you gave me all your pussy, and you even lick my balls" Shit that damn Nate Dogg be blowing them ghetto tunes. He said out load as he headed out the door. Stepping on to the elevator, he felt nervous and excited all at the same time about the new venture he was about to encounter. Ding! The doors open to the main floor. Fresh cooked potatoes, bacon, sausage and grilled steaks smelled up the lobby as the chefs prepared today's brunch menu. While walking by the front desk to pick up his keys, he sees David. Afternoon player, how you doing today? I'm good AC; I left that package in the back seat, the one from Manny. OK that's what it is, thanks bruh, have a good day and be easy, don't work too hard. Where's my Rover? Oh it's parked on the end; I had them clean your bikes too. Shit, you the man! Here's a c note. Thank you Sir. He looks through the glass doors to see how his rides looked. Damn all my rides shinning! Good Job! Alright see you later man, I have to get to work at this club. Later Sir, have a good day.

AC jumps in the Rover and heads to work, when he pulls in the club parking lot, he parks and notice a group of girls heading towards the building as he's heading to the entrance. Hey ladies! Hey what's up! Do you guys work here? Uh, Yeah! So is this your first visit to Dolls handsome? We'll actually this is my first day as your newest bartender. Really! What happened to Debbie? Oh she's the one training me today. OK that's my girl; don't be trying to take her spot. It's nothing like that; Bobby and Vinny just wanted some extra help around the place since business is doing so well. That's cool, so what's your name? My name is Andy but my friends call me AC. Nice to meet you AC, my name is Dylan this is Barbie and Remy. Hi ladies, nice to meet you, here let me open the door for you guys. Thanks, we'll come to the bar and talk with you after we get dressed. OK Dylan. There standing behind the bar was this gorgeous red head with the most perfect teeth and bronze skin, she stood about 5'6" with shoulder length hair, her nice hour glass shape seem to fit perfectly in that black dress. Hey are you Debbie? Yes I am, you must be AC. Yep, that's me. Nice to meet you in person, go let Vinny know you're here and then we can get started. Sure, is he in the office? No, I think he's over by the pool tables. OK, I see him.

Vinny! Vinny! Hey Daz Dillinger! What's up brother, I see you made it. Yeah, Debbie told me to let you know I was here. Come have a seat AC. He stood silent for a moment and observed the club. There was mirrors surrounding the entire building, pink and purple neon lights outlined the 20 foot long black marble tiled runway stage. Three 12 foot brass poles were spaced evenly down the center of the runway, plush hot pink carpet lined the floors and complemented the maple wood grained and purple felt lined pool tables. The bar ran against the back wall and set directly under the Dj booth that overlooked the entire club from the second tier. Pink neon lights outlined each of the 20 steps that led up to the Dj booth alongside the bar. The waitress staff wore black shoes, skirts and black tops that were trimmed with pink frizzles. AC! Have a seat! Yeah, I was just checking the club out. Sit down already! Listen, Deb is going to teach you the bar tending trade, we want you to get familiar with the customers, there is someone selling meth through the girls, we need to find out who it is. Since you will be one of the staff, the girls and other staff will tend to be more open with you. So you want me to be your snitch? See brother you got this thing backwards, once you find out whose taking a cut of our business without our permission and not even paying us taxes on top of that, you're going to off their ass. Got it Daz! Got it Boss! Good, I'm glad we understand each other. Tell Deb I said to start you with the most popular drinks. Oh! I almost forgot to tell you, your shift ends at midnight. OK Vinny, no problem.

He makes his way back over to the bar. Why does Vinny call you Daz Dillinger? Do you rap or something? Nah I don't, but I never asked him. Daz is with the pound right? Yep! I don't get it. Me either, just forget about it, it's not that serious Deb. Let's get started then, they want me to start you with the most popular drinks. Let's see, Hennessy, Crown, Makers Mark are the most popular with your browns. Most customers just want it with coke or on the rocks, sometimes with cranberry. So if someone asks for a Crown and coke I just mix it. Well yes and no, each bottle of liquor has a stopper on it, which measures each drink to pour at 1.5 ounces. The correct way is to get a rocks glass, sit it on the counter, put a few ice cubes in it, pour in the Crown then add like a half ounce to an ounce of coke, stick a stirrer in it and serve it. That's it! Yep! Easy huh! The Vodka's and Gin are usually mixed with cranberry, OJ and sometimes soda. If someone wants a Vodka and cranberry you take the same steps as you did with the crown and coke, same with a Gin and Juice. This is not as hard as I thought it was going to be. Don't get too happy AC, we still have to do the martinis and Margarita's, most of the girls order those type drinks along with tequila shots. We will cover that later, now we have to get prepared for our midday rush.

When preparing for a rush you want to make sure that all liquors, beers, cups, garnish and ice are stocked. What is garnish? That's your lemons, oranges, olives etc. OK got it! So if you will check that end of the bar, I will check this end. You want to make sure we have at least 2 bottles of each liquor and two cases of every beer. If you will write down what we need, I will give it to the bar back so he can restock it for us. Oh! AC when you get to that end, will you turn the TV up so I can hear the news before we get busy. He walks over and turns up the TV. This is your Five O clock news, just in, is breaking news out of L.A. FBI officials are searching for three female bank robbers known as the pretty gangsters. The following footage was obtained three days ago from a bank they robbed in North Hollywood.

The ladies always dress in black body suits and ride ninja motorcycles. The FBI says, these ladies are armed and dangerous, if you see them please call your local law enforcement immediately, do not attempt to apprehend them yourself. We are estimating the take from the North Hollywood robbery was 2 million dollars, but officials say that at least half of that money has marked bills that can be traced back to FBI Headquarters. Here are some surveillance camera photos of the bandits, as you can see they are wearing Gucci shades and have black scarves over their mouths, all three have their hair up in a ponytail. Again, if you have any clues or know of anyone fitting this description, please call our crime hot line at the number listed below. Oh shit! I swear that looks like Ashley, Lisa and Jewel! What the Fuck! Damn! He begins to pace back and forth rubbing his head and cursing under his breath. Dammit! Dammit! Dammit! I need to figure out how to wash that money.

Yo! Yo! AC! Huh? What you doing man? Count the stock already! Oh my bad Deb, got side tracked. Yeah -yeah, whatever, just get to work new blood. OK I'm on it Red, I'm on it. Hey watch it new blood, you can't be calling me red unless you've earned it! Right now you are not even close, you got it. OK-OK, I hear you, Miss hot tamale. Ha-ha. Oh I see, you a wanna be Eddie Murphy type huh? You aint funny, get your ass to work. Yes Mam! Right away Mam! Let's see here, we are looking pretty good on this end, all we need is one case of bud and two bottles of Goose. What about garnish? Oh didn't check that, hold on. Looks like we need lemons and olives, everything else is good to go. OK, you are going to run that side of the bar for now and if you have any questions just let me know. Alright; will do Deb! While stocking the cups he looked across the room and noticed a familiar face, standing there looking in the mirror, was this pretty redbone with the most gorgeous smile and beautiful eyes. She walked with a very confident swagger, her breast and ass were average, but something about her was so damn sexy. Then it happened again, he crunched his stomach muscles to form a six pack as if he was displaying himself to get her attention. She approached the bar.

Hello AC, can I have a Grand Mariner, chilled, straight up? What? How do you know me? Silly it's me, Dylan. Damn girl! You look totally different from earlier. Ha-ha. So you like? Hell nah! I love it! So are you saying you think I'm sexy or you think I'm pretty? I would have to say both but the sexy is definitely winning. Well thank you handsome, now can I get that drink? OK, now what the hell did you want? A Grand Mariner chilled, straight up. OK, One Mariner coming up! He puts a rocks glass on the counter, adds a few cubes in the shaker, pours in the Grand Mariner, shakes it then strains it into the glass. Here you go baby. Oh come on man, I know you're not going to do me like that! Give me a double, I aint no rookie! Damn my bad Dylan, I got you! Here's another shot sexy. Thank you, that's more like it. So tell me about yourself AC.

What exactly do you want to know? Well do you have a bitch? You know; a girlfriend or somebody you're fucking. Let's just say, I don't have a problem getting pussy baby. I'm sure that's not a concern Mr.! So come on, quit bullshitting me. Seriously, there's this one skirt I'm fucking that works here. Oh really! Who is she? Her real name is Sabrina, I have no idea what her dance name is. Stop playing Nigga! You laying pipe to Megan! Who the fuck is Megan? I said Sabrina. Fool that is Sabrina! Well that's her dance name, Megan. Ha-ha. Well in that case, yes that's her. She mad cool yo, I will fuck that Bitch! I'm mad you got the pussy before me. Hey don't be hating on a player, hate the game. Yeah, you did that playboy. I take it you like pussy too Dylan. Don't get it twisted playa, I will ride your dick all night nigga, eat Sabrina's pussy too. Shit, sounds like a date to me baby. AC, if you make that happen, I will suck your dick so good, it will bring tears to your eyes. Damn like that! Yep like that! Say no more, that's a done deal. Yeah I hear you.

Hey Barbie, come here girl! What's up boo? This fool fucking Megan! Who? Him girl! Right here, the bartender! Oh snap, you're not a nutcase are you? No, why do you say that? Because that damn Sabrina have picked some knuckle heads to date in the past, just wanted to know in advance player. I think I'm pretty normal, unless you piss me off then you gone have hell to pay, other than that, I'm cool with everyone. Speaking of the devil, here comes your boo now AC. Hola Poppy! Hey Brina what's up? You daddy! So how's your first day going so far? It's OK, I guest, haven't really had any customers yet. Just be patient, that will all change in the next few minutes, midday rush is about to start. Well, I will be back in a few Daddy; I have to go get ready. Dylan, you got my first round right? I got yours yesterday, remember. Yeah chica! I got you, go get dressed already. So what are you having Barbie? Hmmmm, what do I feel like today? I think I want a glass of wine. Bitch, you know you don't want no wine! Go ahead get that thug passion, quit playing around. Ha-ha! Shut up Dylan, just because you said that, I'm going to get a glass of Merlot. OK Bitch, go ahead, waste your money. Girl I'm going to drink it. AC pulls a new bottle of Merlot from the rack, pops the cork, reaches overhead for a wine glass and pours her half a glass. Here you go B, your red wine. Thank you, kind Sir. You're very welcome, my lady. Man you fools need to cut that shit out, talking about a damn my lady, boy please.

Pssss! Pssss! Hey yall, look at China and Malibu, them hoes aint up to no good. The two girls were sitting over by the stage with a customer, China was only 5'0" but stood about 5'6" in her white knee high boots, she wore a pink dress with diamond studs outlining the edges. Her complexion was pale and seemed even lighter against her silky black hair. Malibu stood 6'0" in her black six inch heels which complemented her black dress that was trimmed at the bottom and up the split with silver studs. Her light skinned complexion looked like smooth peanut butter against her sandy blonde hair. Only one customer sat between them, a very frail looking white male in blue jeans, construction boots and a white short sleeve button up shirt, a link chain hung from his belt to the wallet in his back pocket. On the table sat a cold bottle of bud and a pack of Salem cigarettes, to his left was China and Malibu was on the other. Looking at Malibu and grabbing China by the hand, he said. So what are you ladies drinking today? We want some tequila shots! Hey waitress can you bring me three rounds of Jose' please, along with some salt and fresh lemons. Coming right up! See I told you, they were planning some shit. Why both of them got to be on one dude, his ass is about to get set up. Shut your ass up Barbie, ain't nobody about to set nobody up, girl you be tripping sometimes, I swear. I'm going to check your but into the loony ward and get a check for your crazy ass! Fuck you Dylan! Ha-ha. I love you mommy! Yeah whatever, bye I'm going to make some money, you need to come too, leave AC alone before Megan smacks you up. Ha! Barbie laughs as she walks away. I'm coming! Hold up! Later AC! OK baby.

Here is your drinks Sir, three shots of Jose', salt and some lemons, that will be $63.00. He reaches for his wallet that was barely folded because there was so much money in it. The billfold was stuffed with hundreds and twenties; he reaches in and pulls out a 100 dollar bill. Here you go baby, keep the change. Thank you darling! Yeah, your welcome sweetie! China taps Malibu on the shoulder, leans over and whispers. Did you see all that scrilla?

Hell yeah girl. Do you have one of those pills in your locker? Bitch it's in my boot. Hey ladies, what's the secret? Oh nothing daddy, was just asking her something. So are you ready for your dance? Hell yeah I am! Who do you want to go first? How about you Malibu? Well come here, turn your chair this way so I can get at you. Anything you say sweetie. He turns his chair to face her; she takes off all her clothes and starts to dance. China reaches in her boot, takes the pill from her sock, stands up, leans over the customer's beer and drops it in. She moves towards the customer and whispers in his ear. I can't wait to show you my goodies daddy. SMACK! OUCH! Hey Bitch, what's up? Megan! I'm going to get you for that one. Damn that stings like a mutha! You wait, you going to get yours girlfriend! Girl, stop crying, I'm going to the bar, you want something? Nah I'm good. Well next time then. OK girl. Megan approaches the bar. Hey good looking. Hey baby! Daddy I was so horny last night, I just wanted to come to your place and let you hit it from the back. Is that right? Hell yeah! Can I have some of that chocolate stick tonight? Yep! Ummm! I can't wait! So go get on the stage, let me see you work it. Oh is that what you want? OK hold on; let me go tell the Dj to put on something good. OK.

She walks up the stairway to the booth. Hey Tru! What's up Megan? Can you play some El De barge? Which song baby? I think it's called, Love Me in a Special Way. Yeah I got that CD, will play it after this song. Thanks baby, here's a $5 tip. Thanks Love. Sabrina runs down the stairs and heads towards the stage. Her silver two piece outfit shimmered in the neon light, the 6 inch clear stilettos she wore lit up at every step she took, walking up the stage stairway. The Dj announces her to the stage. OK people this next cut is a slow track by special request, so find your favorite dancer and get your lap dance on. Coming to the stage for your entertainment pleasure is the forever sexy Mega; remember fellas, these ladies work for tips and tips only so please pay the pussy bill. The song plays in the background. "You knew you had me, with your sensual charm, yet your love so alarmed as you walked on by." Megan walked slowly to the pole and leaned back against it while facing AC. She took off her top, massaged her breast in a sensual motion and blew him a kiss. He winks his eye and starts to sing along with the song. "Love me in a special way, what more can I say love me now" Love me now, cause I'm special" Oh shit, sing it boy! Shut up Debra. Go ahead, don't let me stop you! You think you Teddy Pendergrass over here, just keep your day job because you killing that song boy. Ha-ha. Go make some drinks Red!

Megan climbs up to the middle of the brass pole then stops in motion, releases her hands, grips extra tight with her legs, leans back, spins around, slides down to the floor and rolls over into a split. Yeah! You go Bitch! Do that shit! Barbie shouted out across the room. Malibu, China and the customer approach Debra's end of the bar. Hey baby, we're going to the VIP room, he wants a bottle of Moet and 3 glasses, here's the $600 for both of us. OK honey, take room 4 with the 2 couches and love seat, you guys have one hour; I will have the waitress bring over your champagne. Thanks Deb. No problem baby and close the glass door once you guys go in. Megan gets off the stage and heads towards AC. Did you like it daddy? Yeah baby, I loved it, you looked sexy as hell up there. Awww, thanks daddy, guess I will talk to you later, got to go make this money. Yeah go get my cheddar! Man whatever, you silly. It was 6:30pm and the club had begun to fill rapidly, at the entrance were three guys; one whom looked Asian, stood about 5'3" ,wore a blue LA baseball cap, white T-shirt, dickie's and white K-Swiss. Standing around 5'11" with a muscular build, of Cuban descent with black hair and a fade, black shorts, black K-Swiss, black muscle shirt was the second guy. The third male, a pecan brown skinned African American, stood a solid 6'2" in black K-Swiss, khaki cargo shorts and black T-shirt. On his left arm he wore a gold Rolex that complemented the gold link chain around his neck and the gold nugget ring on his right pinky. A neatly taped full beard covered his face; around his head he wore a black bandana, knot to the back under his black Yankee fitted cap

Oh shit girl, look! What Bitch! There's Steel and Jess! Fuck them niggas Barbie, they don't ever give me no damn money. Them your tricks! Dylan you a hater! What the hell ever, you know I aint lying either. The three guys approached the bar. Yo Deb., what the fuck is up? Same shit, different day Steel, what you guys want? Will it be the regular? Yep, let us get three bottles this time, three thousand ones too. Got it babe! Will have it sent to the table. Yo Wes, get three hoes pimpin. Got you bro.! Megan come here baby! Hey Wes, how you been man? Shit it's all good girl, get Barbie and that Dylan chick, come over to the table. Ok baby, I got you. She walks towards the girls as they were standing there looking in the VIP Room. What you guys looking at? Malibu and China's ass, working that customer, that fool throwing all his money at them hoes. Girl you know they slipped his ass a Mickey. Yeah he looks like he's out of it. All I know is, tomorrow when that trick wakes up; he's gone have a headache and an empty wallet. Well that's the price you pay when you fuck with some thieving ass bitches. Yo forget about them, Wes told me to come get you guys. Quit playing Megan, those niggas don't ever ask for me. Bitch shut up and come the fuck on. Yeah Dylan, stop complaining and let's go get this scrilla partner! Ha-ha. Girl, you silly as hell! They make their way over to the guys table. Sit down ladies; we were just waiting on our drinks. The waitress approaches the table. Hello fellas; here's your three bottles of Cristal, some glasses and three thousand ones. Thank you baby, Yo Jess, give her a tip! He reaches over and pulls a stack of one hundred ones from the table and hands them to the waitress. Awww thanks Steel! No problem, it's all good baby.

Deb who are those guys with the Cris? Oh that's Steel with the bandana, Wes in the hat and the other guy is Jessie. They head the 22nd street GD's, pushing Meth, Weed, Guns and chopping Cars is their forte. Damn all that! Yep! Steel is the Boss and Jesse the Capo. I see they getting money. Hell yeah they are! The whole crew came in last Friday night, throwing cash everywhere! It was crazy! It must have been about 20 of them. Damn that's deep! Yep deep! So what's up with Megan? What do you mean? Is that your girl? Oh we just met recently and have been kicking it. Oh kicking it huh? That's what I said Red! OK I hear you Mr. Cooper. Ring-Ring-Ring. Hello thanks for calling Dolls, how can I help you? Hey Deb this is Queen, could you let Vinny know I'm running a few minutes late. Sure thing babe; oh do me a favor, stop by Sunset and get me 12 hot wings. OK girl, I got you. Thanks babe. Damn that guy is drunk as hell walking out of the VIP. No honey; I think he's high, fucking with Malibu, ain't no telling what she gave him. Vinny walks in the front door and comes behind the bar. So how is everything going on your first day Coop? Well it hasn't been too bad. Good brother, that's what I like to hear. Deb how you doing today darling? Doing great Vin. That's good baby; is this guy going to be trouble? No, I think he will be OK. Great, just make sure he knows we don't kid around when it comes to our business. Oh you best believe, I will get that through his skull. OK then, I will be in the office if you need me darling. Later Mr. Cooper! Alright Vinny.

Hey where is that chic I met earlier? I've seen everyone but her. What chic you talking about man? I think she said her name was Remy. Oh Remy, she's slow as hell, always the last one to get dressed. It's about 9 PM now so she will be out soon; her boyfriend should be walking in any minute. Just then; a white male, 5'5" about 165 lbs. walked in the front door, wearing denim baggy shorts, white T-shirt and a blue Dodgers cap turned to the rear with a blonde ponytail hanging from the back. See, there he is now, speaking of the devil. He walks over to the bar, puts a Newport in his mouth, lights it and says. Hey homie what's up with you today? Hey Derrick, I'm good baby. How was work? Shit it was work, know what I'm saying. Yep, got to get that paper! Hey man I'm Derrick, what's poppin? Another day, another dollar is what I always say bruh; I'm AC, nice to meet you. Cool, have you seen my girl Remy, she's usually at the bar by now. No I haven't but Red was just telling me she likes to make a grand entrance. Ha-ha. Yeah that's my Remy, always late as hell. Hey D, you want the usual or will it be something different. Yeah just give me the usual and a shot of rum too. OK baby one MGD and a shot of Bacardi coming up! He downs the shot then sips the beer.

You said your name was AC right? Yep. So who you pick to win the Lakers, Rocket series? Shit! L.A not no damn Rockets! I don't know bruh, Olajuwon be busting ass down low and outside. Plus the Lakers really don't have that much talent this year, I believe Magic is hurt and Eddie Jones ain't no baller like that! I think game 3 is at the Forum tomorrow. Damn, it sure is! My boy got tickets; I'm supposed to be going to that game. Hell nah bro.! You got tickets and you here at work! You tripping! I was going to drive down, but I forgot all about it. Man, just catch that cheap Southwest flight in the A.M. Yeah that's a good idea D. Thanks man! Anytime bro., hey let me know if anybody wants some crystal, I got it for the low. What, are you stupid man? If Bobby finds out, you a dead motherfucker! Man fuck Bobby and Vinnies gwap ass! I got to get my cheese bro... OK I hear you man, just be careful around here with that. Man stop tripping, Remy be serving all these bitches for me, I got this. Ha, ha, OK you got this. Hey look, here she comes now. What's up baby? Nothing Daddy tired of this stripping shit, just don't feel like it today. Awww, cheer up honey cup, I just cooked a new batch. You got anybody asking yet? Yeah China's crazy ass wants some. That hoe done been up for two days straight! How much she want? I got it for her ass, right here! Hold on daddy, damn! That bitch ain't going anywhere! Well here just put these in your boot, I only came by to drop this new batch off so you can serve them hoes. Boss said I got to work a double tonight, some fool called in sick. He pulls her close and kisses her on the lips. Muah! See you later baby, Alright AC, be cool bro and enjoy that ass whipping the Rockets are going to give your Lakers tomorrow. Man what the fuck ever! Later bro.

Steel calls the waitress over. Hey! Hey! Baby come here a minute. Yes what is it? Could you tell the Dj to play some 2pac, oh and some of that Outkast too? Ok anything else? Yeah take this, with your fine ass! He reaches on the table and grabs a hand full of ones and throws them up in the air. She stood and watched in disarray as the money slowly fell from the air and came down all around her. Girl what you looking at, pick that money up Bitch! Are you new! Ha-ha-ha. Leave her alone Dylan! I'm just saying, what the fuck! The waitress turns around, pushes Dylan, grabs a glass of champagne from the table and throws it in Steel's face. Oh hell nah Bitch! Who you pushing! Dylan grabs her by the hair, snatches her back towards the tables; takes her right fist and starts pounding the waitress in the eye. Steel's laughing out loud as he wipes the champagne from his face. Jessie pulls Dylan away; Wes hugs the waitress and says. Baby why the fuck did you do that? We meant no disrespect, come on; let me wipe your face. She really fucked your eye up, that shit is going to hurt like hell tomorrow. Fuck all you niggas, you too Dylan, you stink red hoe! Ha-ha- ha- ha, that girl is crazy as hell! You didn't have to beat her down. Barbie kiss my ass, you didn't try to stop it. I know girl, that shit was funny though! Shut up trick! You stupid, Megan you ain't shit either. Hey don't put me in it, yall already messed up my high. Anyway forget that crazy hoe. Dylan looks up at the Dj booth and shouts. Tru put on that 2pac fool!

OK gentlemen; hope you enjoyed our Friday night fight, Dylan won by TKO! Waitress, she clocked the fuck out of your eye, please somebody, get that bitch an ice pack. This is your night shift Dj, Dj TRU baby. Get your ones ready and keep them drinks coming. Next booty on stage is Malibu from D.C! I still don't know why she wants us to call her Malibu! Anyway please tip the booty on duty gentlemen. Let's get you started with some of that Pac. "You can run the streets with your thugs" " I'll be waiting for you, I'll be waiting" Damn I am so ready to go! What time you get off Deb? Man I have to close tonight! A long night for you then, I'm out at 12 baby. Yeah enjoy it playboy; that want happen every weekend. Bobby just didn't want you to screw nothing up, so he let your ass off early. Ha-ha. Forget you Red. Ha-ha. But I'm so serious man. Yeah, I hear you. Since you leave in an hour, can you cut me some fresh lemons before you go? Sure, I can do that. Thanks a bunch. No problem. Beep-Beep-Beep-Beep. Wonder who that is? He checks his pager. Oh that's my homie Jerm, let me calls this cat. He goes to the end of the bar and picks up the phone to call. Ring-Ring. Hello! What up pimpin! You ain't even let the phone ring! Man whatever; look playa I was trying to see what was good with you on the game. My nigga, I forgot all about it. I'm going to catch the A.M flight on Southwest. I'm at work now, but I get off at midnight. OK, so let me know what time you getting in; we will come scoop you up. OK Jerm, see you tomorrow bruh. Later pimp.

Deb why isn't there a security guard on the floor? Man that dumb ass probably in the back getting head or something; he ain't never where he supposed to be. Wow, that's how yall do it here? To tell you the truth, Vinny been trying to get rid of his sorry ass but he can't find a replacement. Shit, I know a few dudes that will be glad to have that job. Well, have them come see Bobby or Vinny Monday then. Cool, will let them know. Its 12 Red, I am out of here lady, see you Monday. OK baby, be safe and enjoy your weekend. He walks over to the door and waves good bye to Megan. She waves back. Coop walks outside, gets in the Rover and head home. It's the weekend, the tourist fill the casino at The Towers wishing for that lucky hand or spin of the reel. Manny greets the patrons as they enter the lobby.

Hello ladies and gents welcome to Towers Casino; please let any of the staff know if you need anything, I wish you all lots of luck and remember as long as you are gambling all drinks are on us. AC pulls up and leaves his car with the valet. Yo what's up player! How was your first night at work? It was cool man; I met that connect whose pushing the meth. Wait, it gets better Manny! Get this! How about, Vinny wants me to help them knock off the dealer. That fools pushing the crystal in the club without their blessings. Wow! Damn brother, those fools serious. Hell yeah! You think! So what are you going to do? Shit I just met the guy; he has his girl doing the dirt. She is one of the dancers at the spot. So will it be a hard kill? No, that guy is clueless, fool thinks he's untouchable; enough of that already, did you see the news? Some of it, why? I'm talking about the bank robbers out in L.A! Oh yeah, the bitches right? Yeah, I think that's Ashley and Jewel upstairs. Get the fuck out of here! Why you think that? Man they left a black duffle bag in my place last night, that shit had exactly 2 million dollars in it. Coop! What fool! You kidding right! Hell no man, I got the damn money. Damn! They said that some of it was marked right? Yep! So I need for you to wash it through the casino.

Then you need to move your ass soldier, go get it the loot, we take all the money from today's count to the bank vault at 1am. It's on the way to the money room now to be counted, so hurry the fuck up! OK, I will be right back! He runs to the elevators. Manny picks up the house phone and calls hotel security, Ring-Ring- Ring. Hello this is security. Hey Hector this is Manny bro.! What's up Chino? I'm good bro.; I need for you to tell the clerks to put aside 2 million dollars. I am bringing a cart over with 2 million in fresh bills that one of our patrons won; he wants all old bills, so we're going to swap it for him. Cool, I got you Manny. Thanks Hector. AC gets to his place and finds the door cracked open. What in the Hell! I know this bitch didn't break in my shit! The pillows from the couch were thrown on the floor; dishes from the cabinets were broken in the sink and all over the floor. He ran to the master bathroom and pulled the lid off the back of the toilet. There in zip lock freezer bags was 1 million dollars he stuffed in yesterday after he turned off the water and removed the flush assembly. Across the dining area in the guest bathroom was the other 1 million, stuffed in the other toilet. He grabbed the money, put it in the duffle bag and went back downstairs.

Walking off the elevator still breathing hard, he made his way to Manny. Here it is bro.! Cool, put it in this cart, I will take it to the cash room, go wait for me by the cashier's window. Manny pushes the cart down the back hallway; he approaches the door to the cash room. Knock! Knock! Yo Hector! It's Me! The door opens. Oh hey bro., just put it on the table, we will add it in the count. Great, thanks again man. Yeah it's no problem, here are the old bills, we put them in the push cart for you already. Thanks; let me get this on the move, later dude. The wheels sounded like they were hitting every bump and crack as he rolled the cart towards the cashier's cage. Coop stood there waiting patiently as Manny approached. Damn! This cart is noisy as fuck! Here you go bro..! That didn't take long at all amigo, thanks I got it from here Manny. OK, I'm going over to the front, come by when you're done. AC steps up to the cashiers window, excuse me I want to exchange this cash for a cashier's check, I don't think it's safe to be walking around with all this cash on me. Sure, that want be a problem Sir. He takes the cash from the cart and slides it under the window. Who shall I make the checkout to? You can make it out to Andy Cooper. Thanks, one minute Sir, we will have you on your way. She prints the check and hands it to Mr. Cooper. Here you are Sir, all set. I really do appreciate it, I feel so much safer now. Thanks again, hope you have a great day. Your welcome, good day to you as well.

While making his way over to the front entrance, he started singing. Money! Money! Money! Moneyyyy! Some people got to have it! Some people really want it! Some people really need it! But my black ass really got it! Hey! Hey! Money! Money! People don't let money! Money! Money! Fool! Shut your crazy ass up, man you stupid. Manny my main man! I'm rich dawg! You might be rich, but you gone be a dead rich nigga if we don't handle this business. Damn can a brother enjoy himself for one minute! Yeah your minute is up! So what's our next move? Well the club is already in motion and so is the meth dealer. Denna and Nina will need to make their moves tomorrow on both the escort service and video store. I'm taking my ass to bed, I have to catch a 9am flight to LAX tomorrow, Jerm got tickets to the Lakers vs. Rockets game. When are you coming back? Sunday morning or afternoon! Alright I will call the twins and give them the go ahead. Oh yeah, tell Big Will to come by the club Monday, we can put him in play too. See that's what I'm talking about! We're about to make some things happen in Sin City! These fools aint ready for us Coop! Manny go hit the blunt dude, calm your ass down, sometimes I think you like violence a little too much. Anyway I will get up with you when I come back Sunday, oh can you check the cameras on my floor; somebody broke in my place today. I have an idea who it was, but your top flight security aint doing us no damn good with their sorry asses! Yall need to quit being cheap, hire somebody to walk every floor, I'm tired as hell, goodnight dude. Later soldier, I will take a look at the tape in a minute. Yeah please do that, I might have to choke a bitch out! I'm on it brother.

The night is warm, the air is filled with the sound of loud music and car engines, white smoke rise over the top balcony from the bikes doing burn outs below on the strip. Ashley, Jewel and Lisa sat on their patio passing the blunt to each other. So what's our next move Ash? I don't know yet Lisa. Well I think we should go to Miami and kick it with my cousin for a while. That sounds good Jewel. Do your people have room for us? Yeah bitch because I'm not sleeping on one's floor! Girl hell yeah! Truck got a damn mansion and two yachts. What! Oh your people sling dope or something? Yeah and bitch what kind of name is truck? My cuz use to play pro ball for like 9 years until he got shot in the leg, he straight girl. Did you tell him we are wanted by the motherfucking FBI! Ummm no!

OK, so what are we going to do when the news comes on and put us on blast. Jewel I think you should tell him, so there want be no surprises. Hell! He's going to find out eventually, it's all over the news. Yeah but they don't have our faces remember! So don't let your nerves drive you crazy. They don't have shit! I guess you're right, what you don't know want hurt you. OK, so we're not going to tell him. What about the money? I searched that place good earlier and couldn't find a damn thing. AC ain't giving us that money back girl, forget it. I say we go talk with him, let him know what's going on. Fuck it, let's go now then, we aint got shit to lose!

They get up, leave the balcony and head to the elevator. Lisa you think he's going to be mad about us breaking in his place. Bitch what do you think! Look girls, the way I see it, we don't have anything to lose. Let's just be straight up with him. They get in the elevator and go down to the 44th floor. Ding! The door opens and there he was standing in front of his place just about to go in. Hey! Hey! AC! Oh hell nah! I know you bitches aint got the nerve to be running up on me. Look man it's not like that, can we come in and talk. Why should I do that? How do I know I can trust yall bank robbing asses! That's what we want to talk to you about. He stands there, looks at them for a second. Alright come on in, Ashley don't make me wish I would of smoke your ass the last time! We cool man, we cool. They all walk in and have a seat in the living room. OK ladies, what's up? It's like this man; we need some of that money back so we can head down to Miami. Oh now you fools want to run, how many banks you guys done hit? Too many man, too many. What's in it for me? Why should I give you anything? You don't have to, but we really need it. Say I give you half and when I need a favor, I can call on you guys for anything. What do you mean anything? Anything bitch! What part of that don't you understand?

So what's it going to be? Fuck it! OK we're in! Good! Ashley meet me downstairs at the cashiers cage in like 20 minutes, I cleaned the money and got it made out to me in a check. Damn how did you do that? Don't worry about my business, just be there in 20. OK we will be there man, 20 minutes. Yeah, now get the fuck out of my place. Alright! Alright! We're going. He goes to the kitchen, fixes himself a drink then picks up the phone to call Jerm. Ring-Ring! Hello! Hey J! What's up Coop! Pick me up from LAX around 11am tomorrow at the Southwest terminal. Cool bruh, I got you. Later man! Later bruh. Coop dials the front desk. Ring! Ring! Towers how can I help you? Hey Manny, it's AC. Damn fool you aint sleep yet! Hell no dog! Jewel and them came to my place, we had a long talk. What you guys talk about? Money! What else! What about it? I'm going to give them half to go down to Miami. Really! You sure about that brother! Yeah man, I made a deal to give them half the money and they will owe us a favor. Nigga you stupid! I hope you didn't trust those bitches! Man it's all good, trust me Manny. Yeah OK! Anyway they are on the way down to the cashiers cage to get the money, can you have the casino front it and I will replace it when I come down in the morning. OK bruh, are you sure? Yeah fool! Just do it! He hangs up the phone, heads to the bedroom and lay across the bed.

Girl we going to Miami! Woo-hoo! Yeah Girl! So, when are we leaving Ashley? I'm so ready to go bitch! Hold on chic, let's get this money first, then we can decide that. OK, it's been like 18 minutes anyway so let's go downstairs. The girls put on their shoes, walked to the hallway, locked the door, got on the elevator and headed down to the cashier's cage. Jewel let's not call your cousin. Why not? The less people that know about it, the better! Cool, I got you girlfriend. Ding! The elevator opens and the ladies walk out. Hey Manny! What's up ladies! Coop told me you were coming, just go over to the cashier; I will be over in a minute to give approval for the money withdrawal. Thank you Poppy! Damn, look at that line girl! It's not that bad Lisa. Yes it is! Well let's just get in it before more people come. OK let's go.

They make it over to the cashier's cage and wait patiently in line when someone called out Ashley's name. Excuse me, Ms. Marciano! A white male standing 6'3" in blue jeans, white button up shirt, brown cowboy hat, snake skin boots and a blonde goatee; stood there in front of her with two other guys that were dressed similar. Yes how can I help you, how do you know my name? He reaches over and grabs her by the arm. The other males grab Jewel and Lisa by the arm also. Well Mam I'm going to need you ladies to come down to the police station with me for questioning in some events that you are suspects in. What! Wait! What are you talking about! I think you know exactly what I am talking about Mam. Man this is some bullshit! Ashley screamed. Yeah, you cowboy, tight jean wearing motherfucker! Let us go! We aint did shit! Ladies I suggest you calm down; don't make this any harder than it has to be. Everyone in the lobby had stopped what they were doing to watch the ladies get escorted outside. Lisa screamed out in a loud voice. Manny this is fucked up! Tell your boy this was some file shit! He looks at them and shakes his head in empathy.

Oh Shit. Manny says under his voice then picks up the phone to call AC. Ring-Ring-Ring. Come on fool, pick up the phone. Ring-Ring-Ring. Yeah hello! Hey Coop! What man? Did you call one time on Ashley and them? No, what in the hell are you talking about! Bruh the pigs just came and got all three of those bitches while they were standing in line. Dude stop playing, I'm trying to sleep. Fool aint nobody playing! Damn are you serious! Yeah man, them hoes gone with one time! Did they get the money? Hell nah! They took them hoes out of the line before then. That's crazy! I know! Tell me about it! She thinks you set them up. What! Man, fuck that hoe, goodnight bruh, I've heard enough. Alright Coop, just wanted you to know your hoe got popped. Bye Manny! He hangs up the phone. Click! Duck and Loon walk in the Towers and approach his desk.

Hey what's up soldier? What's up, when did you guys get here? Just walked up and seen the cops putting three fine ass bitches in the wagon, what the hell was that all about? Duck you wouldn't believe it if I told you. Shit we can believe anything that happens at the Towers. Shut up Loon. Where you guys coming from? Man we're headed over to Club Beach, just stopped by to see if you wanted to hang out. We got a VIP section reserved already on the top level. I'm going to pass tonight bro., don't get off til 5am. OK then pimp, hold it down. Yep, I will get at you cats tomorrow about that business. What business? The new mission knucklehead! Oh yeah, see you then brother. Come on Loon; let's go catch some new skirt. They head out the door into the warm Vegas night where the pulse of the city was waiting to baptize them in its sea of sin.

CHAPTER 12, THE BEACH.

Hey Duck, isn't it your turn to be the designated driver? Shit, man I'm getting fucked up tonight. Your ass can be the driver. Hell nah! Let's just leave the cars here and take the Towers limo. That's the best idea you've had all week Looney, let's take the stretch black Navigator. Bet! Where the hell is it? Look, there it is, over by the curb, yeah I see but where's the damn driver? Come on; let's go to the limo already, he might be inside. The guys walk over to the Navi. but as they got closer it was clear that no driver was around. Damn man, I don't see anyone over here, maybe the driver is on break or something. Yeah you might be right, hell let's just wait in the back, leave the door open so he sees us when he comes back. Damn! Looney you got all the good ideas tonight! Ha, ha, whatever open the door already. Hmm! Hmm! Hey did you hear that? Duck pulls the limo door open. Hmm! Hmm! There she was, legs wide open, bare feet up in the air, black skirt pulled up to her waist, white blouse unbuttoned, long silky black hair fell to her shoulders from under the black drivers cap. Hmm! Hmm! She moaned as the black eye shadow teared down the side of her light brown skinned face. There between her legs, you could see the back of this big burley man with a head full of long chino braids that ran down his back. Hmm! Hmm! Hmm! Oh Hell Nah! Look Duck! Look! Oh shit! Loon is that Will! Hey Will! Will! Hmm! Hmm! Will! He jumps up!

Man what the fuck you nigga's want! Close the damn door! Ha-ha. Man you eating out the limo driver, you sneaky bastard. Damn baby, don't stop! Wait baby! Wait! Yeah Will, finish your lunch. Shut up Duck! She gets up, puts on her panties and stands outside of the Limo. Damn you fine as hell driver. Big Will how long you been here dog? We headed to club Beach; we tried to call your ass earlier. Don't worry about that partner, I was busy. Where's the rest of the crew? Manny has to work til 5am and Coop's asleep, he's going to L.A tomorrow. What about the twins? Haven't spoken to them! So did you reserve the VIP nigga? I ain't kicking it with no squares man. Yeah bruh, we all good, tell yo bitch to start the navi and let's roll playa, you sneaky motherfucker. Ha, ha, don't be hating Looney tunes. Man I aint hating, but for real though, let's go already. Oh, what's that right there man? What? That right there? Man what are you talking about? You got some hair in your teeth bruh. Nigga quit tripping! Duck come here! Look! Yep! You do bruh. Shit I was all up in that kitty boy! Ha, ha! Yeah you was my nigga. Man let's hit the club. They all take a seat in the limo, Will taps on the tinted window behind the driver's seat. Tap-Tap. Hey baby, drop us off at the Beach.

She started the Navi. And turned on the interior blue lights that reflected softly off the leather cream interior. One long couch lined both sides of the 20 foot cab, there in the center sitting on the black carpet was a black marbled mini bar that was stocked on all sides. A marbled cabinet set against the back of the driver's seat; it held all the champagne glasses and flutes and shared the space with a stainless steel mini fridge, a long sunroof expanded the entire length of the cab. Red, blue, green and purple neon lights danced off the shiny black exterior of the Navi as it rolled towards the strip in slow motion.

She opened the sunroof and turned on the radio, it was a clear warm night and the stars were clear as day. In the background, you could hear the Refugee's over the surround sound system. "Ready or not, here I come, you can't hide." "I'm gonna find you and make you want me" "You can't run away from these styles I got oh baby" " Cause I got a lot of them." Hell yeah boy! That's what's crackin! Man I love the damn fugees! Ready or not! Here we come! In a dope ass ride! Ha-ha. Duck you crazy as hell. That's your version? Nah bro., it's our version! Sin City is about to be ours Will! OK calm down; let's make a toast, crack that Henndog, Looney give me some glasses. He reaches in the cabinet for three glasses. Here you go dub. Thanks! Will pops the Henn and pours three glasses. They all pick up their drinks, Big Will speaks. This is a toast to new shit! May all of our dreams come true, God have mercy on those that stand in our way, we drink for AC, Manny the twins and to death before dishonor! This is our year baby, we will own the 702! Cheers motherfuckers! Loon and Duck shout. Hells yeah! We drink to that! Yo roll the window down fool; we're about to turn onto the strip, let's see if some fine bitches out tonight. Duck you ain't got no game man, so why you want to see some girls? Fool, kiss my ass, stop hating on a player. Oh, so why I got to be hating, you know it's the truth bruh! Look there's three chica's right there standing in front of the Rivera, do yo thing pimp! Go ahead playa! Well what you waiting on? Man I got this, don't rush me; hey driver pull over. Will and Looney sit back and watch in amusement as he calls the ladies over to the limo.

Hola ladies! Hola! This fool speaks Spanish now! Loon says to Will. Come here for a minute. The girls looked at him and kept walking. Come on, don't act like that, we stopped to see if you guys wanted to party with us tonight. Oh yeah, we don't talk to strangers. See now you playing games. Seriously though, come here. The girls walked over to the Navi. OK we're here, now what? Well my name is Duck and these are my boys Will and Looney. Hey ladies! Hi guys! So, what are your names? I'm Jackie this is Jamie and that's Shawna. Hello nice to meet you ladies, where are you guys coming from? What! You must be blind dude. Isn't it obvious, we have our work clothes on, don't you pay attention! Look there's no need to get smart at the mouth about it, I was admiring your beauty not your clothes. Do you guy's waitress at the casino? No silly, waitresses don't wear black slacks and black shirts, we are black jack dealers. Shit! Dealers, that's even better, what shift you guys working, we can come play at your tables sometimes. It varies but we are on break right now for an hour.

Damn that's too bad baby, I was going to invite you all out with us. Oh really, where exactly are you guys going? To the Beach! Really! I love that club, maybe we will come by when we get off at 2:30 tonight. Hell yeah, do that, just look for us upstairs, we will be in one of the VIP sections. Cool will do! Nice meeting you fellas, don't get too fucked up before we get there. Well we can't make that promise, but we will have a bottle on ice for you. OK, deal. The ladies wave bye to the guys. They roll up the window and pull off up the strip, merging into the late night traffic of tourist and locals alike. Yo Loon roll up a blunt pimp. For sho, I got you playa. Will give me that chronic sack you holding bruh! I know you got one. Man you need to start bringing your own shit! Why, when I can smoke yours. Ha-ha. Here fool. Roll that smoke up, next time we smoking your stash. Alright, alright, quit bitching already. The radio plays in the background. " Lord it so hard, living this life" " A constant struggle each and every day" "Some wonder why I rather die, Then to continue living this way" "But I want accept, that this is how it's gone be" "Therefore you got to let me and my people go".

Yeah I'm digging the southern music man; that Cee Lo from Goodie Mob be blowing boy. Duck what you know about the dirty south nigga! Yo ass from Iraq or some shit like that; ain't you fool! Will! Bruh I know you not trying to hate, you big Sumo wrestler, pineapple eating ass. Ha-ha-ha-ha-ha. Yall fools tripping, hurry up with that blunt! You need to put on some of that Master P. What? Who the hell is a Master P? Man this gangsta ass nigga from New Orleans, dude on some other shit, but yall fools aint bout it, wait a few months though. Everybody gone be bumpin that shit! I'm bout it, bout it, is you bout it, bout it! OK, OK, I here you talking that crazy shit dub! Pass me the damn blunt, how bout that! You bout that! Ha, ha. Hey man you need to brush your pussy eating teeth before you hit this blunt too! Nigga that's my weed, you aint got to smoke none of it! Give it here; let me show you how I can smoke it with these pussy eating lips. Yo crazy ass acting like you don't eat no pussy.

Here bruh! Keep that! I'm gone roll my own smoke, you and Duck can have that. Give it here then and stop talking shit! Hold up let me hit it first then you can get it. Looney takes a long pull off the blunt, inhales then exhales the smoke through his nose. He whispers in a low voice. Damn, did yall hear about that Tyson fight coming in September, the city gone be crazy that weekend! It's gone be bitches everywhere, all the movie stars and ball players too. Yeah I heard it on the radio the other day; all those motherfuckers are going to be mad as hell for buying those tickets just to see Mike knock a fool out in 45 seconds. Man Duck, forget the fight, all the fun is gonna be at the after parties. While you talking about it, we should do our own after party and get some of that dough too. The way I see it! It's going to be so much paper here that weekend, everybody can eat off it. Big Will you might not be as dumb as you look after all my nigga. Fuck you Looney! I'm just playing man, that's a good idea though. Let's talk to Manny and Coop about it this weekend and start making moves on it. Hey your girl is driving slow as fuck! We aint at the club yet! Really, I'm saying, it's only a few blocks! Knock- Knock-Knock. She rolls the divider window down. Yeah what is it? Can you speed up baby, we're ready to party and you driving slow as hell. I'm sorry Teddy bear; I thought you guys wanted me to drive slow. No baby, just speed it up OK. OK Teddy bear. Please stop calling me that!

Damn pimpin, she sounds like she loves your big ass; you ate that cat good huh! Damn! Look at that line! Boy the skirts out deep tonight! The Navi drove up slowly to the club entrance; the patrons in line were all pointing and staring to see who was getting out of the Limo. The neon club lights reflected off its shiny black coat and dark tinted windows. Sky blue lights lined the silver step boards that ran along both sides of the Navigator. They pulled up to the VIP entrance in front of the red carpeted walkway; the doorman walked up to the Navi and opened the limo door. Will, Looney and Duck stepped out onto the red carpet. The doorman was dressed in an all-white suit, black shirt and white Versace shades that complemented his olive Italian skin; he reached out and shook their hands. Welcome to the Beach gentlemen, will you guys be needing a table or do you already have reservations. Oh we already reserved one player in the upstairs section. OK gentlemen, right this way. He took them to a stairwell that led to the upstairs VIP section.

There in front of them was an open door to a dark hall of stairs, smell of marijuana consumed the airway, the bass from the clubs music bounced from wall to wall and black lights lit the entrance at the top of the stairs. As they made their way to the entrance, loud screams and roars from the energetic crowd sent an adrenaline rush through their bodies as they entered the club. Everyone it seems was rapping along with the Biggie Smalls track that the Dj had just put on. " First things first I poppa freaks all the honies" "Dummies playboy bunnies those wanting money" " Those the one's I like cause they don't get nathan but penetration" " Unless it smells like sanitation garbage I turn like doorknobs' " Heartthrob never black and ugly as ever" "However I stay gucci down to the socks" Yeah now this is a damn party Loon, what section are we in? Right there man by the balcony, the table with the three bottles of Cristal and the Martel baby. OK that's some pimp shit right there my nigga. Good job boy!

Damn look at all those people on the dance floor. Everybody is having a good time, they drunk and high as fuck too! Duck you high as hell too. Yep and I'm gone be drunk too as soon as we pop them bottles, so hurry up, open that crissy Will so we can get our drink on. My man, you aint said nothing but a word! He pops the gold bottle and pours three glasses. Here we go my niggas, let's drink up and get this shit poppin! Looney speaks out. First we got to make a toast! Man your toasting ass, hurry up; what are we toasting to already. Ha-ha. OK, this one is to Money and Bitches! Hell yeah, we'll drink to that. They all touch glasses simultaneously then proceed to drink.

Speaking of women, let's get some over here! It's your turn dub, I pulled three from the Limo already player. OK watch me work son. Son! Oh you from New York now pimp? Man shut up and watch this. Damn, look over there Will by the VIP bar. VIP was dark and smokey with red velvet rope tying off each section, white leather couches and oval glass tables that sat on grey stone, made each section look identical. Amongst all the smoke, music and patrons a short gorgeous silhouette stood out amongst the rest. She wore fitted CK jeans, black fitted top and black 5 inch heels. Her silky black hair was braided in two pony tails that stretched the length of her back and complimented her smooth caramel skin complexion. OK I see her bruh, watch me in action. Big Will whom already stood tall, looked over the crowd and made eye contact with her. The two connected and he was lured closer by her inviting smile. It was as if no one else existed at that moment, the two became closer by the second. Then there it was. Hey young lady, I couldn't help but to notice that you were watching me from across the room. Wow, oh really, me watching you? Yeah weren't you! Yeah, but I caught you looking too Mr. OK so I was, anyway what's your name Ms.? Oh my name is Sky. Sky! Is that short for something? I know your mom didn't name you Sky. Well let's just say that's all you get for now. The rest is on a need to know bases. Ha-ha. So that's how you want to play it. Well my name is Will; would you like to join us at our table for a drink? Sure!

The two walk over to the table. Hey fellas this is Sky. Hi Sky! I don't mean to be rude but what kind of name is Sky? Duck be quiet man. Yeah be quiet, ha, ha. Looney what are you laughing at; you was going to ask the same question. Ha-ha. Your friends are too funny; his name is Duck, his Looney and yall laughing at me. Be for real, I know you're not serious. Ha-ha-ha-ha, well you got us on that one Sky. Fuck it, you want some crissy? Come on sit down and drink with us. So where's your friends, I know a sexy lady like you is not out all alone. Actually I am supposed to be meeting my boyfriend here, he told me to wait upstairs in VIP by the bar. How long have you been waiting? Not long. Not long? What if he comes and you're not there, then what? Shit! He will be alright, I'm enjoying myself; damn this Crissy is good, I've never had any before now. Welcome to the big leagues baby, this is how we party! Damn I'm hungry! Will, you and Loon want something to eat? How about you Sky? No I'm good man. Me too bruh! Yeah let me get some wings Duck. No problem where's that damn waitress! Hey! Hey! Waitress over here, we have an order. Yes what can I get for you Sir? One order of hot wings, a T-bone steak, medium well and a loaded baked potato. Anything else Sir? No that's it, oh some A-1 too. OK, got it coming right up. Thanks!

Are you enjoying yourself lady? Yeah, you guys are cool. So is your man here yet? Nah, I don't see him. Well, let us know when you do, I don't want to have to fuck some nigga up tonight over no bullshit, yah dig. It's really not that big of a deal Will, I'm just having a drink with you guys, if I was doing something wrong I could see why he would get upset but I'm not. Hell, he's probably running the streets with that dumb ass crew he rolls with. Oh yeah! What crew is that? Steel and his goons from the GD's set. Yeah I heard of Steel, but never met him. That fool is crazy; I don't know why Brian runs with them anyway. Whose Brian, is that your dude? Yes, he runs the cartel part of the crew. OK that's what's up, your dude getting paper then. How long has he been doing that? Shit for like 3 years now, first he did the Cali drops, now he's over Texas shipments too. So he well connected then, yall eating good I mean. Man he is! That nigga don't be spending money on me really, not like I want him to anyway! I say make your own paper, why females always think they have to get doe from a man, get your own cash baby. Well I'm in school getting my engineering degree. Now I can dig that baby, how much longer do you have? Two years left. That's not that long, hey fellas she's going to school to be an engineer, finally a skirt with some since! Ha-ha. What's that supposed to mean Loon? We're always running in to the gold digging type hoes, it's good to meet a chic that's trying to get her own. OK I understand. Duck pop that Martel, let's take some shots dude.

Hand me those cups man, so I can pour these shots. You want one Sky? Hell yeah don't leave me out, I ain't no punk. He begins to pour. OK one for you, one for me, one for you and one for the lady. Alright on the count of three, drink up! One, Two, Three! They all take their shots. Then the Dj says. OK people; it's time to slow it down and get your grind on; here's some Mary j for you. Oh this is my shit! Sky screams out and grabs a champagne bottle from the table, holds it to her mouth as if it were a mic. " Life can be only what you make it" " When you feeling down you can never fake it" " Say what's on your mind and in time your find" " That all the negative energy, it will all be released" " You'll be at peace with yourself, for real". Shut up Sky, you fucking that song up, let Mary sing that baby!

You make sure you stay in school because you aint no damn singer! Ha-ha. Fuck you Will. Ha-ha. I'm so serious though! Look, here comes our food. The waitress approaches the table with both hands full. OK here's your wings Mam, Steak and potato with A-1 for you sir. Thanks baby just add it to our tab, send over a bottle of Jose' too. No problem Sir, enjoy your meal. Damn do you smell these wings, ummm, mmmm, my fucking eyes are watering; these suckers are going to be hot as hell! She picks up the first wing and begins to eat it then a voice yells out. Sky! Sky! Hey Bitch, didn't I tell you to wait for me by the bar! Hey Brian, stop tripping! Tripping! Bitch you tripping! Why are you over here with these niggas, I told you to be at the bar! The guys all spoke up at the same time. Calm down bro.! Fuck yall man! I aint your damn brother! Baby take it easy, I was just kicking it with these guys until you came. What! Fuck that; get your stinking ass up! Come talk to me man, right now Sky! Come here! Stop yelling B! Hey Sky are you good? Yeah, I got it Will. She gets up to leave the table. Come on Bitch! You know what! Kiss my ass Brian! What! Smack! He quickly smacks her in the head.

Sky falls over the table; jumps back up and grabs the crissy bottle. Bop! She swung and hit him in the head. Brian fell seemingly unconsciously to the floor head first, landing on top both his hands. She jumps from the table and starts kicking him in the ass. Huh! Huh! Huh! Take that you punk ass nigga! Huh! Huh! She keeps kicking. Brian jerks and starts to moan as he awoke, he reached in his pants by his dick, pulled out, turned over on his back so he could face the person kicking him then with one quick reaction. POW! He pulled the trigger of his 22 and shot her right between the eyes. Sky's lifeless body fell backwards on to the table. Damn! This nigga done shot the bitch! Loon yelled out. Brian got up on his feet and ran for the exit. Duck checked her pulse to see if she was actually dead, there was nothing. Her cold still body laid there as patrons ran for the exits, security ran to the table but it was too late. Damn what the fuck happened guys! She was kicking it with us, then her boyfriend came, they started arguing, to make a long story short. He smoked her ass! Dude ran away after he popped her, do you guys have cameras in the club? Yeah! Well I suggest you check the tape man and do what you need to because the cops will be here soon. Sorry this shit had to happened at your club but me and my partners have to get the fuck out of here. Wait! Yeah what's up? What's your name man? I'm Will and this is Duck and Looney. Do you guys know her boyfriend? Nah never heard of him. Later dude; good luck with this mess, come on fellas. The guys leave the scene of the crime. Damn she was fine as hell too, this mark ass fool had to go and smoke her. Duck you a hoe! She's dead man aint nobody getting that ass now.

They approached the exit, ran down the dark stairwell and exited out onto the red carpet. The crowd of patrons jammed the parking lot in a panic from the shooting incident. The cops were fighting their way to the entrance as the excited patrons continued to exit the building. Man where's your girl with the Limo? I know! I know! Just shut your mouth and look for the Navi so we can get the hell out of here Duck. Hey! There it is over by the curb, come on let's go. They quick timed it to the Navi... Damn what's all the commotion about fellas? Was there a fire or something? Just start the limo already and get us back to the towers baby. We will tell you about it on the way. OK Teddy bear, on the way to the towers we go. Ha-ha- ha-ha. Man you got that bitch waiting on you hand and foot. We gone start calling you silver tongue nigga! Ha-ha-ha-ha-ha-ha-ha! Loon and Duck laughed loud and continuously as the limo pulled off! Alright Eddie and Martin yall got jokes huh!

Awww Will, we just fucking with you bro.! Yeah OK, both your asses need to go buy some game! Oh wanna be pimp asses! How yall some pimps with no hoes? Nigga that's like MC Hammer without the dancers and no baggy pants! Broke and lonely! Matter of fact Looney, your game so weak, you couldn't get a piece of ass in a whore house if you had $500 taped to your forehead sitting in the lobby in front of the bitches! Ha-ha-ha-ha-ha-ha-ha, that's fucked up Loon! What you laughing at Duck? You could be the only man on a beach full of nude women and you couldn't get no pussy even if you had an elephant's dick! Man, fuck you Will! Yeah, yeah, don't be quiet now, because I rolled on yalls ass. Ha-ha-ha. Now what! Damn, dude fucked that chic up at the spot! Don't change the subject D! Seriously that shit gone have the streets hot than a motherfucker and we was in the middle of it. Yeah might as well be prepared for that shit storm, its gone come our way sooner or later.

The limo pulled up to the towers front entrance. It was around 8:30 am, AC and Manny were both out front talking as the guys stepped out of the Navi. What's up fellas? How was the club? Any hot chicas? Yeah, where's me and Manny's skirts? Yall didn't bring us no girl's bruh? Shit! Wait till yall hear what happened! Go ahead, you tell them Will. Hold up, let me light this blunt first, I got a feeling this aint gone be no good news. Coop pulled a blunt he rolled last night from his top pocket. Yo let me get a light Loon. He reaches in his front pocket to get the lighter but it isn't there. Man I don't have one, must have dropped it somewhere. Here you go nigga, use mine. Thanks Manny. He lights the blunt, inhales, hold it, exhales, takes another pull, holds it and blows it out. OK, let me have it, what the fuck went down? Hurry it up; I have a plane to catch. So we kicking it in VIP, crissy flowing, music jumping, you know everybody is feeling right. I spot this cute skirt over by the bar, to make a long story short. She was waiting on her nigga who was nowhere in sight and it really didn't seem like dude was gone show up after a while anyway. Skirts name was Sky! She comes over to the table with us, haves some drinks, conversation, food and we had a few laughs you know etc. Yeah, yeah, go ahead. We gets to talking about her dude, she tells us he runs with this cat name steel. Her man supposedly runs cartel for the Texas route now but started with Cali and worked his way to more territory. Hmm, I know that name Steel, can't put my finger on it right now though. OK go ahead, what about him?

Earlier we ordered some food, it had just come to the table but soon as it got there, Sky dived into the wings. Then her nigga shows up, talking all kinds of shit! They go back and forth with the arguing and carrying on. Dude smacked her upside the head; she fell on the table, got up, took the crissy bottle and bashed the nigga in the head. What! Hell yeah, playa fell out cold, face first on the floor. Sky started kicking the man in the ass and talking shit then he woke up, turned over and blasted this bitch right between the eyes, she fell dead cold on our damn table. Dude name was Brian I think! He hauled ass out the back exit, the club crowd went crazy trying to leave the building. We left out the VIP exit and came straight here, after security asked us about the shit. I mean this just happened not even an hour ago. Damn! That's fucked up! Do they have it on tape? Manny everything in Vegas is on tape! Um, show you right, well I have to get going but we all good at the strip club Will. You need to come by Monday so we can get you in on security. Duck and Loon get with the twins this weekend; jump on that escort service and video store gig. We got work to do fellas, Manny I will call you tomorrow to see what's what. They all step up one by one and give Coop a handshake and a hug. Alright AC, have a safe trip bruh, tell Jerm we said what's up. OK, thanks fellas; get that shit done, time to get this money. We got you player. He steps into the Navi. Hey baby, I know you get off soon, but can you drop me off at the airport? Yes sir, no problem, we will be there in 15 minutes.

Yo Loon tomorrow as soon as you get up, call Denna and you guys go take care of the escort situation. Duck you and Nina jump on that video store gig; we have to put both of them in play tomorrow. Whatever you guys do! Don't fuck this up! They both speak at once. Yeah, yeah, we got you Manny. OK cool, I will talk with you guys tomorrow, I'm going home to get some sleep. Yeah we headed in too man. Alright fellas, you guys get home safe. The city streets were quiet again; traffic had disappeared as night turned to day. Bus stops had begun to fill with the city workers that made Vegas tick during the day. Delivery trucks crowded the back alleys; street sweepers cleaned both sides of the strip. The day shift dealers and wait staff entered the casinos as the night shift passed them by, headed for the exits. Ladies of the night stood on every other corner barefoot, holding their pumps in hand as they waited patiently on that trip to their next destination. Another sin city night had ended and a new one was on the horizon.

CHAPTER 13, MAY.

The sound of loud lawn mower engines and weed eaters made it hard to stay asleep. It was midafternoon on this hot sunny day, just outside his window was a picture perfect view of the apartment's Olympic size pool surrounded with beach chairs, tables and cabana's. The clock had struck 1pm when his radio alarm sounded off. "Listen up!

Listen up! Sin City, its 1 o'clock lunch hour baby! Boy it feels like June outside and we are only two days from May! So you guys already know that if we don't get enough rain this May that we will be going into another summer on a water drought. Damn it's going to be some brown lawns out this summer, unless you got that green to pay the fines baby, I advise you not to waste water. Anyway enough of that, let's get into some music. Call or fax in your lunch hour request in the next 10 minutes, in the meantime here's an old school hip hop track from Whodini. " Five minutes of funk, this aint no junk" "So pull your bottom off the tree stump" "Ladies real pretty, from city to city" " Now we getting down to the nitty gritty" " We going to make you wet and make you sweat" " Just to see how funky you can get". He sits up in the bed, stretches his arms, turns his neck to the right, to try and crack it. He starts to sing along with the radio. Five minutes of funk this aint no junk, mmmmm, hmmmm, five minutes.

Ring-Ring-Ring. Hello! Hey fool what's up, I just spoke to Denna, did you call Nina yet? Man I'm just getting up good, I aint even brush my damn teeth! Then hurry your ass up Duck, let's get this thing popping already. Loon I'm on it, don't worry partner. So when are you and Nina going to the escort joint? Around 6 pm, they open at 3pm I think. Man I think you need to go earlier like 4pm or close to it. Why you say that? Because the manager will probably be in then, plus they open at noon knuckle head not 3! Yeah whatever! How you know? Don't worry about all that, I know! Well we will hit you guys up later and let you know what happened. Alright bro. later!

Ring-Ring-Ring. Hola! Hey sis! Hey bro., what took you so long, Denna said you were supposed to call a while ago. Shit I just woke up, hasn't even been 30 minutes. Yeah out there running them streets last night, I heard about you guys crazy night. Crazy! More like Physco! Ha-ha. I hear you man, so what's the move D? Well you need to call the agency and set up an interview today. What's the number? Hold tight sis, I have to get the phone book and get it from the yellow pages. Good luck bro.! I hope you know the name because it's like two dozen escort agencies listed, if not more. Yeah I wrote it down when we had the meeting; I just have to find the damn paper. He searches his pants pockets, kitchen drawers, end table and finally he says. Oh Damn! I remember now, it's in my wallet. Hold on Nina, will have it in a second. Duck grabs his wallet off the night stand and opens it, there folded neatly beside five crisp twenty dollar bills was the piece of paper. OK here it is, let's see, that says Angels. He flips through the yellow pages for the number. Angels, Angels, Angels, hmm this must be it, Angels Escorts off Sarah; 702-222-0000. Did you get that Sis? Yep I got it, I will call you right back, let me call them and see if I can get an appointment. OK sis. They both hang up the phone. Nina starts to dial the agency. Ring-Ring-Ring-Ring.

Hello, thank you for calling Angels Escorts of Vegas; we are currently unavailable at the present time. Our business hours are Sunday through Saturday from 3pm to 3am. Please leave your name and the reason for calling, we will return your call as soon as possible. She hangs up the phone. Ring-Ring-Ring. Hello! Hey bro., they're not open yet, the message says they open at 3pm. Well it's like 1:45pm now, I'm going to take a shower and put on some clothes. That's what's up man, go do your thing; I will call them back like 15 minutes til 3pm. Alright sis, later. Duck hangs up the phone and leans against his kitchen counter; he looks over at his stove that hasn't been used in months. The white finish was still clean and the silver around the eyes was shining as if it were brand new. A matching toaster and microwave sat adjacent on the maple wood finished counter that wrapped around the entire kitchen to form a U shape. Empty pizza boxes sat on the part of the counter that was used as a bar. At the other end was a single door white refrigerator, which was home to eight beers, a loaf of bread and half a jug of orange juice. A black futon with a wood base was sitting up against the wall in the living area, across from it was a 52 inch floor model TV. The tan carpet that covered Duck's apartment complimented his brown king sized bed which just happened to be his only other piece of furniture.

He runs the water to take a shower, goes to the bedroom; pulls out a blue and white adidas sweat suit and white adidas sneakers. The bathroom mirror fogs up, the steam rises to the ceiling; Duck closed the door behind him so the heat would stay in the bathroom. He stepped into the hot shower, the water ran over his body from head to toe, with soap in one hand, wash cloth in other he begin to wash and sing. " I saw you and him, walking in the rain" "You were holding hands and I'll never be the same" "There you were begging to me, to give our love another try" " You see baby! You without me! Is like cereal without the milk! You, You just a squirrel trying to get a nut! I saw you-you-you baby, walking in the rain. You and him! Come here; give me back that coat I bought! Give me those keys too! You can catch the bus bitch! "For the first time I saw your face, girl you know I had to have you" "I wanted to wrap you in my warm embrace, visions of your lovely face" " Let's chill, let's settle down, that's what I want to do" "Just me and you" Let's Chill, Let's Chill baby that's what I want to do. Ring-Ring-Ring. Damn it! Who the hell is it! Ring-Ring-Ring. He steps out of the shower, grabs a towel, wraps it around him and heads to the front to answer the phone. Ring-Ring-Ring. Hello! Hey bro., why you sound likes you breathing hard? Because I was in the shower, I just ran up here, what's up? Well I called and got an interview set up for 4pm today. Cool, I will come get you in a few, let me get dressed. OK, see you then.

After hanging up the phone, Duck made his way in to the kitchen, opened the fridge got the loaf of bread and took the peanut butter and jelly off the fridge door. He began to make himself a sandwich to take with him on the drive over to Nina's. He wrapped the sandwich in a paper towel and left it on the counter. The floor was wet from the kitchen to the living room where he ran to answer the phone after jumping out of the shower. Standing there only in a towel, he looks down at the wet kitchen tile, decides to drop his towel and wipe up the mess. Stepping on the towel, pushing it over the floor to dry up all the water, he then steps onto the carpet and makes his way to the bedroom and starts to sing while putting on his clothes. "Make my shit the chronic, I want to get fucked up" " I want the bomb, I want the chronic, I got to get fucked up" "I want the chronic". He thinks out loud. OK time to get busy, got the p&j sandwich, wallet and let's see; where's my keys? Duck gets his keys, locks the apartment door and jumps in the truck to go pick up Nina. Beep-Beep- Beep-Beep. Damn whose paging me? He looks at the pager. Shit that's Loon, I'll call his ass when I get to Nina's.

Nina only lived two blocks away from him up Maryland parkway by the University, which was close to all the restaurants, grocery stores, bars and shopping centers. The area stayed busy with traffic from the students and faculty that attended the University. Every fast food joint in the city aligned the parkway on both sides of the street from Tropicana to the Boulevard Mall. Duck pulled up to the curb in front of her building. A black gated door made of cast iron sat in between the 8 foot red brick wall that surrounded the 8 private apartments; four units were downstairs and the other four upstairs. In the center of the courtyard was a 20 foot by 16 foot pool which went from 3 feet to 10 feet deep.

He entered the courtyard and approached the first apartment to his left on the bottom level. Knock- Knock- Knock. She opens the door. Hey bro.! Hey Sis are you ready to go? Hold up let me put on my pumps. She runs to go put on her shoes. What do you think? Do I look like a prostitute? Nina wore a bright red fitted dress that hugged every curb of her sexy coco cola bottle shaped body, a long silky single black braid hung down the center of her back, red lipstick complimented the contrast of her bronze skin, black hair and hazel eyes. Standing there in red pumps with a 6 inch silver stiletto heel, Nina was indeed breath taking. Damn! Sis you look amazing baby! Yeah you like? Cool, let's go make this happen. Where's the agency? Oh it's in that business plaza off Sarah and Maryland parkway. OK, that's not too far. They both get into the truck. Bro.; turn that air on dude! Ha-ha. I got you sis. So here's the plan, you need to try and get a job answering the phones most important, tell them you can work out calls a few nights a week too. Man I aint selling my pussy, how is that going to work? We will set up the out calls and just give you the money to turn in. Hell yeah, that rocks! Let's do this shit! Ha-ha. You crazy girl! Did Coop go to L.A? Yeah he left early this morning. How long is he staying? Just until Monday, he has to work at the club that night. Get your mind ready sis; the agency is just up the block. Boy I stay in full gear, call me readymade bro.! Ha-ha. Yeah, do you want me to go in with you? Nah I'm good, just sit back and watch me work player, player.

They pull in to the business parking lot in front of the agency suite. OK sis here it is, go do your thing. I'll wait right here in the A.C. Boy don't let this piece of shit over heat! Whatever, take your ass in there and start selling some pussy. Ha-ha. Fuck you! I'm out!

She reaches over and gives Duck a pound, wish me luck. Nina exited the vehicle and made her way towards the buildings entrance, double glass doors with brown tinted glass had been propped open with wooden door stops; old gray commercial carpet lined the long narrow hallway. Adjacent to the entrance was a blackboard that listed all the buildings occupants in white letters, by the name Angels it read suite 212. An old mildew smell fogged the hallway of tan steel doors, a silver plate read suites 100-200 to the left and suites 200-300 to the right. She walked right towards room 212, passing all the mysterious closed doors along the way. It seemed unusually quiet for an office building then there it was; suite 212. Above the door were two security cameras and on the right side of it was a security key pad sitting under a doorbell with a white speaker box. She pushed the button. Ding-dong. Ding-dong. A soft female voice speaks. Yes how can I help you? Hello I am scheduled for an interview. Yes are you Nina? Yes I am. OK dear let me buzz you in, turn the knob when you hear the buzz. Buzzzzzzzz. Nina turns the knob and enters the office. There behind a tan steel desk with a wood top finish was this 300 pound blonde female in a blue sundress. She was the opposite of her soft sexy voice. Rolls of fat; swung from the bottom of her arms and was in layers around her neck that was purposely hidden by that long blonde hair. The walls were bare and held no pictures of any sort, a black TV stand was home to the monitor for its security system, two black office phones sat on the desk beside a rolodex; note pad and can of pencils.

Here have a seat Nina, let's talk. You are very attractive! Thank you! Sorry I didn't get your name. Oh I'm sorry baby, my name is Paula. Well nice to meet you Paula. She reaches out to shake her hand. Now when did you want to start? I am available as soon as you need me. Have you ever worked as an escort before? Yeah a little but I mostly booked the appointments for the girls when I was in New York. Oh really, how did you like that? I loved it; I made good money booking girls! What hours would you be available to work the phones? Anytime Paula, anytime! Hmmmm. Well I tell you what, I can use a few days off. I'm here every damn day, all day! Do you want to answer phones or do escort? Well really I can do both if need be. Damn aren't you just the sweetest thing honey! Let's say you work two nights a week as an escort and take three days on the phones and I take four. That sounds good to me, how does it pay? Oh girl I was so glad to finally get some help I forgot about that part. Honey we charge a $175 agency fee off all calls. The hourly rate is $500 an hour; we get $175 off every hour call. Out of that you get $75, the more you book the more you make. Cool that's pretty damn good! When do I start? Come back tomorrow this time, I will train you on the rules and how we do it in Sin city. OK Paula, thanks a lot girl, I will see you same time tomorrow. Your welcome and welcome aboard pretty lady, our clients are going to love you. Really! You think so? Child yes! Gone home now, rest up, you got a busy day tomorrow. OK, later. She heads out the door and back down the smelly hallway to the exit where Ducks waiting. Beep-Beep-Beep.

Aww man, damn! What's wrong dude? I forgot to call Looney when I got to your place; that fool has been paging since around two, before I picked you up. Well just stop at the gas station on the corner, they have pay phones. Yeah I'm going to do that, shit I need to start carrying that big ass mobile phone I got; it's just sitting at home on the charger. The two pull off and head towards the exit, makes a right on Sahara, go a quarter of a mile and stop at the gas station to use the pay phones. Let me call this fool, before he blows my pager up! Sis give me some change out of my ash tray. Boy you got like $5 in change in this joint, here! I'm going to get me a slurpy while you calling Loon. Duck makes his way to the phones located on the wall of the corner of the building. Hmm, where's that number?

He looks through the pager, ahh here it is. Ring-Ring-Ring. Hello. Hey Bro.! Man what the fuck took you so long? I had to pick up twin and forgot to call you back, my bad man. Anyway what's good? Me and Denna got to be at the video store at 7pm tonight, when we get done, let's meet as Sam's Town and talk this shit through, so we will have our ducks in a row when Coop gets back. Cool that's a plan; did you want to meet at margarita Ville? Yeah we can do that, let's say around 9pm then. OK bruh, see you later. Oh, how did things go with the escort gig? Shit I guess she got it! What! Man, ask her what happened? Look, you tripping man, go and handle your business, we can chop it up at 9. Cool! Yeah cool, see yah at nine punk! Bye doosh bag! Click! He hangs up the phone. Where the hell is this girl at? Duck walks in the store looking for Nina. There are five people in line, two at the slurpy machine. All five slot machines are occupied, three patrons walking around the store but no Nina. Dammit! Where is this woman?

Ohhhh! Ohhhh! Ohhhh! OK! OK! I'm sorry lady! I swear! I'm sorry! A voice screams out from the men's room. D opens the door. Oh shit! Stop sis! Stop! What the fuck are you doing! Stop you're going to kill him! This fool had the nerves to grab my ass! Can you believe this ignorant little punk! Sis! Take your knee out of his back; lift his head out of the toilet. Please don't drown the poor man sis, please sis; come on let him go. Hey man you need to apologize; you fucked with the wrong one today. Blurrrr-Blurrrr-Blurrr. Blimeeee-Blorrrryyyyy. What! I can't hear you punk! Take his head out of the toilet and maybe you can sis! Finally she takes her knee off his back and lifts his head from the toilet. Uhhhh, ewwwww! Damn sis! You could have flushed the toilet! Ewwww, Weeee, dude you just ate some shit and piss! Uhhhhhh ha-ha-ha, come on twin! Let's get the fuck out of here. Ha-ha-ha, now what punk! She laughs in his face. Bet you want fuck with this bitch again, punk ass! Nina and Duck run out of the store and jump in the truck. Ha-ha-ha, Sis you crazy than a motherfucker! What, I had to teach his ass a lesson. Duck speeds out of the parking lot. Where we going man? I'm hungry. Loon wants us to meet him and Denna at Sam's Town around 9, it's like six now. Well we got a few hours, let's go over to Sunset and get some pizza and hot wings, shit that sounds good to me.

Ring-Ring. Yo who this? Fool what kind of way is that to answer a phone? Oh hey Denna. Hey bro., so are you riding with me or you coming to get me. Girl the video store is down the street from my crib, it's only like two blocks up from Odyssey records. OK, so what's that supposed to mean? I swear sometimes you slow sis, I don't know how the Army gave you a Top Secret clearance. Fuck you! Ha-ha. You know I was just playing. Yeah what's the move dick head? Just pick me up from Odyssey Records, I'm going to walk over there and buy this new Mac 10 cd that just came out. Alright, I will be there in twenty minutes, so move your ass. Girl I will be ready, I'm walking out now. Bye, see you in a few. Loon walks out his front door and heads to the sidewalk, the smell of hot iron and tar fill the air as the construction crews continue working on the Stratosphere. Down on his end of the strip, the scene wasn't all neon lights and big casinos. Every other patron was a homeless person who more than likely got caught in the underbelly of this city of sin. Rather it be from drugs, alcohol or the cities number one addiction, gambling. The strip held hostage, those lost souls waiting for that next shot, hit or jackpot. Old hotels that once were marque were now reduced from daily rates to hourly. On this end the ladies of the night tricked for dope and alcohol not for money or pimps. The pawn shops took the place of banks, condos were cardboard boxes and strip clubs became adult video stores and go-go booths. Police rode in their cars not on bikes like they did on the neon side of the strip. Oh there was no pirate shows, dancing waterfalls, volcanoes, amusement parks or white tigers. If you came this far up the strip then and only then would you start to see what was outside of the fantasy land we called Las Vegas. Looney occupied a small two bedroom apartment just one street over from this end of Las Vegas Blvd., A cozy neighborhood where all the locals knew one another.

Loon walked around the corner and up one block to Odyssey records, one of Sin City landmarks. You could see the artistic billboards on top of the record store of Snoop, Tupac, Too Short, 702 and many other artists on a daily basis. Right across the street beside the gas station was the famous Olympic Garden one of the sexier strip clubs in the city, known for its ladies and several octagon stages. He approached the store and walked in to what seemed like a whole different planet, the cold air was a refreshing feeling coming in from the 100 degree heat. There in front of him were all genres of cd's, to his left was the checkout counter, on the right was all the local artist music and cassette tapes. Straight back on the rear wall were the vinyl records, but much as he wanted to get lost in this sea of music, time wasn't on his side. He walked up to the clerk. Excuse me! Excuse me! Could you tell me where that Mac 10 cd is? Sure we have the new releases right here behind the counter. Cool! Can I have one please? Sure will there be anything else? No thank you, that's it. Would you like a bag Sir? No thanks just the receipt will be fine. Then here you are sir; that will be $15.99. He hands her a $20 bill. Thank you, here's your cd, receipt and your change. Have a great evening and come back to see us. I surely will and you have a great evening as well.

He exits the store and the Vegas heat smacks him in the face. Damn it's hotter than a mother out here, where is that woman! The strip is backed up with cars from the weekend traffic; a homeless guy is standing at the corner with a bottle of Windex and newspaper, trying to wash front windows of the cars that stopped there at the corner for red lights. Several horns blew at the girls washing cars in the lot of Olympic Gardens. Loon walks to the sidewalk in front of Odyssey to look for Denna's car in the oncoming traffic. A horn blows from a candy apple red BMW with gold bbs rims and drop top. As it gets closer, you could hear the loud music from the car system. 702 and SFP was bumping the speakers. "Boy you know, you never had a love as good as this" ' My love is the shh" 'Bomb baby, bomb baby" "My love is the shhh" She pulls up to the curb. Get in poppy! Awww you showing off huh sis! I like this right here baby! Got the new car scent tree on the rear view mirror, smelling all good in here, I see you with the cream leather seats, pyramid sound system, wood grain dash and steering wheel. Damn! You doing it sis!

Man, shut up and let's go get this gig. Where's the place? Don't make me pimp slap you girl. Whatever! Wow! Wow what? You have on a dress! Yeah and! I mean, you hardly ever wear dresses. Well I am today, what you think? It looks good on you; the green matches your shoes and your bronze complexion. Thank you bro.! Yeah I like those Gucci shades too, you think you sexy with your hair blowing in the wind. Aww fool, I am sexy! Ha-ha. While you playing and trying to look all cute, you need to put this top back up and turn on the motherfucking AC. It's hot as hell girl! Man you aint touching my top, just deal with it. OK, that's how you gone treat me. Shit at least we aint in a hummer over in the desert trying to dodge bullets and land minds. Ha-ha-ha-ha-ha, Amen to that sister! They both give each other a high five. Alright all jokes aside, let's get to business, just ahead on your right is going to be a blue stone building, that's our mark.

The right side of the building is the video store and the other is where the window dancers are. Dude what in the hell is a window dancer? You know dancers that strip behind a window for money! Wow really! Guys pay girls to do that? Men are such perverts. Yeah forget that, slow down and park right here on the side of the building, I will wait here while you go and handle things. She pulls into the crowded parking lot and parks beside the building. Patrons gaze at them as they walk by the beamer, one guy really stood out amongst the rest. He was two cars down from where they had parked, leaning against a dark green 95 Cadillac with tinted windows and shiny rims. He was a tall white male dressed in white linen shorts and top with brown leather sandals and straw hat, with his hands in both front pockets, he started walking towards them. Hey sis, you see this cat walking up right? Yeah I see him. Where's your tool? I got the 22 in my bag, the 357 is under your seat already loaded. Alright check it! I'm going to lean down and get it as you step out the car and greet him. Got you bro.! Denna opens the car door and steps out. Hey there miss, lovely car you got right here. Why thank you! Why, you're quite welcome! What year is it? Looks like a 96 model. Actually it's a 95. Loon reaches under the seat and gets the piece, sticks it in his pants waist line, opens the door and steps out the car. Hey baby you ready to go inside! Yeah this gentlemen, was just complimenting us on the car. Oh thanks man. Your welcome partner! Denna and the guy were both standing behind the vehicle. Well nice meeting you folks. He pulls his right hand out to shake hers.

She reaches to shake it; he grabs her hand and pulls her towards him in a fast jerking motion, puts his arm around Denna's neck with her back towards him, pulls a knife from his left pocket and sticks it to her throat. Hey man, what the fuck are you doing! Just calm down there hero, yall give me the keys and there want be any problems. Cowboy, you picked the wrong two today. Are you sure you want to do this? Look boy! Unless you want this here bitch to die, I suggest you give me the damn car. OK, OK, listen man, she has the keys in her purse, just get them yourself. Now we're talking! Ouch! Oh shit! What the fuck! Denna took her left foot and dug her heel in his foot through his sandal; he dropped the knife and released her from his grasp. Loon pulled out the gun and pointed it at him. Unless you ready to die Cowboy, get in that damn caddy and get the fuck on! Hey alright, I'm going man, I'm going, please don't shoot! Then get on then! He turns around and runs to get in his car. Bang! Bang! Loon shoots twice in the air! The cowboy ran back to his car and fell down trying to get to get away. He jumped in his caddy, starts it and pulls off. Skkrrrrrrrrr! The thief skids out of the parking lot onto the street. Beep! Beep! He almost t-boned a car as he sped into the passing traffic.

Wow! You believe that just happened! Ha-ha-ha. That fool peeled out fast too! Yeah, Cowboy probably wet his pants after you shot that 357! A few patrons had come out from the store to see what all the noise was about. Denna and Loon were walking towards the entrance laughing at the fiasco. Oh Fuck! Loon screamed. What's wrong bro.? I put this dang hot gun in my pants! Damn that shit hurt! Man you tripping, get it together. She said jokingly. It aint funny sis! Ha-ha. Yeah I'm sorry. Come on let's go take care of this business. Alright put your game face on, let's do it. I'm ready sis. They stop in front of the door and regroup. A glass door with security bars, an open 24 hour sign and Adults only neon letters dressed the entrance. Dusty sky blue paint shaded the stone brick building. Adult Videos and Live Peep Show Girls marque the side of the building written in big red letters. Loon opens the door and they walk in. A mildew smell was in the air, the lights were dim and gloomy shadowing rows and rows of video tapes and DVD's. Over by the counter was a doorway that had a red neon sign over the door that read peep show $10 for 5 minutes. Blue curtains hung from the crescent doorway that led to the private viewing rooms which was separated by a 6' by 6' Plexiglas window that divided the patron and entertainer. Black carpet complemented the red walls and grey leather love seats in each of the seven booths. Behind the counter stood an old white gentlemen; maybe in his late 60's. He wore thin wire framed glasses that hung sideways off his nose, short stubby white hairs covered his head and beard, bronze orange looking skin clung to this man's body and was wrinkled at his elbows, hands and neck. The green polo shirt and jean shorts made him look even more superficial against his skin and white hair.

Loon and Denna approach the gentlemen at the counter. Hello Sir. Hi, how can I help you folks? Well actually I called earlier and spoke to someone about the cashier's job and a security job for my cousin. Oh yes dear, I remember speaking to you. Well how soon can you guys start? How soon do you need us? Hell to tell the truth! I can use both you right know! Wow, hmm, well I guess I can start now, what about you Loon? Hell yeah! Wait Sir! How much does the job pay? Well cashiers make $11 an hour and security $12 an hour. Do you have any more questions Mam? No Sir, I don't. So you folks want the jobs or not? You told me over the phone both you guys were prior military. Yes we are Sir. Great I'm a Vietnam Vet myself, Airborne Ranger U.S Army, Ft. Benning. Whoa! Nice to meet you soldier; we both are 82nd Airborne and Air assault. Well I'll be damn, we gone get along just dandy then aint we young bucks! Yes Sir! OK then, let's get you guys started. Oh my name is Keiser by the way! I'm Denna! Oh I'm Loon! Loon did you say? Yes! What kind of name is that son? Ha, ha, let's just say I got it while working with my unit in the desert. In that case I can understand soldier. So Loon your job will be to make sure the premises are safe, no steeling and watch for the lot lizards. What in the hell is a lot lizard? Ha, ha, that's a $20 prostitute, they try and work my customers when their walking the parking lot. Hell if I don't keep them lizards away, the damn customers want ever come in! Damn bitches out there soliciting $20 blow jobs!

Ha ha no shit! Hell yeah soldier! Them damn nasty woman are a trip! OK, I can handle that sir, say no more. Good hold on a minute; let me get you a shirt. He reaches below the counter and gets a blue shirt with security on the front and back. Here you go young buck, put that on. Miss can you work a cash register? Yeah; no problem! Well come on around here, let me show yah what keys for what. She makes her way behind the counter. These 3, right here are for DVDs, $10, $15 and $20, videos are $9. The bottom key is for the peep show rooms, it's 7 rooms, each room has its own key on the register. When someone pays for a peep show you press the PS key for however many shows they buy. Oh Loon right over here on this glass display case is the security monitor. A 10 foot long counter display case made of glass stood 6 foot high in front of the store. Behind it was a 2 foot high platform that made the employees appear taller than they really were. Yo I appreciate the job old timer, but I'm not wearing no security shirt. How about, I just wear my shoulder harness and a security badge. What do you mean; you're not wearing the shirt! I'm not wearing it and lower your voice Serge, I aint your son. If you want me to take the job, that's the only way I will do it, if not, you can give it to someone else. Loon, stop tripping man! I'm not tripping Denna, I just aint wearing no damn security shirt. OK soldier, I don't have a problem with that, just get the job done. He extends his right hand out to Loon and they shake on it.

Excuse me! Excuse me! Excuse me Mam. Gentlemen approached the counter. Yes, how can I help you? I would like to buy a peep show. OK, how many do you want Sir? Just one! One peep show, that will be $10 Sir. She rings it up on the register. Here's your receipt Sir, you will be in booth 5. Thank you baby! Your welcome sweetie! He walks to the peep show area and takes a seat in the 5th booth. The window shade comes up, A red door opens and a gorgeous 5'1" dark skin beauty with a flat stomach, black shoulder length hair, c cup breast, size 35 ass and brown eyes; stood there in a light green two piece outfit trimmed in white with white knee high stiletto boots. The dancer's peepshow room was plush with wall to wall red carpet and an 8 foot brass pole that was in the center of the 8 foot by 8 foot entertainment area. Hello baby, how are you doing tonight? The dancer said to the customer. I'm doing great sexy; your looking good as hell up there baby. So am I just dancing for you tonight or do you want me to get nude? Hell, let's take it all off today! OK, whatever you want daddy, just put the $50 in the money slot and I can get started. Buzz-Buzz. Yeah what's up baby? Keiser I'm doing an extra 10 minutes; got a nude show. OK darling, will mark it down. Who was that? Oh that was Chocolate the dancer in booth 5; she just got an extra $50 to go totally nude. Oh that's what's up. Yeah, so anytime they buzz the front desk and request more time, just put it in the log book by their names. Alright will do! Beep-Beep. Damn this is Manny paging. Hey sis give me your mobile phone so I can call him and see what's up. She hands Loon the phone, he calls Manny.

Ring-Ring. Hello! Yo what up Manny! Hey Loon what's up! Over here at the video store with Denna working and shit. Working! Yep! Damn you fools started already? Yep dude hired us on the spot. That's cool as hell right there pimping. So you guys are in position then? We will be by the end of the night, old timer teaching us how to run shit. That's what's up, so hit me when you guys leave there then. I'm gone to call AC and let him know our status. Ok, later Manny. Later bro, tell sis I said what up! Alright! Click! Yo Manny said what up. Yeah what did he want? Nothing just checking on things, you dig. I dig. Oh shit! What Loon! We have to leave at 8:30pm to meet up with Nina and Duck out at Sam's Town. Damn, I forgot all about that! What time is it now? Like 8! Hey Serge! Serge! Yeah what is it youngster? We have to leave at 8:30 tonight for a prior arrangement. Well damn! You two running out already, aint even been here a day yet! It's not like that old timer, we just made these plans earlier and we have to keep them. Well I tell you what, come back in tomorrow at 7pm; make plans to work a whole shift. They both said at the same time. We got you Sir, 7pm it is! Good, now go meet your friends and don't do nothing I wouldn't do. They both head to the exit in a rush, jumped in the beamer and speed off the lot. After traveling 5 to 10 miles over the speed limit the entire way they finally arrived at their destination, just off Boulder highway; there it was off in the distance sitting like a City among a sea of cars, trucks and RV's. Sam's Town; Hotel and Casino, a favorite spot for the locals and the lucky tourist that happen to venture away from the strip. Great food, great drinks, awesome customer service and a delicious seafood buffet were just a few things that made it a town's favorite.

Nina and Duck entered the loud casino, slot machines chimed, jackpot bells rung, guys and girls alike yelled to the top of their lungs celebrating the bets they placed, hoping to win big. Most walked around in sorrow after losing their paychecks and even worse, their life savings. Laughter and glee burst from the jovial patrons waiting in the buffet line. Cowboy hats surrounded the craps tables as they tried their luck with the role of the dice. Cigar and cigarette smoke fogged the air and always left a discussing smell in the waitress hair after a long day of serving drinks to the gamblers and other casino patrons. On the other side of the hotel, through a sea of people, smoke and loud noise. There set a vision of beauty, a large bar decorated with pink and blue neon lights, bamboo straw, tiki mask and a large seating area under a big bamboo umbrella. Pink letters over the bar read Margarita's two for one every day, they made their way through the crowd and smoke filled air to this oasis. Hey where do you want to sit Nina? Let's get a table, Loon and sis will be here in a few. Yeah you right, how about this one? Yeah that's fine. A young lady walks over to them.

Hi folks my name is Jay, I will be your waitress today, what can I start you guys off with? Hello Jay, let me get a large hurricane. For you Sir? Let me get the Volcano, yeah the Volcano. So that's one hurricane and a Volcano? Yep that's it. Coming right up guys, do you want any appetizers today? Nah we're good for now. OK, be right back with your drinks. Yo sis that was some crazy shit you did today! What are you talking about dude? The bathroom incident! Ha-ha-ha, that fucker was trying to molest me in the store, grabbing my ass and talking dirty too, like I was his bitch! Ha-ha. Yeah he ended up being the bitch though. Bet that fool want grab another girls ass. Man he probably still embarrassed from what you did to him. What I do? Flushing his ass in the toilet! That fool deserved that poppy, I mean really, he was wrong. Yeah he was. Enough of that, it's in the pass. Hey did you hear about that Tyson fight coming in September? Hell yeah! You know I'm gone be there; me and Denna! So what, you acting like me and the fella's aint coming. I'm just saying, I got tickets already, my girl is fucking his sparring partner so we in like Flynn poppy! Yeah that's what's up right there Sis, Jerm supposed to be hooking us up ring side. What Jerm? Jerm fool! Oh Coops boy from L.A? Yeah! Motherfucking Jermaine, hmm, what that hustler doing for it? Shit, he got this A&R gig with some record label out there. Really! He making moves then, I like that. She looks down at the menu.

Yo ,Yo, Yo! What up Bitches! A loud deep voice shouted out. Oh snap, what up Denna! What up Loon! Yall just sneaking up on folks! We good! So what's popping with the drinks? The waitress should be back with ours in a minute, we just ordered. She needs to hurry that ass up! For real, I'm ready to get right! Calm down Denna, she's coming, here she is now. Alright Sir, you had the Volcano, Mam you had the-the-the, Damn, wait a minute, are you the one that had the hurricane, I swore it was you in the red but you guys look alike. Ha-ha, it was her baby; I just got here but let me get one too. No problem, one more on the way. What are you having Sir? Let me get that great white, with pina colada. One great white and a hurricane coming up; any appetizers? Yeah, bring us some fully loaded nachos with extra hot peppers. OK, will do. Hey guys what happened over at the escort service? Sis it was a piece of cake, this big fat lady is running things over there and she hates it on top of that. I start tomorrow on the phones; the guys are going to set up fake dates a few nights a week on the out call side. I was wondering how you were going to do that Sis? That's smart though, keep it gangsta! You know how we do it sis. Denna, you and Nina are two nut cases, that's why both your asses single today. Fool, nobody asked your opinion; with a name like Loon we know your ass is crazy. Damn right! Crazy as a bat, so don't fuck with me! Ha-ha. Shut up man, you stupid. Shit, we all a little loony. Ha-ha-ha. Duck shut up man; you're the worst of us! Yeah-Yeah. Whatever Nina! I know you're not talking after that incident today! Man be quiet! Umm-hmm. That's what I thought. So guys how did the video store gig go?

Oh that was a trip! We almost smoked this cowboy in the parking lot for trying to jack Denna's beamer; this fool pulls out a knife and stuck it to her neck. What! Girl yeah! I put this 6 inch stiletto heel through his damn foot too! What! Girl he started running like a little bitch, Loon shot two rounds in the air, that fool dang near piss his pants getting in his cadi. That's crazy; what side of town is that store on? It's on the north end of the strip. Shit, no wonder, did you guys get to see about the gig though. Yeah we started working today, we just left. Well tell us about it. It's an easy gig, this old vet runs the joint, soon as he heard we were prior Army we got the gig. Yeah that was easy I bet. What are you guys doing? Denna's on front counter and I'm doing security. Is the Vet cool though? Yeah he's straight, looks like an old beach bum with white hair and orange skin. Oh that type. Yep! Loon that should be an easy takeover, it doesn't sound like it's too secure. Not at all, it's a piece of cake job. Damn, where's that waitress with my drink? Dude she's still over by the bar. Fuck this, I'll be right back. Man where you going? Leave him alone Nina, you know how he gets.

Duck approaches the tiki bar and taps his waitress on the back. Excuse me! Yes what is it? Where are our drinks, we've been waiting a while. Oh I'm sorry sir but we had to go get the pina colada mix from the cooler, the bartender is fixing them now. OK, I'll wait and take them back with me. Are you sure? Yeah it's no problem. Well I'm sorry you had to wait. Thanks for the apology because I was getting pissed. You look like you were coming to bust me up when I saw you walking this way. No I wasn't, but I was thinking about it! Ha, ha, you're so crazy! What's your name? I'm Duck and yours? Oh I'm Jay. Well it's nice to meet you Jay. You're a sexy young lady, do you have a boyfriend? Thanks and no I don't. Just can't seem to find that perfect guy! Good luck with that baby, nobody is perfect. Well I'm perfect! Oh really! Tell me what makes you perfect Jay. Let's see, I love myself, I think I'm the perfect person. My smile, hair, skin, walk, personality, everything about me is perfect. You think you are the definition of perfect? Yes I do! Shit! Bitch you crazy as hell! I can find like 10 flaws with you right now that will make you less than perfect! I don't want to be the one to give you the bad news baby, but you aint perfect. Well that's your opinion Duck! Here's your drinks hater! She shoves them in his hands. Ha-ha-ha-ha. Why I have to be a hater Jay? Hater! He stands there looking at her as she walks away. Ha-ha. Have a good day perfect girl, thanks for the drinks. Yeah, yeah, bye hater! He takes the drinks and head back to the table shaking his head with a grin on his face.

Hey sis, here's your drink! Thanks baby! What was the hold up? They had to get some more mix from the cooler. We saw you chopping it up with the waitress, you bout to hit that huh? Hell nah, aint even tried, that bitch told me she was perfect! Ha-ha. Stop playing bruh! Man I'm so serious, the fucked up part about it all is, she really believes that. Are you talking about that waitress that waited on us? Yep! Perfect! That hoe done fell and bumped her head. Hell, she aint got nothing on me and my sister, we perfect! Not even close sis. Nina and Denna give each other a high five. Seriously though guys, cut the small talk, I'm ready to pull this long hustle, you dig. Hell yeah Loon, I'm so ready to run Sin City. Yeah fellas, this city aint ready for what we got! Damn right, it's time to get money. Shit I'll drink to that! Nina shouts. They all lift their glasses and Make a toast. Here's to the new Kings and Queens of Sin City, the players playground. Then they all say. Death before dishonor!

OK, listen up, I got a joke! Oh boy, here we go! Shut up Loon and listen, go ahead Duck. OK, what's six inches long with a head on it? What! That's easy! Your little ass dick! Ha-ha. Nope, wrong Nina! Six inches long, hmm, man I don't know. Yall so slow! What's the answer man! They all yell out. It's a one dollar bill. Awwww, Booooo, that was wack! Ha-ha. Man you need to stop with the jokes. Yeah whatever, yall know that joint was funny. Man that joke was not funny! Loon you just mad because you don't have skills like me. Look bruh, you're not Eddie Murphy alright. He looks at him, shakes his head and laughs. I still got love for you, even though you got them dry ass jokes. Man, kiss my ass! Ha-ha. Come on dude, don't be getting all mad and shit. I'm cool bruh. Loon stands up. So people what's next? I'm not sipping on no fruity ass drinks all night, let's go have some fun. Hey you guys want to come with me and Nina? Come where sis? Well, we were invited out to Lake Mead; we're going out on the party boat tonight. Party boat, that sounds fun, who's the Dj? Loon looks over and asked Nina. Oh, Ted the guy throwing the party, said it was one of the Dj's from club Drink. Oh those cats are cool, that shit is going to be dope, I'm down let's do it. What about you Duck, you down? Hell yeah fool, let's go. Hold on knuckle heads, we have to pay for our drinks. Man sis, yall go pay for them, I'm not going back over there by Ms. Perfect, that chick got issues. Ha-ha. OK, you guys meet us out front. OK, cool.

Loon and Duck made their way through the crowded, noisy, smoke filled casino. Hey man, I think Sabrina is going to get Coop in some shit he can't get out of. That's funny you said that Loon, I was thinking the same thing. I hope we off that bitch sooner than later, something is not right with that skirt. Well one thing is for sure. What's that Duck? Home girl got bruh pussy whipped! I don't know man, if she had him so whipped, why he aint take her ass to L.A then. Fool, because he's a Ho and he's with Jerm too! Man them niggas probably knocking back ten skirts each this weekend. Ha-ha-ha. Yeah you right bruh. Dang where's the girls, I'm ready to crash this yacht party already. Man give them a few minutes, you know how they like to take their time and shit. Hey, don't be doing that crazy ass Looney dance tonight man! Fool that's my signature dance; gets me all the ladies! Ha-ha-ha. Yeah OK!

You just mad you don't have the skills that I do on the dance floor bruh! That's what it is! Man stop kidding yourself, I got them John Travolta moves. Yeah, exactly! Travolta! Dude, that's like, 1970's! Ha-ha. Just watch your boy at work tonight Duck, you might learn a few things. He starts to bob his head and look at Duck. Hey what yall clowns doing! Oh hey girls! Where the hell you guys been? Paying the bill that you knuckle heads walked out on! I thought we asked you to pay it sis, I didn't want to go back around that crazy waitress. Yeah we almost put Ms. Perfect down for the count! Chica was running after us screaming all loud through the casino like we meant to leave without paying. Damn my bad sis! Uh, huh, don't worry; yall fools owe us! We got you! Now let's get to that party on the lake. Yo! Yo! Valet! The valet attendant ran up. Yes Mam! Here are our tickets; can we have our cars please? Yes Mam, we'll be right back. Hey Loon I'm rolling with sis in the beamer, you and Duck can ride in your truck. Oh that's how you going to do me sis! Yeah man, we can't role up to the party with you guys in the car, people might think we are all dating, that right there will mess my groove up with the fellas poppy. Yeah-yeah! Whatever! OK, here are the cars! Alright ladies, we will meet you at the yacht, we have to make a quick stop on the way. Hurry up, don't be coming all late man; where you two going anyway? We're going to pick up Will; you know we can't party without bro... The girls get into the red BMW; drops the top, puts the peace sign up to the guys and yells out. Hey tell Will to bring some of that indo! Yeah we got you! Don't forget! The ladies speed off the lot. The valet pulls the black F150 up. Here you are Sir. Thanks man! Hey Loon, give the lil niigga a tip! Here lil man, go buy you some lunch with this $5! Thank you Sir. The guys jump in the truck and pull off.

Hey Duck, you buying my first drink the next time we at the club too bruh. Man, what are you talking about? I'm talking about me tipping the valet for parking your truck! Dude, are you serious? Hell yeah, why did I have to tip somebody for parking your shit, noticed I said, your shit! Ha-ha-ha. OK man, I got you. Cool, that's all I'm saying, I do you a solid, and you do me one. Loon shut up about that man, it's over I got you. Alright it's done. He opens the glove box, starts pulling out papers and moving everything around. Hey Loon, what in the hell are you doing? I'm looking for the cologne bruh. Where you got it stashed at, I want use it all. Dude it's under the arm rest, next time just ask! OK my bad. He lifts up the arm rest. Let's see what my brother got in here, Hmm, OK, I like this one, that Cool Water! He opens the bottle and splashes some on. So did you get that waitress number back at the spot? Who? You know! Oh Ms. Perfect, hell no, she got issues. What you mean? Trust me, anytime a girl thinks she is perfect, it's going to be problems. Give me an example bruh. Example! I got one good one for you. Well let's hear it? The way I see it, no one is perfect, to say you are perfect is to say that you never make any mistakes! That everything about you is perfect and everyone should follow you, do as you do or say because you are the perfect person, that's bullshit! Yeah bro., you got a point there. In so many words, that bitch just told you that she was insane. Ha-ha. Hell yeah, now you get it. Got it! Plus she will always be alone as long as she believes that, I don't have time for no crazy ass skirt. They give each other a pound. I can dig it. Yo stop at this Terrible Herbs so we can call Will.

They pull into the gas station off Lake Mead Blvd.; Loon jumps out the truck, walks up to the pay phone and dials the number. Ring-Ring-Ring. Hello, who is this? Hey Dub! This is L, what's crackin? What's up homie, I'm chillin, what's good? We about to go crash this yacht party that the twins invited us to on Lake Mead. You down? Man hell yeah, where's D at? He's in the truck we're on Lake Mead Blvd. now, you coming to meet us out there. Man yall fools need to come pick me up, I plan on getting fucked up tonight brother. Hold on! Hey Duck! What? Will wants to know can we come pick him up?

What's wrong with his truck; why can't he drive? Nothing, he just wants to get wasted. Man, tell that fool we on the way. Hey dub, we on the way. Alright bro., see you in a minute. We should have just stopped by anyway before we hit Lake Mead. Hell nah! Will be tripping sometimes about people dropping in unannounced. Yeah I hear you, but its right up the block, it couldn't have hurt to stop by, that's all I'm saying. They drive up the street a mile or so and pull into the Rancho neighborhood. Damn which house is it? All these cribs look alike, same color and everything. I know right. Stop, its 2254, there it is right there on the left. He pulls in the driveway and blows the horn. Beep-Beep. Out walks Will. Oh shit! Hell nah!

What the fuck! Loon and Duck jump out of the F-150. Man why did you cut your hair off! Time for a change man, plus this Vegas heat felt hotter than an oven with all that hair on my head. OK, you look cool though brother, rocking the fresh baldy like me pimping. Alright fellas, let's go have us some fun. Will I always knew you looked up to me, that's why you did it right, go ahead tell the truth bruh. Ha-ha. Loon shut your ass up fool! He smacks him in the head. Hey smack your on baldy! Stay off mine, you got your own now bruh. So did anyone hear from AC? Yeah Manny called earlier, he spoke with him. Cool that's what's up. Hey aint you suppose to start at the club Monday? Well I have to go speak with the owner and see if he got a spot for me. Dude if Coop set it up already, trust me, you're good man. I hope so because I'm ready to make some moves and get this paper. Hell yeah, no doubt! Loon and Duck gives him a high five.

As they get closer to Lake Mead they can see the yacht at the pier, its white lights lit up the dark sky over the manmade lake. Guys and Girls approached the yacht in groups and some in pairs. Hurry up man and park this truck! Hold on! Hold on, we're almost there. They pull into the lot and park beside a charter bus. Wow, look at all that ass over there, man we just hit the jackpot! Duck you're a hoe! Hey neither one of yall busters have room to talk! Let's go meet some chics. They jump out the truck and walk towards the pier. So who's throwing this party? Some dude name Ted. Ted! Yeah that's what sis said, why you know him Will? No don't think I do, who's the Dj? Man look, none of that even matters, I see girls, hear music and I know they're drinks on the boat! That's all I need to know, Fuck the rest, Loon came to party! As they got closer to the pier they seen Nina and Denna waving them on. Hey come on fellas, hurry up! The music was blasted and the crowd was rowdy. OK people this is your Dj, Dj Prince baby and tonight we are going to party until the sun comes up, so get your drink on, groove on, smoke on or whatever you do! Oh yeah there's an open bar tonight so all drinks are on us baby! Yall ready! The crowd screams. Yeah! The yacht pulls away from the pier as Blackstreet and Dr. Dre plays over the speakers. "I like the way you work it" "No diggidy, you got to back it up" Yeah this is a party right here baby. Nina what's good sis? Everything cool Will, did you bring that indo? Hell yeah! Well what are you waiting on poppy, light it up.

As the yacht entered the dark open space under the hot Vegas sky, its shinny white coat shimmered under the white lights that lined the outside of the three level cruiser. Women in two piece swim suits were stationed throughout the boat in designated areas serving free beer and handing out bottles of champagne. Nina, Denna, Will, Duck and Loon gathered at the bow with a six pack of beer and two bottles of Moet, overlooking the lake and sipping on their beers. Denna spoke out. Fellas, you guys have to tell me how the fuck you let a chica get smoked in front of you and yall didn't do shit! Yeah that sounded kind of fucked up to me too sis. So tell us guys! Man we was just kicking it having a good time as usual, she came over to the table after Duck or Loon approached her at the bar, I forget who it was. To make a long story short, her nigga came in and seen that she was kicking with us. Dude got jealous, started calling her names and smacked the chic. She busted his ass in the head with a bottle and started kicking him while he was on the floor. We was laughing because she was working his ass over, next thing we knew, it was a Bang! Then her ass was dead on the table, he hauled ass out the door and that's how it went.

Damn! That's crazy Will! Yeah tell me about it. Man that fool was embarrassed that his girl was beating that ass, that's all, but for real though, as soon as we lay eyes on that fool we have to smoke him, if we don't, he's going to do us. Loon you always want to smoke somebody. Sis you think that fool aint going to pull out on us when he see us! Hell no! Yeah OK, you crazy then. Tell her Duck! Yeah, we're like motherfucking witnesses to the crime so he's going to try and make sure we don't talk. Then its curtains for that cat at first sight no questions. Yep no questions! OK, yall have a point, just make sure that it's clean, we don't need any heat on our crew, especially with this move we're making right now. Oh sis, you forget, we're professionals baby. Yeah Nina, we got this! Awww, be quiet Duck! Loon, pass me that bottle of Moet.

The temperature had risen from 98 to like 105 degrees, guys started taken off their shirts, some ladies got naked and went to the lower level and started jumping in the lake. Damn! You see that bruh; I'm going downstairs to join the party. Hold up Will, we coming to nigga, you can't have all the pussy bruh! The guys left the girls and went down to the lower level to join the swim party. Hey Will, leave that blunt! Oh here sis, I forgot all about it. Yeah you got pussy on the brain that's why! Whatever Denna, you guys coming down? Nah, we're good right here, away from the madness. I hear yah! Wait til you hit that chronic, I bet your butt will be down then. Ha-ha, oh really! Beep-Beep-Beep. Who the hell is this paging me, this time of night? Beep-Beep. Nina checks her pager and sees that it's Manny. Damn sis it's Manny, well you can't call him, aint no phones out here. We're only going to be another hour, he will have to wait. Beep-Beep-Beep. Shit, he sent a 911 page! Come on, let's go tell the guys. They both headed downstairs to tell the fellas.

Wait sis; let's see if the Captain has a phone. What! Oh, good idea Nina! They walk to the other side of the yacht to speak with the captain. Excuse me Sir! Yes, how may I help you ladies? You wouldn't happen to have a phone would you Sir? Yeah I have one right here. Please, please, can we use it? Sure no problem, here you go young lady. Thank you so much! It's not a problem. Denna takes the phone and calls Manny. Ring-Ring-Ring. Hello! Hey what's up poppy? Where are you guys at? We are all out at Lake Mead. Oh that's why I couldn't reach you guys, are the fellas with you too? Yep, Loon; Duck and Will. So everything is cool with both gigs right? Yep! Cool, tell the fellas that the club shooting made the news so expect some heat! Damn! Alright, I will let them know. OK, later.

Here's your phone back sir and thanks again. Awww, it's no problem, are you ladies enjoying the party? Yes we are! That's great; you guys enjoy the rest of your evening. He reaches out to shake their hands. They both shake then head back through the high energy crowd to the other end of the yacht. Oh girl this is my song! Hell yeah! They join the crowd and start to sing along with the music. "California....Knows how to party" "California...knows how to party" "In the citaaaay of LA" "In the citaaay of good ol' watts" "In the citaaay, the citaaay of Compton" "We keep it rockin! We keep it rockin!" Nina handed the bottle of Moet to Denna and stopped to take off her shoes. She continued to dance barefoot to California Love while Denna danced with both hands in the air, one holding the Moet. The entire yacht was filled with energy as the Dj had the party rocking. Yeah party people; once again, this is Dj Prince Baby! You got 30 minutes left before this thing ends so get your party on! Yo if you're in the water, get your ass on the boat because we heading back to the pier! OK, I can't hear you! Everybody say! California, knows how to party! In the citaaay of LV! Yeah that's it! We just getting started people! We got the limos waiting in the parking lot to take everybody to the after party at Club Drink. Once again this is your favorite Dj! Dj Prince baby; let's get it poppin! The Captain waited for everyone to bore the yacht before heading back to the pier.

Loon, Duck and Will get back on the yacht then head upstairs to meet the sisters. There in the middle of the crowd smoking on chronic, drinking Moet and dancing the night way was Nina and Denna. The guys walk up behind them. Hey woman let me hit that blunt! Loon yelled out behind them. Nina still dancing; turns around to see who it was, smiled and passed the blunt. Oh shit this is my jam! Big Will yells out and starts to dance and sing along. "Aint nothin but a G thing baby" "Two loced out niggas and we crazy" "Death Row is the label that pays me" "So please don't try to fade me". Hey pass the blunt already! Chill Duck, here you go player. Loon I'm going to start calling your ass Smokey, old greedy ass! Ha-ha-ha. Bruh you crazy, hit this and stop crying. He takes the indo, takes a long toke, holds it and exhales. Yo as soon as we get back to land, I'm taking my ass home. Why? You tired already man? Hell yeah, fool it's like 1am and we didn't get in until late last night remember. Yeah I remember, but that doesn't mean you have to be a pussy and go to bed early. Fuck you Will! I'm just saying Duck! I think he's right, I say we all should rest tomorrow, you know, take Sunday off. Yeah you know we start those new gigs too, not to mention we have to meet AC when he gets back. Yeah, you're right Denna! The boat pulls up to the pier. Damn we're back already!

They all continue to stand in the middle of the dance floor, the music had stopped and what was once a yacht full of rowdy patrons became just a big dirty boat. Well let's get the fuck out of here family, the party is just starting to pop and you fools want to go to bed. Man I knew I should of drove my own shit! Loon; shut up and bring your ass on! Come on sis! I know you want to go over to club Drink! Yeah, but we have to get focused on this gig man; we can go kick it later this week. Awww man, take me home, all yall are acting like some old people, and we just got off a party boat, a yacht, not a damn RV! That's it, I'm shutting up! Take me home! Loon, Duck and Will get in the truck, Denna and Nina jumps in the beamer. Duck pulls over to the BMW. Hey sis drive safe, we will see you guys tomorrow. OK bro., see you guys later. She spins out the lot and takes off down Lake Mead Blvd. He drives the truck across the lot and jumps the line of cars waiting to enter the highway, his F150 taillights disappeared into the dark desert night as he drove away.

A yellow taxi pulled up to the Towers drop off zone, all was quiet at 2am this Monday morning, Limo's we're parked in the off duty lot, only one valet was on the clock. Another week was about to begin and things had gone back to normal after the last few busy days. He steps out of the taxi, stretches his arms and cracks his neck. Ahhh, home sweet home! The driver walks to the back of the cab and retrieves AC's bags from the trunk, here you are Sir. Thanks my man! No, thank you Sir! He takes the tip Coops given him and gets in the cab, Manny comes out the building. Hey punta! What's up playboy! Shit, how was L.A? Man it was cool but the damn Laker's lost. Yeah I saw that! Fuck it, I had fun anyway. That's what's up. Yo we got everything in place and ready to go. Oh yeah, there wasn't any problems? Nah, nothing we couldn't handle. Cool, well check it homeboy, I got to get some rest so I can hit this club later, did you remind Will about coming by tonight? Yeah, we all good. Alright, I will holler at you later then. OK brother, I get off in like 3 hours, I will get up with you tonight when you get off from the club then player. Alright, that's what's up. He enters the lobby, all is quiet, no patrons in sight, restaurant is closed and there's only one attendant at the front desk. He continues through the lobby, boards the elevator and goes up to his place for some much needed rest.

Alright ladies, get up! It's chow time! She bangs on the steel door and looks through the small 1 foot by 2 foot Plexiglas window. The room was made of concrete from the floor to the ceiling to the concrete benches; a 20 foot by 20 foot area with one stainless steel toilet and sink, 30 female inmates occupied this Clark County Jail holding area awaiting their first court appearance. The officer opens the door and a trustee pulled up a cart that held the breakfast trays. OK ladies, get up and form a line, come get this chow! Listen up for your names too, I have the list for court today, if I call your name you will be in the 8am session. All of the ladies had become restless after not being able to wash or even change clothes for two days. An unforgettable order filled the air of this small congested area that held 30 frustrated females. They form a line and proceeded to get their meal trays. Hey bitch! I know you didn't jump me! Get the fuck out of the way! Hey! No one talks but me ladies! So shut your damn pie holes! If I have to tell you again, trust me, you want like the results. Now eat and shut your damn mouths! Two boiled eggs, an orange and oatmeal was the menu for the morning. Not a sound was made as the inmates sat on the cold floor and concrete benches to indulge in this jailhouse morning special. Listen up ladies! If I call your names you have an hour from now to get ready. Jackie Mason, Olivia Santana, Ashley Marciano, Debra Brown, Jamie Scott, Jalisa Monroe, Albany Richards and Jewell Cox. So finish your meals, I will be back in 45 minutes.

Damn Ash! What you think this shit is about; I know they don't have anything on us! I know they don't either; let's just see what happens and don't say shit without a lawyer. Lawyer! Bitch what lawyer! Ha-ha. Jewel you crazy girl! Ha-ha. No for real, Lisa you got a lawyer, I know I don't. Hell no bitch, I aint got no lawyer. Do you have one Ash? No, but I know one we can call if we need one. So let's just hold tight and see what happens before we make that move girls, OK, we got you sis, I'm ready to change these damn stinking ass clothes and wash my ass. Please don't remind me Jewel, this is killing me. Girl look at all these hoes and dikes in this motherfucker, just waiting to jump our pretty asses. Lisa shut your crazy ass up, you know you like pussy too. Yeah, but not no hard butch looking chic though, you know my type Ash. Both of yall crazy, are you going to eat that orange Lisa? Yep! Here you can have mine Jewel. Thanks baby! You're welcome. Damn this bench is harder than a mother! Hell, tell that big bitch over in the corner to let you use some of that big ass she got. Ha-ha-ha. Jewel be quiet before you start some shit up in here. Fuck that hoe! She fat! Ha-ha. They all laugh out loud. Yo that chic so big she has to walk sideways to get through the damn door. Ha-ha-ha. Bitch you stupid! Jewel! Ashley calls her name in a loud voice to warn her. OK Ash, I'm done. They lean against the cold concrete, sit their empty trays on the bench, close their eyes and lean their heads against the wall.

Morning shift is just starting at the Towers; the hotel manager is looking over his daily check list to make sure everything is in place. A Latino male dressed in a suit and tie approached the counter. Hello Sir, how are you this fine morning? I'm fine Sir, welcome to the towers, how may I help you? Well I'm Detective Espinoza. He reaches for his wallet and shows the manager his badge. What can I do for you Sir? Well we caught a breaking and entering case here Friday, after watching the surveillance tapes, we have found the suspects and have them in custody, I'm here to speak with the victim, Mr. Cooper from the 44th floor. OK Sir, give me a second to call him. Thanks.Yeah it's not a problem. Ring-Ring-Ring. Hello! Good Morning Mr. Cooper, it's the front desk. Morning, what can I do for you? We have a Detective Espinoza here for you. What? Damn! What does he want? It's about the break in. Damn, OK. Do you want me to send him up Sir or are you coming down? Nah, I will be down in ten minutes. Thanks Sir, I will tell him to wait in the lobby. Fuck! Fuck! Fuck! AC shouts out loud. I got to deal with this motherfucker this morning! Dammit! He slips on some sweats, slippers, a T-shirt and heads downstairs.

Ding! He exits the elevator and heads into the lobby seating area. Well hello there Mr. Cooper! Hey Detective, what's up man? Looks like you having problems with the ladies again AC. What do you mean? Well I checked the tape and we got the robbers red handed, it was three ladies that broke in your place, an Ashley, Jewel and Jalisa. Yeah me and Ashley fucked around a few times, she left something at my place and broke in to get it, we got into it earlier that day; she got upset, left it there. So did she find what she was looking for? Yeah they all came and apologized later for breaking in, you can drop the charges, we all good. Are you sure? Yeah man, it's no biggie, you can let them go. OK, I will call the D.A and let her know; you need to be careful with these ladies man, for some reason you always seem to pick the crazy ones. Detective, thanks for the advice but I'm good, will there be anything else? No that's it; enjoy the rest of your day. OK, you do the same Detective. They shake hands and go their separate ways.

Coop heads back to the Condo, Espinoza goes to the front desk to call the D.A. May I use your phone Sir? Sure just dial 9 to get a dial tone. What time is it? It's 7:40 am. OK thanks! He dials the court house. Ring-Ring-Ring. Hello, District Attorney's Shaw's office. Hi this is Detective Espinoza, can I speak to Ms. Shaw please. Sure hold on Sir. Hello this is Shaw. Hi D.A this is Espinoza. Hi friend, what can I do for you? We got a case that has been dropped from today's docket. OK and which one is that? The breaking and entering at the Towers with the three young ladies, Ashley, Lisa and Jewel. I'm familiar with that one, why is it being dropped? I just spoke with the victim, he and one of the accused are dating, he says she left something there and went back to get it after they had an argument. Who's the victim? Oh you're not going to believe this! It's Mr. Andy Cooper! What? No kidding! AC from the Cologne Company? Yep! Boy he just don't have any luck with the ladies, well OK, I will let the judge know. Thanks for calling, I will speak with you later, I have to get to court. OK Ms. Shaw; thanks again. They hang up the phone.

Knock-Knock-Knock. The prisoners stand up. OK ladies, if I called your names earlier come forward; it's time to hit the court house. The Guard opens the steel door. A prisoner shouts out. Shit, it's about time! Hey shut your pie holes! Get in line so we can put these cuffs on you, Ashley, Jewel and Jalisa you guys step over here on the other side of the white line. All three ladies walk over across the line. Ladies this is your lucky day, your charges have been dropped. Yes! Thank you Jesus! OK calm down ladies, go over to the desk so you can get your personal items, the rest of you ladies, hold out your hands so we can put on your bracelets, we have a long walk to the court room. The office clerk; pull their items from the file area. Ladies sign these release forms for your personal items. He placed the three gold envelops on the desk that the ladies had assigned to them during in processing; they all signed the release forms and followed the officer out to the release area. Alright ladies, try to stay away from this place, you're too pretty to be stuck in here with these animals. Bye officer! Bye ladies! The sliding doors open, they walk outside to meet the 100 degree Vegas heat. Damn! It's hotter than hell out here! Ashley puts the envelope up to shade the sun from her face, Lisa puts on her shades and soaks it all in. Jewel, falls to her knees and begin to kiss the sidewalk. Muah-Muah-Muah. Thank you Jesus! Girl you are so crazy, get your ass up and let's catch this cab. Ha-ha. Bitch you crazy. I'm happy, stink and hungry! Ha-ha. They all laugh and walk to the curb. Hey I'm asking that taxi driver to stop by Carl's junior. Whaaaat, I know that's right girl! Several taxis wait by the curb for released inmates and courthouse patrons. Hey there's a free van taxi right there, come on yall, let's get the hell away from here. They get in the cab. Hello ladies where to? Take us to Carl's junior first, then to the Towers baby! Ha-ha. OK, Carl's junior it is. Ha-ha. He laughs over and over out loud and pulls away from the courthouse.

Excuse me! Excuse me driver? Yes Mam? What's your name? Oh I'm Alex. Hi Alex I'm Jewel this is Ashley and that's Lisa, can you take us to the Carl's Junior over on Maryland parkway by UNLV. Sure! Great, thanks Alex! So when we get back to your place, I will call Tank and let him know we're coming to Miami. Hey, we still need to go and pay AC a visit. Why? Girl we need that money before you even think about calling your cousin. I know that's right Ashley, Jewel just ready to get to that good weather. Shut up Lisa, your ass ready to get down there too. Hell yeah; you think I aint! Look, we all are ready but we're not leaving without that cash baby. The driver pulls into the drive thru.

Hi welcome to Carl's Junior, may I take your order? Hey Alex, pull up some and let down the back window. OK Mam. He pulls up. Yes let me get a number 1 with a coke. What do you want Ash? Get me a number 2 with a sprite. OK, how about you Lisa? A number 1 with a tea. OK, let's make that, two number ones, a number two, one coke, a tea and a sprite. Thank you; please pull forward for your total. He drives up to pay and get the ladies order. Hello, your total is $12.89. Here you go Alex. She hands him a $20 bill. Thanks Ashley. He hands the cash to the cashier. Here's your food Sir and your change. Thank you, come again. Alex hands the bags and change to the ladies then pulls away from the window.

Alright Bitches! It's time to eat! Jewel you are so stupid but hand me my food bitch! Ha-ha. Yeah uh, huh, Lisa. Would you ladies like to stop anywhere else? Nope, just head to the Towers! OK, we will be on our way, soon as these knuckle heads in front of us get out the way. Beep-Beep-Beep. He blows the horn. A white 62 impala was in front of them with dark tinted windows, a black rag top and was sitting on 100 spoke chrome Dayton's with white wall tires.

The front and back right passenger doors of the impala opened, two brown skinned, tattooed Latino men with bald heads, standing about 5'6", dressed in white tank tops that where tucked in their oversized khaki colored dickies that was held up by a black canvas belt. Their khaki pants flared big enough at the cuff to cover their entire Chuck Taylor shoes. The driver's door opened and another brown skinned Latino male stepped out dressed similar with the exception of his black loc shades. He went to the back of the car and leaned against the trunk of his impala. The other two approached the taxi, one on the driver's side the other to the passenger's side. Yo cabi, what's your problem homes! You are in our hood, we run shit around here, you got that! The gangster yelled to the cabi as he leaned over the driver's side window. Yeah I hear you man, but I need to get these ladies home and you guys are holding up traffic. Ha-ha-ha. The gangster standing on the passenger side laughed. Didn't you hear my cousin when he said this is our hood and we run shit! Yeah I did. No, I don't think you understand! Look man I don't want any problems. Oh, it's too late for that homes, you see, all you got is problems now bro... Hey man, come on, we just want to leave. Leave! He reaches in the taxi and snatches the keys out of the ignition. Hey give me my keys back! Ha-ha-ha. I tell you what Mr. Cabi! You can leave but the chica's have to stay with us homes!

What! Fuck you! You burrito eating motherfucker, we aint staying with yall fools! Ha-ha. This one got a mouth on her Poncho. Jewel just be quiet! Shit, fuck that, you be quiet; I'm not staying with these punks Ash! Oh yeah! Yeah nigga, go fuck yourself; me and my girls are going home, move that piece of shit car so we can go! The third gangster gets up off the trunk of his impala, reaches behind his back and pulls out a nine, then walks towards the taxi. Yo Poncho do that fool, me and Chino got these bitches. Well you heard him homes. Poncho pulls out a chrome 357 from the small of his back, sticks it in the drivers face. Give me all the cash and don't try no funny stuff cabi! OK, OK, man here, take it! Chino points his gun at the girls in the back seat. Come on ladies; that goes for you too, give it up! Don't make us smoke you over no fucking money! Hurry up! Alright, alright, hold on! Lisa reaches in her purse to get what cash she had. Here this is all I have! Thank you little white bitch, give me that watch too and that ring! He snatches the watch off her wrist and pulls the ring from her finger.

This is really some stupid shit! Jewel screams out. What's your name punk, its Poncho right! You a dumb ass Mexican! I aint giving you a damn thing, kill me motherfucker, that's what you do. Ha-ha. This one is a firecracker homes! OK, then bitch! POW! He pointed the 357 to her chest and pulled the trigger. Blood scattered all over the back seat and rear window. Scared, Ashley bows her head and begins to prey. Father, please forgive them. POW! POW! Chino placed his nine to Ashley's head and pulled the trigger twice. Blood and brains hit the back of the front seat. Oh fuck! The cabi yelled out as some of the brains landed on his face. Please man, don't kill me! Please! POW! Poncho shoots the cabi in the chest. No-no-no-no-no, please! Why God? Why! Lisa cried for mercy, after she witnessed the massacre. Please don't! Come here you pretty white bitch!

Hector pulls Lisa by the hair and drags her over Ashley's dead body, puts the gun to the back of her head then pulls down her jeans with his right hand. Come here; let me see if you got some good pussy, little white bitch. She cries and lay there shaking, scared shitless. Hector bends her over the seat and shoves her head in Ashley's lap, took out his penis then fucked her right there in the parking lot of this bloody crime scene. She screams a deadly cry as he fucked her. Noooo-Noooo-Nooooo. Poncho walks up and pushes him on the shoulder from behind. Yo Bro.! Let's get the fuck out of here po po is coming, come on homes! He jumps up off Lisa; she continues to shout while her head was lying in Ashley's lap. Why! Why! Please, please, kill me, kill me; kill me now! POW! Hector shoots her in the back of the head and runs to the impala with his other two comrades, they spinned off up the parkway. Hey homes you want some of this Carl's junior, it's still hot! Chino you greedy bastard, damn you took the food too. What! Shit, they wasn't gonna eat it. Ha-ha-ha. They all laugh and continue driving up the parkway. We showed them fools, huh homes! Yeah this one will be on the news esse'! MS for life homes! They all yelled out while holding their guns up in the air out the window speeding down the parkway.

Knock-Knock-Knock. Damn, I aint gonna get no sleep today, who the hell is that now! AC yells out. Yeah who is it? Hey baby, it's me Sabrina! He opens the door. Hey baby why didn't you call me before you came over, I was trying to get some sleep. Awww, I'm sorry but I missed you. Yeah is that right? She hugs him then gives him a big kiss. Yes it is! So what were you doing? I was lying down but I might as well hang that up now. Poor baby, are you hungry? Yes I am. What do you want me to cook for you, pancakes, waffles, eggs? Ummm. How about a ham and cheese omelet! OK baby, I got you, anything else? Yeah throw some raisin toast on that plate too. Alright, go relax sugar and let me get started; oh can you turn on the TV before you go in the bedroom. Sure. Thank you sexy! She turns on the front right eye of the stove, takes a large frying pan from the bottom drawer, walks over to the fridge and gets the raisin bread, ham, cheese, eggs, butter, onions and green peppers.

The TV is playing in the background. Hey this is J&J Beepers, we have the best prices in town, come see us today at one of our seven locations. I'm JJ! The King of Beepers! Coming up on your news at 11. Four found dead at fast food restaurant on Maryland Parkway, Las Vegas one of the fastest growing cities in America, how are we dealing with the increase in traffic and our shortage of water. That and more, next on your local news at 11. Good Morning, I'm Katie Strong reporting for your local news at 11, according to a national survey we are among the top 5 growing cities in the United States. In the last few months we have built more houses than any other state in the nation, our traffic has doubled and it takes twice as long to get to your destination than before. We have been experiencing more and more water shortages in the last six months. Damn babe, are you listening to this? Sabrina shouts out to AC from the kitchen. Yeah I hear it, shit, I don't know why everyone is moving to this crazy ass place, there aint no jobs unless you're in the union or know somebody. All of them will be unemployed and sick at home with the runs from drinking this nasty ass water! Ha-ha. Babe you crazy! Ha-ha. You know it's the truth Sabrina! Yeah you're right.

In this morning's top story we go live to news anchor Bill Durst over on Maryland parkway at the sight of a four body murder. Thanks Katie! Hi I'm Bill Durst reporting live from the crime scene, four people were found brutally murdered just a few hours ago! All we know right now is that three females and one male are amongst the dead.

The names of the victims, has not been release because authorities are still trying to contact next of kin, but we have Detective Espinoza here on the case. Can you tell us anything at this time Detective, do you have any leads? Well I know for a fact that the three female victims were just released only a few hours ago from Clark County detention center regarding another case. AC runs up front to see the TV. Oh shit! Brina turn that up! Hurry up! OK, OK! She grabs the remote from the counter and turns it up. We have spoken with all the employees and some patrons from this establishment but no one claims to have seen anything. If anyone watching, seen or heard anything could you please contact me Detective Espinoza at the Las Vegas Police Department. Thank you Detective. Well there you have it Katie, no leads yet in this horrific crime scene just minutes away from the University. Thank you Bill.

Damn baby I think those girls were Ashley, Jewel and Lisa! What! Stop playing like that baby! No I'm serious they got locked up over the weekend and that same Detective came and spoke with me this morning about them breaking in my place. What? Why would they break in your place? It's a long story, I will explain later. He starts pacing the room. Fuck! Look for a card bay with that Detective's name on it; he gave it to me this morning. You look up here; I will look in the room. OK daddy. AC runs back into his bedroom, Sabrina starts to look in the kitchen and the living room. Hey I found it baby on my night stand; I'm going to call him. OK baby, your food is almost done, come eat something before you call. That detective isn't even at his office yet, he was just on the news, remember. Yeah you right, I'm coming!

She fixed his plate and puts it on the table. Do you want apple butter for your raisin toast sweetie? Yes please! OK, here you are, oh OJ or milk? Neither; let me get a cold beer babe. Alright baby, a cold one it is. Thank you Brina! Your welcome! Get your plate and come join me. I'm coming, let me get this mess cleaned up before I join you. Hurry up; I'm waiting on you before I start. Awwww, you're so sweet! OK, here I come. She come joins him at the table. Hmm, this is delicious! White girl can cook I see! Hold up player; I'm Italian, not white, there is a difference. Oops excuse me! My bad! Ha-ha-ha. They both laugh out loud! Now tell me about them breaking in your place. Really! You want to hear that now? Yes really! Damn, can a brother finish his food first; you can talk and eat at the same time AC, come on, let's have it! Umm this is good, baby hand me the hot sauce please. Boy if you don't start talking you're going to be wearing this hot sauce, come on spit it out already.

Girl you just nosey! Well let's hear it! Alright remember when they all came over and that bullshit happened. Yes! Well she left her bag over here and it was full of money! What! How much money? Two million! Shut the fuck up! No for real! So where is the money? Where do you think? Oh you kept it! Actually I was going to give her some of it back, like half of it. Well did you? No. AC! Wait let me tell you what happened. Please do! I had the cashier make her out a check, but when she went to pick it up the police arrested all three of them for breaking and entering before she could get the money from the cashier downstairs. The cops saw them on the Towers surveillance tape from the other day. Damn that's fucked up baby! Yeah that Detective came by and asked me what I wanted to do about it because he had them in custody. What did you say? Shit, I told him to drop the charges. Now you see why I think it's them, plus he said that he knew the victims from another case that he was working earlier today. Wow! That's not a good sign at all; you need to call him as soon as you get done. I am. They both stop talking and continue to eat in silence.

AC gets up from the table and walks in to the living room to use the phone. Ring-Ring. Hello, Las Vegas Police Department, how can we help you? Hi, Detective Espinoza please. Hold one second. Ring-Ring. Hello this is Espinoza. Hi Detective, you have a call on line one. Thanks, I got it. He hangs up the receiver and presses line 1. This is Espinoza. Hi Detective, this is Mr. Cooper. Hello AC, what can I do for you? Man I seen you on the news at that crime scene, please tell me that the victims were not Ashley; Lisa or Jewel. Yes, I'm afraid it was AC. Damn, damn that's crazy! Did you get the suspects yet? No, we don't have any leads right now, but if you hear anything and I mean anything call me as soon as you do. Yeah I will; no problem Detective. Alright man, you be safe, I will call you if anything comes up. Oh before you hang up, do you happen to know either one of the girl's next of kin? No, I just met them recently; I knew they all came here from LA. OK, I will look into that. Thanks. Click! They both hang up.

Well what did he say baby? Yep it was them. He hangs his head in sorrow, she runs over to hug and comfort him. Sabrina it just seems like motherfuckers are dropping dead all around me, this shit is crazy! Don't get angry at yourself baby, it wasn't your fault. I know that, but it's a bad omen surrounding me and I'm not about to get shot for nobody! It's just a sign for me to stay strapped and watch my back, if a fool looks at me wrong, he's getting dealt with! You getting carried away baby. Bitch I aint getting carried away, I'm just saying, I will be laying fools down, aint going to be no talking! She kisses him on the cheek, shakes her head and walks away. Just be careful baby, I'm here for you no matter what, you want some of this chronic Dylan gave me last night? Hell yeah, I need to ease my mind after that bad news!

He walks over to the end table in the den and picks up the bong. Do you want to use the bong baby? No it's rolled up already, where's the lighter? There's one on my dresser by the watch case. OK, sit down, relax baby, I will be right back. She leaves the room to go get the lighter. I don't see it baby! It should be by the Movado case! Oh I see it! Well get it and bring your ass in here then! Hey who are you talking to like that with your bald ass head! You! Don't make me put this two piece; upside your head punk! Yeah, yeah, whatever, come over here and light that smoke up with your sexy ass. They both sit on the couch, she lights up the blunt, he takes a pull from the chronic, holds it in, looks at it and passes it back to her then exhales the smoke through his nose. What time do you have to go in tonight Brina? I have to be there at seven baby; why? Me too, so we might as well go in together. That's cool. Who's driving me or you? We can take the Harley; I haven't pulled the big hog out in a few weeks. Hell yeah, I can't wait! Let's leave early so we can ride a little before we go in. You know, that's a good idea girl, we can leave at 5 and ride over to Green Valley or something. The TV is still playing in the background. Can you turn the channel please baby?

Sure where's the remote? Right here! Turn to the box, let's watch some music videos. Cool, are you going to order a video daddy? Yep, that DPG! New York, New York! Ahhh, you just want to see Snoop kicking over the buildings and shit! Hell yeah baby, that shit was gangsta! Well, can I order one too? Yeah, what do you want to order? The playas anthem! Big Poppa baby! I love it when you call me Big Poppa! Alright, alright, that's a good one. They turn the channel to the videos and wait for the code to show for their desired songs. Baby! Yeah what's up? How did you like working at the club the other night? It's cool; I still have to get use to calling you Megan at work. Ha-ha. Don't worry, you will. You got skills on the stage though! Oh yeah, you like how I work it daddy? Yes Mam I do, I think you should come give me a dance right now. Oh is that what you want? Hmm, mm, come over here and strip for me. She slides over next to AC and grabs his chin with her right hand, leans in close and gives him a kiss on the lips. Muah! That's all you're getting. Why baby? Because I know you fucked Ashley after I left, didn't you? Awww girl, quit tripping, no I aint fucked that slut. Yeah whatever AC! Look at you! Your head is sweating! So! It's hot in here! Boy stop playing, you know that bald ass head starts to sweat when you lie. Ha-ha. What! Girl you crazy! Don't be smiling at me, you know I'm right! So tell me, I want get mad at you. I don't know what you're talking about Sabrina. Uhhh! Men, yall aint about shit! Wait, wait, wait! So you calling me a liar? If I told you I didn't fuck that woman, I didn't fuck her. Well I guess we will never know the truth since she's dead now! Huh AC! Man you tripping Sabrina! I aint dealing with this right now! He gets up, goes to the bedroom and slams the door.

Don't get an attitude with me AC! Just tell me! She runs to the room door and starts to knock repeatedly. Damn girl give it a break, if you don't want to believe me, then kick rocks! Take your white ass home! Crazy Bitch! You don't need to smoke no more weed if it makes you paranoid like that! Damn! Fuck you AC! She kicks the room door; turn around and walks towards the front door. Don't even think about speaking to me when you come to work tonight either! She walks out and slams the door. Bam! Then screams once she got in the hallway. Motherfucker! AC comes out of his room to see if the coast was clear. Wheeeewwww, that girl crazy! He makes his way to the front door to make sure it was locked. It's going to be a long night, I can see it already.

Ring-Ring. Who could this be calling now? Hello! Hey what's crackin playboy? Yo what's up Will? Not much brother, just wanted to know what time I needed to drop in later? Oh yeah, come around 7pm tonight, the Boss should be in then, did you catch the news at 11? No, I was knocked the hell out bro., why, did I miss something? Man those three chic's that partied with us a few days ago; got mercd! Who Ashley and that fine ass Jewel? Yep they got popped over on Maryland Parkway by that Carl's Junior. Oh that's Hector's turf from MS; I bet he knows who did it! Isn't he Denna's cousin or something like that? Yep that's her blood cousin, we need to pay him a visit and see what he knows. I don't know AC, if we don't have anything to do with it, we should leave it alone, Attention is something we don't need right now bro... Yeah you right, but those girls didn't fuck with nobody. Alright, don't say I didn't tell your hard headed ass, either way I got your back bro, you know that. I already know playa; I got to get off this phone though pimp. Cool, catch you at the club later then. Alright, later Will.

AC picks the phone back up and dials Denna's number. Ring-Ring-Ring. Hola, whose speaking? Hey Denna, this is AC! Hey poppy what's happening? How was your trip? I'm good sis, the trip was awesome. That's good, so what's up? Is something wrong, you don't just call out of the blue, is it about the gig? No, Manny told me that the gig was good to go. Right, so come on what is it poppy? Well do you remember Ashley, Jewel and Lisa? No, I don't think I've ever met them, you guys were telling me about some chic's that were partying with yall the other day I think. Girl you tripping! You and Nina were here with the chics too. Ha-ha-ha. Oh those chica's! OK, what about them? Sis, they got smoked this morning over on Maryland Parkway. Oh shit, that was them on the news? Yes! That's messed up man, did they catch the killers? No not yet, that's why I called, isn't the parkway your cousin's turf? Yeah, his crew runs that area. We need to talk then sis and not on the phone. OK that's cool, when and where do you want to meet up? How about in an hour by the landing strip, that parking area off Sunset. Sunset? Oh the area where you park to watch the planes land and take off? Yeah! OK bro., see you in an hour. Cool! He presses the receiver, waits for the dial tone and dials the valet. Ring-Ring. Hello, Towers valet. Hey this is Mr. Cooper, could you bring my Harley up please? Yes Sir, it will be waiting on you. What time are you coming down? In the next 20 minutes man. OK, it will be ready. Thank you! He slips on his work clothes, then gets a beer from the fridge and turns it up, walks over to the deck to close the blinds and lock the doors, turns off the TV and heads downstairs.

It's Monday evening and the delivery trucks are pulling into the club lot to drop off the weekly beer and liquor orders. Vinny and Bobby are standing at the back door to check the invoices; both the drivers park and start unloading their trucks. Hello gentlemen; how's everything? Just fine Sir, where do you want us to put your order? Follow me fellas. Bobby walks in the club to show them where he wants the product. Tori! Tori! What the fuck are you doing! Get your naked ass out of the kitchen with that shit! Smoke your weed somewhere else. One of the dancers was in the kitchen naked, leaning against the stainless steel cutting table smoking on a blunt. Damn girl, put some clothes on and go out back at least. OK, I'm sorry Bobby! I swear these fucking girls has shit for brains sometimes, sorry about that guys, just put it over here by the walk in. No problem Sir, we have two more loads to bring in, and then you can sign for it. Alright thanks, you fellas want a sandwich or something for the road? No we already had lunch, but thanks Sir. Yeah, you sure? We make a mean cheese steak! Yeah we're good. OK then, just give the invoice to my brother when you come back in, I have to go up front, take care guys. Will do Sir.

Hey Tori! Yeah Bobby! Come here! She stood only 5'3" with brown caramel skin, a perky size c breast, small waist, round bottom and short black curly hair. She walks in the office behind him. Yes Bobby? Come in and close the door behind you. He took a seat behind the desk in his big black leather chair, leaned back and put his feet up on the large desk top. Tori stood there naked in her black stilettos with a blunt in her left hand, she softly pushed the door closed with her right. Let me hit that before you smoke it all. Her naked body looked hard and firm but was soft as cotton, as she got closer to him; her nipples had seemed to get larger with every step. Tori leaned over the desk and stuck the blunt in his mouth. Bobby grabbed her hand and pulled her around in front of him. She stood there looking at him with her large puppy dog eyes waiting for instruction. While taking a toke off the blunt he unzipped his pants and pulled out his hard penis, took his feet down from the desk, turned the chair towards her and leaned back. She dropped to her knees and leaned in closer. He grabbed her by the neck with his left hand and gently eased his dick in her mouth while pushing her downward. Ummmm, Ummmm, that's it baby. Ummm, Ummmm, yeah I like that. Slow down take your time baby, Ummm, Ummm, that's it. Knock-knock. Damn who is it? It's VIN! What you doing Bobby? Come in Vinny and lock that door behind you. Ummmm, Ummm, yeah baby that's good. Damn bro! You're holding out on me. Shut up man, can't you see I'm busy!

Vinny walked over to the desk and begin to rub Tori's pussy as she had her ass arched up in the air, his fingers begin to get dripping wet from the erotic juices her vagina released. Damn fuck this! Vinny reaches in his back pocket, gets a condom, pulls out his hard Johnson and slides the Trojan on. Tori arched her pretty caramel ass up a little higher as if to say come and get me. He dropped his pants to his knees, got behind her and penetrated her wet pussy. With both ends full, she could barely make a sound, a soft moan was the best she could do. Hmm-mm, Hmm- mm. Tears begin to run from her eyes as she choked from Bobby's dick hitting the back of her throat. She tried to run but to no avail, she just backed up more on Vinny's hard rod. The scene was getting intense, Tori could barely breath and snot was coming from her nose, she started smacking her hand on the desk and pulling Bobby's shirt to make them stop. Hey bro., you see that, the little girl can't handle it. Awww, what's the matter Tori, you want us to stop. She looks up at Bobby and rolls her eyes. Ohhhhh, Ohhhhh, Ohhhhhh, Ohhhhhh, Ohhhhh, Ohhhhhhh, Shit! He released. She lifts up and spit it on his pants. Vinny kept pounding it from the back but she pushed him off. Hey; what the fuck! I wasn't done! You're done now man, I'm tired! You and your brother are crazy. Ha-ha-ha. That was good as hell Tori! Yeah-yeah, whatever, I'm not paying tip out for two weeks! Yall tried to kill my black ass! Ha-ha-ha. OK, OK, we got you. Yeah I know you do! She looked at them and wiped her mouth with some napkins that were on the desk then walked off. Bye! She left the room.

AC walked off the elevator helmet in hand, sleeves rolled up just above his biker gloves. A white tuxedo shirt, black slacks, black socks and black shoes complemented the black shinny helmet. Hello Mr. Cooper! Hey Man, how's your day going, is my bike ready? Yes Sir, it's just outside the entrance. Thanks man, have a good evening. You too Sir! AC puts on the helmet, jumps on his Harley starts it and cruises off down the strip towards Sunset Ave. Traffic moved surprisingly smooth that day, all the lights happened to be green as he approached them from Flamingo all the way down to Tropicana. He came upon the sign that read thank you for visiting Las Vegas. As he passed it and merged over to the left turning lane, traffic had cleared just enough for him to turn on to Sunset. After going two miles up the road, there on the left he could see her cherry red BMW parked in front of the fenced landing strip. He pulls up beside her, the noise from the departing planes pierced the air all around them, every two minutes it seemed.

Hey AC, you cruising today huh! Yeah had to pull out the hog Sis! I like it! Thanks! So what's up? Why you got me way out here on Sunset? Thank you for coming. Yeah, you know I was coming to see what my brother wanted, now let's hear it poppy. Well I need you to go visit your cousin and see if he knows anything about that murder that happened on the parkway earlier today. Who Hector? Yeah! Man I have to catch up with that Punta; he's hard to keep up with bro.! It's important sis; I need to know who's responsible. Alright-alright, give me a week or so to find him, I will call my aunt and see if she knows where he's at. OK Denna, thanks a lot! Yeah anytime poppy. Well I have to get to work at the club, what time are you going to the new gig? Ahhh, around 8, I have to pick up Loon's butt too. He gets off the Harley, walks over to give her a hug and kiss on the cheek. OK then, I will talk to you later; tell Loon to hit me up when he gets a chance. Alright poppy. She starts the beamer and pulls off up Sunset towards Henderson. AC heads the other way, back towards the strip.

AC speeds up the strip pass the welcome to Las Vegas marquee sign, radio blasted while weaving in and out of traffic. He makes a left at the light and turns up Tropicana, travels a mile and goes over the bridge, merges to the right lane and turns right onto Industrial Blvd., passing In and Out Burger. The road was clear at this time; no cars in sight the speedometer read 115 MPH as he raced up the hot black pavement towards Dolls. A 10 minute ride had turned to 5 by the time he pulled onto the parking lot, parked the Harley. While walking towards the club, he started singing Guy's, Peace of My Love. "Even though I hate to leave her" "But I cried as I walked out that door" "That door I cried" "Temptation is asking me to stay" "But I've been through the same thing before". He walked in the club and Deb was already stocking the bar.

Hey AC! Hey Red, how you doing baby? I'm doing great man, how was the trip? Man I had a ball, but the Lakers got their butts kicked, Hakeem showed his ass! Yeah I saw it on the sports channel. So what's new? Nothing we just have to put up all this stock, the trucks came today. Damn, how much do we have? Man, get your ass over here and help me, quit asking questions. Alright Red, don't make me pop that ass. Ha-ha-ha. I like my ass smacked! Girl you crazy! Where do you want me to start? Go bring that hand truck from the walk in; it has all the beer on it that we need to stock. OK, I will be right back; can you put my helmet behind the bar? Yeah sure, let me have it. Night shift was about to begin, the day shift crew was clocking out and the night team was coming in. The dancers at night were sexier, the staff more experience, a total transformation from the day time crew. Girls walked in by groups of four, five and six, hair, make up and nails were done before they clocked in. Bobby and Vinny believed that their dancers should come into work looking beautiful; they wanted the patrons to be impressed by their beauty, even when they were in their street clothes.

Hello ladies! Hi Deb! The ladies rush to the dressing room to get dressed and ready for another nights work. Excuse me! Excuse me ladies, coming through! He pushes the dolly from the back and through the club on the way to the bar. Damn girl, whose that fine ass motherfucker? Poison; don't waste your time baby, Megan already got him. What, that skinny bitch! He needs some of this nice ass and thighs baby! Girl shut up! Don't tell me to shut up Dylan, I'm serious. That man wants a real women like me baby! Ha-ha. Whatever, come on bitch, let's get dressed. Megan think she's a damn model, I'm gone take that nigga! Watch girl! Yeah whatever Poison, come on here. AC approaches the bar with the dolly. Alright Red, here's the beer, I'll be right back. Got to get the liquor.

AC heads back to the stock room; one last girl comes in the front door, hair pulled back in a ponytail, wearing a long red sun dress and sandals. Hey Red! Hi Megan! You look tired girl! No I'm good! Is AC here yet? Yeah he's in the back. OK thanks Deb! The two meet each other in passing. Hi Daddy! Girl you a trip, I aint fucking with you today! Come on baby, I'm sorry OK! He stops and stands there, looks her up and down. Why should I accept your apology Sabrina? Because I was high and wasn't thinking straight. No you was acting up! I know, I know, so do you forgive me? Yeah I guess? Thank you! Muah! She gives him a big kiss. I love you daddy! Sure you do, now go get dressed Megan. Awww whatever! It's Sabrina to you Mr.! Man bring that damn liquor over here before we get too busy to put it up, Megan take your ass to the back! I'm going Deb! Hey Red, don't be talking to my woman like that! Whatever! Yall can make love at home, we're here to make money dude, Get busy!

He makes his way to the bar with the liquor. Thank you slow poke! Red shouted. They put away all the stock and get ready for the night crowd, the dancers all come out on the floor and prepare for tonight. Deb! Hey Gia! What's been up bitch! Where the hell you been? I've been working over at Crazy Horse. Crazy Horse over on Flamingo? Yeah girl! Man that place sucks! Tell me about it, but I had to work somewhere girl. Oh yeah, your ass was on suspension for a month huh? Yep! I miss you guys so much! You better behave this time Gia! I know! Bobby put me on the no drinking list for my first week back. Thank God! Aww shut up Deb! Ha-ha. Girl you are a straight fool on that liquor! Hold on, do you want your coke on ice or straight up? Ha! You funny! Ha-ha. Just playing, here take this bottle of water. Bye Deb, I'm going to get me some dances, your ass got jokes tonight! Bye-bye Gia, I love yah! Deb wipes down her area and prepares for the night shift crowd. Hello people this is Dj Cutta! Welcome to Dolls, home of the most beautiful ladies in Sin City! Poison stand by, your first up baby! Gentlemen, our Monday night specials are $3 domestic beers and $3 Tequila shots until midnight! So get juiced up and loosen them pockets baby, because it's time to have some fun the Vegas way! Poison standby!

Coming to the stage gentlemen is the lovely Dominican beauty, Poison; remember that these ladies work for tips and tips only, so please pay the pussy bill! Table dances are $20, VIP's 300, please tip the waitresses as well as the bartenders, we all work hard for the money, for your entertainment pleasure. Again, welcome to Dolls! The club begins to fill to capacity, standing room only; patrons crowd the bar to where it's elbow to elbow; some familiar faces start to filter in. Yo what up Coop! Hey what's going on D? You know me man, trying to make this money, I got that meth and some chronic if anybody ask bro.! OK man, just be careful; don't let Vinny catch your ass. Dude I got this, don't worry about the kid. OK kid, be careful. Yeah I know! Hey, I seen the Rockets did the Lakers in man, didn't we bet on that game? Man I aint bet your ass! You sure man? I think you owe me a drink or something! I don't think so! Dude I think so! Man are you going to harass me all night about that game? Naw man, you can just give me one free drink and I want bring it up again. Alright, only so I want have to hear your big ass mouth no more. Cool, now we talking! Yeah whatever! Dude can you make it a vodka and cranberry? Sure, I guess.

He puts a rocks glass on the bar, adds ice, and pours in a shot of vodka and a dash of cranberry, a lime and a stir stick. Thank you brother. Yeah don't mention it. Damn there's a lot of hoes in here tonight man; naked girls everywhere, you a lucky motherfucker AC! Yep this is the best job in the world! Hell yeah bro.! They give each other a high five. Remy makes her way through the crowd and over to the bar. Hey Honey! Hey sweetie, what's up? Let me get about four grams, Sasha and Missy want some. He reaches in his sock and pulls out four small baggies. Here you go sweetie. Thanks honey! Muah! She gives him a kiss. Hi AC. Hey Remy. She walks off into the crowd. D, you must do pretty well with that Meth? Hell yeah, a couple of G's a week dude, these girls pop it all the time so they can stay up and get that paper. Yeah I'm starting to see that now. If you want in man, let me know, you can cash in when I'm not here, we can split the profits. No shit! Yeah dude, I'm serious, just get at me. Alright, I will think about it. Cool, let me get another drink too. Got you coming up but you're paying for this one punk. Awww man, how you gone play me! D kiss my ass! Ha- ha. I'm just fucking with you bro.! AC spots Will's large frame towering over everyone in the club as he's approaching the bar.

Yo, Yo, what's up soldier? Yo what up Will, hold on a second. He stands there behind the patrons at the bar waiting for AC to come around. Here's your drink D! Thanks dude! Hey Red, I will be right back, I have to run to the office for a minute. Alright rookie, hurry your ass up! Coop leaves the bar and tells Will to follow him. Come on man; let me introduce you to Vinny and Bobby. They force their way through the crowded club and over to the office door entrance. Knock-Knock. Come in! Hey Boss, this is my friend Will I told you about. Hey Will, how's it going man? I'm Bobby and this is my brother Vinny. Hey, nice to meet you guys. Come in, have a seat. Will walks over to the desk and sits in the chair. Hey Will, holler at me before you go, I will be at the bar. OK brother. AC leaves the office, makes his way back through the crowd and over to the bar. Hey rookie, who was that wrestle mania looking brother you took in the office? Oh that's my home boy Will. Why? You want me to hook you up Red? I don't know about that, he's your friend, so that means he's a ho! Girl you want me to hook you up or not? Nah, I'm good. OK, I will introduce you two when he comes back out, that way you can do your own talking. Yeah-yeah, whatever smart ass! Ha-ha. You know you love me Red! Shut up Coop, make some drinks!

So Will, AC tells us you guys served together in the Army. Yeah we served 4 years together. That's a good thing; did you get any bodies while you were in the desert? Too many to count man, I still have nightmares about that shit. He also says you're looking for a job. Yeah, I need to get to work. Have you ever worked at a strip club before? No, but there's a first time for everything. True indeed Will, true indeed, how many hours can you work a week? I'm open anytime, any day. That's good; I tell you what, come in Friday with AC, I will have something for you then. OK, no problem, thanks a lot man. Your welcome, see you Friday big guy. Will gets up and heads back out into the club. The waitress is standing at her station waiting to put in an order with red. Hey Deb, can I have four shots of tequila for table 6? Yes baby, coming right up. Hey Sexy! Hey Sexy! Hey new bartender, I'm talking to you. Oh I'm sorry, what can I do for you baby? Let me get two Corona's, with limes please. No problem, anything else? Yeah, what's your name? My name is AC. Hi AC, I'm Max. Hi Max, nice to meet you, you said you wanted limes right? Yes Sir! OK, here you are, two Corona's with limes. Thank you sexy, I will come and talk with you later. Ha-ha. Alright, Max. Byeeee. She gives him a wink as she walks away.

Will finally makes his way back to the bar. Hey bro., do you know what you're doing back there? Come on man, I got this, so how did it go, you get the job? Yeah, I start Friday! Cool, you want a drink before you leave? Leave! Who said I was leaving, all this pussy! Let me get a double shot of that tequila! Ha-ha. Alright bro., here you go, don't fuck anyone up! Oh I got one thing on my mind brother, see you later. OK man! See, I told you he was a ho and you wanted to hook me up with him! Awww Red, this is a strip club, be easy. Yeah whatever! Hey baby, get these shots, what are you waiting on. Don't get mad at me when they don't tip your ass, these drinks been ready! You're taking 20 minutes to bring four shots! OK Deb, I hear you! God! Don't call on God, get this order. Excuse me! An older gentlemen, tries to get her attention. Yes, what can I get for you Sir? Can I have a Manhattan? Sure coming right up.

Do you want Makers Mark or the house bourbon? Makers, is fine. Coming up. She puts a martini glass on the bar, picks up the vermouth and pours a dash in the shaker along with a shot of Makers over ice, shakes it and pours it into the martini glass and drops in a cherry. Here you are sir. He takes a sip. Why thank you darling, it's delicious! You're welcome. He slides her a crisp $20 bill. Aww thank you! She blows him a kiss. Alright Red, I see you over there flirting with the customers. Shut up AC, mind your business. Hmm, mmmmm. Megan finally makes her way to the bar after being harassed by some drunken soldiers over by the stage. Hey Daddy! Hey Baby, you look sexy than a motherfucker in that two piece. Ouch, I want to bite that ass! What are you drinking tonight? Let me get a double shot of tequila daddy. One double coming up, you want lemons and salt too? No, that's for pussies, give me mine straight! He sits a shot glass on the bar and pours a double shot of Jose'. One double for my baby! Thank you daddy! Your welcome Megan! See you later daddy, I got some customers waiting. Later baby! She turns around and struts back into the crowd.

Gentlemen, Gentlemen, get your ones ready, we have a birthday girl in the house tonight! Coming to the stage is the lovely Brazilian beauty, Sasha from Rio. It's her 25th birthday, so make sure you pay the pussy bill and show her some love! Coop runs into Deb at the register as she rings up her order. Yo Red, I'm leaving at 4am partner, what time you get off? I get off at 4 too man. Well we got 30 minutes, what time is the next shift getting here. Calm down rookie, they clock in at 3:45am, so start cleaning your area and make sure everything is stocked up. OK Deb, I'm on it. Yo bro I'm out man, see you tomorrow. Alright Will, be safe man. Yep always, later bro... 10 minutes had passed and the shift change was about to take place, Deb stood there looking at AC with her drawer in hand. Come on Rookie, get your drawer and let's go to the office so we can cash out. OK, I'm coming, hold up. He pulls out his drawer and followed her to the office after the next shift came behind the bar.

Vinny and Bobby counted both the drawers down to match the sales receipts. Red and AC sat there and waited for them to finish. Bobby stops counting and looks up at AC. Hey AC your drawer is $150 over; you didn't ring up something somewhere. Damn my bad man, shit was so busy tonight I must have lost track. Don't worry about it this time, it will show up during inventory. Just pay more attention when you're working a busy night, it could of been worse. OK, no problem Bobby, will do. Cool, well that's it guys, you can clock out now. Deb and AC get up from the desk, punch out and leave the office. Coop gets Sabrina's attention as he is walking towards the door and waves goodbye. She waves back and blows him a kiss. He grabs his helmet from behind the bar, exits out to the club parking lot and mounts his Harley. Vroom-Vroom-Vroom. He pulls over by Deb, who is standing in front of the club by the valet, smoking a cigarette as she waits for her ride. Later Red, see you Friday. OK AC, have a good one. He and his hog cruise off the lot.

The Towers is still quiet compared to the weekend, barely any people were out as he pulled up to leave his bike with the valet. Emanuel is standing out front taking a cigarette break. My brother from another mother! How was the skin joint? Ha-ha. What's up Manny, it was cool man; Will came through and hung out for a while after he got the gig of course. What! That's what's up bro., so everybody is in place then. Yep we in full gear! Hell yeah, time to get paid playboy! You heard about Ashley and them right? No, what about them? Man they got smoked this morning over on parkway. Shit, that was them on the news! Yep! Damn who did it? They don't have any suspects but we got an ear to the streets you dig, Denna's cousin Hector run shit on that side. OK, so she's going to talk with him and see what he knows then? That's the plan. So what's going on with you amigo, did you get some sleep? Man hell no, I got like four hours. What! I know you're about to go wet that pillow up bro! Ha-ha. Manny you a stupid motherfucker boy! Oh wanna be Eddie Murphy ass! Man Eddie aint got nothing on your boy, my jokes way funnier! What! Dude you must be high! I'm going to bed on that note, later Manny. Goodnight AC! He walks into the building and heads up to his place to crash after a long day. Yo! Yo! Man put that Harley up what are you waiting on? Manny yells at the valet. You must be sleep walking, wake your ass up and do your job son! Damn! I swear these young guys are lazy as fuck! Manny shakes his head and walks back into the building.

Two weeks had past; everyone fell into play in their new positions. Ring-Ring. Hello, thank you for calling Angels escorts! Yes, I would like to book an escort. What kind of girl are you looking for sir? A tall brunette with big breast! Are you looking at our booklet right now? Yes! You must be talking about Brandy! I think that's her. What time did you want her to come out and where to? Can you send her in the next hour and I'm staying at The Salt Palace, room 687. OK we're all set; Brandy will be there in one hour Sir. Your rate will $500, we accept cash and all major credit cards. I will be paying by Visa, do I pay now? No wait until she gets there and then we take your payment. OK! Thank you again for calling Angels, enjoy your date. Nina hangs up the phone and switches over to answer the next call. Ring-Ring. Hello, thank you for calling Angels escorts, how may I help you? Hey Sis, it's me! Hey Denna, what's up? Do you have Aunt Rosario's number? Yeah it's 702-303-4455. Thanks babe, how's work chica? Girl it's okay, they make crazy cash over here. Really! How much is crazy? Like $8,000.00 a day sis. What! You're lying! Hell no and these guys just give it up with no problems, not even a complaint! Wow, that's a lot of money Nina! Ring-Ring- Ring. The phones continue to ring. I know right; look I have to go sis the other line is ringing. OK bye, call me when you get off babe. You have to tell me some more. Bye Denna!

Ring-Ring. Hola! Hola Auntie! Hey, is this my Denna? Yes Auntie. How have you been baby, where's that sister of yours? I'm doing great and Nina's at work right now. Working huh, that's good, you guys need to find Hector a job! I-yi-yi, that son of mine. Where is Hector Auntie, I've been trying to find him. Did you go to the Valley? No, what for? He's usually over there with his little girlfriend. What girlfriend? I think her name is Selena, you know her Denna. Are you sure? Yes her brother Priest has a tattoo shop over in Green Valley. Oh yes, I know her, thank you Auntie! No problem baby, tell your mother to call me, I baked her favorite cake today. Okay I will. Alright, bye-bye baby. Denna hangs up the work phone. A few customers roam the isles searching for their favorite skin flick; she looks around for her partner and spots him in the back. Loon, come on Punta, let's go! I'm coming mean ass, hold your horses, I had to load my clip. Lock that safe back girl, you know old timer be tripping about that shit. I know, I had to put my drawer in, plus he's coming right back, we can't leave until he comes behind the counter anyway. I'm ready to go, where the fuck is he at? He's taking a dump. Hey Old timer! Loon walks towards the restroom calling out to Keiser. Old timer, what you doing bruh? He opens the bathroom door. Damn! Man what in the Hell crawled up your ass and died! You need to take a laxative or something this don't make no sense. Bruh you stink! Whoa!

Hey watch it young blood, your shit and sweet. It may not be, but I don't smell like a 3 day old dead dear! Ooh weeeee, you need to be shame of yourself. Make sure you wash your ass, toilet paper is not going to help you bruh! Damn! He walks out of the restroom. What's wrong Loon? What's wrong! You don't smell that! No, smell what? Keiser walks out of the restroom. Kiss my ass soldier! Ha-ha. Did you wash your ass? Ha-ha. Bye old timer, we're out of here, have fun. Denna and Loon leave the store and jumps in the beamer. Dang I'm glad this day is over sis! Yeah this was a slow one. What are doing when you get home poppy? About to crack this bottle of Goose I got and hit some chronic. Man your ass is forever smoking. Yep. She looks over at him and shakes her head then starts the car. Why are you shaking your head at me? You smoke too nigga! Yeah but not every damn day! Girl, put this car in drive and take me home, I'm not in the mood for this right now. Well I was just saying! Yeah whatever sis, save it! Fuck you Loon! She spins off the lot and makes a left onto Las Vegas Blvd.; Loon reaches over and turns up the radio as she speeds down the strip. The two are now silent as they journey home after another long day on the job. Denna drops the top, Loon reclines back in his seat; the Beamer fades in the distance on the way to its destination.

CHAPTER 14, JUNE.

Beep-Beep. Denna blows her horn outside of Nina's apartment, the door opens, and she sticks her head out. I'm coming sis, wait a minute. Hurry up girl! She runs out wearing a white UNLV T-shirt, red shorts and white sneakers with her hair in a ponytail. She comes out, jumps over the door into the passenger's seat. Wait! Hold up! I know you didn't just jump in my shit like the damn dukes of hazard! Aww, quit tripping, you got the top down. Yeah, that don't mean jump in crazy! Awww, poor baby, I'm sorry and please tell me why you have on that ugly Raiders T-shirt? The same reason you have on that Running Rebels shirt. Yeah whatever, you just hating that's all. My Raiders shirt is the shit. OK, yeah I hear you; now tell me where we're going? I've been trying to catch up with Hector's ass for 3 weeks and can't catch him, so it's time to take a ride to the valley; Auntie told me he's dating Selena. Who, Priest sister? Yes, how did you know? I didn't, but I do know Selena. Well, that's where we're going. Cool and why are we looking for him again? AC wants to know if he had any information on that murder about a month ago. What murder? Ashley, Jewel and Lisa remember?

Oh yeah, on the parkway; hmmm, Denna, isn't that Hector's turf? Uhhh yeah! Why do you think we're going to visit him? Hold up sis! I'm not shooting my cousin! No crazy, we just need to find out who did it and why? What if he did it? If he did I'm sure he has a good reason. Good reason my ass! Cuz will kill a bitch just for telling him no!

You know I'm telling the truth Denna. Ha-ha. Yeah that Punta is a little off his rocker! 20 minutes had passed and they finally made it to Green Valley. We're here, now where we going? To Priest tattoo parlor, maybe he knows where Hector is. OK, it's just up here on the left. She drives down a few blocks then pulls in the lot, parks in front of the door, they exit the vehicle and walks into the tattoo parlor where they see a couple of guys sitting in the front room. Hey homes it's your go, kick the ball Punta! Come on man, you can't get none on Madden! I'm the champ Punta! Hey homes you look like somebody fucked you up with that band aid under your eye. Shut up fool, yours going to look worse than this after you get those two tats on that ugly mug of yours.

The girls interrupt the fellas. Hey Chino! Poncho! Where's my cousin? Oh shit! Look who it is homes! What's up Denna! Nina I like that shirt homes! He's over there with Priest getting another tear drop tatted on his skull, look, I got mine already Mommy! Yeah, yeah, it's about time you became a man, it took you long enough esse'. Ha-ha. Be quiet Chino, you only got one more body than I do, I'm gone catch that ass this weekend homes. Watch! They walk over to the surgical chair where Hector is sitting. Hey what's been up Priest? Hola ladies, how you been? We've been good Priest. Oh what's up my two favorite cousins, Ma told me you called a few weeks ago. What brings you two all the way out to Green valley? Well cuz, my crew is trying to find out about this murder that happened on your turf about a month ago. Murder? Yeah! Who wants to know again? My crew. Hmmm. How those fools doing, AC still running things? Everyone is cool and yes, AC is still the Boss. That's cool; tell those fools I said what's up, yall need to come party with us sometimes, we haven't gotten together in a minute cuz. Yeah we got this long job we're pulling right now, it got us all tied up.

We really need to know about this hit cuz. OK, who got hit? It was three ladies and a cab driver. Oh that's who you're talking about, we did them fools our self, that's why we here getting these tear drops, got to add that rank, you understand the game cuz. We could care less about them hoes Hector, but why did you do it? Did they try to rob you or something? Hell no, we had the munchies and went to Carl's Jr. to get some drive through, we got our food, pulled up to the exit and those fools were behind us. They started blowing the horn and being disrespectful, so we got out the impala and handled them. One girl was talking all kinds of shit and saying she would fuck us up, we tried to laugh it off but she got out of hand so we did what we had to do. That's it! Yeah, that's what happens; you know I don't waste time talking cousin. Thanks man I appreciate that, we just wanted to make sure the girls didn't have any beef that we had to handle. Beef! Shit them pretty bitches wasn't no gangster's cuz! Actually those hoes were from Cali and did about a dozen bank jobs before they moved our way. No shit! Man we could of used those chica's on our team cuz, damn! Well it's kind of too late for that Hector huh? Whatever Nina! Alright, take it easy guys we're out of here. Nina and Denna hug their cousin and head towards the exit. Peace ladies! Hey cousins where you two headed? We headed to Sunset Park to meet the rest of the crew to shoot some hoops and down a few beers. OK, be safe and tell Auntie I said hello. Alright, later cuz. The girls exit the parlor and get back into the beamer. See sis, I told you Hector was crazy! He smoked those poor girls for no damn reason! Shit! I'm glad he's my cousin! Ha-ha. Me too Nina, Me too! They both laugh and head up the highway towards Sunset Ave.

The Rover and F150 sit in front of the Circle K on Sunset Ave, just walking distance from the park. Duck is standing behind the truck loading the cooler with ice. AC, Will and Manny sat in the Rover listening to Too Short, while smoking on some chronic. Loon walks out of the store with two cases of beer and singing. "Walking down the street smoking indo... sippin on gin and juice" "laid back". Hey Duck, hold off on that second bag of ice bruh; let me put this beer in first. Come on then slow poke. I'm coming pimp. He sits the beer on the tailgate and rips them open from the top. Here you go bruh. Duck takes the beer and starts loading them in the cooler, Loon opens the other bag of ice and pours it over top; they close the cooler and get in the truck. Yo Coop, let's go man. The guys start the vehicles, back out and head over to the park.

Duck turns up his Alpine sound system as they leave the lot, bumping MC Eiht."Wake your punk ass Up for the 93 shot. MC Eihts in the motherfucking house... gyeah" " And it aint nuthin but a Compton thing yall" "And we aint nuthin but niggaz on the run" "And this goes out to my niggaz... gyeah". They pull into Sunset Park and cruise over to the ball courts as the music continued to bump. "A fucked up childhood is why the way I am" "It's got me in a state where I don't give a damn, hmmm" "Somebody help me, but nah they don't hear me though". Hey Coop Park over there by Denna, there's her car right there! OK, I see it Manny. They pull up beside the BMW; Duck turns off the music and parks the F150 by the Rover. Nina and Denna are on the court already shooting free throws.

The fellas get out of the trucks and go over to the court to join the sisters. What's up fellas! Hey girls, I see yall warming up huh! Hey Manny, you ready to ball amigo? Am I ready! Come on Nina, I'm like the Latino Jordan girl! I stay ready! Yeah if you're Jordan, I'm Magic! Manny you aint got no game boy! Yeah I can bust you up Coop! Come get some! Look, not one of yall fools can see me on the court! Will please, you know your game is weak! Ha-ha. Let's shoot already, first two that make it from the three point line gets to pick teams. Duck why you want somebody to shoot all the way from the damn three point line. Because all of us can make a dang free throw, that's why. Alright, give me that rock! Loon goes to the three point line and shoots a jumper. Bing! Nothing but iron! Will shoots, he puts a high arch on it, they all watch as it comes down. Swish! Nothing but net! See that's how you do it people! Just like that! Nothing but net! Denna steps to the line and launches her jumper. It sales through the air, hits the back of the rim, bounces up 2 feet, comes down, hits the front of the rim, then falls in. Yeah! Yeah, get some! Wow! Really! That was luck! Shut up Manny, don't hate! OK, let's get it crackin! Will and Denna choose your teams, it's half court 3 on 3 and the game goes to 12, each basket counts as 1, the first team to 12 wins.

Will, you go first. Cool, let me have Nina. I pick Loon. OK, give me Duck! Yeah, yall are about to get smashed Denna. Whatever Duck, let me have AC. Oh, so Jordan is on the bench, OK I got next. No shit Manny, who else is next! Ha-ha. Go on the other end and practice your jumper Jordan! Ha-ha. Fuck you Nina! Nina you and AC shoot for the ball. AC steps up to the free throw line, dribbles the ball, picks it up, pauses then releases his shot. Swish! All net! Yeah let's go! Ball out! Loon steps out of bounds under the goal so he could pass the ball in. Nina is guarding her sister, Duck is guarding AC and Will is on Loon, they run back and forth over the half court. Denna fakes to the right, goes back to her left and stops in the corner. Loon passes her the ball, she sets her feet and launches a jumper from the corner, it hits the top left of the back board and banks through the net. Yeah, good shot baby! Loon and Coop shouts. Denna goes to the top of the key to take out the ball. Loon is posted down low, AC at the free throw line. Loon signals for the ball up high, she passes it to him; he backs Will down, turns right and shoots a hook shot. It goes up and hits the front of the rim and rolls in. Yeah baby! Let's go! AC takes the ball out, Denna runs up to get the pass. AC cuts across the court and swings back around under the goal, she passes it to him, he goes up for a layup, finger rolls it off his left hand. Smack! Will slaps it on the back board, grabs the ball, and passes it out to Nina at the top of the key. She release a high arc jumper, it falls through the net without touching the rim. Oooooh! In your face Denna! Manny yells from the sideline.

Duck takes the ball out up top, passes it in to Will. Denna runs over and picks his pocket. AC runs up the middle, she passes it to him as he enters the paint. He elevates and two hand dunks over Nina as Will tried to block it from behind. Damn get some! Loon yelled as he ran to the top of the key. Denna runs over to the top right of the three point circle, he throws her a bounce pass; Nina goes for the steal and miss. Denna takes off for the paint and makes a layup. 10 minutes had pass and the score was now 10 to 7 in favor of Denna's team. Will has the ball and faces up with Loon; he does a cross over move on Looney, leaves him at the top of the key and pulls up a jumper. Swish! He makes a pretty jumper. Duck takes the ball out; Nina runs up and gets the bounce pass. Ducks runs by her, she bounces it to him; he cuts through the paint and lays it off the glass. Yeah, let's go baby 10-9! Will shouts. Nina takes the ball out, Duck post up AC down low, Will runs to the free throw line to get the pass. Loon reaches in and slaps it away for the steel, Coop cuts to the basket, Loon hits him with a dime, AC goes up for the uncontested finger roll. Yeah baby, 11-9!

Denna takes the ball out. Will and Duck double team her to stop the pass from coming in, they jump up and down, she tries to throw it down low, it hits Will on the leg. Duck picks it up, throws a bounce pass to Nina down low, she lays it in for an easy layup. 11-10 baby, let's go! Damn! Come on team, we need one point, let's get the rock! Let's go! Loon yells. Duck takes the ball out, AC crowds him and tries to deflect the pass, he misses and Duck gets the rock to Will. He runs to the paint, stops and pops for an easy jumper. Damn! Come on yall! Let's play some defense, it's tied up! AC yells. Nina takes the ball out, AC and Loon double team her to stop the inbound pass, and they move left to right to mirror her every move. She tries to pass over their heads, AC catches the rock; Loon run to the post, Coop passes him the rock. Denna run towards him, Loon passes her the ball, falls to his knees and lands on all four. Denna is coming his way full speed, she steps off his back and goes up for the two handed slam. Dunk! She rattles the rim as the ball falls through the net. Ohhhhhhhh! Shit! Will! Denna just dunked on yall ass! Wow! Manny screams as he runs on the court to give her a high five. Man that was some bullshit! Where they do that at! Awww Duck, be quiet and take your loss like a man. Will and Nina just laugh and walk off the court. Good game guys, Denna you was wrong for that shit sis. Ha-ha. You know you liked that move Will! Yeah whatever, I need a beer. Sis you crazy! Nina don't be made baby, I love you! I'm not mad, you just crazy. She laughs as they all walk back toward their cars.

Manny and Coop pick up the cooler from the back of the truck and take it over to the bench by the cars where the rest of the crew is sitting; they all take a beer and start to converse. Hey Denna, did you ever catch up with you cousin? Yeah, we just spoke to his ass today. Dang, you just catching him? Hell yeah, I told you that fool be on the move. Well, what did he have to say? Did he know anything? Yep! OK, what! He said him and his partners did it. What! Why he do that? Hector claims they were talking shit and causing problems, they tried to talk with them but one of them kept mouthing off so they did them in. Damn your cousin got a quick temper. Hell yeah, aint no talking when you fucking with that fool, you got to step up or get dealt with! I see! So it was just random then, no contract or anything like that? Yep random. That's all I needed to know, everything is cool then.

What you mean, everything is cool AC? Since it was a random hit, that means no one was looking for the girls. Those bitches had a lot of money and I didn't want to catch no beef from somebody we didn't know about. Oh, I dig it. So you just made an easy 2 million then bro... Hell yeah! That's what I call a come up! That's nothing; we stand to make that a week once we take over the Delgato operation. Do you think they have any idea we're coming? Manny, they don't have a clue, by the time we hit them, we will have the whole thing sewed up. How much they pulling in a week at the club? Nina the last time I counted, it was like 70 to 85 g's a week! Damn, that's some serious cash flow poppy! What are they doing over at Angels? We're averaging like 6 to 8 g's a day. Damn, they make that much selling pussy! Yep! Shit there aint no reason a bitch should be broke, if you can make that much off your pussy! Loon shut your crazy ass up! Nina I'm saying though, it's the truth. Duck, which hotels do the customers use the most? Man most of them are on the strip and it's mostly tourist. Really! I would have thought you guys had a lot of locals. Will, I thought that too, but it's nothing like that brother.

It's a few regulars that live out in the Lakes, Spanish Trail and some in Summerlin, most of them only call like once or maybe twice a month. 90 percent of our clients are tourist, mostly because of the brochures and adult magazines we put ads in. Yo, these motherfuckers are pulling in a lot of dough off pussy! Will, pussy makes the world go around my nigga! You can say that again Manny! Denna, what are the numbers from the video store? We're good for about 5 to 7 g's a day Coop! That's like another 40 to 50 g's a week right there bro.! Hell yeah Loon, make sure nobody robs that shit! Ha-ha. Don't worry about that Coop; I got a full clip for any fool that step up. They might come in with bad intentions but I promise you, them fools will leave in a body bag! Hell yeah! Lay that ass down baby! Duck shouts out. We still need to find the connect on the drug tip though, do you have any idea yet? Not really, I know about Dupree and one of the girls from the club helps her boyfriend push a little in the club but no major players have come up yet. Me and Will are keeping our eye on things, they will pop up eventually.

That's really the last piece we need to secure before we can lock this thing down, I say we bring in a buyer to stir things up and see what happens! Hmm, that's a good idea Nina, but who? We already have the whole team on this thing. You guys are making a big deal out of nothing. We just need to go visit my boy Dupree; he will tell us everything we need to know! Yeah, you sure about that Duck? Hell yeah or I wouldn't of said it! So let's go see him then! When you want to go AC? Right now nigga, time is money! Cool, yall rolling? I'm down! Me too! We have to go wash fellas, ladies don't go anywhere, smelling like this, so we will get up with you fools later. They head to the beamer. What about you Will? Nah, I got some plans already. Hold up twins, let me catch a ride. Come on then poppy, hurry up!

Will, runs over to the BMW. So it's us four then! Yep! Let's take a ride to the south side my niggas! Hey, do you even know where he is Duck? Man that money hungry fool is always in the same spot, he aint trying to miss no money! I hear you, so where is that? Right off MLK drive, over by all those Churches. Churches! What is he doing over by the Churches? Manny, just chill my brother, it's all good, he runs his operation from the back room of a church. Wait, let me get this straight! Dupree and his crew are selling drugs out the back door of a church? Yep, that's right Loon. Man that nigga going to Hell in a hand basket, that fool done lost his mind! Fool we already in hell, we in Sin City remember, they don't call it that for no reason! Yeah AC, this is Sin City but that don't mean we have to be devils. Loon just shut up, you going to hell right along with all of us, so enjoy your life while you here my brother. See that's crazy talk, I'm done with it! Let's go find this dude.

They start up the Rover and the F150; take a 15 minute drive up Sunset, then to the strip and down Tropicana to the interstate 15 South exit. As they traveled down I-15 to the spaghetti bowl, the Las Vegas strip of Casinos fade away into the distance. They drove another 3 miles down the interstate then exited off on to MLK Blvd... Alright Loon, get your gat ready player. Duck I stay ready, no need to worry about that. Hey check behind us and make sure Coop is still following. He looks in the passenger side mirror and spots the Rover about three cars back. Yeah he's still back there. Cool! Man you weren't lying, this is like a village of Churches, it's one on every block, this is crazy. Your boy Dupree kind of smart, the cops would never expect a drug dealer to be posted up over here. Yeah, it was a smart move. Which one is he in? Look for a tan brick one with a red wooden fence. Hmm. Turn right here, I think that's it at the end on your left. He swings a right turn and goes to the end of the street. In the rear view he could see AC turn on to the street a few seconds later. Yeah, stop right here! This is it! He parks the truck by the curb, Coop pulls up and parks behind him.

They turned off the trucks, cock their pistols, get out and tuck the guns in their waist bands. The crew; walk on the church yard and take the sidewalk to the rear of the building. Three feet in front of them leaning against the wall, was an older gentlemen standing by a red door. Hello, how can I help you young men? Where looking for Dupree? Is he expecting you? No Sir, he isn't? Hold on then. He knocks on the door. What's your name young man? Duck Sir. A small window slides open at eye level on the door. Yeah, what's up Deacon? Could you inform Mr. Dupree that a young man by the name of Duck is here to see him with three guests. Hold on! The voice in the window disappears for about 10 seconds then the door opens. Deacon steps aside and points at the door. Right his way gentlemen. Thank you Sir! They walk through the door down a long narrow hallway.

Off to the right, a bright light was coming from a doorway along with a lot of noise. Come on man it's your play, count them bones already! Oh hell no, I know you didn't just play that! Wait, look! Is this a double five! He holds the domino up in the air then slams it on the table. Bam! Domino! Give me ten bitch! You see it! Ohhhh! The other three guys at the table yelled. AC, Manny, Loon and Duck approach the entrance and walk in on them. Well, well, if it isn't my homie Duck! What's up man! Dupree stands up to hug his friend. How the hell are you Pree? I'm great my man! I see you got the crew, what up Loon! What's good pimpin? Making this paper baby, making this paper! Oh Pree this is AC and Manny! He extends his right fist and gives them a pound. Nice to meet you fellas. You too player. So what brings your crazy ass to the South side D? Remember that time I called you about that strip club and moving some dots? Yeah, yeah I do. What about it? Shit, we trying to make some moves, but can't get to where we need to be you dig? I dig! All we need is a connect! Well to be honest with you homie, it's not that easy. Come in, sit down; make yourself comfortable. He says while sitting back down at the table. You fellas want a beer or something? Sure! Hold on! You, lil man, get my folks a beer! He tells a short teenager sitting in the corner.

We realize it's not an easy request but we have to make this happen, my nigga. Let me tell you how this thing works homie. The guys you asked me about, the Delgato's, have to give you their blessings before you can even touch the product I'm pushing. They only deal with Weed and Coke, no hard or meth or any other shit. I don't even get it from them, there's a guy by the name of Diego that has the product, but you can't do any business with him unless Bobby or Vinny OK's the shit. Damn! Where's this Diego from? He's a crazy ass punk from Colombia. This guy has a fake right eye; that joint is like a purple ruby with a diamond pupil, right under it, he has a long nasty scar and he's missing his right pinky! Dude sounds fucked up! Loon that aint the half, word is he got the pinky chopped off when he was 12. His cousin gave him a key to move in 48 hours. Diego couldn't get the job done, so he cut that fucker off! So his cousin gave him another chance, 48 more hours! He failed again and this time got cut under the right eye. The cut was so deep; he had to get 30 stitches! Third time came and his cousin told him he better sell that shit or he would wish he were dead! Well Diego had finally locked in a buyer, they meet up to make the transaction, all seemed well but this fool got jacked for the key and got shot in the leg. Cousin got word of it and was so pissed, he took a hot branding iron and poked Diego's right eye out. Damn, that's some cruel shit! Sure is Duck! The guys set there with blank stares on their faces as they listened to the rest of his story.

That's an interesting tale, now how do we get in on moving some of this weight? Bobby and Vinny choose who they fuck with, them cats never ever touch product! It's five people in Sin City that they deal with, I run the South side, Steel has the North side, Fat boy has the west side, Paco runs the east and Rose has the strip. We pay a $10,000.00 tax once a week to the Delgato's, each one of us has a certain day that we have to drop that envelop full of cash off to them at the club. Rose pays the highest tax because she runs the strip, her payout is $25,000.00 a week this is the baddest sister I know in the game. She's like 5'9", brown skin, keeps a nice short cut, hour glass shape, brown eyes and some sexy ass lips. Bitch is fire! Why does she pay so much? Isn't it harder to sell to tourist then to locals? Duck her operation is top tier pimp, Rose has one dealer in every casino on the strip on her team. Each one of them where's a purple wedding band laced in green ruby's on their left ring finger. If you want some coke or weed, let the dealer know, they then give you a marked chip and you go to a location and pick up your package but you have to tip them for this info, you dig? Dig it!

Manny looks over at AC then clears his throat. Ummm, hmmmm. So how often do you guys meet Diego to re-up? Shit, we re-up once a week! We get the location a week before from the Delgato's when we go pay tax. All the bosses have to re-up on the same day, no matter what! If we're late to a re-up or even miss paying taxes; our connect is over immediately and the punishment is death! The only time all the bosses see each other is during re-up or at the end of the year for our annual Christmas party. Damn, they have a smooth ass operation going! I told you I was getting paper Duck; this is some serious cash bro., wrath of God money. You should see my crib out in Spanish Trail; got the pool, cars, bitches, and all that man. That's what's up D, make sure you invite us over for your next pool party or cook out my man. You know I got you pimp. Hey you guys good? Want another beer, some smoke? Nah, we straight bro., appreciate the information, we have to bounce. OK fellas, be easy. Later Pree. They walk back down the narrow hallway through the red door, pass the deacon and out to the trucks.

Where you headed Duck? I'm about to take it to the house man, I have a date tonight. Oh snap bro man got a hot date! Shut up Loon, you rolling with me or you riding with Coop and Manny? It's like that man, you just gone kick me out your ride huh? I see how you are! Nah, it's cool, just playing, I will ride with Manny and AC, be safe man and don't be trying to take the bitch pussy! We know how your ass can get! Man whatever, you fellas hold it down. Alright D, be safe boy. Later! Duck gets in the truck and pulls off. OK boys! What's the move? Get in Loon! I'm coming pimp, I'm coming! He jumps in the back of the Rover and they coast up the street. So what did yall think about what Dupree said? It all sounded good to me, I'm ready to take over this city! Hell yeah that's what I'm talking about Loon! Let's get this cheese baby! You guys do know that this means war right! Shit AC, it aint no war if the other side doesn't know their under attack.

That's a good point Manny but hear me out. OK, go ahead brother, we're listening. Once we knock off the Delgato's, all their business and territory will belong to us. We become the motherfuckers in charge, this means we are now the target and you can best believe somebody is going to try us, we must prepare for war. Yeah I dig that! I say we start forming allies right now, we need a crew on the street to bust some heads and let everybody know we mean business. Who do you know that we can trust to do that Manny? Yo we should put Hector and his crew down, them fools mean business and their like family anyway. Yep, I agree with Manny, AC. Hmmm. That might just work guys. Man it will work, just tell Nina or Denna to speak with him and it's a done deal. Hey I got some weed back here, either one of yall got a blunt? Nah! Nope me either, but I will tell the twins to set that up ASAP. Damn man, go to that store on the corner, I need to roll this up.

He pulls the Rover onto the store parking lot and rolls up beside a black Corvette with the T- Tops off. Loon jumps out and runs in the store. Holy Shit! AC you see that! Hell yeah! Damn that bitch is fine! There she was in the driver's seat of the Corvette wearing a white two piece swim suit, white shades, sandy blonde hair and red lipstick. Her caramel skin looked smooth and soft to the touch as it spread evenly from her legs, to her stomach, her arms and juicy breast. Manny leaned out of the passenger window. Hello sexy! Hi! What's your name baby? Gina! Hi Gina! I'm Manny! Manny! Yes Manny! Nice to meet you Manny. So where are you headed gorgeous? I'm going to a pool party out at the Lakes. Damn is that right? Can me and my boys come with you? I know you have some sexy ass friends, fine as you are. Ha-ha-ha. No I don't think that's a good idea. Why not? Because. Because what?

He opens the door, gets out and walks over to her car. Well I don't think my boyfriend would like that. Shit, he doesn't have to know, I'm not going to tell him, are you? Ha-ha-ha. AC laughs in the background. Loon comes out of the store and gets in the Rover. What is that fool doing bruh? Be quiet Loon, he's getting his groove on. Yeah, she gone smack his ass watch! So what's it going to be gorgeous? I told you! Hey Nigga! Hey Nigga! A deep voice shouts out. Manny stands up and away from her car door, looks around. Yeah you nigga! Hey, are you talking to me bro.! Yeah fool! What's the problem bro.? I aint your bro. nigga, why the fuck are you talking to my bitch! Ha-ha-ha. Oh this fool is about to get his ass whip over some pussy. Shhhh, shut up Loon, Manny got this. You sure bruh! I got my shit cocked! Yeah he's good. OK, if you say so! He pulls out the weed and starts to roll the blunt. Manny looks at the gentlemen. Wait man, all this isn't necessary, my bad, I will step off. He backs away from the car.

All 5'11", 285 pounds of this big bald headed black male walks off the sidewalk towards him. Yo stay where the fuck you are bro.! I told you everything was cool! Fuck you nigga! Aint shit cool! She opens the door and gets out of the car. Baby chill, everything is cool! He pushes her back in the car. Sit your ass down bitch; I will deal with you in a minute. But baby! Shut up bitch! He points his finger in her face. Click! Click! He turns around and the cold steel of Manny's nine is on the tip of his nose. You see brother, what we have here is a fucked up situation. I have your life in my hands right now, but your stupid ass may die today because you wouldn't accept my apology. The weather is nice; you got a nice ride with a bad ass bitch behind the wheel. She looking all sexy and you guys are headed to a pool party to have a good time. I want you to do me a favor brother, look behind me in this truck. Do you see these two guys? Yeah, I see them. Good! Well they are packing, same as me; you on the other hand, take this as a joke. It's not a game out here player, I see your out of town plates and shit, that tells me you don't know any better. So listen, listen good! Out here on the West Coast; you will get smoke for looking at a fool wrong player!

Let this be a lesson to your ass! I'm not gone kill you, you get a pass this time but you will remember this day! POW! Oh shit! Oh shit! Owww, Owwww, you motherfucker! Manny shoots the ear ring off her boyfriend's right ear, blood is dripping non top all over his shirt. Oh my God! Baby! Baby! She screamed. Yo enjoy that pool party; you might want to get some band aids for that ear, oh nice meeting you Gina! Manny gets back in the Rover then screams at the injured victim. West Side Fool! Be prepared next time, you mark ass nigga! Ha-ha-ha. Boy you crazy as hell. AC and Loon tell him as they pull off the lot. Yeah that dumb ass, lucky I didn't kill him. I bet he wishes he were dead right about now though! Ha-ha. Pass me that blunt up here; I need to smoke after that episode. Yeah I bet! They make a left turn onto MLK Blvd. and merge into traffic on their way back to interstate 15. Vroom-Vroom-Vroom. An engine revs up behind them. Man what the fuck is their problem? Can't they see the lights red! Loon looks out of the back window. Man yall aint gone believe this shit! What! It's that fool and his bitch from the store! All three guys reach for their guns; AC puts the Rover in park. Oh he wants to see us!

Vroom-Vroom-Vroom. Gina revs up the engine again, her boyfriend is sitting in the passenger seat holding a blood soaked towel to his ear, to stop the bleeding. What the fuck are you doing baby? He said to her. We have to get you to a hospital and their fucking holding up traffic! Baby the damn light is red! So what! Loon, Manny and AC exits the vehicle and walks back to her car. Click! Click! They cock their pistols! Yo do we have a problem? I can finish the job right now bitch! Now I ask you again, do we have a problem! No! Just get the fuck out of the way so I can get to a hospital. Ha-ha. This girl got some balls Manny! Loon laughs and points the gun at the couple. Take your ass around bitch, your boyfriend aint our problem, we can send his ass to the morgue instead, if that's what you want! Hey baby, pull the fuck off! He yelled at her. That's what I thought! Manny lowers his gun and waves her on. Go on; get the fuck out of here! She pulls out from behind them and speeds up MLK, running the red light. Vroom-Vroom-Vroom. Skeeeerrrrr! She peels out. Ha-ha-ha. That chica was crazy! Take me home AC, this day has been too damn much. Let's get out of here fellas. Coop shakes his head as they all get back in the Rover and head up the I-15 towards the strip as the sun sets and neon lights illuminated the desert sky. The Casinos lit up the skyline with an array of colors as they got closer to the Las Vegas Boulevard exit.

A few days had passed and it's now 11am Tuesday morning, Paula is sitting in the office writing out an ad for the Vegas Adult Magazine when Nina walks in. Good Morning Paula, what are you doing? Hello Nina, awww, I'm just writing out this ad for some new girls, it has to be in for publication by the 15th of the month. Oh OK, how many girls are we looking for? Honey there is no set number, really the more we have the better. Wow, I thought it would be the other way around. No child, we have to fill the cat house too, not just our escort service. Huh! What cathouse? Angelica's out in Pahrump! What's that? It's a legal whore house honey, open 24 hours a day and we try to keep at least 15-20 girls on staff. Wow! Yeah, I thought you knew baby. Nope, I had no idea! Well now you do, shit loosen up sweetie, it's nothing. So do the girls work escort and at the ranch? No honey, come over here and have a seat next to mama, let me school you on the business, you are obviously lost.

Ha-ha. Nina laughs, walks over by Paula and sits on the desk. She opens an issue of the Adult magazine, see this page right here? Yes. This is our business, Angels Escorts and Angelica's Bunny Ranch, open 24 hours a day; we provide limo service to and from the ranch. Whenever you come in to work, look in the lot and there will be at least 2 limos parked on the first row, we have three, two Town cars and a Navigator. We pick the guest up from their hotels and take them out to the ranch for a small fee. The ladies live on the ranch with their own rooms and there is a house mom to make sure all their needs are met as far as food and other amenities. Damn seriously! Yes Honey! Do the girls make a lot of money? They average $1,000 to $2,000 a day. How does the company make money? Oh we get $300 from every guest for the trip, plus 40% from each date the ladies book, last year we did 15 Million. Right now we're doing 75 to 100 thousand a week; honey there's no place like Nevada when it comes to the sex industry, it's the second leading industry after gambling!

Now do you get the picture Nina? Yes Mam, I had no idea we made so much fucking money doing this shit! Honey, pussy makes the world go around; I will chat with you later, I have to go across town and pay for this ad. OK Paula, can you bring me some hot wings back? Child there's a menu in the drawer, call it in. She gets up, grabs her purse and heads out the door. OK, did you want me to order you something? No I already ate; thanks anyway, see you in a bit. Your welcome, bye Paula. She picks up the phone and makes a call as soon as Paula leaves. Ring-Ring-Ring. Hello! Hey bro., what's up, it's Nina. Hey Sis, what's going on? You're not going to believe this! Believe what? My boss just told me that the Delgato's own a bunny ranch out in Pahrump called Angelica's and it's pulling in heavy clams! Stop playing; get the fuck out of here! No I'm serious! What are heavy clams? How much! Like 100 g's a week! Damn that much! Yes that's what I said!

Well Nina, you have to get out there and check out the operation. No problem AC, I got it covered already bro. Cool, that's a good girl sis, hit me back when you take care of that and fill me in. Alright bro., chat with you later. Click! They hang up; Nina walks over to the corner of the room and turns on the radio. Hello people, if you're just tuning in, we are giving away two tickets to the Las Vegas Cowboys football game this Friday. All you have to do is be the eight caller and you win two 50 yard seats for this playoff game against the Arizona Rattlers, start calling now and let's see who will be the winner of these 50 yard line tickets. Ring-Ring. Hello, thank you for calling Angel's Escorts, how can I help you today? Hi I would like to book two escorts for a bachelor party. OK Sir, I can help you with that, did you have any special girls in mind? Yes, I would like one black girl and one Hispanic. Sure, we can make that happen, when did you need the girls Sir and where? Tonight at the Palace around 11pm. I have just the two ladies for the job, your total will be $1500.00, we accept cash and all major credit cards, you can pay your bill when the girls arrive; I just need your name and your room number sir? Oh my name is Richardson and I'm in room 2284. Alright, you are all set for 11 tonight. Perfect, thanks a lot. No problem Sir, enjoy the party, thanks again, goodbye!

Nina hangs up the phone then dials another number. Ring-Ring. Hi, thank you for calling Sunset Pizzeria! Hi I would like to order a medium cheese pizza and 20 hot wings. Sure, will there be anything else with your order Mam? Yes, add a coke please. OK, your total will be $16.89, what address will we be delivering to Mam? It's 2437 Sahara Ave., Angels Escorts. Thank you, it will be there in 30 minutes. Thank you! No problem, enjoy your food Mam. She hangs up.

The office door opens and in walks Paula. Hey girl, did we get any bookings? Yeah, we got a few. Good, we should have had more than that by now, maybe this new ad will bring us some more ladies to help out business. We are doing pretty good but can do much better. Is it hard to hire girls for the ranch? Not really, this is Vegas baby, girls move here just to sell that pussy honey! Why, because the money is so good? Yep you got it sister and it's legal too! I want to go? When can I visit? Child your little nipples are getting hard! What's making you horny girl? The sex or the money! The Money, what else! Yeah, that's what they all say. I tell you what young lady; I have a house right next door to the ranch because the bosses want me to keep an eye on things out there.

Here's my keys, go downstairs and have one of the Limo drivers take you out to the ranch for a visit, while you're there go to my place and get my purple suitcase, it's in the living room already packed. I'm staying up here for a few days and left it home by mistake this morning, I really need it. What! Really! Yes! Knock- Knock. Damn, who could that be? They both look at the camera. Oh, it's my food. Nina opens the door. I have a medium cheese pizza and 20 wings for this address. Oh, it's mine baby, here's a twenty; that should take care of it. Thanks; let me get your change. No you keep it baby! Thanks, Bye-bye! She takes the food and starts to close the door. Oh wait, Mam your coke! Oh thanks babe! Nina grabs the soda and walks inside.

Here are the keys honey, take that food with you, I need my bag! She runs over to the desk to grab her purse, sits the food down, puts her bag over the right shoulder, picks up the food with the left hand and stuffs the coke in her purse. Well get on honey, it's a 45 minute drive! What, 45 minutes! Yes, now get! OK, OK, I'm leaving! Nina grabs the keys from Paula and heads out the door, down the smelly hallway and outside to the limo. As she gets closer to the Town car, a white gentlemen short in stature wearing an all-black suit and hat approaches her. Hello Mam, how can I help you? Oh hi! Paula said for you to take me out to Angelica's. Sure that's not a problem, here let me get that food for you.

He opens the car door, and then takes the food from her. Thank you! Your welcome, I didn't get your name. I'm Brad! I'm Nina, nice to meet you Brad! Yep! He closes the door and gets in the driver's seat. Off to the bunny ranch we go, so are you going to be working out at the ranch Nina? No! Lord no! I work at Angels, I answer the phones. Phones huh, well that's an easy job right? Yeah it is. The Limo cruises off the lot and heads out of the city towards the desert. Hey do you want some pizza or some of these wings Brad? Sure, I will take a slice. She opens the box and hands it over the seat. He grabs a slice. Thanks Nina! Ahhh, it's no problem, I'm not going to eat it all anyway. Ummm. This is good, where did you get it? It's from Sunset! They make the best pizza in Sin City! Hell yeah, I would have to agree! I have to eat there at least twice a week! Wow, can I have another slice? Sure just keep the box up there, hold on, let me get a few slices and you can have the rest. She grabs two slices from the box. OK, it's all yours. Cool, thank you Nina! Yeah, don't mention it.

The scenery changed from big hotel casinos, pyramids and castles to a two lane highway filled with miles and miles of desert. Thirty minutes had passed during this long boring scenic ride then there off in the distance sitting all alone was a big white Ranch house, surrounded by a rusty steel fence and dirt parking lot. As they got closer, a large Neon light that read Angelica's lit up the front entrance of the ranch. Brad pulled the limo off to the left of the house and parked in front of a grey double wide trailer. OK, Nina this is Paula's place, that over there is where all the magic happens, the world famous Angelica's! Wow, is this where she really lives? Well it's one of her places; she has a kick ass 4 bedroom house out in Spanish Trail in the city.

Look we don't have much time; you better go in and get that bag. Yeah, you're probably right Brad. She jumps out of the back seat, heads up to the double wide, walks in and see the purple bag sitting by the door. Nina stops to take a look around at this place her boss called home. The room was filled to the ceiling with tons and tons of unpacked boxes which hid the floral designed wallpaper, dark brown carpet covered the small area of the floor that was still visible. She picked up the bag and headed back outside to put it in the limo. Ahhh, I see you found the purple bag! Yes I did! He takes it and puts it in the trunk. Thanks Brad, wait a minute, I'm going over to Angelica's to meet the staff. OK doll, take your time, I get paid either way babe. Thanks, I want be long. She walked up the wooden steps and entered the brothel.

The music is low and the room is dark, red leather barstools surround the bar. Three sky blue sofas align the back wall which matched the curtains over the doorway beside the bar. A tall white gentlemen; with a brunette ponytail, wearing a black T-shirt that read Angelica's attended the bar. Hello Mam what can I get you? Oh no, I don't want anything; I just came to introduce myself. Cool who are you? I'm Nina, Paula's assistant. Yeah is that right? Uh huh. I just started a month ago. Well welcome aboard Nina. Are you going to be working out here too?

I'm not sure yet, right now I'm at Angels setting up dates. Cool, since you're here do you want to meet the girls. Sure.

Hold on a minute then, let me page them on the intercom. He presses a button on the wall behind the liquor shelves and speaks into a small receiver. Attention, can I have all ladies to the front please! All ladies! You could hear the girls coming, as they got closer the clutter of their footsteps over the grey marble tile sounded like a stampede of horses. She looked up and there they were. 15 of the most gorgeous ladies she had ever seen; in a range of several nationalities. They all gathered in front of the bar and waited to see why he paged. Evening girls, I wanted you guys to meet Nina, she's Paula's new assistant and will be helping with daily operations here and at the main office in the city. One by one the beauties walk over to Nina and introduced themselves. Hello I'm happy to meet all of you! Which one of you ladies is the House Mom? Oh that's Nancy; she's over at the cashier's booth, that window just over by the couches.

You are very pretty Nina, are you sure you don't want to work here with us girls? One of the ladies asked her. Awwww thanks, but I don't think I can handle it. OK, if you change your mind, we will show you the ropes baby! Thanks, I will remember that, nice meeting all of you. She heads over to the cage to meet Nancy. Hello Mam, how may I help you? Oh I don't need any help, I wanted to introduce myself, my name is Nina, Paula's new assistant. Well hello gorgeous! Welcome to the company sugar! Nancy a short Asian woman sat there in glasses, a red wig and a blue silk pull over gown. Why thank you! Your welcome sugar! When you get back to the city tell Paula to call me. Yes Mam, I will. Alright thank you! Bye sugar, come back and see us.

Ding-Ding. A bell hanging over the front door rung as two gentlemen entered the bar. Bye ladies! Bye Nina! She walked out the door and back to the limo. So are you ready to head back now Miss? Yep, let's go Brad. Nina stepped in the Limo as Brad stood there holding the back door open for her. OK buckle up, we're headed back to Sin City! He closes her door and gets in driver's seat. The limo pulled off the dirt parking lot, leaving a cloud of dust as the sound of small rocks hit the fender and a cloud of dirt filled the air.

Over at the Towers, Coop's looking over his balcony and sees three ladies getting out of a white cadi that stopped at the light on the corner. The temperature at the time was around 115 degrees at 5pm, down below; work traffic began to congest the strip. AC opened a cold beer and sat in his lounge chair on the balcony watching the ladies. All three of them stood about 6 feet tall, blonde hair, big breast, red pumps, white fitted dress, red purse and white shades with red lip stick. One stayed at the corner, another crossed the street to the other corner, while the third girl walked up the strip. Traffic was almost at a standstill during this five o'clock hour, the ladies didn't want to hold up traffic and draw attention, so while at the corner they only made eye contact with single gentlemen who came up to the stop light. In less than five minutes both working girls were quick on the job as they disappeared from their assigned corners for 30 and 40 minutes at a time. While walking the strip the third working girl had only managed to pass one casino before she was lured up to a hotel suite, by a gentleman with a hand full of $500 dollar chips. After all, just one chip would be a great start to her day, but a fist full was worth the hustle of a potential mark. He watched from his balcony in amusement as the ladies worked this area like trained professionals, the street walker had just vanished into the casino when his phone ringed.

Ring-Ring-Ring. He runs into the kitchen to answer. Hello! Yo Coop, what's up Pimp! Yo, what up Will! Man I need you bro.! Yeah, for what? I got these two bad ass girls coming over man and it's just me, you can have the other one. Man what the fuck ever, I aint messing with no duck! Bro., she's fine as hell, their sisters! Hell, if they were not sisters I would try to bone both their asses. Come on bro., help me out! Manny is at work, Duck is too and Loon already got a bitch at his crib. Alright, what time are they coming? They supposed to be here at 7! Cool, you need me to bring something? Yeah get some of that henn dog and alize'. Oh you want that thug passion. Yep! What are we going to eat nigga? Man get the drinks, I'm seasoning some chicken for the grill right now. Hell yeah, that's what it is; see you in a bit pimp. Later! He hangs up from Will and dials the front desk.

Ring-Ring. Hello front desk! Yo Manny, what's up! AC, what's crackin! Yo, can you have them pull out the Ninja? Oh boy, it's on today huh! Where you headed homie? Will got these two skirts coming over and I'm gonna run side man. Dude, I hope they aint ugly, Will be picking some dogs sometimes bro.! Man; I will leave his ass at home with them mutts by himself, forget that! Ha-ha-ha. Alright man, I got you. What time you want them to pull it? Next 30. OK, see yah in a few playboy! He puts on the khaki dickies, a black wife beater, black k-Swiss, black L.A fitted cap and his silver and black Movado watch. AC walks over to the balcony and closes the slide doors, turns off the lights, then head downstairs.

Ding! The elevator door opens. There he is! My man Coop, you ready to go meet that mutt Will set you up with, make sure you take a bone. Manny shut your ass up, yall got my bike yet. Nah, it should be around any minute. Oh guess what amigo? What? How about Nina called me this morning and told me that the Delgato's have a bunny ranch called Angelica's out in Pahrump bro.! Damn, those motherfuckers are making a ton of fucking money! We need to hurry up and crash that party Coop! Oh it's going to be a big score my man, a big one! Hell, I can't wait! Be patient Manny, be patient, once we gain power, you are going to be my right hand man, right? Come on dog, you know I got your back! Yeah you better after all we've been through together, you got to cut this job shit lose though bro.! I mean how's it going to look if my Capo is working a 9-5 dog? Homes cut it out; I'm leaving this joint as soon as we knock off those two grease balls. That's what I'm talking about homie! They give each other a high five. Yo, here's your bike now! Don't do nothing I wouldn't do Coop, later be safe bro., tell Will I said what's up too. Alright, later home boy. He walks outside to his bike, unhooks the helmet from the seat and mounts the ninja. AC turns his L.A fitted around to the back and slips on his helmet, starts the ninja and speeds off the lot. He makes a right on the strip and heads north down the boulevard towards Freemont Street.

A strong aroma of hot coals, mesquite wood chips and grilled chicken filled the air. The Sun has set and the temperature dropped about 5 degrees to 100 from 105. Will starts preparing the patio table for his guest, pasta salad, corn on the cob, grilled tiger prawns and grilled chicken was on tonight's menu. The music playing in the background had set the mood for a perfect evening. Ding-Ding-Ding. He runs to answer the door. Well hello handsome! Hi Selena, you're looking sexy in that dress. Thank you Will; oh this is my sister Toya. Hi Toya, nice to meet you; come in ladies make yourselves at home. Where do you want me to put this bottle of wine baby, I know you told me I didn't have to bring anything but I couldn't come empty handed. Well thank you for being considerate, here I will put it in the fridge. OK, here you go babe. Thank you, oh the food is almost done too ladies, I'm just waiting on the chicken. Ummmm. It smells really good! So Toya, my friend AC should be here shortly. I hope he's cute, the last time I had a blind date that nigga was uggggglllllyyyyy! Ha-ha-ha-ha. Right sis! Yeah child, that brother was a monster! Ha-ha-ha. Nah, my boy straight. Yeah, I'll be the judge of that! Vroom-Vroom-Vroom. Hey that sounds like him now. What, he rides a bike! Yep, I think he has two or three of them, do you ride Toya? Boy please! I got a Harley, that's the only way to ride. Yeah that's cool, AC has a Harley too. See, you guys are going to get along great and you haven't even met yet. Ummm-mmmm. Slow down cowboy, we'll see in a minute.

Knock-knock-knock-knock. Its open bruh, come in! He walks in with two brown paper bags. What's up Dub! You got it playboy! Where do you want this Henn and Alize? Yo, just put it on the counter, I have to go check on this chicken. Not a problem, go handle that, I got this, yo, you want a drink right now? No I just opened a beer. Cool! Oh damn, my bad ladies! He stops to acknowledge Selena and Toya, sitting in the living room, Selena wore a white sundress and matching white Gucci sandals with an ankle bracelet made of sea shells on her right leg, her hands and feet were both manicured with French tips, sandy brown micro braids fell to her shoulders and complemented that pecan tan skin.

Toya was standing there in the center of the living room, a red two piece sectional formed an L shape in front of the glass coffee table, soft white lighting from the chandelier mirrored her image in the maple wood panel floors. Her caramel skin tone made the purple sundress she was wearing stand out even more, standing there barefooted with her hair pulled back in a ponytail; she resembled a young sweet humbled Sade. My name is AC, how are you ladies? Hello AC, I'm Toya and that's my lovely sister Selena and we're doing great. How about you? Me, oh I'm enjoying life baby! Well that's good, Will told us a lot about you. Is that right? Hmm, hope it was good. Yes, it was all good. So which one of you lovely ladies am I suppose be blind dating? Ha-ha-ha. Take a guess? Ok let's see, since you are wearing my favorite color and your sister looks most comfortable over there on the couch, I would have to say it's you Ms. Toya! She shakes her head to say yes. Good guess Mr.! Thank you, so can I make you ladies some thug passion? Sure I will have one, how about you sis? Sure! Cool coming right up.

He reaches in the cabinet to get four glasses, pulls the ice trey from the freezer and puts a few cubes in three of them, pours half Hennessey and the other half Orange Alize'. OK ladies, come and get some of this thug passion! Ha-ha-ha. Alright 2pac, we're coming to get that thug loving baby! They both head into the kitchen to get their drinks from AC. Whoa. What you guys got going on in here playa! Thug passion baby, get you beer so you can toast with us! Hold on; let me put this chicken on the table. Will takes the pan of grilled chicken and placed it on the table with the other dishes, picks up his beer and joins the others. Let's do it baby, get them glasses up! They all lift their drinks and toast. Here's to Will, Selena, Toya and me the one and only AC, may this be the start of a beautiful union. Yeah, we'll drink to that! Cheers! Hey the food is ready people, grab your plates and help yourself. Ummm. This looks good Will! Thanks Lena! Let's see how it taste! Yo, Toya, my man can cook baby don't even trip. Ha-ha. Ummm, Hmmm. Let me see what this chicken taste like. She picks up a piece and bites into it. Damn this is actually good sis! Good job Will! Sis you can keep this one! Oh yall crazy for that one, but thanks baby. I'm glad you like it though.

Man put that damn beer down and get some of this thug passion my nigga, here let me hook you up playa. He fixes him a drink. Thanks bro.! Yeah don't mention it, drink up! Oh turn that up baby, that's my jam! The radio plays in the background. "Boy you should know that... I got you on my mind" "A secret admirer... I've been watching you" "At night I think of you.... I want to be your lady baby" "And when the time is right... Give me a call boo" "Because I've been watching you.....". The girls run into the living room, kick their shoes off and begin to dance, Will and AC walked over to join them in this jovial celebration. Yo I love this song; it just does something to me! Yeah, what does it do to you Toya? Hmmmm. It makes me want to just get naked and dance in the mirror! Oh yeah! Shit, there's a mirror right over there! Ha-ha. You wish AC! Hey I was just trying to help baby. Yeah whatever! Ha-ha-ha. Will she said it, not me! Man you crazy, I aint in it dawg! He continues to dance with Selena.

Its cool AC, I'm not tripping baby. Oh, I was about to leave too. Why were you about to leave AC? Because, I don't deal with no Bitches with attitudes girl. Awww nigga, shut up with that NWA shit! I'm just saying! Didn't I say it was cool; OK I hear you girl, damn. So I see you rode your 1500 over? Yeah I love to ride! Do you ride? Yeah I have a Harley. Huh, no shit! Yep! Cool we should ride out sometime. Yeah we can do that. What are you doing when you leave here? I don't have any plans. Hell we can ride now, why wait? I didn't want to be rude and leave my sister. Girl she's grown, plus they probably want to be alone anyway. Yo dub! Yo dub! What's up Bruh? Hey, me and Toya are going to take a ride, we'll be back in an hour or so. Cool, you guys be safe, and bruh, take your time. Ha-ha. I got you covered my brother. Hey come on Toya, let's go burn out! Let's go then baby, I'm ready! She puts on her shoes and walks outside with Coop.

Jodeci's Forever My lady is playing on the radio. "Forever my lady... It's like a dream" Will starts to sing to Selena. I'll be holding you tight, all through the night. This dream is ecstasy.... Boy you making up your own words but I like your voice though, keep singing. Ha-ha. Be quiet then baby, let me sing. He whispers in her ear and walks her back towards the couch, she falls back as he starts to kiss her and run his fingers through her hair. Selena slides her legs open as Will moves his right hand down below and pulls her panties to the side. Ummmm-mmmmm. I like that baby.

He massages her vagina slowly in a circular motion until it becomes moist. Ummmmm, mmmm. Stop playing with it and put something in it baby. Ummmm, mmmm. I want you inside me! She says out loud. You sure you want it baby? Yeah nigga, give it to me! Selena unzips Will's jeans and pulls out his dick; he lifts up and slowly thrust it down inside her sugar walls. Ummmm, mmmm. That feels so good. Ummm, mmmmm. Damn that feels good. In then back, in then back, in then back, then in again, he pushes for the next 25 minutes until her sugar walls turned to a creamy syrup. Uhhhhhhh, ummmmmm, mmmmmmm, mmmmmmm, dammmmnnnnnn baby, dammmmmmm, oooohhhh, I LOVE YOUR ASS! She screamed. Yeah I bet you do, you just like my doggy style. Ha-ha-ha. Be quiet nigga; you stupid! He laughs, gets up and goes to the bathroom to wash his dick. Baby, bring me a towel please? I got you, you want it wet, hot or cold water? Yes, hot water please. Will walks in the bathroom and washes up, then brings Selena her wet towel. Thank you darling. You're welcome. Vroom-Vroom-Vroom. Coop and Toya pulls in the driveway. It sounds like their back. Ha-ha. Not a second too soon, huh baby?

Knock-Knock. It's open man! They walk in. Toya undo her hair and let it hang down. Ooooohhhh, weee. It smells like straight ass in her! Yall been fucking! Ha-ha. Oh snap! Toya be quiet! You crazy as hell girl! I'm saying they could have burned some candles, light some in scents, hell spray some Lysol, and I'm not sitting on that couch! Selena what is that? Is that your coochie rag? Girl, go to the bathroom with that, yall some freaks! Sis shut up; get your stuff so I can take your crazy ass home. Hey baby! Baby! Yeah, what's up Lena? I'm leaving, I have to drop my crazy sister off, I will call you when I get home. OK baby! The sisters get their bags and head out to their car. Toya come on here with your crazy ass. She drags her by the arm and head outside to the car. Bitch why did you embarrass me like that! Because, that was nasty Selena! Girl shut up and get in the damn car, that's why I don't like to take your ass nowhere, I swear! Bitch you still nasty, yall could have went in his room.

Vroom-Vroom. Selena starts the car and pulls out of the driveway. I'm leaving your ass home next time. They continue to argue as she drove away. Yo nigga, you tap that ass on the couch, didn't you? Man why you aint use your room. Bruh, don't even go there with me about what I do in my house! Ha-ha. I'm just saying dawg, was it good? Hell to the yeah nigga, I knocked that cat out of the park! They give each other a high five. My man! Yo thanks for the food and everything, I have to hit the club in a few hours, so I will see you next week at the 4th of July get together. When do you go back to work anyway? I don't go in until tomorrow. Oh that's what's up, I'm off tomorrow. So next week then. Alright Coop, later. Later bro... He walks AC to the door and they dap each other up. Coop gets on the ninja and head back over to the Towers to get ready for work.

CHAPTER 15, JULY.

It's a warm summer night on the Vegas strip, AC's white Land Rover, Denna's red BMW and Ducks black F-150 cruise behind one another up the parking ramp of Caesar's Palace. They make it to the top level and park beside the edge to view the Vegas skyline. Duck, Loon, Will, Denna, Nina, Manny and AC all step out of the vehicles. They stand to the edge and prepare to see the annual 4th of July firework display that will illuminate the dark sky over the Las Vegas strip. Looking down from the top of Caesar's parking deck you could see the Planet Hollywood globe rotate below as patrons line up outside to see the fireworks display. Manny sits on the tailgate of the F-150 beside the beer cooler, the sisters jump on back and join him, Loon, Will and Duck jumps in the back and sit on the side rail. AC gets in and leans against the cab. Yo, what's in the cooler? Let's see, we got some brewskies and some St. Ides. Hey did you guys hear that new St. Ides commercial with Nate Dogg? No Loon! Check it, homeboy was like. "I went to the corner store... You know what I'm looking for....." "St. Ides...... St. Ides...." Nate put the G Funk on that shit homie! Yeah, Nate do be killing it. So what you want Loon? St. Ides Manny, what else. What time do the fireworks start? I think they start in the next hour poppy. What time is it now Denna? It's 9:15 AC. Thanks baby.

So Nina, did you ever get out to that bunny ranch? Man I went like a few weeks ago. Well let's hear it! Hold on poppy, hold on; let me get one of those cold brewski's. Here you go baby! Thanks Manny! Well go on with it chica! AC don't make me drop kick you in the head Punta, why you rushing me? Because you will forget Nina if I don't stay on that ass. Yeah, yeah, anyway, so I go out there to the desert and it's like this big ass white ranch house, I go inside to check things out, up front is set up like a bar. That's the area where the girls come out and meet the customers, the bartender was cool as hell; he had all the ladies come out so I could meet them. Damn, I swear it was like 20 bitches! All of them were sexy too; then I met Nancy the house mom. Hmmmm. So do you think the bartender or Nancy could cause us any problems down the road? Well Coop, the bartender, we definitely will have to handle, but Nancy will be an asset. Then there it is, he's on the list. Loon, Denna how are things over at the store? We have everything under control on that end but the old timer will have to go! Don't you think so Denna? Yeah he will be a big problem if we let him stick around. OK, put em on the list. Duck what about the other drivers over at the agency, are they in deep enough to make any noise. Hell no bruh, those fools in it for the pussy, they want cause any problems. Well on my end; Will and I pretty much got things covered. The only targets from the club will be the bosses; everyone else will fall in place after the takeover. So when are we taking down the bosses? Manny I was thinking early December, maybe that week before Christmas, I'm still putting the final job together though; I still need to meet the players from the drug cartel before we can move forward.

The only ones I've met this far or know of is Steel and we already knew Dupree, so that leaves Paco, Fat Boy, Rose and Diego! We just need to keep our eyes and ears open at the club, because they all have to come by every week to make their drops. That's true Will, so we should be able to identify and meet all of them next week with the exception of Diego. Yeah that's going to be the tough one, meeting that Punta! Hmmm. I think I know a way to stir things up so we can get him to show his face. How are you going to do that poppy? Give me a few days Denna to iron out the kinks and I will let you guys know something, I may need your cousin Hector for this one too. Cool, just give me the word and you got him. Thanks sis, Manny hand me one of those St. Ides bro.! Pop! Pop! Bam! Bam! The fireworks illuminate the dark skies over the Vegas strip, creating a unique show over every casino. Down below crowds of adults and kids alike enjoy the combination of loud booms and neon color creations that danced across the Sin City skyline.

Hey Duck, when you get back home, call your boy Pree and find out when his next re up date is and the location. Sure I'm on it! Nina call Hector and set up a meet on his turf at the Crazy Horse for tomorrow night. OK got it! Which horse AC? The one by the bridge or the pink building on the parkway? The pink one. OK! Loon jumps off the truck and walks back over to the edge. Damn look at all those people! Man do you ever wonder how the damn strip is filled with tourist every week and weekend; I mean if you think about it, this is some impossible shit! Getting people from all over the world to fly in and gamble their money away at hopes of the American dream, way out here in the middle of the damn desert. You can't tell me that Gangsters don't make the world go around! Hell, look at this! He turns around and holds out his arms, so that the sky line of the strip is behind him. A Gangsters paradise! Yes it is and it's about to be all ours my nigga, all ours. They all stand up, look at the skyline and open their arms too. Then say. All ours baby! Shaking their heads and smiling at each other as the fireworks continue to illuminate the skies.

Good Morning! Wake up people! This is your AM shock jock KC and you're tuned into WCEP your favorite Hip Hop and R&B station; it's official baby! Tyson is fighting in September at the MGM Grand and The Row just announced that they are having an after party at club 662. So Sin City get your paper right and your gear fresh baby, it's about to be a night to remember. You got a few months to stack your paper, take off work or do whatever you need to, here's a hot one for you, from Ice Cube. Today was Good day! AC rolls over and turns up the radio, wakes up Sabrina. "Just waking up in the morning, got to thank God" " I don't know but today seems kind of odd" " No barking from the dogs, any smog and momma cooked a breakfast with no hog". Baby why did you wake me up? I'm tired, can I get a few more hours? No Brian get up, you aunt laying your but in bed all day! Come on woman, I'm about to make some breakfast. Make the bed for me, when you get up. He slips on his robe and walks into the kitchen. Sabrina rolls over and turns the radio up louder. "Had to stop at a red light" " Looking in my mirror not a jacket in sight". Sabrina! He yells from the kitchen. What! Turn the radio off and get your ass up! Don't make me come get you! Alright, Alright, I'm about to make the bed. Cool, how do you want your eggs? Fried hard! OK, you want raisin toast or white? Raisin!

Sabrina makes the bed and goes into the restroom to wash up. The sausage links are in the pan simmering, he pulls the raisin toast from the oven. He places two plates on the table, put eggs and toast on each, takes the 4 sausage links from the pan and placed two on each plate, pulls the OJ from the fridge and fix two glasses. Hey baby, the food is ready! OK, I'm coming! Sabrina comes out of the room in a wife beater, red boxer shorts and hair tied up in a red silk Louis Vuitton scarf. AC sits down at the table. Let's eat up baby! Hmmm. That smells good daddy! They sit down to eat breakfast. Thanks for cooking daddy, what made you cook. Shit, I was hungry as fuck last night, but was too lazy to get my ass up and fix something. Ha-ha. Boy you crazy. I'm serious, my damn stomach was growling all night. Well either way, thanks. Ha-ha. You're welcome. Oh, I almost forgot, Vinny wants you to call him today! Who? Vinny your boss! Oh! What does he want? I think he needs you to cover for him or something, I'm not sure. What time is it? It's 2 o' clock. Hand me the phone. He dials the club number.

Ring-Ring. Hello! Yeah may I speak with Vinny! Whose calling? This is AC! Oh what's up brother, this is Vin. Hey how you doing man? Sabrina said to call. I'm good brother, listen I have some people coming by tomorrow night that I need to introduce you to. OK. So I will need you to come in about an hour early, you and Will! OK Boss man, we will be there. Great, see you tomorrow then. Click! Well, what did he want daddy? For me and Will to come in an hour early tomorrow to meet some people. Oh really! Yeah, wonder who it is? That's a good thing daddy, no matter who it is, trust me!

Yeah we'll see about that baby. He picks the phone up and dials Denna's number. Ring-Ring. Hola! Hey sis! Que pasa AC! Did you speak with Hector? Yeah, he's coming tonight; we're meeting at the Crazy Horse on the parkway right? Yep! OK poppy, see you there. Later. Click! He hangs up and calls Will. Ring-Ring. Hello! Dub! What up Coop! Yo, we have to go in an hour early tomorrow; Vinny wants us to meet some folks. Who we meeting? Man I have no idea! Alright whatever, we'll see tomorrow I guess. What you getting into tonight? I have to meet Hector about that business remember. Oh yeah! Well get with me later. Alright my nigga. Knock-Knock. Dang, who the hell is that? Yeah who is it! It's your Granddaddy; open the door Punta! Manny use you're damn key, I'm not getting up! Man open the door, I left the keys at my desk. Baby can you please go let that fool in? Yeah, I got it daddy. She walks over, opens the door, he walks in. Hey Sabrina, what's poppin baby! Hey Manny! Yo bro., get off the couch and put some clothes on! Dude it's almost three O clock and you still in your robe! Kiss my ass Manny, what the fuck do you want? I'm on break, I need to smoke something before I go back, let me get some of that chronic you got stashed. You can have that blunt on my dresser, I rolled it last night. Cool, that's why you're my man, you always keep it 100! Yeah, yeah, whatever. I'm serious Coop! Bruh shut that crazy talk up and go get that smoke before I burn it. Ha-ha. You would do that; wouldn't you? He looked at AC and laughs as he enters the bedroom to get the blunt. Alright, I got it and I'm gone! Thanks homie! He yells as he exits the condo. Ha-ha. Look at this nigga, yeah you welcome Manny! Remember you owe me one! Yeah later, I got you though! He screams from the hallway as he enters the elevator.

Ring-Ring-Ring. Jesus that phone is driving me crazy! Baby can you get that please! I got it daddy. Hello! Hey can I speak to AC. Sure may I ask whose calling? This is Duck. Oh hey Duck, it's Sabrina, how are you? I'm good baby, how about you? I can't complain; hold on here's AC. Daddy its Duck. OK, I will get it in the bedroom. OK! Coop walks in the bedroom to take the call. What's up bruh? I got that info. From Pree! Cool, what's the deal? Their meeting Sunday at the EQ Warehouse plaza off Tropicana and Industrial, in building 675. Alright, thanks man, I got to get ready to meet Hector in a few, I will hit you later. That's what's up bro., peace out. AC slips on some khaki shorts, black wife beater and his black and silver Jordan slippers. Hey Sabrina, are you working tonight? Yeah, I go in at 8! Well lock up for me when you leave, I have a meeting at 7 across town. No problem daddy. Thanks! Hey can you call the front desk, tell Manny to pull the Rover up? Sure babe. She picks up the phone and dials the front desk. Ring-Ring. Hello front desk! Hey Manny, this is Sabrina. What's up Brina? Coop wants you to pull the Rover. No problem, when does he want it out? Hold on. Daddy! Daddy! Yeah! He wants to know when? Tell him now baby! He says now. OK, I got it. Thank you! Bye Manny! Your welcome, see you later. Click! AC gives Sabrina a kiss, smacks her on the ass and heads downstairs to his car.

Traffic is heavier than normal for this time of day on Maryland Parkway, the red beamer moves in and out of traffic trying to get over to the right turning lane. They catch a break when someone lets them cut in front of them. Denna and Hector make their way into the plaza and pulls up in front of the Crazy Horse club, a small dirty pink brick building located at the back end of the parkway business plaza. They exit the car, lock the doors and walk inside to find a table for their 7 o'clock meeting with the Boss. The smell of old cigarette smoke and recently shampooed carpet met them at the door. Dirty foggy mirrors mounted the walls behind the bar and stage area of this small 3000 square foot adult night club. A small staff of 10 girls and 1 bartender outnumber the 4 customers that were shooting pool over in the corner. Behind the bar stood a 6'3" slim built white female, wearing all black with her blonde hair styled in a bob.

Hector and Denna approach the bar. Hey Slim, what's crackin homie! What's up fucker! I'm pissed at you! Come on mommy, don't act like that! Don't mommy me, lil fucker! Excuse me Lady, what can I get for you? Oh my bad slim. This is my cousin Denna. Hi Denna, I don't mean to come off mean, but your cousin is full of shit. Ha-ha. Yeah

I hear you on that sister but he means well. Hmmm. You don't have to take up for him baby but enough about him, what you having honey? Oh let me get a shot of goose baby. Hector are you having the regular? You know it! She fixes a shot of Grey Goose and one Crown and coke. Here you go guys. How much do we owe you slim? The first one is on the house baby. Cool thank you. Your welcome!

Hey cuz let's sit over there in that booth. He looks back at slim. Thanks again baby! Fuck you Hector! Damn mommy! OK, I see how you are, I will make it up to you, I promise! Bye lil fucker! Denna laughs, picks up her drink and heads over to the dark corner where several booths sit alongside the wall of dirty mirrors, he follows. They have a seat in the mahogany wood finished benches with the mahogany table top. So cuz what kind of job you guys got going that's using up so much man power that AC has to use my services? It's really big cousin and there's going to be plenty cheese in it for you and your crew if you want to get down. Hey, I'm here for you familia, if you're in, I'm in! Where's your boy? It's 7 and I'm ready to handle this business cuz! He should be here any minute. Hector picks up his drink and takes a sip. Look there he is walking in now. AC walks in the club and stops to look around. Hey AC, over here! She yelled. He sees them and gives her a head nod to confirm, walks over to the bar, orders a beer then heads over to meet them.

Hector stands up to greet him. What's crackin AC? It's all good Hec, how you been homie? He leans down and hugs Denna. Shit on that paper chase homie, you know how it is. Yep I can dig that. So did Denna fill you in? Yeah a little. AC takes a seat in the booth beside Denna across from Hector. Well this is the business; me and my crew are in position to take over the Sin City underground. I'm talking prostitution, drugs, strip clubs, hits all that shit! I have my people in place to run all the top spots as soon as we knock off the current bosses. I still need a team on the street to take care of the dirty work, bust heads, pick up money all that shit you dig! Homes say no more, count us in. How much money we're talking? I figure 40% of the take on collections and each hit will have its own price anyway. Hector stands up. AC stands up. They look each other in the eye, stick their hands out and shake on it. I'm all the way in homie! Cool! Welcome to the crew Hector. Thanks, when is the first job? I like that, a man about his business! He looks over at Denna. Sis you OK over there? Yeah, I'm good poppy. Oh and to answer your question, I need you to handle something this coming Sunday. They both sit back down. Lay it on me!

All the drug bosses will be going to re up at this location, I need you to jack one of them for their shit. We need to meet their supplier and I know this will get his attention, so take the car, money and all the dope. Don't smoke anybody; just leave their ass by the road or something as long as they all get the message. Hector don't kill anybody! I got you homes, no bodies. I got you. So where is the location? Its building 675 over on industrial and Trop. in the EQ Warehouse section. OK, I know where that is. Who are the marks? It's the five Sin City drug bosses, Fat Boy, Paco, Steel, Rose and Dupree. Which one do you want me to hit? I know Dupree, Steel and Fat Boy's sloppy white ass. Hell, you can jack anyone of them except Pree, he's down with us. That fat ass white boy, that's my mark! Hey, whoever you want homie! Yeah we're going to make that slob wet his pants. Just remember no bodies and wear mask, you got to keep your identity secret if you're going to get paper with us. It's done homes. Cool! They all get up, finish their drinks and head outside. So are you clear on everything Hector? No questions? Yeah homes, I'm good, let's do this bro... Sis are you good? Yep, I'm fine poppy.

The three of them are standing on the sidewalk in front of the Rover. Hector, again thanks for sitting down with me amigo, I'm looking to make some major moves with you my friend. Hey any friend of my cousin's is a friend of mine; I'm ready to make those moves homes. AC walks over and hugs Denna. Him and Hector shake hands, he gets in the Rover, starts it, let's the window down and says one last thing. Alright then guys, take it easy, Hec call me after the job for further instructions. See you later sis! Hey man I need your number, wait a minute! Hector shouted to him before he could pull off. Oh Denna, write it down for him! OK I got you! AC winks his eye at her then pulls off. Beep! Beep! He blows the horn as he leaves. Denna and Hector get in the beamer; she grabs a pen from her door panel and a piece of paper, writes the number down and hands it to Hector. Cool, thanks cuz, now let's get the fuck out of here! She starts the BMW and speeds off the lot.

It's another hot summer day in the Mojave' deserts Sin City and over at Dolls the Vodka is flowing as Bobby and Vinny entertain their guest. Sounds of laughter fill the air from the four gentlemen sitting at the bar as Deb pours the spirits and tells the occasional joke or two. Will and AC walk in the back door looking for the two bosses, they hear noise coming from the front of the club, which was strange because they wasn't open for business yet. Upon entering the main club area they could see Vinny and Bobby sitting at the bar with two other gentlemen, they approach the jovial fellas. Deb sees them coming. Hey AC, Will! Bobby and the other guys turn around. Hey fellas; come over here and meet Smiley and Sam!

What's up fellas, nice to meet you, I'm AC. I'm Will. Guys, Sam and Smiley are here from Costa Rica, they bring new girls down every 4 months. Wow, no shit! There are some nice bitches in Costa Rica! Ha-ha. We know, you got to come visit sometime. What did you say your name was again? AC! Yeah, let us know when you guys want to come down AC, we will make the arrangements. Cool, that's what's up Smiley. We brought six girls down this time, their downtown getting, ummm, how you say, uh sheriffs card? Cool, can't wait to see them! Sit down fellas, what you drinking? Let me get a Vodka and cranberry. How about you Will? Vodka and OJ. Deb take care of that baby; look, I know you guys want to know why we called you in early today. Hey, I know you have your reasons boss! Listen to this guy! AC, you're a real charmer brother but seriously, from now on, I want you and Will to handle the import end of things. What do you mean by import Bobby? Ha-ha. Where did you go to school, don't you know what import means? Sure I do, but my question is, what are we importing? Ha-ha-ha-ha-ha. All the gentlemen start laughing except for AC and Will.

Deb; give these guys another round. Coming up boss! We import pussy fellas! How do you think we stay ahead of all the competition! We have girls coming in from Costa Rica, Germany and Thailand every other month; Sam and Smiley are the point men. They fly over to meet our contact in whichever destination, choose the girls, fix them up with passports then bring them over to work for us. We have four houses in the city for the girls to stay in; those are the ones that will be working here at the club and for the escort agency. Our bunny ranch out in Pahrump is for the girls that want to sell that pussy all day. So you see when it comes to pussy, we mean business! Hell yeah! Shit we'll drink to that! Ha-ha-ha-ha-ha. Vinny stands up. Here let's take a drink to the pussy! They all raise their glasses and say out loud. To the pussy! Then drink up. Now do you fellas get it? Oh yeah, we got it! Good!

Listen up and listen good, on the middle of every month these two guys will be bringing us a delivery, you two will be responsible for that delivery. Make sure they get their permits, clothes, shoes and place them in one of the houses or at the ranch. Do you understand? Yes we got it. Oops, I almost forgot! Please check their papers and make sure they don't have any STD's or no crazy shit like that! We want good, clean product gentlemen; that's how we make our living! AC and Will raise their glasses to acknowledge him. OK Vinny, we got it. Great! Now you two exchange numbers with them two and go take care of business. Sil should be back with the new girls in a few, make sure their all squared away gentlemen. Vinny and I need to make a bank run before we open, you two are in charge of the girls. See you fellas later, Sam, Smiley, have a safe trip back. Alright Vin we will, go handle your bank business, we'll see you fellas next time. The brothers down their drinks then rise to their feet. OK, later gentlemen. Vinny and Bobby, shakes every ones hand then leave for the bank; Sam and Smiley finish their drinks. Well fellas, it was nice meeting you guys, we have to be leaving now. Got to catch a flight to Thailand in the next hour or so. They gather their belongings off the bar; shake Will and AC's hands and head outside to the Limo that has been waiting on them for the past hour. Later fellas, I guess we will see you two next month. Yeah, sure thing my friend, be safe and don't get into any trouble. Sam and Smiley walks outside. Bye fellas! Deb shouts as they walk out the door. See you later baby!

Beep-Beep-Beep. AC's pager is going off; he takes it from his waist and looks at the number. Hmmm. This is Loon, wonder what this fool wants? Hey Red, could you hand me the phone baby? Sure, here you go sweetie. Thanks! Ring-Ring-Ring. Hello! Yeah can I speak to Loon? Hey Coop, this me bruh! What's up pimp? Man this old timer over here getting on my nerves about some bullshit, I am about to do his ass in a minute, I just wanted you to know that! Man; chill the fuck out! It's too early for that shit, you'll mess everything up! I'm just saying Coop! I'm about to kill em! Man if you do that fool right now, we gone have to do everybody else too and we're not in any position to profit off any action right now. Boy you lucky I got love for you, this nigga was about to get one to the dome. I swear, I was gone leave his stinking ass on the toilet with one in em! Calm down bro... I'm calm man, just because I don't want to fuck up our paper. Ummm. But when it's time, that nigga gone get his, I swear. Yeah, until then be easy! Alright man, I got it; let me get back to work. Later! He hangs up the phone. Click!

Man let me calm my nerves. Loon starts to sing. "Some... times in our life. We all strife" " We all have sorrow....
but if we or wise" " We know that there's always tomorrow.... ""Lean on me... When you're not strong". Hey
Loon! Loon! Loon! Man what do you want? The two are standing outside in the parking lot. Come here for a
minute young buck. He walks over to the back of the building where old timer is standing. What's up man? You see
that black Chevy right there. I see it, what about it? You telling me you can't see it rocking. Huh! Well damn, it is
rocking! Hmmm, mmm. That's one of them lot lizards, she done got by you and caught her a trick! Now they're in
my parking lot sucking and fucking! I swear, I don't know why I hired your ass boy! Old timer; shut up and watch
me handle this here situation! Loon pulls out his nine and cocks it, walks up slowly behind the bouncing Chevy. The
windows were up, engine on and ac blowing. While standing there behind the car he could see a man's head
leaned back in the driver's seat, a woman's body is arched over the arm rest and her head is moving up and down
in his lap. The guy's right arm is across the back of the seat and his hand is clenching the head rest on the
passenger's side as she continues to go down on him.

POW! POW! POW! Three shots ring out and shatter the back glass! The trick shifts to drive, press the gas and
runs into the side of the brick building, the woman jumps into the back seat and ducks for cover. POW! POW!
POW! Three more shots sound off and one hits the driver's tail light! He jumps out of the car, pants down to his
knees and falls to the ground screaming. Please, please don't kill me Sir! Please! The woman is still hiding in the
back seat; old timer runs and opens the back door to get her out. Loon, goes and stand over the half-naked
gentlemen there on the ground, he points the nine at his dick. Look motherfucker, the next time you want to trick
off; don't bring your ass on my property! Do you understand? Yes Sir! Yes Sir! Consider this your final warning, next
time I will shoot that little scribbled up dick off your nuts! OK Sir, I'm sorry! Get the fuck out of here! He jumps in
the Chevy and burns rubber off the lot, almost hitting several cars in the oncoming traffic. Loon turns and looks at
the little frail woman that old timer is holding by the arm; she has her head down, he walks over to her and points
his gun in her chest. Bitch don't you ever bring your crack head ass back on this property again and tell your whore
friends the same thing! Yes Sir! I will stay away, I promise! Good, let her go Keiser. He releases her arm and she
walks off the lot, Loon runs up behind her and kicks her in the ass. Run bitch! Don't walk! OK Sir! I'm sorry Sir! She
runs across the street! See old timer, that's how we do shit where I'm from! He looks at Loon, shakes his head,
puts his hands in his pockets and walks inside. POW! Loon fires a shot in the air and goes inside behind him.

Keiser walks over to the counter. Denna what's wrong with your cousin, that boy needs anger management. Ha-
ha-ha. Keiser why do you think we call him Loony? Shit I know now baby! I know now! Hey, you guys go ahead and
take off early, I got it from here. What! Are you sure K? Yeah Denna, go ahead, Loon done made my pressure go up
with his crazy ass, I've had enough for one day. Loon is leaning against the counter listening to them. Awww, stop
crying old timer, you use to be the same way back in the day! Hell, I'm too old for that shit now youngster, go
ahead you two! Get out of here! Alright, see you later old timer, get some rest and take them pressure pills. Hah-
ha-ha. Loon stop being mean and come on! Just kidding Keiser, thanks and take it easy. Yeah- yeah, bye go home
already. They collect their things and head outside to the beamer. Yo D, let's stop by the wooden nickel and get
some of those $3 drinks. Cool, I'm down. Are you treating? Yeah, I got it! Hey, want you let me drive the whip?
Denna looks at him and rolls her eyes. Come on stop playing, I aint gone wreck your shit! You better not poppy!
She throws him the keys. That's what I'm talking about baby, let's ride out! He walks around to the passenger's
side, opens her door, then goes around to the driver's side and starts the beamer. She turns on the CD player and
bumps her 702 cd. "I'm gonna keep it real, how you make me feel" "Boy you give me chills, baby." Denna you love
that 702 huh? Yeah boy, that's my jam! She turns it up a little louder. Hold on my favorite part is coming up. She
sings along. "You know how I do... And you know how I flow" "Can I get your name and number... cuz I like your
steelo".

Loon cruises off the lot and heads up the strip towards the Rivera Casino. Denna let's back the top and puts on
her shades as the hot Vegas wind blows through her long silky hair. Up ahead on the left, the parking lot of the
Wooden Nickel Casino was full of rental scooters and four wheelers, patrons crowded the entrance to the casino.
Everybody was trying to take advantage of their $3 drink specials, a common night spot for the Las Vegas locals.
Loon and Denna enter the lot and find a park over by the Pepper mill which set adjacent to the nickel. Damn! It's a
gang of folks out here tonight sis! Yeah I see that, come on let's go inside, I'm ready to get wasted! They get out of

the car and join the line of impatient patrons waiting to enter the casino, the hotel security steps outside and speak to the patrons. Alright people, we're going to open the side entrance, the bar is packed on this side. Awwww Mann! The crowd yells. Hold on people! We got it covered; both the side bars are now open and you guys can drink til you pass out! Just don't puke on the carpet, take your drunk asses to the bathroom please! Ha-ha-ha-ha. Just kidding, follow me people; it's this way to the side entrance. The rowdy patrons gather and follow him around back, the doors are open and you could see a large sea of people covering 90% of the main casino and bar area. Loon and Denna made their way to the side bar before it got swamp with the others.

Hello guys, what are you having, we got $3 vodka, gin and tequila. Let me get two shots of tequila. Got you! Mam what are you having? Hmmmm. Let me get a sea breeze. Cool one sea breeze and two shots of tequila coming up! Excuse me miss! Yes! Can you make hers a double too? Sure! Loon you know I'm not a big drinker; don't be trying to get me' fucked up! Chill out girl, I got you. Yeah you better! Ha-ha-ha. He pats her on the back and smiles; you're in good hands baby. Here you go guys, do you want to pay now or start a tab? Yeah, start a tab. OK; I will need a credit card Sir. He reaches for his wallet and pulls out the visa card. Here you go baby! Thank you Sir!

Drink up Denna! Come on, you sipping that drink. Uhhhh. You trying to get me fucked up poppy! She takes her drink and turned it up. Yeah, that's how you do it Dee! Drink yours Loon, what you waiting on? Ha- ha-ha. Loon laughs then drink his shot. Hey, another round over here baby, make them both doubles. Sure! Are you hungry Denna? Yes a little. What do you want, some wings or something? No, do they have nachos? Excuse me baby, do you guys sell nachos? Yes we do. Great, can I have an order please, with extra dip and salsa? OK, I got you babe. Man this is crazy, I can hardly move around, all these damn people in here! Both bars were packed, along the walk ways and all the slot machines were filled with patrons. Waitresses could barely move through the casino among the people standing elbow to elbow. Four rounds and a few hours later. Poppy! Poppy! Let's go! I am fucked up! Hey bartender; can you close out my tab? Sure, one minute Sir. Damn, those shots got me feeling good; I'm too messed up to drive D! Can you drive? Hell nah poppy, I'm not wrecking my shit! So let's get a room here at the casino then and sleep it off. OK poppy, whatever. She said in a drunken slur.

Come on; let's go to the customer service desk then. They get their drunk asses up and head over to the front desk to get a suite. Hey Mam! Yes, how can I help you Sir? Can we get one of your suites? Sure, we have smoking or nonsmoking, king or queen size. Cool, let us get that king size. King size, will you be paying by cash or credit? Credit. Here, you can put on this one. Loon you better keep your hands to yourself. Denna what are you talking about, shut up that non sense, your ass is drunk. I know what I'm saying poppy, don't be trying to get none! Ha-ha-ha. Me, trying to get some, you make sure you keep your hands to yourself! Ha-ha. You funny, I can put my hands anywhere I want! Yep, that's exactly what I'm saying; I know you want this girl. Shut up Loon! I'm just saying! It is what it is! Come on poppy, I need to take a shower and get in the bed. Hold on; let me get the key first girl! Here you are Sir, your room is on the 35th floor, just go down that hallway and you will see the elevator at the end. Thank you Mam. Come on Denna, let's go. He escorts her on that long awaited journey down the hallway to the elevator.

They exit off onto the 35th floor and entered the hotel suite, a huge King size bed captured the center of the room; dressed in a red and gold comforter with big matching pillows. Black carpet with large gold diamond designs complemented the gold couch and black floral Rose prints imprinted on the fancy wallpaper. Loon walks in with his right arm around Denna's waist. Alright baby, sit down, take off your shoes and go take a shower, the robes are right here in the closet. OK poppy. He goes over to the curtains and slides them back to reveal the beautiful Las Vegas skyline. Off in the distance the Excalibur Hotel Casino dominated the Vegas strip with its large Castle towers and larger than life statues of several Magicians. Green beams of light illuminated the opposite corner as a huge gold lion stood there as keeper of the night. Heavy water drops hit the ceramic bottom of the shower stall, steam fogged up the bathroom mirrors, a sexy hour glass silhouette appeared through the steamy glass shower doors as Loon entered the restroom. Hey Denna! Yeah poppy? You want some company? See, I knew it; your ass was up to no good! Come on, stop tripping, can I join you or not? Uhhhh! You better not tell my sister about this! I promise I want tell anyone! Well come on, I need my back washed anyway. He quickly removes his clothes, looks at himself in the mirror and smiles then joins her in the shower.

Denna's, wet bronze, soapy skin, was both gorgeous and inviting; Loon grabs her by the waist from behind and pulls her wet body close to his. Ohhhh, what's that sticking me poppy? That's what you've been asking for baby. Hmmmm. And what is that? This chocolate stick! Ha-ha. I like chocolate poppy! He reaches around in front of her and starts to play with her pussy; she tilts her head of wet hair back and leans on his shoulder. Hmm, mmm. You like that baby, don't you? Yessssss, don't stop poppy, don't stop. She turns her around to face him, they begin to French kiss, Denna jumps up into his arms and wraps her legs around his waist, Loon pushes the shower door open with his left elbow. Ooooohhh. Where you taking me baby? Shhhhhhh. He carried her across the suite and gazed in her eyes as her skin lit up from the glow off the Vegas skyline.

Awwww fuck! Damn, this window is cold as fuck poppy! Shhhhhh. He tells her to be quiet. Uhhhhh, Uhhhhh, Uhhhhh. She sounds out as her wet backside moves up and down against the large window that overlooked the Vegas strip. Ummm, hmmmm. That's how you like it baby? Yesssss poppy, yesssssss! He lets her legs go, her feet touches the warm carpet. No poppy, don't put me down, what are you doing? Stop talking so much, turn around girl. Ohhhh. You think you can handle this huh! Stop talking. He bends her over and slips his black love inside her pretty wet clean shaved vagina. Uhhhh, Uhhhhh, ummmmmm. She moans as she braces both hands against the window overlooking the neon lights and miles of traffic down below. Damn baby, you got that wet pussy, hmmm, mmm. This thing is juicy girl! You like that huh poppy? Love it baby, love it!

She slings her hair to the side, looks back at Loon as he continues to stroke it from the back. Hmmm, mmm, Hmmm, mmmm. Yeah daddy! Give me that dick poppy! Yeah, this is your dick baby! After 30 penetrating minutes all the water on their bodies had turned to sweat, the side of Denna's face was now against the window, her hands on her ass, one on each cheek, holding them apart. Ohhhh, give it to me poppy! Give it to me! Uhhhh, shhhitttttt! Whose pussy is this poppy! Whose pussy! This is my pussy baby! My pussy! Hell yeah poppppppiiiiii, oooooohhhhhhhhh, yessssssss, yesssssssss. I'm about to cum poppy! Ohhhhhhhhhhh, Myyyyy God! Shhhhhhhhhhiiiittttttttt! Uhhhhhhhhhh, Uhhhhhhhhhh, Uhhhhhhhhhh. God Damn baby, that was good. Ummmm, mmm. We have to do this again. Yeah poppy, we definitely have to do this again. Hell yeah, that was the bomb baby. Loon lay on the floor in front of the window, she lays her warm body on top of his, they lay there chest to chest, he could feel her heart beat slowdown from its rapid pace. The smell of shampoo from her wet hair was the last smell he would experience before both their eyes closed for a long nights sleep.

Today the temperature index had reached 118%; the sun was setting over Sin City. On the corner of Tropicana Ave and Industrial Boulevard; 8 bikers gathered in the parking lot of in and out burger. Hector is standing there in front of the 8 black ninja bikes along with the 7 other riders. The guys gather around him, all of them dressed in black from their shirts, shoes, helmets, jeans and gloves. Alright my brothers, listen up! This is the move! Me and Poncho are going to scout the warehouse for the mark, Chino you take the other brothers, wait for us across the street at the I-hop. You got that Chino? Yeah Hector, I got it homes. The location is like a mile and a half away from the I-hop. Here Chino, take this cell phone and wait for my call, once we make the mark, I'm going to hit you on the cell. OK homie! When you get the call, start the bikes and be ready to ride. Me and Poncho will be tailing the mark, so you guys need to pull out in front of them before they get to the stop light. So do you want us to smoke them homie? No brother! No bodies! Damn mannn, I need another tear drop homes. Chino, if you catch a body, I'm going to put a bullet in your ass myself! OK, I got it Hector, no problem esse'. Good, let's ride Poncho, time to get this thing crackin, guys let's go, wait for us across the street.

Yo Hector, hold up homes, we have to wait for Marcia. Where the fuck is she man? In the bathroom homes, Oh, here she comes now! Running towards Chino was a slim female dressed the same as the others but wearing red lipstick, eye lashes, short red hair and two tear drops tattooed under her right eye. Come on chica, get on, time to ride baby! She gets on the back of Chino's bike, puts on her black helmet then taps him on his left leg. Vroom-Vroom-Vroom-Vroom. The bikes pull off the lot and head up industrial across Tropicana, Hector and Poncho continue a mile or more up industrial toward the warehouse complex. Chino and the others hang a left into the I-hop parking lot to await his call. The white lines on the black pavement begin to blur as Hector and Poncho continued down industrial pushing 115 miles per hour, two minutes later, they arrive at the warehouse location.

Three white gentlemen dressed in suits are standing outside of the main entrance; a dark blue armored truck is backed in to the open garage. Parked out front is a white Tahoe, black Bentley, green Range Rover, white Town car limo, black hummer and a red Benz. Hector and Poncho cruise pass the warehouse and park three doors down to keep an eye on the location. Yo Ponch, look at that fucking Bentley bro.! Yeah that sucker is hot homes! Which one is Fat boys? He drives that Tahoe. OK, the big man must drive the Bentley. Yeah I know, I would be pushing that motherfucker too homes, if I was him. Ha-ha-ha-ha. Hell yeah. Hector laughs and shakes his head. What time is it Ponch? It's 7:45 right now. Hmmm. They should be finishing up by now. I think they are man, look. Just then a few doors down, a tall black female dressed in a black pants suit and red heels with a red blouse to match walked over to the Bentley. Hell nah homes, Chica is pushing the Bentley! On her shoulder, she carried a big blue duffle bag; she popped the trunk and threw it inside. The gentlemen posted outside the door waved to her as she pulled away from the warehouse.

The front door opens and out walks a short Latino male, wearing white slacks, snake skin boots and a green silk shirt, A tall African American gentlemen dressed in all white walked out beside him.. Hmmm. That must be Paco right there homes, walking with Pree. Both guys were carrying green Army duffle bags as they exited the building, Dupree heads over to the Range and Paco to the Benz. That Punta must be making some loot too homes, driving a Benz and shit. The two speed off the warehouse lot onto Industrial Boulevard. Out walks Steel and Jesse carrying two black duffle bags, they placed them in the back of the Hummer, Steel walks back over to the entrance and speaks with the fellas posted outside the door. Hey my man, do you have a light? No man, none of us smoke! What, that's crazy, none of you fuckers smoke? Nope! Damn, alright then man, you dudes take it easy. Later!

Jess starts up the Hummer, Steel jumps in the passenger seat; they leave the lot in an opposite direction than the others. Hector picks up his phone and calls Chino. Ring-Ring. Hello! Yo homes, get the boys ready! Got it boss! The garage door moves up a little further, the truck backs all the way in, A huge 6' 2" white male wearing about 400 lbs., dressed in a number 34 Raiders jersey, khaki shorts and white K-Swiss with a bald head exits the garage with two, big blue duffle bags. He makes his way over to the Tahoe and tossed the bags in the back. Yo that's the Punta right there homes! Hector says to Poncho as he pulls out his cell phone to call Chino once more. Ring-Ring. Hello! Yo the mark is driving a white Tahoe, be ready to pull out in front of him, we will be in the rear, send three bikes out in front of the truck. Be sure you pull up on the driver's side with Marcia, send two of the other guys to the back to switch with us, place the last guy on the passenger's side. OK, we're on it. Hey Chino! Don't shoot anybody! OK, OK!

Fat Boy starts his Tahoe and proceeds to exit the lot, Hector and Poncho wait a few minutes before they follow, he turns onto Industrial, gets about two blocks before they pull out behind him. The two lane side street is clear of any other traffic; cars pack the warehouse lots of industrial business parks along the way. As the Tahoe gets closer and closer to the intersection of Tropicana, the two bikes traveling behind starts to gain ground, his front windows are down, left arm hanging out of it and right hand on the wheel. Beep- Beep-Beep. He blows his horn as three bikers pull out in front him before he could reach the light. Vroom- Vroom-Vroom. Chino and Marcia pull up alongside of him; two more bikers pull off the I-hop lot and roll to the back of the Tahoe, another biker pulls up to the passenger's side. Beep-Beep-Beep. What the fuck are you fools doing! Move your damn bikes!

Hey shut the fuck up, Fat Ass! Chino puts his nine to Fat Boys forehead. Put the truck in park! Do it right now, fat ass! OK, OK, I'm doing it! He puts the Tahoe in park. Get your ass out, now! Come on! He steps out of the truck, Marcia gets off Chino's bike, gets in the driver's seat. Hector pulls up to where Fat Boy's standing. Vroom-Vroom. He stops in front of him as Chino is holding him there at gun point. Hector pulls out his 357, looks at Chino. Go ahead bro., take the Tahoe to the chop shop, we will catch up with you later. Awww fuck, come on dude, don't chop up my shit! Hector points the gun at him. Shut up Fat ass! Give me your cell phone! Right now! Give it to me! He hands the cell phone over.

96

Chino looks over at Marcia, gives the signal, a simple head nod, he pulls up with the three bikers waiting in front at the light. Marcia puts the Tahoe in drive then follows them across Tropicana and up Industrial. Hector scrolls through Fat Boy's cell phone and finds Diego's number, then dials it. Ring-Ring-Ring. Hello! What's up Fat Boy, did you forget something? Yo, this aint Fat Boy homes! Then who the hell is it? What do you want? Listen up Diego, we have your shit! What shit! We got your dope homie, if you want it back; me and you need to meet. What! Do you want money! No homes, no money, we need to meet! We have some business to discuss. Fuck it; meet me right now at the warehouse over on... Hector interrupts. I know where you are homie, we can't meet there. Meet me in 2 hours on the top parking deck of the Rio. Good, I will be waiting on you motherfucker! Hey calm down brother, that's no way to treat somebody that's holding your money! Oh yeah, big man! I will see how big your balls are, this is Diego! Nobody messes with Diego! Ha-ha-ha-ha. You haven't met me yet homes. Click! Hector hangs up the phone. Here you go fat ass! He throws the cell phone at Fat Boy. Vroom-Vroom-Vroom. Hey wait! How the fuck am I going to get home! Walk fat ass! Vroom-Vroom. Hector and Poncho spin off and head up industrial behind the others.

A half mile down from the intersection the bikers meet up at a big red and yellow warehouse, the vicious loud barking from two white Pitt Bulls would detour any stranger from venturing behind its 10 foot tall privacy fence. Three red colored garage doors concealed the workers chopping up several stolen vehicles from the night before, sitting there out front on the gravel lot was Fat Boy's white Tahoe. Hector and Poncho pull onto the lot, the automatic gate closes behind them; Chino is at the Tahoe with the back gate open. They ride over and park beside the truck, so what's in the duffle bags homes? I don't know boss, I was waiting on you before I opened them. Alright, go ahead, open them up! He opens up the first bag, damn; look at this shit! Inside the first bag were ten blocks of cocaine wrapped in red paper.

Hector walks over to the truck, pulls out his switch blade and sticks it in one of the red packages, puts it to his nose and inhales. Hmmmm. Yeah brother, this is some good blow, open the other one. Chino opens the other bag and finds another ten blocks. Shit, this is $500,000.00 worth of snow brother; fat ass is moving all this in one week too. Hey, go ahead, close it back up bro., let me call AC. Ring-Ring-Ring. Hello! What's up Coop; got that mission covered. Cool, where is it? Right here at my shop. How much work was he carrying? Man, it's an easy half a mil here. That's what's up, when and where are we meeting Diego? In like an hour and a half on top of the Rio parking deck. Sweet! Stay there at the shop; wait for my call for the next move. OK Coop, I will be here bro... Alright, will talk to you in a few Hec.

AC slips on his black slacks, black socks, black Stacey Adams, wife beater and red button up short sleeve Louis V shirt. He walks in the bathroom, splashes on some Cool Water cologne and puts on his black Louis V shades. Knock-Knock-Knock. Yeah, who is it! Knock-Knock. He grabs his wallet and heads to the door. Who is it? It's Nina! He opens the door. Hey sis, what's up? I was in the area, just stopped by to see if you wanted to grab a bite. I don't have time right now baby, I'm on the way to meet this connect. What connect bro.? The drug supplier, your cuz just jacked him for his product. Oh yeah, when did he make that move? Hell, about an hour ago. Damn, who's rolling with you? Nobody sis, you want to roll? Hell yeah, I'm down, let's go. Are you sure? Yeah, why you ask that? Because you got that sexy black dress on, high heels and shit! Hair all long and sexy, got your lip stick on too. Look bro., don't get it twisted, I got my 22 in my purse and the nine strapped to my thigh! So cut the crap and let's roll already! Ha-ha-ha-ha. That's why I love your ass sis! Come on, the Rover is waiting downstairs. He locked the door behind him and they entered the elevator. Ding! The elevator door opens to the lower level, they walk off, the Towers lobby smells of fresh baked bread and cinnamon from the mall bakery. All is quiet before Nina's heels and Coop's Stacey Adams clash with the marble tiles that dressed the Towers lobby, their four feet sounded like horse shoes galloping across the Atlantic City boardwalk.

As the two got closer to the exit, the double doors swung open, they walk out into the sea of night heat, tourist traffic and patrons that crowded the busy Las Vegas strip. Hey Nina, want you drive sis, I'm going to sit in the back. What kind of mess are you trying to pull AC? No, it's not like that, me and Diego never met, so when we roll up on them and you're driving, we will catch them off guard. How will we know what he looks like? Dupree told us how he looks and baby trust me, he want be hard to spot! Ha-ha-ha. Why you say that bro.? This guy has a purple ruby eye with a diamond pupil, plus he has a scar under it, how are we going to miss that shit! Wow! That's crazy!

Alright, let's roll and get this thing popping. Where are we going again? To the top parking deck of the Rio. OK, let me put this clip in before we take off. She reaches in her purse and gets her clip for the nine, slides it in, cocks it and puts it on the safety. Damn you ready for war aint you! Hell yeah poppy! You know how we do it! Ha-ha-ha. For sho! Hey turn that AC on; it's hotter than hell tonight. She rolls up the tinted windows, turns the AC on high and turns on the disc changer. Snoop Dogg's Murder was the case was thumpin in the Bose surround system. Yeah, that's the jam right there Nina, turn that up some more! "As I look up at the sky, My mind starts trippin, A tear drops my eye" " My body temperature falls, I'm shakin and they breakin tryin to save the dogg". Nina pulls off into the busy Vegas traffic and head towards Flamingo Boulevard. "Pumpin on my chest and I'm screamin" " I stop breathin, damn I see deamons".

They finally make it to Flamingo Blvd. ten minutes later, in the distance across the bridge over interstate 15; you could see the red and blue towers of the Rio capture the night skyline over the other buildings on that side of the city. Nina cruises through the lot of tourist, RV's and cars to the parking garage entrance, after 35 levels of driving she reaches the top deck. The view of passing cars on the interstate below, show an amazing light show against the backdrop of the Las Vega strip. Off to the North end of the deck set a black Lincoln Town Car Limo, A tall white gentlemen dressed in a black suit and tie stood about 6'6", his large body over shadowed the back car door he was leaning against. He tapped on the back window as the headlights from the Rover got closer to them. Slow up sis, that must be him over in that Town car. She stops about 15 feet away from the limo.

The huge gentlemen opens the back door and out stepped Diego, wearing all white linen, sandals, a long black pony tail and full beard, his eye sparkled as the Rover headlights reflected off his diamond pupil. Nina put the truck in park, exited the vehicle, walked to the rear and opened the door for AC. Diego walked half way between the limo and the Rover then stood there waiting in front of the bright lights. Coop took his 357 from the seat, stepped out of the vehicle and stuck it in the small of his back, snugged under his belt. Nina closed the door and walked to the front of the truck as he followed; she stopped and posted in front of the Rover between the headlights. AC continued on to the halfway mark where Diego was standing. Click! Clack! Sounded as he approached the Drug lord. Whoa! Hold on! I'm clean! AC yelled out. The big guy had his gun pointed at him. Who the fuck are you and where's my dope? Wait a minute, you one eyed motherfucker! I have the product, so I ask the questions around here. My name is AC; I take it you are the infamous Diego. Yeah, so what! You see Sir, me and you; we have some business to discuss. Then in a deep Latin accent, Diego says. Man, I don't even know who the fuck you are, so how do we have any kind of business? Well let's just say, some of your product is showing up on some of my turf. Look AP! Whatever your name is, I have permission from the Sin City crime family to put my shit where I want, when I want! Oh is that right? Yeah and you're not one of them, so you need to give up my shit before I have my man here put two holes in your head.

I don't think you know who you're talking to Captain Jack! My family will make sure you lose that one good eye you have left Pablo! Listen we are both business men, let's work this thing out so we all can leave alive and happy. Go ahead, speak, I'm listening. First, tell me what turf you are referring to, this turf you say my product is on. I'm talking about over on industrial, club Dolls. Ha-ha-ha-ha. You say your family owns that property? Yes the Delgado's! Hmmm. I know them well my friend. So why are you pushing on our turf if you already know not to fuck with Vinny and Bobby! Shit brother, I'm a part of that family, we have an alliance. Yeah and what's that? No dope gets sold in Sin City unless it's approved by the brothers, we have five bosses that supply the city; I'm their supplier. Oh, so you're the connect for the guys that come in and drop off the padded envelops every week. Yes, exactly, I see you have been paying attention. I always keep my eyes open Diego. That's good my friend, what exactly do you do for Vinny and Bob? I make sure the club is safe and there is no one trying to infiltrate our network. Is that right? Did I stutter? No; wait a second!

He turns around and reaches out to the tall gentlemen standing by his Limo. Scotty, give me the satellite phone! He lowers his gun then reaches in the back seat and comes up with a large grey phone. Here you go boss! Thanks Scott! Let's call Vin and Bob, AC! I would love to tell them we've had this run in. Sure, go ahead, knock yourself out! He dials the number. Ring-Ring-Ring. Hello, thanks for calling dolls. Hey Bobby, Is this you Bobby! Yeah, who wants to know? Hey man, it's Diego! Hey what's going on man? I was calling because I'm at this bar I like to visit every now and again. OK, what about it? I just ran in to this guy that says he works for you over at dolls, he goes by AC!

Oh yeah, he's one of ours, started here some months ago, some new muscle we hired to help keep an eye on the place, keep motherfuckers in line. Buy that physco a drink on me will yah! Alright, I will Bobby, holler at you later my friend. Click! OK, so you were telling the truth, welcome to the family. Thank you Diego! Now where's my shit? Ha-ha-ha-ha. Hold on a minute. He picks up his cell phone and calls Hector.

Ring-Ring. Hello! Hector! Yo Coop, what's the move bro.? Alright, take the Tahoe back to the warehouse and remember to stay low. Wear a bandana or mask to hide your face when you drop that shit off. OK, got you amigo, we're leaving now! Later! Click! Diego hands his phone to Scotty. Hey call the warehouse, tell them to expect a visitor, he will be driving Fat Boy's truck, take it and park it in the garage. Doing it now boss. Oh, one more thing! Call Fat Ass when you're done and tell him to come pick it up and that he owes me 50 g's for finding his dope! Ha-ha-ha-ha. You got it! Yo AC, why don't you guys join me for a drink or two downstairs at the bar, I'm treating. Sure, let's do that! Nina parks the Rover and they walk over to the elevators and head down to the casino.

CHAPTER 16, AUGUST.

Beep-Beep-Beep. Horns blow constantly as traffic slows to look up at the new MGM billboard of Iron Mike Tyson's mean and unforgettable snarl. The figure was huge and dominating as it towered over the corner of Las Vegas Boulevard and Tropicana, promoting his upcoming September 7th WBA Heavyweight Title bout against Seldon. Man look at that shit, you know Mike getting paid! Dude got his face on the MGM billboard and I just heard on the news that anybody living in Las Vegas want be able to see the fight unless they buy a ticket to the fight. What? Stop lying Loon! I'm serious Coop! Them fools gone black out the fight on TV if you live in Vegas, we can't even order it! Man that's some ol bullshit! Well were going to be sitting ringside anyway, so fuck em! Ha-ha-ha-ha. Yeah, that's what the hell I'm talking about baby! Yo L, make this left on Trop., we need to go down to Boulder Highway and check out something. Damn nigga, you should have said something two blocks back, all this damn traffic! Dude; stop bitching, move this cadi over; when you painting this thing anyway? It looks like a grey ghost with this damn primer on it. Oh you got jokes! Nah, I'm just saying bro.! I'm getting that blue candy paint next week. Oh yeah, whose doing the job? Carlos over in North Town. I bet your ass gone want to drive it then nigga. Man whatever; hurry up and catch this light! He speeds up to catch the yellow light before it turned red. Vroom-Vroom-Vroom. Loon speeds through the light then cuts in front of a car off to his right; he sees blue lights in his rear view. Damn! What's wrong pimp? Fucking one time is behind us! The police officer pulls up behind them and speaks through the intercom system.

Driver, pull the vehicle over now, turn off the engine and put both your hands out of the window; passenger, put both of your hands out of the window as well. He picks up his hand radio and calls dispatch. Dispatch this is unit 578, I have two black males pulled over on Tropicana, just off of Vegas boulevard. The suspects are in a grey color Cadillac, model looks to be a 1995, please send backup; suspects appear to be gang affiliated. Man this is some bullshit; do you have your gun with you Loon? Hell yeah, it's under the damn seat. Fuck! I have my shit too! Yo, just be cool bro. Roger that 578, back up is on the way, please proceed with caution. The officer exits the car and makes his way to the caddy. Driver, can I have your license and registration please; leave your left hand on the wheel, get your documents using your right hand please, passenger keep your hands out the window. Loon reaches over to get his documents from the glove box. Excuse me officer, can you tell me why you stopped us? He takes the documents from him but ignores the question. Put your hands back out the window please Sir! He walks back to the patrol car.

Yo, I'm not going to jail bruh! I swear, I will smoke this fool if he starts tripping. Loon be cool bruh, be cool! He runs Loons license and plates. Dispatch can you run a national on this guy, he's coming up clean locally. Sure 578, hold on one minute. Dude what the fuck is he doing back there? Man we just need to remain cool and don't give him a reason to trip, you know how one time is around this bitch. Yeah, yeah, I know, but the longer he takes, the worst it looks for us. 578, we have a Lionel Harris, prior military with a secret clearance and no criminal record, this guy appears to be a friendly 578. OK, thanks dispatch.

A second officer pulled up behind them and exits the vehicle; he walks over to the other patrol car. Hey man, everything cool here? Yeah buddy, I got it, the suspect is prior Army with no criminal record, I'm just going to give him a warning. Okay man, I'm going to take this other call. Alright buddy, later, be safe. He walks back to his car and takes off. Yo that other cop just pulled off, we straight man, he didn't even ask us to get out of the car, just keep cool. The officer walks back to the caddy. Here you are Mr. Harris, next time you cut in front of another vehicle; please use your signal light, we don't need any unnecessary accidents Sir. Yes Sir, I will and thanks. No! Thank you for your military service Mr. Harris, stay out of trouble and be safe, you are free to go Sir. OK, later officer have a good day. He walks back to his patrol car. Whew, that was close bruh! Man, I'm glad he didn't search this damn car! Yeah our black asses would be on the way to jail right now. Shit, not me nigga, I'm pulling out on them fools ASAP! Boy you crazy, let's get over to boulder already!

Man turn on the damn radio or something, I'm tired of this same old cd you playing. It aint nothing wrong with your hands Coop, go ahead and turn it bruh. He turns the radio on. Don't make me knock your ass out Loon. You know I'm too fast for you bro! Ha-ha-ha. Man whatever! He turns on the radio. What's up people, this is Mona Simone, your Five O'clock drive Dj! This just off the news wire. A local Mother reports that her two sons are missing; both of them are in their mid-twenties and go by the names Pharaoh and Monk. Detectives spoke with both the Mom and Monk's girlfriend; neither has seen or heard from the brothers in several months. LVMPD says they don't have any leads at the present time and if anyone has seen or heard from the brothers, please call Las Vegas metro. Shit, them niggas aint coming back fools! Huh AC! Yeah they might as well forget about them niggas. Yo, you sure your girl Sabrina is not going to snitch! Man you worry too much; I got her under control bruh! If you say so Boss, if you say so. They turn onto Boulder Highway and drive a few more miles. Yo pull in over there at that pawn shop.

They pull up to the pawn shop. AC, what in God's name is you getting out of the pawn shop? I'm not getting anything bruh, I have to see if this person told me the truth. What person bruh? This dealer I met at the club, where I work. They get out of the car and make their way into the old smelly pawn shop, as the door opened a bell rung to alarm the clerk. Ding-Ding. Hello gentlemen, what can I do for you today? Hello Sir, I'm looking for a fella name D. D! How does this D look young man? A white guy about 5'6" long hair usually keeps it in a tail. Oh you talking about my grandson, well hold on a minute, I'll go get him for you. Thank you Sir! No problem. Oh who may I tell him is asking? My name is AC Sir. OK, be right back. He walks through the employee only door. Man this is some old shit in here boy! Nobody is going to buy this stuff Coop, damn, look at this radio! It has to be 1970's; this thing has an eight track player! Wow, they can't be serious! Ha-ha-ha-ha. Loon you crazy!

Does it look like I'm joking, they wonder why nobody comes in this bitch; this looks like some Sanford and Son shit! Where's Lamont! Ha-ha-ha-ha-ha-ha. Old dude right there is the white Grady, good googley goo! D walks up front to greet the gentlemen. Yooooo, what up man! Hey what's up D! Man you know me, on that hustle, trying to stack them chips. Oh this is one of my partners, Loon. L this is D! What up man, nice to meet you. I'm good, nice to meet you too D. So I was thinking about that offer you made me the other day. What offer man? Oh hold on, come back here with me. He heads back through the door and they follow. Yo grandpa, I'm going to lock the door, we have some business to handle real quick! Alrighty junior! Junior! Why he called you junior? Oh I'm named after my father. Loon sometimes I forget why we call you Loon, but I swear you always find a way to remind my ass. Ha-ha-ha. Shut the hell up Coop! So you want to move some meth huh? Yeah, but it depends on how much you can give me and what my take is going to be? Dude you can have much as you want, I just need the order 72 hours in advance, you got me. Yeah I got you. As far as your cut; we can do a 60-40 split, I will cook it and deliver it to you, we will have to re up once a week though. At first it will be a little up and down with your order until you get a feel for your customers and how much they want every week, once you figure that out, it's smooth sailing. Cool and what about the sales you and Remy are getting at the club; will I get those or not? Check this out bro., because I like you, this is what we gonna do. She can still push the shit but it will just come from you, really at the end of the day we are all in this together, at the end of the week you can give her our 60% take, we can keep it rolling from there. Is that a deal you can work with brother? Yeah D I can definitely do that my man.

They give each other a pound. So when did you want that first order bro? Hold your horses man, I have some moves to make before we can start, but it want be long now. Ok, that sounds like a plan Coop, just let me know when you're ready. No problem D, I will as soon as things are in place. We'll I have to be going my man, keep hustling; I will see you when you stop back by the club then. Cool, you guys take it easy, nice meeting you Loon. They leave the pawn shop and get back in the caddy. So what the fuck was that all about? We need to have a foot hold on the drug trade all over Sin City, we got the weed and coke locked, and my man D is going to make sure we can supply the meth end of it. OK, I got you Boss man, that's some smart business. I know dog! That's why I'm the nigga in charge. What the fuck ever man, you crazy! Ha-ha-ha. They both laugh out loud as Loon turns onto Boulder Highway and heads back in to town.

It's another busy summer weekend on the strip, the adult porn star convention is in town for the next three days and the after party for tonight's event is going down at the Towers own Club Ritz. Manny is sitting at his desk admiring the scenery as the people crowd the lobby; three topless girls make their way over to his desk. Excuse me Sir, we seem to have misplaced our tops, did you happen to see them anywhere? Ha-ha-ha. No ladies I haven't seen anything that even resembles your tops. Awww that's too bad daddy, we were going to ask you to put them back on for us. Why ladies! Why would you want to cover those beautiful works of art up, there so pretty and perky! We don't want to get in trouble by that police officer over there. Baby this is Las Vegas! Sin City! Didn't you hear? No hear what? That what goes on in Vegas! Stays in Vegas baby! Ha-ha-ha-ha-ha-ha. All the girls along with Manny laugh out loud at the same time. Yeah, we did hear that! So enjoy Vegas ladies, now go forth and enjoy the night, show the world your lovely breast, they want be perky forever! Thank you daddy, are you coming to party with us? I can't right now ladies, I have a few more hours at work, I promise I will come and find you as soon as I get off though! Awww, you promise! Yes, I promise! OK, let's go girls. They walk over to join the crowd heading to Club Ritz. Bye bye, daddy! Bye girls!

Ring-Ring-Ring. Hello Towers! Yo Manny, what the hell is going on downstairs, why are all these people walking in our parking lot? What! I'm looking over the balcony right now; I see groups and groups of people coming to the Towers. Oh man, its adult porn star weekend, the after party for tonight is at the Ritz. Man, stop playing! I'm serious Coop! Hell, I just met three topless chics with some pretty ass breast. No shit! So is a lot of skirt down there? Hell yeah, I can't wait to get off work; I'm going to the party, you coming bro? Hell yeah! What time do you get off? In like an hour and a half. OK, I will meet you when you get off. Alright. Click! AC hangs up then makes another call. Ring-Ring-Ring. Hello! Yo Duck, what's popping man? Aint shit AC, just playing some Dominoes with Loon and Will crazy ass. Check this out D! How about the adult porn star convention is in town this weekend and the after for tonight is at Club Ritz downstairs, I just spoke to Manny and he says the skirts are out down there too. Dude quit fucking lying!

Bro., I'm serious as hell; I'm going down when Manny get off in like an hour, yall fools coming over? Hold on! Yo Loon! Will! This is AC, he says that there's a porn star party downstairs in his building tonight at the Ritz. Oh, I heard something about that! Well yall down or what? Hell yeah nigga! Let's roll out! Cool! Hello! Yeah! Yo we're on the way bro.! Alright, I will see you guys in a few then. Click! He hangs up. Manny stands up and walks over to the crowd of people. Hey my man, hold up! He stops one of the patrons. What do you want? You can't come in here like that dude, I'm sorry. Why not? Because, we don't allow any pets of any sort in the Towers, you will have to take that thing and put it in its cage and come back without it! That's some bull if I ever heard any! Look, you can take that big ass snake home and come back or I can ban both of your asses, it's up to you my man! OK, I'm going, I will be right back. That's cool; just leave that big motherfucker home! What the hell is it anyway? It's a Boa! Damn, don't those things eat people! Yeah, only if you get in their way or make them mad! Yeah that's a big fucker, please hurry! Take it home dude! Yeah, yeah, I'm going.

The lobby had filled to its capacity with groups and groups of white blonde and brunette females, who all seem to have big double D breast and juicy lips. All kind of guys trailed behind them like dogs in heat on a hot summer day. The pimps and hoes paraded through the crowd as if it was their kingdom and everybody else was just visitors in their world. Pink, Blue, Green and even Yellow mink coats and hats draped over every pimp as they paraded in their domain. There were White hoes, Black hoes, Asian hoes, Thai hoes, Latino hoes and even Russian hoes, not a patron seemed out of place among the crowd of their peers. Corporate America had their automotive, computer, electronic and clothing conventions while the Underworld of America's oldest profession held their annual adult industry convention. Yes Vegas is truly the best of both worlds.

David enters the building to start his shift. Yo Manny; how was the shift? Hey what's up David! Oh, it wasn't bad; this porn star party is just getting started. Yeah, I see it's looking crazy right now. I really didn't have any problems though, I'm glad you're here so I can go party too! Ha-ha-ha-ha. Don't get in any trouble Manny! Trouble! That's exactly what I'm looking for D, trouble! I'm waiting for AC to come down and we're going to show these suckers how we do it in Vegas! Another voice sounded out, interrupting their conversation. Man, stop talking that junk, you can't have no party without the crew. Oh shit, what's poppin fellas! What's up Will! Loon! Duck! Where the fuck did you fools come from? We just got here; AC called and told us about the party. Hey keep my name out of your mouth fucker! Coop walked up on them. Ha-ha-ha-ha. Just kidding, what's up fellas! What's up Coop! I'm ready to crash this party and catch some new skirt, you know there aint nothing like some strange! Man, yall some man whores! Duck shut the hell up with your whoring ass! You don't have any room to talk bruh, Loon you worse than me! Well that might be true too! Ha-ha-ha! Shit, let's go do this already! They all start walking towards the Ritz.

The line in front of the club was extra-long as patrons waited impatiently to enter. Yo, watch this fellas, just follow my lead. Manny lead the guys to the front of the line, a 6'4" Latino doorman dressed in a black suit, stood there monitoring the VIP entrance. Hey Carlos, how you doing tonight pimp! Manny what's crackin fool? Me and my boys are coming to crash this sex party bro.! Come on around through VIP man, we got you, Pierre is at the VIP section tonight, just tell him to give you the company booth and three bottles. Cool, thanks my man, we will save some skirt for you too! Ha-ha-ha-ha. Thanks fellas, you're so kind. Yeah, don't mention it! Ha-ha. Will you stupid for that. What, I was just joking Duck! I know man, come on with your slow ass. The guys walk inside; go down a flight of dark narrow stairs; at the bottom you could see a flickering red light coming from its small doorway. When the fellas reach the end of the steps, they are greeted by a short sexy female in a red body suit. Hi gentlemen, welcome to Club Ritz, do you have reservations for a V.I.P booth? Yes we do babe, I need to speak with Pierre. OK Sir, he's right over there. Alright I see him, thanks hun. They make their way across the room through the crowded dance floor and packed bar.

A short stubby man in a red blazer stood in front of the VIP booths, He sees Manny coming. Oh hell no! I know this isn't Emanuel! Yep, what's up P! Aint shit up fool but my $100! What $100? Dude, don't play stupid! You bet me on that UNLV vs. RENO game! Oh yeah! Man, I didn't even watch that game, who won? Not you fool! So pay up! Pierre, I got you bro., stop worrying about that $100. Yeah, when you paying up? I tell you what, let's go double or nothing! Yo Manny! Yeah what's up Will? Can we sit down first before you and Pierre start that betting and shit! Oh my bad, go ahead fellas. Pierre moves the velvet rope aside and let the gentlemen in. Now what's the bet Manny? Let's double down on the Tyson fight next month. Shit you crazy as hell Manny! I'm not betting against Tyson, that fool is going to knock Seldon's ass out! Yeah, I agree on that. Well, what then? OK, let's bet on which round the fight ends in. Hmmmm. Pierre scratches his chin with his right hand and thinks about it. OK, I'm down with that, I say it goes three. Is that your bet, round three? Yep! OK, I'm going to take round one. Seldon might be a little soft but he aint that soft Manny! Look, you want to go double down or not! Yeah, I'm in. Cool, let's shake on it. The guys both reach out and shake each-others hand, Pierre waits for him to pass before he replaces the velvet rope.

Manny walks up into the booth with the others. Alright, let's get this party started, we need some chica's over here fellas! Will, calls the waitress. Excuse me sweetie! Yes Sir, what can I get for you? Let me get one bottle of Moet and two bottles of Cristal. Will there be anything else Sir? Yeah, add one bottle of Grey Goose please, a pitcher of OJ as well and some cranberry. OK, I will be right back with your order Sir. Thanks sweetie! Your welcome, but you don't have to thank me, it's my job. Hmmmm. Well excuse the fuck out of me! She aint getting no tip from you huh Will? Ha-ha-ha-ha. Loon laughs as he steps down from the seating area and walks over to the velvet rope that was surrounding them and three red couches with a large steel top table. A group of ladies stood in front of the ropes, dancing by themselves and laughing among each other. Hey ladies! Yeah, what's up? Hi my name is Loon. Hi Loon! What kind of name is that? It's a nick name! Hmmmm. Loon like Looney tunes? Yep! So why they call you that? Yeah are you crazy or something, we don't talk to physcos! Ha-ha-ha. All five of yall got jokes I see, why don't you guys come join me and my fellas up here in VIP? Why should we do that Mr. Looney? He-he-he-he-he. All the girls giggle amongst the group. I figured you ladies wanted to sit down and have a drink instead of standing there staring and talking about people. Well, since you put it that way, come on girls let's go join the nice gentlemen and his friends; I still have to work on that name though. My mother would slap me if I told her I was dating a guy named Loon. Oh you still got jokes, huh baby, that's OK; I got something for you! What, I was just joking! Yeah, don't try and change it up now little lady. Why are you being so mean Looney, I was just playing handsome.

The girls started dancing and screaming when the Dj played the next song. Yeah baby! This is the shit, right here! "Fuck Bitches, Get Money" "Fuck Niggaz, Get Money" " Fuck Bitches, Get Money" " Fuck Niggaz, Get Money" " Fuck Bitches, Get Money"" Fuck Niggaz, Get Money". The entire VIP section is now standing, ladies are up on the couches and the fellas were on the floor in front of them. Yeah get Money! They all scream. The club is filled wall to wall, standing room only. Everybody's singing along with the music. " You wanna sip Mo on my living room flo" " Play nintendo with Cease-a-leo" " Pick up my phone, say poppa not home" " Sex all night, mad head in the morn" Pop! They pop the cork on the Moet and Cristal and start drinking from the bottle as they passed the champagne around to each other. "Spin my V, smoke all my weed". Yeah party people; this DJ MikeTech! We got this party jumping! Shout out to all the sexy porn stars in the house tonight! "You wanna be my main squeeze baby, don't cha" " You wanna give me what I need baby, want cha". The crowd screams. Fuck Bitches! Get Money! Fuck Niggaz! Get Money! Alright everybody when I say party people, I want yall to say, get money. Let's go! Party People! Get Money! Party People! Get Money! We came here to party, People! Get Money! Yeeeaaaaahhhhh! DJ Mike Tech in this Bitch! Let me hear yuh! Party People! Get Money! Party People! Get Money! Yo AC! What's up Duck? See that short dude over there by that chic in the red dress. Yeah, what about him? That's the nigga from Club Beach that shot that girl. No shit! Yep! Hey Loon! Will! Yo what's up! Isn't that guy right there by that chic in the red dress the dude that shot Sky that night? Where bruh? Right there man, look straight ahead. Oh yeah! That's that fool! Man, let's go do that punk! Hold up Duck, he knows how you, Loon and Will look. Damn, I want that fucker man! Yeah, were gone get him, just hold tight.

What was that suckers name Loon? I don't remember man. Do you remember Will? Yeah, I think she called him Brian! Yeah that's it! Hey Coop, his name is Brian, she called him B too. Alright, let's handle this before he spots us over here. So what's the move? Hey Manny! What's up AC? Do you have your knife on you? What kind of question is that bro., I don't leave home without it. Good, we're about to use it. Will, you Loon and Duck go ahead start the car up, we're about to take care of this chump right quick. Alright, you guys sure about this? Man if we don't get him, that fools going to get one of us, this is some business that needs to be done, you dig! Cool, say no more, we will be outside by the car. I don't get it Coop! What don't you get Duck? Why the fuck are you going to get in the car, you live here, you can just go upstairs! I want to be out of sight, out of mind, once the job is done! We're going to shank his ass in the bathroom. When you told me who he was, I started watching him; he's serving dope to cats in the bathroom. The chic in the red dress came over and asked him something, then she went back over to this guy she's with, whispered something to him, he then goes to the bathroom and Brian goes in behind him. They both come out, one after the other in less than two minutes.

How many motherfuckers you know can use the bathroom in less than two minutes, in a crowded club like this? So how are you two going to get him to come in the bathroom? We're going to wait for the next buyer to approach him, and then Manny is going to go wait in the bathroom. Once Brian comes in and waits for the customer, Manny is going to walk out of the stall and shank his ass. Yeah that sounds easy, how do you know someone is coming to buy some dope? That's the easy part bro.! I'm going to be the buyer; first I'm going to walk over to the girl in the red dress and her friend, then start a conversation. He will see me talking to them and assume what I want him to, that's when I will approach him for some product, and then we will make our move. Trust me; that greedy fool is going to fall for it! Alright, that's a tight ass plan but why are you leaving the building afterwards? You live here! Because, by the time they find that fool, I don't want to be anywhere in the building, out of sight, out of mind, that way, none of us will be suspects. Let's go fellas! Loon, Will and Duck go get the girls from the couch and exit the club. Come on ladies, we're about to leave, it was nice meeting you all tonight! Awwww, but the party isn't over! Yeah I know, but we have to be someplace else in the next hour. OK, bye guys! The guys leave the girls standing in the crowd, then moved to the front of the dance floor and disappeared into the sea of people. OK Manny, are you ready? Yep, let's do this. Cool, wait for me to make my way over to the couple before you go in. I got it covered, go ahead and make your move.

AC makes his way over to the lady in the red dress and her friend. Hey, how are you guys doing tonight? I'm good! The lady replied. Yeah, I'm cool. The guy replied. How you doing man? I'm doing pretty good man; look I know this may seem kind of odd, but I wanted to know if you were a porn star Mam, you look so familiar! Ha-ha-ha-ha. No I am not. Oh, I am so sorry, please accept my apologies guys! Ha-ha-ha-ha. The couple laughs. No it's OK, you're good man, and this is, a porn star party after all. Ha-ha-ha. Yes it is! Anyway, sorry to bother you guys, oh one more thing! Yes, what is it? Where's the restroom? The lady in red points. Oh its right over there, see that short guy! AC turns around and looks, then points. Yeah right there. Yep, it's right on the other side of him. OK, thanks! He walks off. Manny leaves the VIP and heads in the bathroom. Coop heads over towards Brian as Manny closes the bathroom door behind him. Yo what's up my man? Not much, what's poppin?

My friend over there in the red dress told me that you were the man. It depends on what you're talking about. Shit, I just need some blow my man. How much are you trying to spend? I got $100. Cool, I can do that. Alright, you want the money now? No, just meet me in the bathroom, I'm going in first, then you come in like 30 seconds after. Alright, got it! B walks in the bathroom, Manny hears the door opens and peeps through the silver restroom stall door, thirty seconds pass and in comes Coop. Yo, lock the door behind you man, I don't need anyone to walk in on us while we handling this business. AC locks the door, then leans back against it and reaches in his pocket for the money. Brian reaches in his front pocket, AC grabs his arms. Yo! What the fuck are you doing nigga? Let me go! What the fuck! Manny burst from the stall with his knife in the right hand and grabs B around the neck with his left arm! Yo! Get the fuck off of me! Brian tries to get away! Uh! Uh! Uh! Uh! Manny shanks him, four times in the kidney! The blood spot on the back of his shirt begin to get larger and larger by the second as AC held him there and watched the life leave his body.

That fucker is done Manny, come on let's wrap this shit up. Manny turns around and opens the stall; AC walks the lifeless body over and places it on the toilet. He locks the stall from the inside, then gets down on the floor and slides under the door to exit the stall. The two gentlemen go to the sink and wash up. Manny wraps the bloody knife in some paper towels so that none of the blood would hit the floor. He sticks it back in his back pocket; they unlock the bathroom door and walk out. The music is louder than ever and it seems as if more people had joined the already over-crowded party. Come on bro.; let's go out through the VIP entrance, the exit doors are right beside the parking lot. They make their way up the narrow stairway to the outside. Alright Carlos; thanks for the love man! Hey, anytime Manny! You guys be safe, don't try and sleep with all this pussy tonight! Ha-ha. Later man, we will leave some skirt for you bro.! Yo! Hurry up fools! Will shouts from the truck, AC and Manny make their way over to the F-150, jumps in the back and Duck pulls off the parking lot and disappears into the busy traffic on the Las Vegas strip. Boom! Boom! Boom! The canons sounded off as the pirates tried to sink each-others ships at Treasure Island nightly scripted show. Beep-Beep-Beep. Horns blew at tourist who stopped driving because they were amazed by the 30 foot high flames erupting from the Volcano at the Mirage. Crowds and crowds of people congested both sides of the strip, a sign that Sin City was again filling people's lives with an illusion of entertainment that was only a front for its corruption.

Over on Sahara Boulevard, business was starting to pick up. Ring-Ring-Ring. Hello, thank you for calling Angel's Escorts, how may I help you? Yes, I was calling about your ad in the Adult Magazine. OK, which ad was that Mam? Oh I'm sorry, the one for escorts! Yes, are you interested in that job Mam? Yes I am. Well what's your name sweetie? My name is Shawna. Do you have any experience Shawna? Yes Mam. Oh sweetie, I am so sorry, my name is Paula, you don't have to call me Mam. OK Paula, how soon can I start? That depends on how you look and how much experience you got sweetie! I have three years-experience in New York as an escort. That's good, but this aint the Big Apple, we do things a bit different in Sin City sweetie. How so? I tell you what, why don't you come in for an interview and I will see what we can do for you sweetie. The address is right there in the ad, what time is good for you? Hmmmm. I can come in the next hour or so! That's fine Shawna; I will see you in an hour then. Alright, do I need to bring anything? Yes, bring your I.D and your health card. OK, but I don't have a health card yet! Go ahead and come anyway, if you get hired then you can go get that health card. OK, thanks. Yep, no problem sweetie. The office door knobs turns as the sound of keys rattle before it swings open. Well hello, Ms. Nina, how are you today sweetie pie? I'm good Paula, what about yourself? Baby the phone has been ringing off the hook! Oh that's a good thing right! Yea it is. So did we book a lot of dates for today? We did a few, but most of the calls were for the job placement ads we posted, I have interviewed several girls already and a few more are coming in shortly. That's great! I hope we got some pretty ones. Ha-ha-ha-ha. Well, some of them are, but some of them aint! Wow! Yeah sweetie, that's the business, too bad we can't use the ugly ones too.

Yeah I'm glad we don't have to use them, business would really suck then. What sane guy would spend money on an ugly duck! Ha-ha-ha-ha. Sweaty you will be surprised; my Momma always told me that there is somebody for everybody. I must admit, I've done seen most of it all when it comes to men buying pussy! Anyway, enough of that talk, I have a big job for you today. Oh yeah, what's that Paula? The Boss called today and said that we had some new girls come in from over-seas; I need for you to go over to the boarding house and pick them up. I don't know where the house is Paula. Well this one is in Summerlin; we have three others besides that one. What do you want me to do with them, once I pick them up? Take them to the store and let them get their personal items, then take them to the Fashion Show Mall after that, make sure you show them what they need as far as clothes and shoes.

Okay Paula, where are these ladies going to be working? Two of them will be working for us and the other three will be going to Dolls, so hurry up and get going, we don't have all day! Paula, I can't fit all those girls in the truck with me and Duck! Child, take the Limo, this is company business, oh, hold on sweetie, one more thing. She reaches in her purse and pulls out the Visa card. Here put everything on this; bring me back all the receipts please. Do you want me to drop them off at work later too? No, we already got that taking care of, now hurry. OK, OK, I'm going. Nina grabs the card, puts it in her purse and walks out the door down the long smelly hallway. There standing in front of the entrance smoking on cigars was Duck and the Limo driver. Hey sis what's up, where we going? Oh you're staying here bro., I have to go meet some new employees, Paula told me to take the Limo. Well, I guess that's my cue brother, I will catch you later on. He puts on his black hat, turns away from Duck and follows her over to the Limo. Alright you guys, be safe, I will get up with you when you come back. He puts the cigar back in his mouth and leans against the brick wall outside the entrance.

Ring-Ring-Ring. Hello, this is Dolls. Hi Boss, this is Paula. Hey Paula, what's up? You should be getting the two new girls sometime today. Well that's great, thanks honey. Your welcome, I will talk with you later. Sure thing doll. Click! He hangs up the phone, it's a slow Tuesday night at Dolls, the 50 girls outnumber the 20 customers like 2 to 1, most of them are sitting at the bar getting drunk and killing time. Hey AC! Yeah, what is it Poison? Can I have a double shot of Crown Royal and a shot of tequila please? Yes Mam, coming right up! Here you are baby, a double Crown and one tequila shot. Malibu and Max walk over to the bar. AC! Yes ladies. Where is Deb? Oh she's off because it's a slow night and Vinny only schedule one bartender. Oh, so our first drink is on you tonight then right! Ha-ha-ha-ha. You got jokes Max! Come on man, one drink! I tell you what; here are two shots of tequila on the house. Awwww, thanks baby! Here you go, this is for you. Malibu reaches in her garter belt and hands him a twenty dollar bill. Thank you baby! Wait bitch, I know you aint trying to shine! Fuck that! Hold on baby!

Max pulls two twenty dollar bills from her garter. Here you go honey! Ha-ha-ha. Thanks baby! Your welcome honey, this cheap bitch over here trying to give you twenty dollars. Awwww, fuck you Max! Ha-ha -ha-ha. Got you bitch! Whatever girl, that shit wasn't funny! Come on bitch; let's go see if we can get some table dances from these broke ass fuckers! Thanks again baby! Your welcome ladies. They leave the bar and head over to the stage side tables. Hey bro., it's dead as hell tonight. Will walks over to the bar. What time are we closing? I think we close at 2am tonight Will. Damn, we got three more hours; I'm going to lose my mind. Man, calm your but down, go talk to the girls or something. A few ladies are gathered by the pool tables. Oh bitch, look who just walked in. Who Dylan?

Girl, Fat Boy is here. Shit, that's like $500 a piece right there, go get his ass. Be cool Asia, he's going to the bar. The girls make their way over to meet him.

Yo Coop, look at this fat fucker. Yo, that's Fat Boy right there. Oh that's the mark from the thing with that Diego dude? Yep, that's him. Cool, I got this. Will walks over to the door to greet him. Hey how's it going man? I'm good dude, what's poppin tonight? We have plenty of girls, if that's what you're asking! Yeah I see that pimpin, you must be new here? Well you can say that, I've only been here for a few months. That's cool pimp, I'm Fat Boy. Nice to meet you bro., I'm Will. What you drinking Will, I got you. No I'm good man; I don't drink while I'm on the clock. Alright, I respect that. Fat Boy approaches the bar. Damn where's Deb? Hey Fat Man! What's up Dylan, where's my girl? Oh she's off tonight, that's AC behind the bar. He's cool people man. Yo, what's up man, what can I get for you? I'm good player; let me get a bottle of Moet and three glasses, plus one thousand ones. Coming right up. AC pulls a bottle of Moet from the wine cooler, puts it in a bucket and covers it with ice, sits it on the counter, puts three champagne flutes on top, opens the safe under the bar and pulls out one thousand ones. OK, here you are my man, will there be anything else? He takes one hundred ones from his stack of a thousand and slaps it down on the bar. That's for you bro.! Thanks my man! No problem pimp, oh, can you let Bobby know I'm out here. Sure, no problem. Yo dub, can you go tell Bobby that Fat Boy is here. I got you bro.! He leaves the bar and walks to the office.

Knock-Knock!-Knock. Yeah, whose there! It's me, Will! Yeah, come in big man. He opens the door. What's up Will? There's a Fat Boy here to see you. OK, tell him I'm busy and to give you the thing. Thing? Yeah, can you just deliver the message! Alright. Will walks over to the table to give Fat Boy the message. Hey my man, Bobby says he's busy and for you to give me the thing. That's what's up; I didn't want to get up anyway. He reaches down in the side cargo pocket of his shorts and pulls out a thick envelop. Here take this to him pimp. Will takes the envelope from him, walks back in the office. Here you go Bobby. He hands him the package. Bobby opens it right there in front of him and counts it. Yep all there; like always. He pulls out two one hundred dollar bills and hands them to Will. What's this for? One thing we always do around here is take care of our own, now get out of here and let me finish my business already. Wow, thanks boss! Yeah, don't mention it. He exits the office with a smile as he stuck the money in his pocket.

At the bar, Fat Boy takes the Moet from the bucket of ice and starts to shake it, Asia and Dylan stand up to take off their clothes before the next song starts. POP! The cork fly across the room, champagne spills everywhere as he tries to fill the three glasses. Hey AC, get me another bottle pimp! No problem; got it coming up. He puts the new bottle on ice. The Dj shouts him out over the mic. Yeah, what's crackin Fat Boy, I see you ballin baby! Ring-Ring. Damn, who the fuck is this calling? Fat Boy looks down at his cell phone. Oh this is my boy Chuck! Hey Chuck, what's up pimp! What's happening Big Boy! Shit, at the strip club, sipping on some Mo and tricking on these bitches. Yeah, must be nice. It's all good pimp, what's poppin though? I need to meet you today at the same spot we met at last week. OK, what time you want to do that? Well, I'm at the casino watching this Rebels and Badgers game right now, it's like 2nd quarter now, I'm going to need to leave 4th quarter to meet you at that same spot at the same time as before. Alright, I got you pimp, same time at same spot. Yep, that's right playboy. Cool, see you in a few Chuck. Click! He hangs up the phone.

Hey ladies, take this money and split it up. He stands up, picks up the glass of Moet and turns it up til it's all gone. Aaaaahhhhh. That hit the spot! Girls, take it easy, I will see yall next week. AC my man, nice meeting you pimp, make sure these ladies don't get in any trouble. I got you player, be safe out there in them streets. Oh, no doubt! Fat Boy puts his empty glass on the bar and leaves the club in a hurry. Shit girl, this was the easiest $500 dollars I made all week! Hell yeah, me too Dylan. Hey AC, can we get two double shots of tequila babe? Sure! He places two shot glasses on the bar and pours the doubles. Here you go ladies. Thanks babe! Girl I'm glad that trick came by, it's dead as hell in here child. Bitch, you said a mouth full, I'm about to get dress and take my ass home. Me too Asia! Dylan and Asia drink their shots, then head to the dressing room. Bye AC, see you next time baby. OK ladies, see you next time, make sure you go by the office to turn in those ones. Yeah, yeah, we know. Will comes back over to the bar. Yo Coop, I'm off bro., call me when you get home, I have something to tell you about your girl. What girl? Sabrina knucklehead! Oh, OK, bro. later. Will exits Club Dolls and disappears into the warm Vegas night.

CHAPTER 17, SEPTEMBER.

There's a full moon in the dark desert sky, overlooking the neon lights and miles and miles of traffic, all the Hotels are sold out and casinos filled to capacity. Media vans, trucks, photographers and staff swarm to the MGM grand, a star studded crowd over shadows the everyday tourist and locals as they invade Sin City for this long awaited Tyson fight night. Black shiny Limo's from every casino cruise through the MGM's drop off point to unload patrons and celebrities alike. AC dressed in black shoes, slacks and blue Versace shirt, stood there in the lobby waiting for Sabrina to come from the restroom. Soft white lights reflect off the caramel marble tile throughout the lobby that was overwhelmed with patrons coming to see tonight's heavy weight fight. Sabrina appeared from the crowd of people walking towards AC, her black dress swayed from left to right as the warm air from outside blew through the main entrance doors and across the lobby. She stood an additional 6 inches in stature, wearing her black Louis V heels. Come on baby! I'm coming daddy! Damn you looking sexy in that dress girl, I can't wait to get you back to the house. Ha-ha-ha. Oh yeah, you aint ready for this daddy! She smiles. Yeah, we'll see about that later.

The sisters had just walked over from the gift shop. Hey girl! I like that dress! Hey Nina! Thanks Baby! Yeah, you look hot girl! Thank you Denna! Shit, both you guys looking sexy as always, Denna I love those red shoes, that white dress is hot too! Thank you Brina, Nina picked it out. Yeah, you know we had to be hot tonight girl, all this money in this motherfucker! Girl, Nina's going to catch all the fellas in that purple Prada dress and them hot ass shoes! Man, all you ladies look stunning tonight! He said out loud as he approached the group of girls and gave them each a hug. Awww. Thanks Duck!

Hey, hey, what's up people! Hey, it's about time yall get here! What's crackin, Will! Loon! What's up Coop! Ohhh, OK, I see yall niggas pulled out the black suits tonight! Heyyy, you know me and Loon stay sharp brother; I see you and Duck rocking yall Versace shirts, I like that green Duck. Thanks brother! The crew gathers and head towards the arena to take their seats ring side. Yo Coop, where's Jerm and Manny? Them fools been sitting ring side since an hour ago, they came in the back entrance; I got our tickets right here though, so we straight. OK cool, let's go see Mike knock this fool out then. They continue the long walk down to the arena, cutting through large crowds of excited patrons and celebrities.

The arena is packed to capacity, anybody that's somebody was there, the third row from ringside is empty, except for the four seats that were occupied by Jerm, Tam, Manny and Sophia; Manny's wife. Hey Sophie! Denna and Nina run to hug her at first sight. How have you been Mommie, we haven't seen you in forever! She stands up to give them a hug. Awwwww, hey ladies, I've been good; how have you two been? Girl we're doing great, loving life baby, look at you, you look way to nice for Manny tonight. Ha-ha-ha-ha. Stop it girl! Shut up Nina, don't make me spank you! You know I was just playing bro! She gives Manny a hug, as the group takes their seats. What's up fellas, what took you guys so long? Man you know how it is. Hey Sophie, how are you baby? I'm good AC. That's good, oh this is my girl Sabrina, Brina this is Sophia; Manny's wife. Hello Sophia, nice to meet you. Hi, nice to meet you too baby. Will, Duck and Loon proceed to take their seats, giving Sophia a hug as they passed. Hey guys, you all look great! Thanks sis! Beer! Peanuts! Popcorn! Anybody! Beer! Peanuts! Popcorn! The server yelled as he roamed the isles ringside. Yo little man, over here, let me get some of that beer. Guys, yall want some of this beer? Yeah Jerm, send me one down too. Anybody else besides AC want something? Bro., just get everybody one, I got the tab. Say no more Loon, little man, make that 11 cold ones, make sure we get 5 cups for the ladies. Thank you Sir! He stops, opens the cooler and starts passing down the beers along with 5 cups, covering five of the bottles. Thanks little man, here's a c-note, keep the change. Thanks again Sir!

The announcer enters the ring, the packed arena starts to cheer, and he grabs the mic. Ladies and gentlemen, are you ready for tonight's main event? The crowd roars. Yeeeeaaaahhhhhh! Tyson makes his way to the red corner and stands there with a cold hard stare as the crowd chanted his name. Tyson! Tyson! Tyson! Seldon makes his way through the isle of excited fans, entered the ring and stood in the blue corner. The heavy weight champ stared Tyson down as he rocked side to side beating his gloves against one another, the announcer walks to the center of the ring. Tonight's bout is for the WBA heavy weight title of the world! In the red corner, we have the challenger Mike Tyson! Yeeeeeaaaaaahhhhh! The crowd goes wild! In the blue corner we have the champ, Bruce Seldon! Yeeeeeeaaaaaahhhhhh! The arena continues to get louder.

The ref enters the ring and calls the two fighters to the center. OK fellas, I want a clean fight, no head butting, hitting below the belt or any kind of cheap shots, alright touch gloves and let's have a good fight! They touch gloves and head back to their corners. Yo, Mike is about to knock that boy out! You wanna put a bet on that Loon? Ha-ha-ha. I don't wanna take your money Duck! Denna stands up and screams. Yeah! Come on Mike! The bell rings. Ding! Ding! The two fighters charge each other and meet at the center of the ring. Seldon throws a right hook! Tyson ducks! Seldon throws a left upper cut! Mike ducks and moves to the right! Man, that guy moves slow, he aint never gone hit Mike like that! Shut up Manny! I bet he moves faster than your ass! Ha-ha-ha-ha. Fuck you Jerm! Tyson counters with a right hook to Seldon's face, then a straight left jab to his chin. Thump! Seldon's heavy body hits the mat! Ooooooooohhhhhhhh! The crowd goes bananas; the ref runs over and starts counting. I told you! I told you Duck! That fool can't take Mike! The ref counts. 1..... 2...... 3..... 4...... 5...... 6...... 7....... 8....... 9........ 10........ He turns around, grabs Tyson's right arm and held it high in the air. The entire arena stood up in misbelief and started cheering. Tyson! Tyson! Tyson!

Man, that was some crazy shit dawg, how the fuck is the fight over; I didn't even finish my damn beer! Ha-ha-ha. You aint the only one Will. The crew stood up and started walking towards the exit; all you could hear from every direction were people talking about the dramatic end to the fight. Yo, where we headed Coop? To the club Manny! What club? I heard the Drink was going to be poppin tonight! Duck, what's up with you and that club Drink! Bruh, it's where all the fine girls hang out! Dude, the whole city is filled with bitches tonight, just look around.

Denna slaps Loon in the back of his head as they walked out of the arena. Ouch girl! What was that for! Stop calling women bitches! You better not hit me again; keep your hands to yourself. Oh yeah! What are going to do about it, if I do! I'm gone have you calling my name while you gripping those bed sheets! Ha-ha-ha-ha. Shut up fool! Sis you two are stupid, come on let's go party already. Hey, we need to decide which club we're hitting before we get to the Limo. Hold up guys, Nina has a point. The crew stops in the casino by the black jack tables, people are everywhere, and all the tables are full, tourist are snapping pictures of celebrities from every angle. A large crowd starts to gather in one area, several big gentlemen whom looked like Hotel security dressed in all black suits responded to their radios and ran to the area. An entire group of young guys dressed in jerseys begin to run to the area also. Ohhhh damn, that's fucked up! Gentlemen yelled from the irate crowd.

Several women begin to scream as they tried to free themselves from the area by running towards the front. Hey, what the fuck is going on over there? Hell, I don't know Tam, some fools probably fighting or something; niggas can't go anywhere without acting up. Awwww. Be quiet Will, your ass be doing the same shit. AC, you know I don't get into anything, unless it's necessary bro.! Yeah man, whatever! So, what's the word yall, which club are we crashing first? Hold on Jerm, I'm trying to see what's poppin off over here! Man, fuck that shit over there; let's get the hell out of here. Yo, I'm going to the Limo! Hold up Coop, we're coming. The crew; leave the casino and head to the Limo. That's crazy, motherfuckers can' never go anywhere without fighting and shit! Loon, I know you're crazy ass aint talking! What? Why you say that Manny? Nothing bro., let's go. The traffic outside is unreal, cars are bumper to bumper in front of the entrance as they try to leave the MGM and traffic is at a standstill on the strip. Their driver is waiting for them outside in the stretch Navigator, he opens the back door as the guys approach, and they get inside.

The energy in the air is exciting, Tyson had just won another title, tonight Celebrities are performing and partying at several clubs throughout Sin City, Las Vegas is on full tilt. The crew gathers in the back of the limo, the driver closes the door behind them, and then takes a seat at the wheel. So where are we headed to guys? He asked them. Hey, isn't there an after party at 662? Yeah, I think you're right AC! Well let's go over there first then! Will taps on the drivers back window. Tap-Tap-Tap. Yo my man, we're going to 662. Ok got it! Hey Will! What's up Duck? Tell him to go down Tropicana, down Maryland parkway and over to Flamingo, so we want be in all that damn traffic. Will taps on the window again. Tap-Tap. Yes Sir! Yo, go down Trop to Maryland then over to Flamingo to skip this traffic! No problem sir! He exits the lot and enters the traffic on Tropicana headed away from the strip. Ladies, how did you guys like the fight? Jerm, it was too damn fast for me man! You can say that again Sabrina! Ha-ha. I know, right girl, he did knock Seldon's ass the fuck out though yall. Yeah, he put a quick two piece on that ass Denna. Ha-ha-ha. A two piece, huh Loon? Yep, a right hook then a left jab, that's a two piece! Ha-ha-ha. Boy whatever! So Jerm, how's L.A dude? I love it Will, when you coming to visit? Bruh, just give me the word and I'm there! Cool, let me know when you're ready and I can set it up. Say no more my man! They give each other a pound. Damn, we aint at the club yet? AC looks out of the tinted window.

The Limo had just turned onto Flamingo Boulevard, traffic began to pull off to the side of the road as blue and red lights from police cars, ambulance and fire trucks headed up Flamingo towards Koval. Damn, what the hell is going on with all these damn cop cars and shit? I don't know Duck; can you see anything on your side Tam? No, not really. The driver pulled off to the side of the road and parked the Limo. Hold on; let me go see what's happening. AC exits the Limo. Hold up bro., we're coming too. Will and Manny exits also, they begin to walk a few blocks towards all the police cars, ambulance and fire trucks. A few other people had already left their vehicles and started walking down the sidewalks on both sides of the street headed that way as well. As they got closer to the scene, it became obvious that someone had been injured; several women were sitting on the hood of their cars crying.

A few gentlemen had taken a seat on the curb and were shaking their heads in disbelief. Excuse me, Mam what happened here? AC said to one of the ladies sitting on her car. The medics had just closed the doors on the ambulance; police were putting up black and yellow tape around the scene of the accident. Man, somebody just shot Tupac and Suge! What! Are you serious? Yep, they just put both of them in the ambulance, their headed to UMC now. Damn that's fucked up! The detectives begin to put white numbered cards on different spots of the crime scene. Will walked over to the yellow tape and spoke to an officer. Excuse me Sir! Yes Sir, how can I help you? I heard what happened; they are both okay, right? Well, it doesn't look good man, Suge got shot in the head and Tupac has several gunshot wounds. Damn, man. Will shakes his head. Did you guys catch the shooters? No Sir, we are still trying to figure out what happened. OK, thanks brother. Yeah, no problem. Will walks back over to Manny and AC.

What did he say Will? He said Suge got shot in the head and Pac was shot several times. Man that's some bullshit! AC yells out full of anger. Dude, look at that damn car, that shit has bullet holes all over it! I saw that when I was over there, it looks like a hit to me Manny, that wasn't no drive buy. Yeah bro., all the holes are in the passenger's door, this is going to make Sin City look really bad man, especially if them cats don't make it. What I can't understand is, why somebody would want to shoot them cats, hell, we're on the West Coast at home on top of all that, this is supposed to be the safety zone! Manny, who knows bruh; someone could have had a hit on them or something. Yeah, when you getting money, motherfuckers get jealous and do all kinds of stupid shit. Man, Tupac done been shot like five times, that nigga aunt gone die! He got like nine lives and shit. Yeah, you might be right about that Will. All I know is, the world will never forget this day, I swear man, we can't have anything without somebody getting fucked up! Yo, let's go fellas; I need to smoke a blunt after this shit. Manny and Will join him as they head back to the limo. Dawg, I'm taking my ass home, this done ruined my fucking night, where you guys headed? I don't know Coop, Me and Sophie are probably gone take it in too. Shit, I aint going home, I'm bout to hit up the Crazy Horse Too bruh; I need to get some drinks in my system and look at some pussy! Will you crazy as hell bro., but I feel you pimp. I'm about to take Sabrina to the crib, get me some head and smoke some chronic. They finally make it back to the Limo and the driver is standing outside smoking a cigarette.

What's up fellas, what happened, somebody get in an accident or something? Man somebody shot Tupac and Suge. Get the fuck out of here with that bullshit AC! I'm serious man. He throws his cigarette on the street, stomps it out in disgust and slings his cap on the hood. The girls, Loon, Duck and Jerm get out of the Limo to see what all the fuss was about. Hey baby, what's wrong? Sophie, some bitch ass fools done shot Pac and Suge. No poppy, No!

Denna starts to cry. I'm so fucking tired of fools shooting up shit for no reason! Damn this is some bull, damn, I'm so tired of it sis, just tired. Nina starts to cry, her and Denna embrace each other. Man, did they catch the fools that did it? No Loon, the cops say they don't know yet. Yo, this means war player and you know it! War with who Duck, they don't even know who did it! AC, when did that ever make a difference, bodies are about to drop bruh, believe that! Well, they don't need to start no war in Sin City, aint none of the crews here got beef with Pac or Suge! I don't know where it's going to happen but it is going to happen, my man, I can promise you that! You right Duck; somebody is going to pay for this shit! Tell them Jerm, that aint going down easy in Cali! Man, let's go already, dude take me back to the Towers!

They get in the Limo, the driver closes the door. Hey you guys, me and Brina are going back to my place, yall have fun; I'm not in the mood to party right now. Alright bruh, I understand. Yo, I'm going to the Crazy Horse Too if anybody wants to roll. Ha-ha-ha. Will, you love to look at some ass. Nina, I'm a man baby, what do you expect? She shakes her head. What about you Loon? What about me? Denna looks at him with a serious look. Oh, I think we should go to club Drink since we're not going to 662. Yeah, that's a good idea poppy! Denna says to him. Tell the driver to drop the rest of us off at the Drink. Jerm knocks on the window. Knock-Knock. Yes Sir! My man; after you drop them off at the Towers, take the rest of us to club Drink. No problem Sir; as you wish. He makes a U turn and head back towards the Towers.

A few days had pass since the shooting, it's now 5pm in the evening out in the desert. Ding-Ding. The bell rings over Angelica's Bunny Ranch, a customer enters, the television over the bar is playing unusually loud. Today on your Five O'clock news, the controversial rapper, Tupac Shakur dies of several complications from gunshot wounds, Shakur was shot several times on Sept 7th, a few days ago, after leaving the Tyson vs. Seldon title fight, the shooting took place on Flamingo boulevard and Koval. We mourn the young man today and we will for many years to come, he will be truly missed by his family, friends and fans alike. Reports say that there will not be a funeral and that his body will be cremated instead. Again, today September 13th at University Medical Center, the Hip Hop star Tupac Shukar, passed away from complications due to gunshot wounds he received six days ago. We will have more details later on this sad day in Hip Hop, he will be truly missed. The customer was dressed in a plaid shirt, blue jeans, brown leather boots and a brown Cowboy hat. His tanned wrinkled skin sagged off his cheeks, a long white mustache covered his top lip, a brown belt and a gold buckle that read Nevada was at the center of his 6'4" frame as he approached the bar.

Howdy Sir! Hello, what can I get for you? Well, let me have one of those Jack Daniels and coke if you don't mind. One Jack and coke coming right up, here you go Cowboy! Thank you partner, what you watching on the news there? Oh, that rapper who got shot a few days ago, down in the city, he passed away today. Oh yeah, I heard about that mess they had down there, I just don't get it! Why you want to shoot a man that isn't armed, that's beyond me, that's what I call pure pussy if I've ever seen it haus. He stops talking, picks up his drink and takes a few sips. Yep, I will have to agree with you there cowboy. Hell, back in my day, we would duke it out by hand or have a shootout, you know, the man with the quickest hands wins. Well it's not like that today cowboy, it's guns all over the place, kids even have oozies, nines, Ak's, anything they want, they can get. See, that's just some bullshit haus and we wonder why the kids are killing each other.

He takes another sip of his drink. So, what gals you got working today haus? Man, we have 15 girls working today. God Damn, it's my lucky day, aint it! Yes Sir; looks that way! Well, I want me some brown pussy today haus, you got some sisters or some Latina girls back there? Cowboy, we have a few for yah. So, what you waiting on haus, get em out here! The bartender goes over to the intercom. Selena, Brandy, Trish, Gloria and Marcy to the front please! Haus, I'm feeling good today, how much for two girls buddy? Ha-ha-ha. You sure, can you handle that cowboy? Ha-ha-ha-ha. Haus, I had me some of that good ol moonshine, right before I came here, I can go for hours now haus. Ha-ha-ha-ha. They both laugh. Ok cowboy, it's going to be $1500 for each one. Cowboy reaches in his wallet and pulls out a gold Visa card. Here you go haus, put it on that, take $100 for yourself. Thanks cowboy, the girls will be out in a minute. Alright, I'm ready for em, bring em on!

The ladies come out front and line up alongside the bar. Now that's what I call sexy haus, what's your name darling? I'm Gloria! Hi Gloria, I'm Ronnie, come over here; let me take a closer look at yah. She walks over to him, dressed in black 6 inch heels and a green robe. You are a pretty lil thing darling, open that gown for me sugar! She opens her robe. God damn sugar, you're butt naked, aint you! Ha-ha-ha. Yep! That is what you want anyway, right cowboy? Hell yes, I got some snow for them pretty brown mountains of yours. He rubs his hands through her long silky black hair. Hey haus, I want this pretty brown one, right here! OK, I got you cowboy! Gloria, have a seat over on the couch honey. She walks over to the seating area. Who's your second girl Cowboy? Weeee doggie, what's your name sugar? My name is Trish daddy! Well, where's your clothes honey? All I need is these red boots daddy. Honey bun, you look like a chocolate covered cherry standing there with those big perky nipples of yours, come on over here sugar, join me and Gloria. Haus, she's gone be the one man, I'm ready now. Alright, let's get you on your way cowboy, ladies, the rest of you can go back to what you were doing. Gloria, you and Trish are doing a double. OK, we got you babe, which room are we using? Hell, it doesn't matter, yours or hers, it's up to you guys. We can use mine Trish, my bed is bigger, come on, let's go party baby. They grab Ronnie by the hand and take him back to the room for some fun.

A huge California King Size bed sat long ways beside the wall; on the opposite side of the room was an old six drawer, oak wood dresser and mirror. Perfume, cd's and a few personal items covered the top of the dresser; old brown frizzy carpet complemented the earth tone curtains and comforter. Gloria and Trish walk in and push Ronnie down on the king size bed. Whoa nelly! Lay down daddy; let us take those clothes off of you! Weeeee doggie! I like it ruff ladies! Gloria pulls off his boots and socks, Trish unbuttons his shirt and jeans, Gloria pulls off his pants as Trish took off the shirt and hat. Two small bags of cocaine fall out of his hat and hit the floor. Oooohhh, what is this daddy? Darling that's snow, give it here. Trish picks it up from the floor and hands it to him. Here you go baby. Thank you Darling, now lay back. Gloria pushes him back on the bed and starts to suck on his hard penis. Wow; that feels great, keep that up sugar plum. Shhhh, be quiet, let me do this daddy. Trish stands up and straddles him. Come down here darling, let me lick that kitty. Oh, that's what you want cowboy? Hell yeah! She walks over his face and sits down; Ronnie begins to lick her pussy up and down, inside and out, round and around the clit. Oooohhh daddy, you got some skills!

Ronnie was humming while her clit was in his mouth, his body started to shiver from all the sexual tension. Ummmmmm-Ummmmm. Oh yeah daddy! Oh yeah! That shit feels good! Ummmm-Ummmmm. He continues to shiver, again and again before his body came to a calm peace. Damn, is that it daddy? Gloria lifts up, looks at them both, shakes her head to say. Umm, hmmm. Yep, that's it sis! She gets up and walks to the restroom to spit the cum out of her mouth. Trish roles over on her back; Ronnie opens one bag of powder and sprinkles it on her left breast, he leans over, snorts it off her sweaty brown D cup. Gloria walks back in the room. Ooowww, I want some baby. Ronnie picks up the other bag and hands it to her. Here sugar! Gloria opens the other bag and puts it on Trish stomach, while snorting the coke; she takes her other hand and starts to rub on Trish's pussy. Ohhh baby, that feels so good. Ummmmm, mmmmm, mmmmmm. Yes, I like that! Ronnie snorts the last line and rolls over beside Trish on the bed; she grabs his Johnson and starts to stroke it. Gloria reaches over to get a condom off the dresser, opens it then puts it on him. Trish rolls over and gets on top; she rides and rides and rides for the next 15 minutes. Hey darling, you can stop, I'm on this here cocaine and I aint coming no time soon sugar. Awww, ok daddy, I'm higher than cloud nine right now too, she rolls off and lays on the bed beside Ronnie and Gloria. The three of them, lay there looking up at the ceiling fan spin for several minutes, until they drift away into a cocaine induced sleep.

AC was at his place relaxing when the phone rings. Ring-Ring-Ring. Yeah, who's calling? What's up nigga, this is Mo! Oh hey baby, how are you doing? I'm good! Why the fuck you aint call me yet? Bitch, didn't I tell you what the deal was! AC, you aint told me a damn thing since we closed the office; I've been waiting for your black ass to call me for months. I heard through the grapevine that you got a gig over at that strip club! Girl, your ass is nosey as fuck! Yep, you already know, I don't let shit get by me baby! Yeah, I see, so what's up? What do you mean, what's up? I mean, when are you going to put me down? Give me another month or so, maybe I will have something for you by then baby. OK, that's cool, so did you miss me? Yeah, you know I miss that ass girl! Oh yeah, how much did you miss me? I think about you everyday baby. Nigga, stop lying! Ha-ha-ha. Why you say that Mo? You full of shit

AC, that's why! Girl, I'm serious! Well, I'm downstairs at the front desk right now. Stop playing Mo! Bring your ass down here and see nigga! Fuck that, you lying! OK, hold on player. She hands Manny the phone. Hey, what's up bro? Manny! Yeah, what's up bro.? So, that bitch downstairs for real! Yep! Man, send her crazy ass up to my place. OK bro... Manny hangs up the phone. Hey Mo, go ahead up baby. Alright, thanks baby, it was good seeing you again too my nigga. Yep, you too baby! She makes her way through the lobby to the elevator.

Knock-Knock-Knock. Yeah who is it? Nigga, why are you playing, this is Mo! It's open, come in baby! Coop is sitting on his kitchen counter top, wearing only black gym shorts, Mo walks in wearing her blue Air Max, no socks, white skirt, no panties and blue Swoosh tee shirt, no bra. Her sandy blonde micro braids fell shoulder length and complemented her pecan tan skin tone. Hey baby! Hey AC. Come here girl and give me a hug! She walks over, reaches out and wraps her arms around him. Ummmm. You look good Mo. Thank you. Muah! They kiss each other on the lips. So are you hungry, what something to drink? Sure, what do you have to drink? I got some juice, milk, water and over there on the counter is some vodka and a half bottle of Crown. What kind of juice you got baby? Orange juice girl. Why you say it like that nigga? Because, you act like I was supposed to have some apple juice or some shit. Ha-ha-ha. Boy, your ass is still crazy; just give me the orange juice AC. He gets the OJ from the fridge and hands it to Mo. Thanks; can I have a glass too? Yeah, they're some solo cups right under the counter by the vodka. Where are they, I don't see them. Open that left cabinet door. She opens the door. Oh I see them. Cool, fix me one too, oh, here's the ice. He slides the ice trey across the counter. She proceeds to make two screw drivers, one part vodka, one part OJ, over ice. Here you go honey. AC and Mo take a seat on the couch and sip their drinks.

Damn, it's hard to believe it's almost October already. Yeah, it seems like you just closed the office last week. I know, doesn't it! So, how do you like your new gig? It's cool for now, but I got some other things working that will bring some major cash our way, you dig. I guess! What's that supposed to mean? I'm just saying; don't forget about a sister over here. No doubt baby, you just be patient, I got a spot for you, it's just going to take a few more months. OK, AC! So, how's the marriage life treating you baby? It's alright, I guess, but I want more than just being a house wife. Oh yeah, what is it that you want? You know, I like to party, travel, shop and go to nice restaurants; I want the good life baby! Look at your place, nice furniture, the view, your cars, bikes, you got what I want AC. Well, in a few months baby, you can have all of this too. I sure hope so, I mean, I love my husband but he aint no hustler like you nigga, you know how to go get it! You know, everybody can't be a hustler Mo; that shit has to be in your blood, you have to be almost made into this life baby. You don't have to tell me that, I can see who's made and who's not! Is that right? Yep! They pick up their glasses and take a drink. Just don't forget about me. Hey stop worrying, didn't I say I got you. Yeah you did. So, leave it alone already then. OK, OK, I'll change the subject, what did you think about that stunt they pulled with Tupac? What do you mean stunt, Mo? Yo, don't tell me, you think that nigga is dead! Hell yeah, he dead! Man, Pac aint dead, he done got shot like 6 times before anyway. Girl, that don't make him invincible!

I didn't say he was invincible. Then what did you mean? Come on man; think about it, if he's really dead, why didn't they have a funeral? Those fools think they can tell us anything, talking about they cremated him! Girl you crazy, tell me what you think happened? Listen to this AC, he got shot on the 7th and was stable every day until the 13th, all of sudden, he dies and there aint no funeral. Suge wasn't even at the hospital when he died, Suge aint never seen the dead body! Man, I think the Feds told him to fake his death and leave the country, he already had two attempts on his life and survived, the third time, he might not be so lucky! When his Mom came down, her, Tupac and The Fed made the decision to fake his death, I'm telling you baby! They do that shit with the Mafia, putting people in witness protection all the time, why wouldn't they do it with him! Mo shut the fuck up! OK, you don't have to believe me, but I know I'm right, watch that nigga start popping up overseas and dropping new music and shit, watch! Yeah, here, give me that glass so I can make you another drink, you a crazy bitch, don't tell anybody else that story. Ha-ha-ha. He laughs and proceeds to make her another drink. Whatever! Don't laugh at me nigga, I'm serious. Hmmm, mmmm. I know, here drink up. He hands over the drink, looks at her, laughs and shakes his head.

CHAPTER 18, OCTOBER.

The roads are clear, Nina turns off Tropicana Boulevard and pulls up to the Spanish Trails security gate. At the entrance, gigantic Palm trees, huge Red Granite rocks and dark green grass surround a large man made pond that was home to a few dozen geese. Off to the left of the entrance, several luxurious Billion dollar homes capture the hillside; in this star studded secluded community. Nina drove up the hill and around the curb; pass all the Bentley's; Rovers, Benz's and Jaguars that seem to be in every other driveway. She gets to the bottom of the hill and pulls up to a 12 bedroom, 6 bathroom; brick mansion; that sat on 7 acres of green grass, surrounded by shrubs and Palm trees. A coble stone driveway, led up to a 6 car garage and veered off to the left into a coble stone sidewalk that led up to a 5 foot wide 10 foot tall blue door. An 8 foot tall, black cast iron fence; surrounded 4 of the 7 acres that covered the back yard. It's the middle of the day, the house was empty, no cars in the garages, no girls by the pool, she exits her car and enters the mansion, once inside, she picked up the phone to make a call.

Ring-Ring. Hello, thanks for calling Angel's Escorts, how can we help you today? Hey Paula, it's me Nina. Oh, hey sweetie, did you make it out to the house yet? Yeah, I just got here. OK good, this is what I need for you to do. When you first walk in, you will see a huge 12 foot statue of Julius Caesar downstairs, placed in the center of the wall, dividing the base of the two huge stair cases. Yeah, I see it! Good! Now walk over to the statue and push down on his right hand. Nina walks over to Caesar and push down his hand. OK, I just did it. Great, now wait a few seconds and you will see a crack appear in the wall, right behind the statue, do you see it? She looks behind Julius. Yep! OK, now push on that panel. I'm pushing it now. Alright, don't panic, just stay still.

As Nina stood there, the statue and floor begin to move down like an elevator, after what seemed like three levels, the floor had finally stopped. Wow, I just stopped Paula! Listen and listen good sweetie, you are now in a vault, you have 5 minutes before it goes back up! 5 minutes! Yes Mam! So, what am I doing down here? I need for you to get this week's take. What is a take? Money baby, money! Oh, OK! Where is it? Get off of the platform, make a right behind the statue, you will see a silver vault door, push down on the handle and open it, you will see the money there in a black duffle bag sitting on the table. Nina walks over to the vault door and opens it, she walks inside the vault and see the bag on the table, just like Paula said. I have it! Good, now you have like 2 and a half minutes left before the platform goes back up, if you don't get on it, you will be stuck down there until someone comes home to send it back down, so hurry! Damn, I'm going right now, I can't be stuck in this shit. Yeah, so hurry! Get the money; I will see you when you get back to the office. Alright, bye Paula.

She hangs up the cordless phone and stops to take a quick look around the vault; one wall was covered with rifles and hand guns. Bundles of $100 bills were wrapped in plastic, 50-K was stamped in black ink on each bundle that sat on several shelves of the opposite wall. Wow, there's a lot of guns and money down here. Nina spoke softly then picked up the black duffle bag from the table and exited the grey steel vault, with 50 seconds to spare. After making sure the door was closed, Nina stepped onto the platform, A few seconds had passed and it begin to rise back upward, once it got back to the top she walked away from the statue and exited the mansion. Beep-Beep. A person driving by in a white Range Rover had blown his horn at her as she locked the big blue door and headed back to her car.

Nina picks her cell phone up off the dash and calls Paula. Ring-Ring. Hello! It's me Paula. Hey, where are you sweetie? I'm in the car, on the way to the office. Well, there's been a change of plans. What do you mean? I need for you to drop the bag off to the boss. What? What do you mean, what sweetie, I said I need you to drop the bag off to the boss! I don't know the boss Paula. Oh, I'm sorry sweetie; you never met them have you? No, I haven't! Well, you will today. OK, that's fine. Do you know where Dolls is? Yes, the strip club on industrial? Yep, that's the one. What about it? That's where our bosses work out of every day, so take the bag there, once you get there, go inside, tell them you're dropping off something for Vinny and Bobby from Paula, you got that sweetie? Yep, got it!

Good girl, call me once you're done dropping it off. OK Paula! She drives a few miles down Tropicana until she comes up on Industrial Boulevard and makes a left, Nina calls Will from her mobile.

Ring-Ring-Ring. Yo what up, this is Will! Hey bro., this is Nina! Hey sis, what's poppin? I just got orders to drop off a package for Vinny and Bobby over at the club. No shit! No shit. What's in the package sis? Like $300,000.00! What the fuck! Yep, that's a lot of cheese; do you think it's safe for me to let them meet me? Hell no, that can't happened. Well, what am I going to do? Hold on; give me minute to think on it. Is AC at the club? No, he's off but I'm here now; OK, I got it, just give me the bag when you get here and I will take it to them. Cool; that was simple. Hey, sometimes that's the best way, keep it simple. Alright, I'm about 2 miles away, so be at the door or something, I don't even want to get out of the car. Sis, you have to get out of the car and come in to hand me the bag, we at least have to make it look real! OK but I don't want to meet them. Sis, they don't even come out of the office half the time, stop worrying, we go it covered, I will be keeping an eye on the door until you get here.

Thanks bro., I will see you in a few. Your welcome, I'm going to call Coop, let him know what's going on. Alright, see you in a bit. Later sis. He hangs up and dials AC's number. Ring-Ring-Ring-Ring. Hello! Yo Coop, what's poppin my nigga! Aint shit Will, what's good? How about Nina's boss is sending her over here to drop off a package for Vinny and Bobby. I know you're kidding! Nope, I just got off the phone with her. Damn, you know we can't let them meet her, right! Yeah, I told her to give it to me and I will take it to them. Cool, that was too close, how much is the package? She said it was something like, 300 K! God damn! That much! Yep, that's exactly what I said, bruh, these fools are making money, hand over fist. Damn, we need to have an Intel meeting, before this month is out, so we can see where everybody's at then plan our end game. Yeah, I agree with you there Coop, this thing is way bigger than we could of ever imagined. Now that we know all the major players and allies, it's the right time, when Nina gets there, tell her to tell Denna, I will call the rest of the crew to set a date, time and place. OK bruh, I got you covered, later. Click! They hang up. Will is standing at the end of the bar over by the entrance when she walks in. Hey sis! Hey bro., here's the bag. Thanks. Will takes the bag from her. OK, bye man, I'm out! Wait, hold on a minute! What bro.? AC said to tell Denna we're having an Intel. Meeting at the end of the month, you guys keep your schedules open OK. Alright, I will let her know, later man. She hurries back to her car and speeds off the lot up industrial.

Will walks over to the office. Knock-Knock-Knock. Ummm-Um-Ummm-Um. Yeah, come in! He enters the office. Oh shit, I'm sorry boss! Sorry for what, you never got head before or something? Umm! Damn, she's good too! Umm! Remy was there on her knees, sucking Bobbies dick while he was lean backed in the office chair. Well, what's up Will? Oh, Paula sent you this package. Bobby holds Remy by the back of the neck and looks over at Will. OK thanks; just sit it on the floor, in front of the desk. Umm! Damn, I swear, sometimes I don't know what's better, the mouth or the pussy! Umm-Umm. Remy! Hey, sure you don't want next Will! Ha-ha-ha-ha. Nah, I'm good boss! OK man; close the door behind you, thanks for the package too. Slurp-Slurp. Damn Remy! Ha-ha-ha-ha. Will leaves the office laughing and shaking his head as he made his way back over to the bar. What are you laughing at Will? Awww. It's nothing Deb. Yeah right; I see you're still smiling about something. Oh, I just thought about this joke I heard on Martin the other day, you know how him and Pam be going at each other. Oh yeah, that show is funny as hell.

Dennis walks in the club and approach the bar. Yo what's up Deb? Hi D, aint too much going on right now, where you coming from? Just getting off work baby. So, what are you having? Let me get a corona with a lime please. Coming right up! Hey, what's up Will? I'm good D, how you feeling? A little tired from working all day but other than that I can't complain. I know what you mean brother. Here you go D. Thanks Deb! He turns up the cold corona, drinks nearly half of it in one swig. Say Will, how's AC doing, I'm surprised he's not here today. He's cool bro., he comes in tomorrow, he switched shifts with someone today. Remy had just walked out of the office and made her way over to the bar. Hey baby! There she is, my sweet Remy! She walks over and kisses D on the lips. Muah! How was work baby? Same ol; same ol sugar. Will looks at them both and smiles. Man there you go, smiling again. What are you talking about Deb? You man, all that damn happy shit today! Hey, I was just smiling at these two love birds. Remy rolls her eyes at Will, takes D by the hand and pulls him away from the bar. Come on baby;

let's go sit at a table. Damn, hold on honey, let me get my beer! D grabs his beer off the bar as she pulls him away. Later yall, she wants me all to herself. Yeah, later man! Bye D!

Hey Will. Yeah Deb, what's up? Can you keep an eye on the bar for me, I need to go get something from my locker, it want take me long. Sure, go ahead, I got you covered, I aint making no drinks though. Ha-ha-ha. Yeah and you better not try either! She walks from behind the bar as he takes a seat on the bar stool at the end of the counter. Smack! Ouch! Hey Paco! Stop smacking my ass, you Cuban motherfucker you! Oh, you know you like that Deb! Yeah whatever, just go have a seat at the bar, I will be right back. Hurry up; I have something for you Mommy. OK, I want be long. Paco walks over to the bar and haves a seat by Will. Hey what's up man? What's happening! You must be new here, I never seen you around. Yeah, I've been here a few months. Oh that's cool, I'm Paco my man, what's your name? I'm Will bro... Nice to meet you Will, you want a drink or something when Deb gets back? No I'm cool, don't drink on the job. An honest man, I can respect that.

Yeah, I have to keep a clear head, you know what I mean? That's cool. Oh, I got the hook up on some Versace shit if you like clothes like that. Oh yeah, what kind of Versace, I don't sport no fake shit if that's what you're asking. This shirt is Versace my man, does it look fake! OK, that's hot right there, diggin the purple and gold designs, what kind of hook up you got? Well, I have this chica that works over at the Versace store in the Fashion Show mall man, I give her some blow, and $200 and I get like $2,000.00 worth of shit. Hell yeah brother, that's a deal for your ass right there. Yep, I know right. So, how can I get in on it? Man, just let me know when you're ready, I can meet you up there, introduce you to her, that way you will get the same deal I get. Cool, I can dig that brother. Here, take my number, hit me up when you're ready. Paco takes a napkin from the holder and writes down his number. Thanks bro.! No problem Will, anytime.

Deb makes her way back over to the bar. Hey you Cuban Fucker, what you got for me? She reaches over and kisses Paco on the cheek. He reaches in his back pocket and pulls out a long narrow brown box. Here you go sexy. Boy, what is this? Open it woman! She opens the box to find a gold, chain link, Versace watch. Awwww. Thank you Paco, you're so sweet! Yeah, yeah, I know! Ha-ha-ha-ha. Whatever! Muah! She gives him another kiss on the cheek. Hey babe, can I get a Martel on the rocks, don't feel like vodka today. Yeah, anything for you baby. Oh, see how she is Will, first I was a Cuban fucker, now I'm her baby after she gets the watch. Ha-ha-ha. You a trip Deb. She looks at him, smiles and blows a kiss. Here you are, one Martel on the rocks. Thanks babe, oh, can you let Vinny know I'm here with his package. I'm sure he seen you on the camera's already, trust me on that, here, give it to me; I'll take it to him. Nah, I got it, just let him know please. Well, excuse me!

She picks up the bar phone and pages Vinny. Vinny, Paco is here to see you! The office door opens; Bobby is standing there waving for him to come back. He's ready for you Paco. Thanks Deb, I will be right back. He walks over to the office, goes in and haves a seat at the desk. Well, how are you my friend, how's business? Business is good Vinny and I'm well. Great, that's always good news. Here's your package. Thanks Paco, is there anything else, you act like something is on your mind. Actually, I'm going to need like 5 extra pounds of chronic on my next re-up order, that shit is moving through the hood like crazy. 5 extra pounds Paco, are you sure you can move that extra weight? Bobby, that shit is already sold, soon as it hits my hands, I swear. OK, if you say so brother, just don't come in here with a light envelop next week or that's your Cuban ass. Hey, that's never going to happen boss, I'm the man when it comes to this game. Alright, we will let Diego know, have a good week, see you next time. He gets up, shakes their hands and exits the office.

Will walks out the front door and pulls out his cell phone. Ring-Ring-Ring. Hello! Hey pimp, it's me again. What's up Will? A cat name Paco just came by to drop off a package for Vin and Bobby. Damn, make sure you meet him, it's important he knows one of our faces. Chill out Coop, it's done already, we in the game pimp. Hell yeah, that's what's up my nigga. Cool, later man. He hangs up, walks back inside. Yo Will! Deb! You guys take it easy, I'm out of here, Will; hit me up whenever you're ready to make that move my man. Yeah, no doubt Paco, I will bro... He leans over the bar and kiss Deb on the cheek. Muah! See you next time gorgeous. Alright, you Cuban fucker, thanks for the gift. Your welcome, see yah next time babe, don't get in any trouble. He exits the club. Deb, I see you got you a boyfriend, huh lady? Who, Paco! Child please! I don't know Deb, I think he likes you, you getting Versace presents and shit like that! He always brings me gifts but he aint never smelled this pussy. Ha-ha-ha. You crazy Deb! Shit it's the truth, he's trying too hard, I know he got a bitch for everyday of the week, I aint gone be one of them. I heard that loud and clear, somebody has got to be tapping that ass. Nope nobody, just me and my rabbit!

Oh hell nah, not the rabbit! Yep! You are too damn fine to be single, what's the problem? Sorry ass men who want to fuck every piece of pussy that comes their way, that's the kind of men I seem to attract. See that's the problem, you trying to date some players and you want gentlemen. There's a big difference baby, believe me, but most women don't recognize the real man when he's right in front of their face. Yeah, I hear you big Will, tell me, are you a player or a gentlemen? To be honest, I can be both! Ummm-hmmm. Just like I thought, your ass aint no good either. Well, if you want to find out Deb, I will be glad to take you out on a date. Child please, that will not work, especially with us working together. Hey, suit yourself baby, the offer still stands if you ever change your mind. Yeah, I will be sure to keep that in mind. I'm sure you will. He gets up from the bar and starts to walk off. Where do you think you're going Mr.? I'm going home, my shift is over baby. Oh, you suck! Yeah, yeah, bye Deb. He walks to the back, clocks out and exits through the rear employee door.

Ring-Ring. Hello, front desk, how may I help you? Yo Manny, it's AC. What's crackin bro.? We're having an Intel meeting, the day before Halloween; can we use the Presidential room, like before? Yeah sure, I will go ahead and book it right now. Cool, I'm going to call Loon and Duck to inform them, could you hit up the sisters? No problem bro.! Thanks man, later! Click! They hang up. Ring-Ring. Hola! Hola Denna, this is Manny. Hey poppy, Que pasa? Hey, we are having an Intel meeting the day before Halloween, 7pm here in the Presidential room. OK bro., thanks, I will let sis know. Cool, talk to you later than babe. OK, good bye. Manny hangs up the phone, gets up from his desk, grabs his cigarettes and head outside. Hey what the fuck are you doing! Yeah you, Valet, I'm talking to you! Hey!

The valet ignores Manny, proceeds to put several sets of keys in his pocket. Manny walks up behind him, grabs his red jacket and turns him around. The valet swings a right hook towards Manny, clocks him in the head, he moves in to throw another blow. Manny grabs him by both collars, pushes him back into the key stand; the valet falls over, Manny starts stomping him in the chest and kicked him in the face. Hey, somebody call the police! Yo, get the fuck off of me man! Shut up bitch! Manny leaned over and punched him in the face, again and again, until his face was covered in blood. Two bicycle cops, who were patrolling the area, had just rolled up. Hey Manny, what the hell are you doing, you trying to kill the guy? Manny gets up off of him. No man, this guy was steeling car keys from the rack, this fucker don't even work here; he just has on the jacket! Alright, we got it from here, move away before you kill the poor guy. The two cops walk over, proceeded to pick the bloody and beaten thief up from the ground. OK Mr., you're under arrest for larceny; come on, get up. One officer placed the cuffs on him while the other radio dispatch. Attention dispatch, this is unit 78, I have a suspect in custody, we need a car over at the Towers. OK 78, car 602 is on the way. Thanks dispatch, Manny, call us earlier next time before you kill somebody. Hey, my bad officer, I had to stop this fool before he took off with these cars. Yeah, we understand. The patrol car had just pulled up. OK come on buddy, here's your ride, they put him in the back seat, closed the door, then tap on the driver's window. The patrol car sees the prisoner is secure in the back seat and pulls off.

Manny picks his damaged pack of Newport's up off the ground; pulls out the one good one, sticks it in his mouth, lights it and takes a long hard pull. Damn, look at my fucking shirt. He looks down and finds blood all over the sleeves of his white shirt. Hey, are you alright Sir, there's blood everywhere. A casino patron asked as she was entering the Towers. Yes Mam, I'm fine. Well, you better change shirts son, that one is a mess. Yes Mam. He walks back in the building and heads to the break room to get an extra shirt from the locker. Damn Manny, what the hell happen, you murder a motherfucker or something? I almost killed his ass! Kill who man? Some punk was steeling the keys, from your Valet station, where the hell was your ass at? Man, I had to take a dump; I couldn't hold that shit no longer. So, you couldn't call someone up there to replace you, till you got back? Dude, I wasn't even thinking about that, I was about to do number two right there, if I didn't go right then. Yeah, I tell you what, the next time you leave that booth unattended I'm gone put my size 11 shoe up your ass! Damn Manny, chill! Don't tell me to chill, punk ass motherfucker; because of you, some of our tenants cars could have got stolen, as a matter of fact give me that jacket and clear out your locker! Your ass is fired! Man come on, stop tripping! I aint tripping dawg, you fired! Bye, get your shit and kick rocks! That's some bullshit Manny! He takes off his jacket and throws it on the floor, clears out the locker, slams it and walks off. Fuck you Manny and the Towers!

Man, I swear, one of these young kids gone make me catch a case one day. Manny says out loud as he walked back to the lobby. Yo, where the hell you been fool? AC, you don't even want to know bro... Well anyway, what time is your break, I'm headed over to Wolf Gang's at Caesar's for a bite. Dawg, I don't go on break for like 3 hours. Shit, I aint waiting that long for your ass. Yeah, I already know that much. I'm gone player; I can bring you something back if you want though. No, I'm good Coop. Alright, see you later. AC exits the Towers and head across the street to Caesar's. Ring-Ring-Ring. He runs over to get the phone. Hello Towers! Can I speak to Manny? This is Manny. What's up bruh, this Loon! Hey bro., what's good?

What time is that meeting next week, I forgot already. It's at 7pm bruh and don't be late either! Thanks Manny and I'm never late bruh! Yeah, I hear you Loon. Later man. The two hang up. Manny sits down at his desk to take a breather and relax his nerves, then in walks Detective Espinoza. Detective! Hello Manny, how have you been man? Hell, just trying to make it man. Yeah, I hear you. So what brings you over this way? I need to check Ms. Marciano's personal items for any clues that may give me something on her murder case. Damn, you might be too late Detective; we cleared her place out a few weeks ago. What did you all do with her things? Everything went in the Auction last week. Do you guys keep track of the sales receipts? No, we only accept cash during an auction, sorry I couldn't have helped you more Detective. Hey, it's OK, thanks anyway man. He shakes Manny's hand then heads out the door.

Carlos the doorman for Club Ritz enters the Towers to clock in for work when he spots Manny. Yo amigo, what's going on with you today? Same shit different day Los! Yo, good looking out the other night at the club too bro... Yeah, anytime man, you know I got your back. Boy, the girls were in that bitch that night though! Yeah, I caught at least three skirts at the door. It got crazy later that night though. Why you say that, some fools started fighting or something? Hell no, I wish that was all, we found a fool dead in the men's bathroom stall. Damn, no shit! Yep, that fool was shanked the hell up too. Hey, he must have pissed somebody off that night; you know anything can happen when you claim that G life, here in Sin City, A fool got to be ready for what comes with it. Yep! Alright Manny, I will get with you later player, let me get to work. Later amigo, it's time for me to get out of here anyway. Carlos walks through the lobby pass the casino and to Club Ritz. Manny's relief, David, had just clocked in to replace him.

Three ladies sit in a small moldy office with one desk, a TV, two phones and a book shelf. The youngest of the three sat there nervous as she answered several questions for the oldest woman in the room. Hello sweetie, how are you? I'm doing OK. That's great sweetie, my name is Paula and this is Nina. What's your name? My name is Georgia. Nice to meet you Georgia, is this your first time being an Escort? Yes it is, I'm so nervous right now. You're going to be fine baby, let's get started; first you need to get nude so we can do a body check. OK, do I take my clothes off in the bathroom or what? No sweetie, you can do it right here in front of us, we both have the same thing you got. She stands up to unbutton her jeans, kicks off her heels, then pulls off her pants, Georgia unzips her jacket to reveal her perky c cup breast. You have a nice body sugar but that bush has to go. What do you mean? I mean you have to shave that pussy; nobody is going to eat that with all that hair sweetie! How should I shave it? Baby you can take it all off or leave just a little on top. I never shaved it off like that before. Nina, show her how a clean shaved pussy is supposed to look.

Nina stands up, pulls up her dress and shows her pretty pink clean shaved pussy. See that sweetie! That's how yours need to look. OK, I can do that. Great! You have some gorgeous red hair, that's going to be the thing that separates you from the rest. Thank you, so when do I start? Sweetie you can start tonight but we need to give you a serious make over first, from your shoes to your hair. Go ahead; put your clothes back on baby, Nina is going to take you shopping so we can get your wardrobe straight. Nina, take her by the hair salon too, get that hair fixed. Yes Mam! Paula stands up and gives Georgia a big hug. Welcome to Angel's sweetie; remember to listen to everything that Nina tells you, OK. Yes Mam! Come on Georgia; let's go get you looking like an Angel baby. Here Nina, take the gold visa. Thanks Paula! We will see you in a few hours; she's going to look like a movie star when I'm done. OK, bye sweetie, get going, we have a busy night ahead of us. The two ladies leave the office and head outside to the limo.

Nina and Georgia walk outside and see Duck sitting on the tailgate of his truck rolling a blunt. Come on bro., you rolling with us? Where you guys going sis? I'm taking Georgia shopping and then we hitting the Hair and Nail salon. Man, I aint fucking with no salon! Come on Duck, you don't have to go to the salon with us, just the mall; you know we're going to need you with us to keep them lame ass dudes away. OK, I'm coming. He jumps off the tailgate and walks over to them. What's up red! Hello. So your name is Georgia? Yep, that's what my parents named me. Nice to meet you; I'm Duck. Ha-ha-ha. Like Daffy? I said Duck, didn't I! Alright, calm down bro., it aint that serious. Georgia stood there in her Ck jeans, black heels and yellow jacket, standing about a foot shorter than Nina with a petite frame. Hey sis, if she wants to be a big girl and take it to that level, let me take her there. Duck, you tripping already! Georgia looks at him and rolls her eyes, all three of them walk to the limo, the driver opens the back door, and Nina, Duck and Georgia sit down in the back. Where to guys? Oh, we're going to Fashion Show mall first. Yes Mam! Fashion Show, here we come. He pulls off the lot and takes a right on Sarah towards the strip, the sunroof is open, warm rays from above has heated up the black leather seats. Knock-Knock. He taps on the driver's divider window. Yes sir? Hey man, close that damn sunroof and turn on the AC, it feels like hell back here man! Yes sir, as you wish. The roof slowly closes, the strong current blows from the vents cooling off the limo. After a few stop lights down Sahara boulevard he comes to the Sahara Casino intersection then makes a left onto Las Vegas boulevard, just ahead on the right, three lights down the strip, was the Fashion Show mall.

The drop off zone in front of the mall had several Limo's parked in its waiting area as he pulled up to the entrance, he parked the limo, got out and opened the door for his three passengers. Nina, Georgia and Duck exit the limo. Here you are guys, the Fashion Show mall; I will be parked over in the waiting area with the other limos when you're ready to leave. Alright, thanks man, see you in a few. Your welcome, please take your time, I'm in no hurry. Come on guys, he's talking too much. They leave the driver standing there talking to himself and enter the mall. Georgia, come over here baby, this is our first stop. Hello there stranger! A female voice spoke out as they walked into the Prada store. Hi Stacey! Girl, where have you been? I've been really busy for the past few months. Yeah I bet, how long has it been? Ummm. I think, I was last here in February. Yeah darling, that has been too long, it's October now girl, what can I get you today? Well my friend here needs a nice dress and a pair of sexy heels for this evening. Hmmm. come over here baby, let me look at you; I love that pretty red hair of yours. What's your name darling? It's Georgia Mam. Wow, you sound like a southern belle, where are you from Georgia? Atlanta Mam. OK, that explains the accent, the name and that pale skin of yours. You need to soak in some of this Vegas sun baby, so you can show off that pretty body of yours, come over here, in front of this mirror, let me see what I can do for you. Georgia walks over and stands in front of the tall life size mirror.

Stacey pulls Georgia's long red curly hair from the back of her head around to the front, so that it would fall over her shoulders. I love her hair Stacey, it's so pretty don't you think? Yeah, it's very pretty Nina; let's see, I have a black sleeveless dress or we can try the green pull up. Which do you want to try first darling? Let's do the black one. Good choice darling! Here you are, the dressing room is right over there. She goes into the dressing room to change. So Nina, are you getting anything today? Nah, I'm good for now but I will probably be in next month to get my sister something for Christmas. Darling, that's perfect, we will have some new designs in by then too. See, that's even better, are you going to give me a deal? Don't I always. Yes you do. OK then, lord what is taking her so long in there? Georgia, Georgia, are you OK darling? Yes Mam.

She walks out in the black Prada dress. Wow, that is just stunning! Damn girl, you look like a different person! Duck yelled out from the front of the store. Ha-ha-ha-ha. You guys are hilarious, I told you we could take care of her; I guess there's no need to try on the green one now darling. No Mam, I love this one. Good, come over here; let me find some heels to match it. You know, since it's October and the fall is here; which isn't very cold in Vegas but cool enough, I think you should try these knee high Prada boots we just got in. Ohhhh, I like those! Nina shouts. Yeah, aren't they pretty, come sit down, take those heels off. Georgia takes a seat on the bench and removed her shoes. Here put these on. Stacey hands her some socks. She slips them on. Now, let's see how these look on you. Georgia slips on the right boot, then the left. Now stand up, let us look at you. Wow, if that isn't a model right there in front of us, I don't know who is!

Darling take a look at yourself in the mirror, tell us what you think. She walks over to look in the life size mirror. Oh my God, is that me! Well yeah, you look fabulous darling; Nina, what do you think? Shit, I'm jealous Stacey!

118

Girl, you should be! That girl is stunning! Ha-ha-ha. Nina laughs. We'll take the dress and the boots Stacey. Alright darling, go take those off so I can box them up for you. OK! You sure, you don't want anything Nina? Oh no, I'm good for now baby. OK, I will be right back, how will you be paying? Here put it on this visa. No problem, as you wish, I will be right back with your items and a receipt. Wow, thank you Nina, you guys are so nice for doing this! Don't mention it baby, its part of the job, you have to look like money to catch money baby. OK people, we're all set, here are your items; your card and your receipt are in the bag. Stacey hands over the bags then she and Nina hug each other. Awww. Thank you Stacey, I will see you in a few weeks. OK darling, you guys be safe, enjoy your Holiday season. Nina, Duck and Georgia waves good bye to her, exits the store and head outside to the limo. Hey guys, I see you're all done, where to now? Yo, drop them off at the Salon on Flamingo and Maryland parkway, take me back to the office, you can come back and wait on them after you drop me off. The driver opens the back door. The three passengers get in and take a seat. Alright, first stop Flamingo and Maryland, then back to Sahara. He starts the limo and heads over to the salon so that Georgia can complete her new makeover. This was the moment that Duck didn't want any part of, the reason he went back to the office. The girls were about to spend the rest of their day at the salon, their evening and any other plans was now over.

Another day dawns, its Halloween eve at the Towers, the staff is setting the Presidential up for its 7pm meeting. The carpet was just cleaned, table polished, chairs wiped down and two bottles of Martel along with a box of Cuban cigars sat in the center of the table, alongside a bucket of ice and 7 crystal glasses. AC and Manny are sitting downstairs in the lobby waiting area. So, we got like an hour before the meeting Coop, do you have all the details ironed out for the end game of this thing? Yeah, I'm pretty sure I have all the major players and allies accounted for, we just need to put all our Intel together to complete the plan. Man, I bet you didn't think this shit would be so damn deep. Hell nah bruh, it's so much money and people involved in this thing, we have to get it right the first time. Yep, you're right, there's no room for error.

So, what you decide to do about Sabrina? As of right now, she isn't a threat, so nothing. Are you sure man, she knows plenty of Intel. on us already. Yeah, I'm sure, she can't hurt us! Alright, you know I got your back, no matter what the decision brother. Yeah I know, shit, are you ready to quit this gig and be my Capo? Bruh, that's a dumb question! Ha-ha-ha-ha. Yeah, that's my nigga. They laugh and give each other a pound. Oh yeah, that detective came by the other day wanting to search Ashley's place. Who, Espinoza? Yeah, that was him. Damn, that fool is going to be a problem, what did you tell him? Shit, it wasn't anything to tell him, we cleared that place out weeks ago, auctioned off all her things. Ha-ha. I know he was mad as fuck. Yeah but he handle it pretty cool. Did he say anything else? Nope, just said have a good day and left. Bet that's not the last of that pig, you can count on that. Yo, it's almost time; let's go to the Presidential. They both get up and head over to the meeting room. Hey, did you get the Martel? Yep, I got some fresh Cubans too. Manny, you my nigga.

AC takes a seat at the head of the table, Manny sits off to his left, the door opens, in walks Denna and Nina. Hey ladies how's it going? We're good fellas, where's everybody else? They should be here soon. Dang, this must be serious poppy, we got the Martel tonight! Oh look Denna, Cuban's too. She picks up a cigar from the box and sniffs. Ummmmm. Nothing like a fresh Cuban cigar. Nina, go ahead pull seven of those out, one for each of the crew. Sure. She picks up the cigars and puts one in front of every ones seat. Thanks baby! No problem AC. Manny; how's Sophie? She's doing great Denna. Good. The door opens. Hey people, what the fuck is up! Hey Loon! They all spoke at the same time. Oh yeah, we got the Martel baby! He walks over to the table, picks up the bottle and proceeds to open it. Yo, what are yall waiting on to open the drink man? We were waiting on the rest of the crew Loon. Oh, Will and Duck just pulled up, they should be coming in any second. Cool, go ahead set the glasses up then. Loon puts two cubes of ice in each glass, pours in some Martel and sits one in front of every ones seat, the door opens and in walks Will and Duck. Hey what's up people, I see the crew is all here. Hey! They all speak at the same time. Duck, lock that door behind you brother. OK Coop. All the guys take their seats at the table, pick up their cigars, lights them and starts smoking. Alright crew, we're about to get started, I'm going to let everyone speak, each one of us will share what Intel we gathered from our end of the operation; Nina, we'll start with you.

Oh man, where should I start? Well, let's see; my boss is Paula, she's over Angel's the escort business, Angelica's the bunny ranch and several houses in the city where the girls board. Her staff includes one bartender, several escorts, 15 prostitutes and a House mom out at the ranch where she also has a trailer that she stays at from time to time. The other day, I went to one of the Mansions in Spanish Trails to pick up a week's worth of earnings. Paula had me call her once I got there, when I get inside she tells me to push the arm of this huge Julius Caesar statue to release a hidden panel that was behind the statue. I push in this panel, the statue goes down two levels like an elevator would, I find myself in a steel vault surrounded by a lot of guns and tons of money. On the table was a black duffle bag with $300,000.00 in it, the package she sent me to pick up; Paula said the money was the earnings for that week.

Over at the agency we have three limos at our disposal and a corporate gold visa card that we use to outfit the girls when they first come aboard, we also use it for any other expenses she deems necessary. Duck runs errands for us sometimes and act as security on some gigs; I am now familiar with the phones, customers, ladies and the staff at Angelica's. Me and Duck are in position to take over Paula's spot when the time comes, our marks for this gig is Paula of course, the bartender and the house mom Nancy at Angelica's. They definitely have to go because of the pull they have over the girls. Are you sure we need to off the last two? Yeah there's no doubt about it AC. It seems to me, your boss controls the agencies income and those two the brothel. No Coop; that bitch controls all of it, she hires and fires the girls for the agency and the ranch, Paula is the biggest pimp in Sin City under the bosses. Shit, sounds like we need to knock her off immediately after we take out the bosses, if that's the case. Yep, because everybody will be looking for her to take the chair. OK, consider it done, Paula and her staff is out. AC had made his decision.

Loon, what's up on you and Denna's end? Bruh, it's a piece of cake, there's this old Vet named Keiser running the place and there's seven dancers that do the peep shows, it's really a dump if you ask me but it pulls in some good money. Yeah, it's an easy takeover, I agree Loon, but the place do make money; me and Loon are definitely in place to take it over, no problem. There has to be some changes though AC. Like what Denna? Like painting the building, adding better security cameras, some that work and more outside lighting to make the customers feel safe, if we do that, it can make even more money. Last but most important, we will need more guards, to help keep the lot free of prostitutes and tricks.

Keiser will have to go, he's old and stuck in his ways, a definite problem, if he sticks around. Yeah, I almost smoked that fool a few times! So, is he the only mark? Man, it's an easy operation, aint really nobody else in the way, the dancers all check in with Denna and like her more than they do Keiser anyway. It's done then, old timer goes. Well, it goes without saying, Vinny and Bobby has to go, the Delgato's are more powerful than we eventually thought, they control the drug trade in Sin City, Club Dolls, Angel's Escorts and Angelica's the bunny ranch. Me and Will met Sam and Smiley, two guys that are responsible for shipping several foreign girls in every month to man Vinny and Bobby's businesses. I have befriended Diego, head of the Drug cartel, he supplies the cocaine and weed to the five drug bosses in Sin City, who we found out was Fat Boy, Dupree, Rose, Paco, and Steel; these guys control the east side, west side, north and south. The biggest earner of them all Rose controls the strip; I have yet had a chance to meet the lady they call Rose; we must make it our business to meet this lady before we take out Vinny and Bobby. I want all of you to keep your ears and eyes open for any opportunity.

So, when are we putting the two bosses to bed? Will, I'm looking at the week of Christmas; catch them off guard while they're in the Holiday spirit. Now that some gangster ass shit brother! What about that skirt? What skirt Loon? Sabrina Nigga! Nah, she's cool for now. Man; your ass in love bruh, don't get us fucked up over no pussy. Oh yeah AC, that's what I had to tell you, one of the girls at the club told me that Sabrina use to date Steel. Damn that bitch a groupie bro, I'm telling you. Duck be quiet, your ass would hit it too, if you we're in my shoes. Man, you damn right! That's enough about Sabrina already. Denna, call Hector, let him know I want to meet next week to discuss another job. OK poppy, consider it done. So, we have six marks total to make this thing work and has to be a total success, first two will be Vinny and Bobby, the other four, we will hit that same day, soon after we take the bosses out. We have to act fast before they find out about Vin and Bobby though, that's the only way we can pull it off, that's it guys, and does anybody have something they want to add? No, I'm cool bruh, let's get this thing poppin. Yeah I'm with Loon, let's roll some heads. Oh, we know you're ready Will with your crazy ass, I feel sorry for those fools. Manny, you have something you want to say, you've been quiet the whole time. Bro., I'm just ready to get this cheese, you dig! Yeah poppy, that's what I'm talking about, I say we toast to that! Denna stands and holds her glass up high while holding a cigar in the other hand; the crew rise to their feet, AC speaks. Here's to the cheddar and the crew that's about to run this bitch! Hell yeah! Manny then says. Death before Dishonor! The entire crew repeats. Death before Dishonor! They all drink up. This meeting is now adjourn guys, Denna don't forget to call Hector tonight. I want poppy! The crew exited the room, each with cigar in hand as they made way across the Towers lobby and out into the warm Sin City night.

CHAPTER 19, NOVEMBER.

Good Morning, Las Vegas! This is your AM Jock, Shy C, its 8am and a sunny 80 degrees in Sin City. I hope you guys are getting that Christmas shopping done, Thanksgiving is just around the corner and the Holiday season is here baby. It's also that time of the year when we come together to help out the less fortunate and make sure they have a happy holiday also, we are accepting can goods, clothes or personal items over at the Freemont Street shelter today. I will be broadcasting live from the shelter at 12noon, so come by on your lunch break, donate what you can, I look forward to seeing you there, here's some holiday music to brighten up your day. "Happy Holidays… Happy Holidays… Happy Holidays to you…" "We wish you a happy holiday". Ring-Ring-Ring-Ring. AC turns over in the bed and pulls the covers over his head. Ring-Ring-Ring. Daddy; get the phone!

Ring-Ring. I'm sleeping! Fuck that phone, you get it! Ring-Ring. Damn! Hello! Hey, can I speak to AC! Daddy, it's for you. Sabrina throws the cordless phone at him, it lands on the pillow. Yeah, who's this? Homes get your ass up! Who's this? This Hector homes, get up fool. AC turns over and sits up in the bed. Hey, what's crackin bro.? What time we meeting today homes, I have some other shit I need to take care of, I need to know when and where you want to meet. Doesn't matter, what time did you want to meet up bro.? Hey, if we can do like 11am, that will be cool homes. Alright, let's meet at the Golden Nugget at 11, I have to take something over to the Freemont shelter anyway. Cool homes, what your ass taking to the shelter, I know your gangster ass aint got no heart! Brother, I will always have love for the kid's man; after all, they're our future. Ha-ha-ha. Yeah, what the fuck ever, see you at 11 man. Alright bro., later.

Here, put that back on the charger! Sabrina replaces the phone. Who was that daddy, where are you going at 11 o'clock? Girl you better mind your business, stay out of mine. He rolls back over and goes back to sleep. Thump! Sabrina hits him in the head with a pillow. Hey, stop that shit girl! No, get up! I'm hungry, want you go make us some breakfast. OK, if you promise to get up! Yeah, I have to be awake to eat, don't I? Thump! She thumps him in the head. You don't have to be a smart ass! Ha-ha-ha. I'm sorry baby. That shit aint funny AC! She gets up and pulls the covers off of him. Stop playing Sabrina! Now get your naked ass up! He-he-he. She laughs and runs in the kitchen. He picks the covers up off the floor and jumps back in bed, A few minutes had pass. Daddy, do you want toast and Orange Juice with your breakfast? Yeah babe! OK, it's almost done, you want grape or apple jelly? Grape! OK, it's ready, be there in a second. AC sits up in bed and prepares himself to eat breakfast.

Sabrina walks in the room with a large trey. What the fuck, baby, I know good and damn well your ass didn't fix me no fucking frosty flakes and toast with Oj for breakfast, girl you got to be kidding! Why you say that daddy, what, you don't like frosty flakes? Aint this a bitch, are you serious? Look motherfucker, I can put yours in the trash if you don't want it, don't be acting like you brand new! When did I ever fix you cereal for breakfast? Awwww, poor baby wanted some eggs and bacon huh? She sits the trey down on the bed, picks up her bowl of cereal and starts eating. Ummmm, mmmm. This is so good daddy; go ahead try it, there Greeeeaaaaattttttt! Ha-ha-ha. Fuck you Brina that shit aint funny! Ha-ha-ha-ha. She burst out laughing. Girl, you're a damn trip! She leans over and gives him a kiss on the cheek. Muah! Come on daddy, eat up, it's 9:45; you have to leave in a few. He shakes his head and smirks at her as he started to eat his frosty flakes. See, aren't they great baby? He continues to eat as he looked up at her with empathy.

Ummm. That was good, it's time for you to get up, get ready for your meeting daddy. Yeah, yeah, I'm getting up. He walks over to the dresser, pulls out some clean underwear, T-shirt and socks. Baby, hand me my Fila sweat suit off the chair please. He sits on the edge of the bed to put on his socks, underwear and T-shirt, Sabrina hands him the blue sweat suit off the chair. Thanks baby! He slips it on then goes over to the walk in closet to get his all white Fila's with the red and blue stripe. Damn daddy, you sure are looking sexy in that sweat suit with the fresh baldy too! Ummm, mmmm! AC goes to the bathroom to brush his teeth and freshen up before he leaves. Hey babe, call downstairs and have them pull up the Harley. OK! Ring-Ring. Hello, Towers front desk! Yes, Mr. Cooper wants you to pull up the Harley. Sure, what time will he be leaving? Oh, in the next 10 minutes. Alright Mam, we will have it waiting. Thank you! You're welcome. He walks out of the restroom. Your all set daddy, I just called. Muah! He gives her a kiss. Thank you baby. Yep! So how long are you going to be? Ahhh, maybe a few hours. Well I have to go home and handle some business for my Mom; I guess we will catch up later then. Cool, that's fine, just don't forget to lock up when you leave. No worries daddy, I got you. OK then, see you later baby. Bye daddy. He walks out the door and catches the elevator down to the lobby.

Good Morning, Mr. Cooper, your Harley is ready for takeoff. Cool, thanks man. Sure no problem. AC mounts the hog and heads North down the strip a few miles to Freemont street. As he cruised away from the big casinos towards old Las Vegas, hotels turned into business offices, pawn shops and government buildings. On this end of the boulevard the fantasy begin to look similar to any average American city, 9 to 5 workers wait at every other cross section in route to a frequent destination during their daily lunch breaks. Just over the horizon, among the court house and county jail, you could see the white and gold historic building known as the Golden Nugget and its seasoned counter parts that created the Freemont street experience, which included the famous 4 Queens another Las Vegas landmark. The light had just turn red as he approached the intersection, while sitting there he could see Hector exiting a white 62 Impala parked in front of the Golden Nugget. Vroom-Vroom. He took off through the green light, pulled up behind the impala, parked the Harley and entered the Hotel. Loud sounds of coins dropping and slot machines chiming filled the Smokey casino air, a sea of senior citizens made it look like bingo night at an old folk's home. Just pass the black jack tables and four rows of slot machines he could see Hector sitting in the sports book.

AC cut through an isle of slot machines to bypass the busy senior citizens that had seemed to take over the Golden Nugget, he finally made it over to the sports book where Hector was waiting. Homes, it's about time, where you been? What's up Hector! Shit, everything homes, sit down, have a beer. Yo lady, can you get my friend a beer? Sure, what are you having Sir? A bud is cool. OK, coming right up. So what's the job homes; I'm ready to make some more paper g! Remember when I told you we had to knock off some major players so we can be in place. Yeah, a little. Anyway, here's the job, do you know of the Delgato's? Oh yeah, the two brothers that run Dolls. Yeah, those two. What about them? Those are the marks. Damn, those fools are mafia AC, you sure you ready to take that kind of heat?

The waitress had made her way back over to their table. Excuse me sir, here's your beer. Oh, thanks darling. You're welcome. Like I was about to say, man with my crew and yours combined we can take anybody out. Fuck yeah homes, that's a no brainer, I just wanted to make sure you were ready for all the bloodshed; it's going to be war amigo! My friend, the way I have this shit planned, aint gone be no war, all I need for you to do is knock these two fools off and we will handle the rest. Alright, I got you homes, when you need it done? I want it done the week of Christmas. Damn, that's cold homes; do you want us to hit them at the club or what? No, no, man, it has to look like an accident, not a hit, you dig. Yeah, we can do that, where and when? Well, they go on a bank run like twice a week, I was thinking you guys can wait up the road from the club, follow them and make it happen when they are on the way to the bank or leaving it. I don't care which, just make it happen and remember to wear mask. Shit, that's a piece of cake homes, I already know how we're going to pull it off too. Cool, let's make it happen then. You got it amigo!

They look at each other and give a head nod, raise their beers to a toast then drink up. So what's our take on this job homes? 50 k for each head bro... AC, you the motherfucking man homes, we're going to do them fools up real nice for you bro... They both stand up. Hector, I'm counting on you bro.! Hector stands there shaking his head. I got you homes! Cool! AC puts his right hand on Hector's shoulder. Fuck it, let's do it on the 23rd, two days before Christmas. Shit, that's cool, aint gone be no Happy Holidays for them fools huh? For us, yeah, them fools, Hell nah! Ha-ha-ha. They both laugh. Alright homes, I got to run and handle this business. OK Hector, be safe, I will let you know if anything changes. Cool, later amigo. Hector daps him up, makes his way through the senior citizens and leaves the casino. AC leaves the Sports book; head across the casino pass the roulette wheels and craps tables to the cashier's cage.

Several patrons are standing in line cashing in their chips from today's winnings. Next in line please. AC walks up to the cage, reaches in his pocket and pulls out 10 crisp $100 bills. How are you today Mam? I'm fine Sir and yourself? Oh I'm fantastic, just enjoying the Holidays. That's great Sir, what can I do for you? I would like to get a cashier's check for $1,000.00. Sure, that will be $1,005.00, who would you like us to make it out to? Can you make it out to The Freemont Street Shelter? Whatever you want Sir, give me just a second. She takes his money and proceeds to print out the cashier's check. OK all done, here you are Sir, have a Happy Holiday, may God bless you! Thank you Mam, Happy Holidays to you too. Thank you young man. He takes the check, puts it in his back pocket and heads outside to his Harley, starts it and pulls off the casino lot heading towards Freemont Street. As he cruise pass the sheriff's department and gallery stores on Freemont, the scenery begin to change, everyday patrons and tourist turned into homeless people and desperate crack heads, searching for food, shelter or that next big fix. Half a mile down, on the left, he could see cars lined up, coming and leaving the shelter.

The radio station van was parked by a U haul truck, several volunteers, loaded clothes, can goods and any other donations that the community came to give. A station representative was sitting at the table under a tint collecting all monetary donations. Vroom-Vroom-Vroom. He pulled onto the lot, parked beside the van, got off the Harley and walked over to the tint. Good afternoon brother, Happy Holidays to you. Hey man, Happy Holidays to you too bruh, I got a check I want to donate. OK, we can take care of that for you. AC pulls the check from his back pocket and gives it to the gentlemen. Thank you Sir, if you wait sec, I will give you a receipt for your donation, alright all set; here's your receipt and may God bless you. Thanks. He takes the receipt, puts it in his pocket and goes back to the Harley. Vroom-Vroom-Vroom. He starts the hog and pulls off up Freemont; heading back towards Las Vegas Boulevard on his way to the Towers, lunch hour traffic had started to build up on the strip as he tried to make it back home. Two police officers were ahead at the light directing drivers to detour because of a bad accident on the corner of Flamingo and Las Vegas Boulevard; he rode his bike in between the immobile cars to get ahead of the slow traffic.

He approached the scene of the accident; a body was laying there on the sidewalk covered with a white sheet. A black 300 ZX, T - top, 1994 model, was over on the sidewalk leaking what looked like oil and gas, from the smashed up engine. The hood of the car was peeled back like an open top of a sardine can; the entire passenger side was smashed up against a 20 foot tall steel light pole, mounted on that corner. Blood was on the driver's side of i's cracked windshield, the driver's door was lying there in the street like it had been cut off its hinges. An officer walked over to him. Excuse me Sir, we can't let you enter this way, as you can see, this street is closed. Yes Sir, I do but I live just over there in the Towers, it's no other way for me to get home. Hold on Sir.

The officer walks over to another cop that was standing over by the Ambulance, AC could see them talking and looking in his direction, the officer walks back over to him. OK Sir, I spoke with my Sergeant, he said that you can go down the sidewalk on the other side to get home, just give me a second; I will yield traffic on the opposite side so you can cut across. Cool, thanks officer, I really appreciate it! No problem Sir, once I go stop traffic, just ride to the other side in the pedestrian crosswalk, you can get to your driveway off the sidewalk. Thanks Sir! Yep! The officer walks over to the other lane during a red light, yields traffic so that he could make it to the Towers. Vroom-Vroom. He cruises down the sidewalk over to the Towers then pulls up to the Valet. Hey Mr. Cooper, what's going on down at the light? Man, somebody hit the light pole, it looks like someone is dead too, that car is fucked up; they have a person in the back of the Ambulance too. Damn, I hate to see that. Yeah, me too man, did you want me to put the Harley up? Yeah, I'm in for the day brother, I'm going to fix me something to eat and watch some TV.

OK Sir, have a good evening, I will see you tomorrow. AC parks the hog, gets off, hands his helmet to the valet and goes up to his place.

The sun had just set over the City of Sin, the ladies of the night gathered on every other corner of the north end of the strip to start their shifts. Beep-Beep. Hey sexy, you need a ride? Yeah daddy! Come on then! She stood there on the corner, dressed in blue jeans, black boots and a three quarter long, black leather jacket and white T-shirt. Wait a minute! What's wrong? Come on baby! Are you a cop? No baby, I aint no damn cop! OK, I had to ask, a bitch aint trying to go to jail tonight, my rent is due! She opens the door of the F-150 and slides in the front seat. What's your name gorgeous? They call me Jaguar! Oh, is that the name your mother gave you? She looks at him, slings her long blonde hair to the side, pulls down the sun visor, takes some red lipstick from her purse, looks in the mirror and proceeds to put it on her skinny lips. No, it's the name I gave you, which should be enough! Hey, its cool baby, I was just trying to start a conversation. Yeah, whatever, how much are you trying to spin daddy?

Well, I was thinking something like $100. Shit, that's all! Yep! Hmmm. You can get some head, that's about it for that little bit of money! That's cool with me! What's your name daddy? Oh, they call me Duck. Duck, you had the nerve to ask me about my name and yours is Duck! Ha-ha-ha. Pull over up here daddy, let me see how fast I can make you quack! He pulls the truck over and parks by the curb behind several other cars on the street. Turn the car off, roll up your windows, put some music on too. She begins to rub between his legs. I hope you don't take forever to come daddy, that $100 aint gone last too long , so make it quick; oh yeah, there he is, get good and hard for momma baby. Duck's erection was full grown; Jaguar unzipped his pants and pulled it out. Let me know when you are about to cum daddy, OK. Yeah OK, I got you. Alright now, don't be holding out, you better tell me or I will spit that shit right in your lap. Damn, I said OK, come on, suck this dick baby. She puts her hair back in a ponytail, goes down under the steering wheel and places her cold skinny lips on his dick. Hmmmm. Yeah baby, that's it! Suck it for daddy baby! Oh yeah, suck it baby! Suck that dick! Jaguar stroked up and down with her cold mouth as he held the back of her head by her ponytail. Oh yeah, baby! Oh yeah, it feels so good! Yeah that's it, go slow baby, slow, yeah like that. Hmm, mmmm. That's it, right there baby, don't stop, its coming baby. She strokes slower and slower, Duck tenses up and grabs the steering wheel. She sucks slower and slower. Uhhhhh. Yeah baby, its coming! It's coming baby! Damn baby! Ummmmmmmm-Ummmmmmm-Ummmmmmm. She jumps up and catches it with a napkin. Oh, thank you baby, that just made my day, damn baby, you're good at what you do. Shit, I'm gone call you my head doctor; I need your motherfucking number!

Hold on player, no numbers, you can find me in the same spot whenever you need me; that is my office daddy, now pay up. Its right there baby, in the ash tray. Thank you daddy, come see me again, enjoy your night. Jaguar opens the door, exits the F-150 then scrolls down the boulevard to find another client to satisfy. Duck takes a moment to gather himself; places his dick back in his pants, zips up, starts the truck and heads up the strip to Charleston Boulevard then over to the I-15 exit. Ring-Ring-Ring. Yo, who this? Pree my nigga, this Duck, what's poppin? Duck, what's good fool? Yo, I need a dub sack of that sticky pimp. I got you playboy, fall through. Cool, where you at pimp? I'm at the Church playboy. Alright, be there in a few player! My nigga! After ten minutes he comes to the MLK boulevard exit, pulls off and heads down to the Church infested area.

Duck parks his F-150 in front of the church with the red fence; he picks up his mobile to call Dupree. Ring-Ring-Ring. Hello! Pree, I'm outside player, about to come in. Cool, come on playboy. He makes his way down the sidewalk to the back entrance; Deacon is standing there as usual. Nice to see you again Sir, Dupree is waiting for you in the first room to the left. Deac opens the door and shows him in. Ha-ha-ha-ha. Hell nah man that fool Ezel crazy as fuck! Dupree yells out, Duck walks in the room. Hey my nigga, come in, sit down, you want a brew? For sure pimp. He reaches in the cooler and throws Duck a can of beer. Thanks pimp! Ha-ha-ha. This my movie right here nigga! "See the weed be letting you know" "Evil lurks". That damn Smokey a fool too, oh here you go playboy.

Dupree sits a dub sack of chronic on the coffee table. Hell yeah nigga, let me smell this shit, see what's crackin. Duck opens the bag and takes a sniff. Ooooohhhh, Weeeee! Yeah, this it right here baby! He takes a knot of money from his pocket, peels off a twenty dollar bill and puts it on the table. I told you, I had you fool! Yeah, you keep that sticky boy! What you getting into tonight fool? Man, I'm about to go to the crib, hit this smoke, get some grub and catch some z's, A nigga got to work tomorrow, you dig. Work! Fool, where you working at? Oh I'm over at Angel's

Escorts man, doing a little security and driving for the girls when they book them gigs, you dig. Shhhhiiittttt. That's what's crackin right there my nigga, I might need to order me one of them bitches, what you think playboy? Hey, you get enough pussy already my nigga, aint no need to be paying no bitch! Ha-ha-ha. Yeah, sure you right pimp, sure you right, so you aint never pay one of them hoes man? They aint never offered you the ass on a discount?

Ha-ha-ha. Hell nah my nigga. Go ahead, you can tell me pimp, I'm yo nigga. I aint gone tell nobody. Nah player, I aint never did that. Shit, you better than me, I will pay for some ass, especially if that hoe fine too! Ha-ha-ha. Pree, you a fool playboy, check it though, I will holler at you later, thanks for the smoke my nigga. Yeah anytime playboy, be easy. Duck leaves the room and enters the hall way, Deacon is waiting by the door at the end of the hall. OK young man, you be safe out there in them streets now. Yeah, no doubt, Later Deac!

It's a busy Friday night over at dolls, the parking lot is packed and the line to enter is wrapped around the building. Pink and Blue neon lights from the Dolls marquee sign dance off the wind shields of parked cars and limos that packed the lot. OK people, listen up, we have two lines! This one here is general admission, which is $20 tonight and the other line over there by my man Big Will, is the VIP Line. The VIP line is $100 for guys and $150 for the ladies, so if you want VIP, you need to be over there. Several couples and a few guys leave the line and head over to VIP. Beep-Beep. A horn blows to clear the path, a stretch yellow Hummer enters the lot and parks in front of the VIP entrance.

The driver parks the Hummer, exits the vehicle, walks to the back and opens the door. Red high heel pumps on caramel muscle toned legs stepped down from the hummer. Her hour glass shape was hard to miss under her Red Louis Vuitton fitted dress; black shoulder length micro braids fell to her shoulders and perfectly complemented her hazel eyes and caramel skin tone. She carried, a large Red, Louis Vuitton purse, over her right shoulder as she scrolled effortlessly towards Will. Hello Mam, if you want to enter VIP there will be $150 fee and you will have to go to the end of the line. Excuse me! You must be new here! Sil! Sil! She yells out. Yes baby! Come over here. Sil left the general admission line to see what she wanted. Yes dear! Why is this gentleman trying to charge me to get in, you must not have told him who I was. She said calmly. I'm Sorry Rose, please accept my apologies. Will this gorgeous young lady is Rose. Hi Rose, sorry for the misunderstanding. It's not your fault sweetie; you were just doing your job. Will removes the velvet rope and let her pass. Thank you Sil. Muah! Oh and thank you too handsome. Muah! Your welcome Rose. She entered the club and disappeared amongst the hundreds of patrons, exotic dancers and the cigar smoked filled air. Flashing lights seem to fall in sync with the loud music as its beams danced from wall to wall and mirror to mirror.

All eyes fell on the entertainers of the moment as they captured the main stage and demanded your undivided attention. The Dj controlled every move as the loud music blasted through the speakers as patrons started to tap their feet or bob their heads to the beats per minute. Over 100 female entertainers roamed the floor on a quest to meet a nightly quota. $20 table dances and $300 VIP's topped the menu. Megan is on stage and No Doubt's, Don't Speak is blasting through the speakers. "You and me... We use to be together" " Everyday together... always" "I really feel... That I'm losing my best friend". Megan removes her top, then climbs to the top of the 10 foot brass pole, grips it with her thighs, falls back and spins counter clock wise down to the bottom, then roles off into a split. The patrons surrounding the stage; starts to cheer. Yeah Baby! Yeah go girl! They throw money onto the stage as she rolls over on her back then raise both legs in the air.

The Dj's loud voice comes through the speakers. Once again people, welcome to the hottest strip club in Vegas baby! We have the lovely Megan on stage right now showing her sexy ass, remember ladies and gentlemen, these entertainers work for tips and tips only, please, show them some love as well as the wait staff and bartenders. Rose makes her away across the club to the office. Knock-Knock-Knock. Yeah, come in! She enters the office. Hey baby! Hey Rose darling! Bobby was sitting at the desk while Vinny stood over by the security monitor adjusting the picture. She walks in and gives them both a big hug. Wow, you're looking gorgeous tonight Rose! Awww thanks Vinny! She takes the large red purse from her shoulder and pulls out a thick gold envelop and sits it on the desk in front of Bobby. Thanks darling, how's business on the strip? I don't think it could get any better than this honey! Good for you baby, good for you. It's a nice crowd in here tonight fellas. Yeah, it's the weekend, always pretty busy around the end of the week. Well, I'm headed to the bar to get fucked up, is my girl Deb working tonight? Nah, she requested off, AC is the head bartender tonight, just tell him to put your drinks on my tab. AC! Who the hell is that? Oh he's the new edition to the family, good guy, he knows how to get shit done! Know what I mean? Oh yeah, that's always an asset. Alright, later you two. Muah! She blows them a kiss and heads back into the busy club.

Alright people, get your money right, this is Dj Skillz on the tables, let's give a warm welcome to my girl Poison! The Fugee's; Ready or Not plays over the speakers. "Ready or not, Here I come, you can't hide" " Gonna find you and take it slowly" "Ready or not, Here I come, you can't hide". Rose makes her way through the smoke filled, crowded club and over to the bar. Hey, are you AC? Yes Mam, that's me, how can I help you? She yells over the loud music. Vinny told me to let you know, all my drinks will be on his tab! Oh yeah, is that right? Yes Sir, it is. Hey, whatever the boss says. Yep, that's what he said! Alright, what are you having Ms..., I'm sorry I didn't get your name gorgeous or should I call you Lady in red. Ha-ha-ha. She laughs. That works but I rather you call me by name. OK and what's that? I'm Rose! Really! Yes, why did you say it like that? Because it fits you perfectly. Why thank you AC. Your welcome, now what's it going to be Ms. Rose? Well what would you suggest Sir? What do you feel like, a martini, shot or some liquor? Hmmmm. How about a martini? Yeah, let's do that. Cool, what kind? How about, you surprise me?

He pulls out the shaker, adds some apple pucker, vodka, a dash of sprite and pours it in the shaker over ice. He puts a chilled martini glass on the bar, shakes the shaker then pours the contents in the martini glass and slides an orange slice on the rim. Here you go Ms. Rose! Wow, thank you AC! She picks up the martini and takes a sip. Wow! This is really good! Thank you Rose, I'm glad you like it. So Vin tells me you know how to get the job done. Well, let's just say, I've never had an unsatisfied customer. She takes another sip of her apple martini then puts it down on the bar. Ha-ha-ha. That's one way to say it. Why do you ask? Maybe I want to hire you one day. Oh really! Yes really! AC takes a napkin from the bar and writes his number on it. Well here you are Ms., just in case you ever need me. Thank you. She puts it in her red bag. Excuse me Sir! Excuse me! Another patron at the center of bar calls him. Enjoy your martini Rose; I have to go serve these customers. Oh sure, go ahead, thank you, I have your number, maybe I will be in contact. OK lady, have a good night. He heads down to the middle of the bar. Listen up people, it's last call baby, you got 5 minutes left on the bar, we are about to wind things down. I need all ladies to report to the Dj booth if you're not doing a table dance or VIP. People, be sure to check us out tomorrow for Porn Star Saturdays! Thank you guys for coming out and see you next time at Club Dolls. Have a good night!

A light rain falls over the city on this cool gloomy November evening. Several cars are in the drive way, a few are parked alongside the curb of this two story tan stone house, out in Summerlin. Thick green grass, perfectly trimmed and manicured covered the front yards landscape. The two car garage was opened while the guys stood there talking, smoking, drinking and shooting pool as Manny tended to the deep frying Turkey. Sounds of laughter came from the inside as Sophie, Denna, Sabrina and Nina gathered in the kitchen at the table over a bottle of red wine. Fresh baked sweet potatoes, Ham, Macaroni and Cheese, Apple pie, Collard greens, Corn bread and stuffing created the perfect aroma for this annual Holiday setting.

Loon taps Will on the shoulder with his pool cue. Yo Will, me and Duck against you and AC, for $100! Alright, I'm down! You down Coop? Yep, let's do it! Loon, you know you and Duck is about to get that ass whip, right! Yeah, whatever man, are we playing straight up or last pocket? Straight up nigga! What, you scared to play last pocket Will? Yo, just rack em up Loon! Hell no! Flip for it fool! Duck pulls out a nickel and flips it in the air. Loon calls it. Heads! It lands on the pool table. Tails! Yeah rack em fool, get ready for this ass whipping. Yeah OK Coop, we'll see who's going to be racking the next game. The house door opens. Hey Poppa! Yes Alex, what is it? Momma says, how long before the turkey is ready? Tell your Momma it want be long. OK! Hey come here, where's your manners, aren't you going to speak to your Uncles? The 13 year old and his friend walk down the three steps into the garage. Oh, hey Anthony, I didn't see you behind Alex, what's up little man? Hey Mr. Manny. Alex, the son of Manny was in his spitting image, only a foot or so shorter than his pop, the same brown skin tone, silky black hair and a devilish grin. His buddy Anthony was of Cuban decent from his father's side and half Italian from his mother's side, he was a frail kid, about the same height as Alex, also with black hair and brown skin tone but one could see the curiosity and evil in his dark brown eyes.

Anthony stands beside Manny as he's checking the turkey, Alex makes his way over to the guys at the pool table. Hey little man, what's up with you? Nothing much, Uncle AC, me and my home boy was just upstairs playing Madden. Who's your homey? Oh that's Anthony from up the street. OK. Hey Uncle Will. Alex, what's up buddy? He reaches out to shake his hand. Alex, how you been nephew? Good uncle Duck. Oh yeah, how's school, you getting good grades? Yeah, all A's and B's. That's cool little man, keep up the good work. Thanks Uncle Duck. Alex, your partner looks a little serious over there to be 13, what's his problem? Oh, he's cool Uncle Loon, that's my homie. Oh yeah, your homie huh, what's his name? It's Anthony, Uncle Loon. Yeah, I think we have to see what's up with your homie, his eyes tell a familiar story lil man. Awww Unc, don't start tripping! Oh shit! Watch out! Manny and Anthony both back away from the fryer as the grease starts to pop off the turkey. Manny looks over at the kid. You alright Tony? Yes Sir. Good, stand back some, this damn grease is hot, last thing we want is for someone to get hurt, how's your mother Mrs. Montana doing? Oh, she's fine Mr. Manny; my grandmother came up from Miami for Thanksgiving; so her, my aunts and some of my girl cousins are at the house getting dinner ready. OK that's good, tell her I said hello and to stop by sometime, me and Sophie would love for her to visit. OK, I will Sir. Alex calls Anthony over to the table. Hey homie, my Uncles want to meet you! Go ahead son, they want bite. Manny pats him on the back and sends him over to the pool table by the guys. Alex approaches Loon at the table.

What's poppin lil man? Nothing, just kicking it with my homie for a bit, before dinner's ready. That's cool, so what you and my nephew be doing at school and around the neighborhood? Yall don't be getting into no shit, do you, I bet you fools got a few chica's huh? Ha-ha-ha-ha. The two boys start to giggle; Will turns away from the pool table and looks at the two of them. Yeah, you two are sneaky; I can see it in both your eyes. What do you guys want to be when you grow up? Hell, yall start High school next year, right? Yes Sir. They both say at the same time. Well, what's your plans, College, Military what? Man, me and Tony are going to be some gangster's, we taking over Las Vegas by the time we're 18 Unc! Ha-ha-ha-ha. All the fellas start laughing, including Manny. Damn, you two are going to be trouble already, I can see it! Why do you say that Uncle AC? Shit, because I know who your daddy is! The guys all look at AC with a serious look, then they all turn to the boys, stare at them for a second, Loon and Will both give the two young men a wink, then a head nod. OK back upstairs you two, tell your Mom the turkey will be ready in a second. The youngsters walk up the three steps and back into the house.

Duck, hand me that pan, would you sir? Alright, I got you brother, hold tight. He walks over to the folding table that was against the wall and picked up the large wash pan. Here you go man. Thanks Duck. Manny lifts the turkey out of the deep fryer. Shit! Hey Loon, grab that rack off the table and sit it over this pan. Loon runs to the table to get the rack, Duck puts the pot on the small table beside the fryer; Loon places the rack over the pan. Alright, now we're ready. Manny lifts the Turkey out of the hot grease with the hooks and places it on the rack so that the grease would drain off before he took it inside. Damn, that looks good as hell bro.! AC, you know my deep fried turkeys be on point man. Yeah, you right bro., you be hooking it up. They wait a few minutes then take the turkey inside, Will opens the door and Manny follows. Hmmmmm. Yeah poppy; look at that beautiful turkey! Oh Nina, you're ready to dig in, huh sis? Hell yeah Sophie! Everything else is all ready to go!

Loon, Duck and AC come in behind Will and Manny, the ladies begin to sit all the food on the counter top as Manny placed the turkey in the center of table so he could carve it. Sophie placed the silverware and plates at the end of the counter so everyone could fix their plates. Nina lined up the glasses and started filling them with a few cubes of ice and some sweet tea. The turkey was now sliced and ready to eat. OK everyone; come gather around so we can bless the food. They all came in the kitchen, formed a circle and held hands. Bye everyone! Bye Anthony! He walked out the door and headed home to join his family. Now let's bow our heads. Manny begins to say grace. Father, forgive us of our sins, both knowingly and unknowingly, we ask that you bless everyone here today as well as those that couldn't make it. We thank you for the food we are about to receive and bless those that prepared this wonderful meal Father, in the name of Jesus we pray and thank you for all things. Amen!

CHAPTER 20, DECEMBER.

Hello Las Vegas, this is Katie Strong with your TV news at 11, I'm on the scene today over at a new housing development just off of the interstate in route to Utah. Contractors have been building new homes in this area for the past several months due to the cities rapid growth. You can see, right here behind me, LVMPD has this one home yellow taped off today, two workers found what looked like clothing sticking out of the cement of the homes foundation. The two gentlemen informed their supervisor; he looked into the matter a little further and found out that the clothes were actually on a male body. Crime Scene Investigators are here now digging the body out of the concrete. I had a chance to speak with newly appointed Chief of Police; Mr. Espinoza, about this incident earlier and this is what he had to say.

Hello Katie, I have my best people on this case and I intend to get to the bottom of it, first we must identify the victim so that we can learn more about him and what lead to this senseless crime. I want the citizens of Las Vegas to rest assure that me and my people will handle this matter, as the new Chief of Police I intend to put an end to senseless crimes in our city and put the criminals responsible to Justice! Well Las Vegas, you've just heard from our newly appointed Chief of Police; Mr. Espinoza and his promise to clean up Sin City. I would just to like to say, Chief good luck with your crusade, you have a lot of work to do and we are with you all the way. Once again, this is Katie Strong with your news at 11, see you tomorrow Las Vegas. Coop is sitting on his couch at home, watching everything unfold on TV.

Ring-Ring-Ring. Hello! Will! Yeah, what's up AC? Are you watching the news? Yeah, I just saw it. So, what the fuck was that? Relax bro., that wasn't our guy. Are you sure? Man, I buried that fool myself! I hope your right man, if not; we've got problems my nigga. How deep did you burry him Will? At least four feet. What! That's it? Four feet! Man, you know six feet is the mandatory nigga! Who went with you that night? I think Loon was with me. Alright, when the pigs clear out, you two need to ride out there and make sure that wasn't one of our packages. You do remember which house you used right? Yeah bro., I aint no amateur, just relax, me and Loon will go later tonight to check things out. Good, we don't need anything fucking this gig up; we're this close to pulling it off. I got you bro., later, be easy. Alright man, later.

Ring-Ring-Ring. Hello! Hey Sophie, how are you, can I speak with Manny, this is AC. Oh hi Cooper, I'm fine, hold on. Manny, telephone! OK, I'm coming, who is it? It's Cooper! OK, I'll get it in the room baby. Hey bro., what's crackin? Tell me you seen the news Capo! Yeah, I caught the end, about your boy making police chief. That wasn't the worst part. Shit, what can be worse than that! Man, they found a body out in one of those new homes, off the interstate; you know the ones you pass on the way to Utah! Fuck, are you serious? Yep! Damn, did you call Will? Yep, just hung up from him. Well, what did he say? He said that it wasn't our guy; he and Loon are going to double check later tonight after the pigs are gone. Cool, I sure hope he's right bro.; we don't need that heat right now. You aint never lied about that shit! OK man, I will holler at your ass later, when I get to work. OK Capo! Later!

AC hangs up the phone then makes another call. Ring-Ring-Ring. Yo, what's up, who this? Loon this is AC. Oh, hey bro.; I already know man, I seen the news and Will just called me too. OK, make sure yall handle that, ASAP bro.! We got you bro.! Poppy! Poppy! Come over here; give me some more of that chocolate. What the fuck? Loon! Loon! Yeah bro.! Was that Denna I heard in the back ground? Who? You heard me bro.! Ha-ha-ha-ha. You tripping AC! Is that AC; hi poppy! Girl shut up! Loon, you aint shit bro.! Coop, chill man, it's all good, we cool. OK, just don't let it fuck up our business. Dawg; me and Denna have an understanding. Yeah, that's the kind of shit I'm talking about, right there, you know Denna is not like them bitches you be doggin in the street bro., she will straight do your ass and you know it! Loon whispers to AC in a really low voice. I know bro., but that pussy is so damn good though. Ha-ha-ha. You crazy nigga, don't get your ass shot fool. Ha-ha-ha. I want! Bye man, tell her I said what's up.

OK bro., oh, don't tell the rest of the crew yet. Man, that's yall business, I aint in it, later fool! AC hangs up the phone, turns the channel on the TV, then his phone rings again.

Ring-Ring. Hello! Hey AC, what's going on Sir? I'm good, who's this? This is Bobby! Hey Bobby, what's up man? I need a favor. OK, what is it? Do you remember Sam and Smiley? Yeah, the two cats that recruit the girls. Yeah, those two. What about them? They are flying in at 6pm today with three young ladies from Germany; I need for you to take the club Limo, pick them up and drop them off at the Mansion in Summerlin. No problem, I can do that, where's the Mansion? The Limo driver knows; just tell him you are going to the one in Summerlin. Cool, what about Sam and Smiley? They have to catch a connecting flight to Bangkok. Alright, I will stop by the club around five then to get the Limo. No, you don't have to do that man, I will send him over to your place, and you can go from there. OK, that will work. Cool, later brother and thanks for doing this. No problem Bobby, I will talk to you later. Click! They hang up.

It's a busy evening over at the adult video store, several customers, line up at the counter to check out. Keiser is there all by himself, because Loon and Denna took the day off to go up to Lake Tahoe. Next in line please! A young lady walks up. How are you today Mam, did you find everything OK? I'm fine and yes I did Sir. That's good; your total is $7.95. Here you are. She hands him a $10 dollar bill. Thank you, here you go, $2.05 is your change. Next in line please! The store phone rings. Ring-Ring. Hello, thanks for calling the adult store, can you please hold? Yes. Thank you! Next in line please! Hi Sir, did you find everything OK? Yes Sir; sure did. Let's see, what do you have there? Oh, I just have these two movies. Alright, your total will be $16.87. Here, you can charge it to my Master Card. Alright, no problem. He swipes the card and bags the movies. Here's your receipt. Thank you Sir, come back and see us. Next in line please!

The customer walks up. Did you find everything OK Sir? Click! The customer cocks his revolver. You know what it is old man! Hey, hold on man, I don't want any problems! Shut the fuck up old fool, give me the cash! POW! He shoots the 357 at the wall. Hurry the fuck up! The next time, I swear I want miss! Hurry up! Give it up! The store was empty; Keiser was there helpless with no protection at all. You got 1 minute fool, empty that damn register! Ding! He opens the drawer and pulls out all the cash. Here you go Sir, I don't want any trouble! Put that shit in a bag old man! Keiser gets a white plastic bag and stuffs the money inside. Here you go man! I know you have some more cash in this motherfucker! No, I swear that's all there is! POW! POW! POW! He shoots Keiser twice in the chest then once in the shoulder, his limp body falls to the floor as the blood gushed from his chest at an alarming rate. The thief dropped the duck taped handle chromed 357 to the floor and ran out of the store.

Beep-Beep. Two cars pulling in the parking lot blow their horns at the thief as he ran in front of them crossing the lot, the patron's park and enter the store looking puzzled from what just happened. Oh my God! One of the customers screamed once they seen ol timer on the floor bleeding. Call 911! The other patron picks up the store phone and calls the police. Ring-Ring. 911, what's your emergency? There's a man shot over here at the adult video store on Las Vegas Boulevard and Charleston. OK, calm down Mam, is the man breathing? No Mam, I don't think so. Alright, can you tell me where the gunshot wounds are? There two in his chest and one in his right shoulder. Is he still bleeding? Yes Mam and there's a lot of blood on the floor. OK thank you Mam, we have an emergency squad on the way. I can hear the sirens coming now. Great, thank you for calling Mam, the medics will handle it from here. The sirens get louder as the medics pull up outside.

Two police officers along with three medics walk in to tend to Keiser. Mam, could you please move away from the gentlemen! The officer said to the patron who was kneeling down beside the victim. The medics move in to check for a pulse, one of them kneeled down beside Keiser, check his neck and wrist for any signs of life. Nope, there's not a pulse officers, the body is still warm, time of death looks to be 20 to 30 minutes ago from gunshot wounds to the heart and chest cavity. The officer went over to speak with the two patrons. Excuse me Mam, can you tell me exactly what you saw when you pulled up? Well, a white gentleman was running across the lot dressed in all black with a red ball cap on. How tall would you say he was? If I had to guest, I would say around 5'7". Was he a heavy guy or more on the skinny side? He was definitely a skinny guy; he looked like one of those crack heads. About how old would you say he was? Hmm. Maybe mid 30's! Alright, thanks a lot Mam, you've been a big help. The second officer takes a walk around the store to see if anyone else was in the building. The two medics lift Keiser's body up onto the roll bed, cover him with a white sheet and wheel him out to the ambulance. A detective car pulls up outside as they were putting the body in the back of the ambulance, two black females step out of the unmarked vehicle and walk inside.

Hi detectives! Officers, what's going on here? We have a murder victim. So where's the victim? Oh, he's in the ambulance already. What! How are you going to move the body before we investigate the crime scene, are you fucking kidding me today! You two must be new! One of the lady detectives pulls her radio from her belt. Dispatch this is Detective Casey. Go ahead Casey! We are over at the crime scene of that adult video store murder, the officers moved the body before we got here; the scene is now compromised. OK Casey, I will notify Chief Espinoza, what's the badge numbers of the two officers? Hold on, I will get them; officers, could you both come here for a minute? The officers walk over to the Detective. Dispatch! Yes, I'm here Casey, go ahead. The numbers are 779 and 832. Thanks Detective, we will forward this information over to the Chief. Roger that, over and out! Officers, is there anyone else in the building? No, there wasn't Detective. Did you guys check the dressing area where the dancers work? No we didn't.

Damn rookies, I swear! She pulls out her gun and head to the back. Briggs, I will be right back, keep an eye on these two please. Casey, I'm not babysitting no damn rookies! Fuck em then! Casey proceeded to the back to search the dressing room; she entered the red lit doorway behind the counter then opened the black door that was to her right. No one was in the room but a cigarette was still lit and had burned halfway, sitting there in an ashtray; Casey picked up her radio. Briggs comes in! Yeah Casey, go ahead! Someone was here at the time of the shooting, I found a lit cigarette in the ashtray, I'm going to check the emergency exit and see if I get lucky. Did you find any clues up front? Yeah, I have the 357 but it has a taped handle, this looks like a hit partner. Hmmm. Do you think it's an inside job? I don't know Casey, too early to tell. Roger that partner, I'm headed out the exit now. OK, over and out.

Buzz-Buzz. The alarm sounded when she pushed open the emergency exit, outside by the door was a blue dumpster that hadn't been emptied in what look like weeks. The odor was strong and disgusting to say the least; a small alley way ran behind the building alongside an 8 foot tall fence that led down to the street. Casey searched inside, behind and around the dumpster for clues but to no avail, she moved further down the alley to look for clues and came across one clear 6 inch stiletto, A size 9 for a left foot. She stops, pulls out her camera and take several pictures of the shoe as well as the surrounding area, after taking the pictures, she puts away her camera and slides on a pair of latex gloves. Casey picks up the shoe and head inside to show Briggs, as she returned to the scene of the shooting, she could see her partner bagging the 357. Hey Briggs! What's up Casey? I found a shoe out back in the alley; I think we may have had a witness to the murder. Yeah, looks like one of the girls either seen or heard the shots and ran out back down the alley to get away. Let me have two of those evidence baggies, so I can bag this shoe and that cigarette for some DNA. Here you go partner, I'm done here, I will be at the car. OK, I will be out in a minute, go ahead and call some more investigators to canvas the area surrounding this building to see if anyone seen our witness or the suspect. Alright partner, I'm on it.

Briggs head outside to place the evidence in the trunk then picks up her radio. Dispatch, this is Briggs, come in please. Go ahead Briggs! Can you send a team over to canvas the area for possible witnesses? Roger that Briggs, sending the call out to patrols in the area as we speak. Thanks dispatch. You got it Briggs, over and out. Casey exits the building with her evidence, walks over to the trunk of the vehicle and places it beside the other evidence. Are you ready to leave this joint partner? Not yet, we have to notify the owner so they can close up or whatever their going to do. Dispatch, this is Briggs again! Go ahead Briggs! We need to locate the owners of this place so they can come lock up! Hold tight Briggs, running a property check now. Alright got it, looks like a Bobby Delgato; hold on while we call. Roger that!

Ring-Ring. Hello, this is Bobby! Hi Mr. Delgato, this LVMPD. Yeah, how can I help you? We have you listed as first contact for the property on Las Vegas Boulevard and Charleston, the adult movie store. Yeah, what about it? Well, there was a shooting there earlier today, the detectives are there now and need someone to come take over the property. The clerk that was working earlier has been shot and didn't survive. What! Are you fucking serious right now! Calm down Mr. Delgato, I know it's hard to loose someone you're close to but we need you out at the property so the detectives can continue their investigation. Fuck! I don't believe this! I'm on the way! Click! He slams down the phone. Briggs you there? Yeah dispatch! Mr. Delgato is on the way! Thanks dispatch! No problem Briggs, over and out! Roger that dispatch.

Back at the Towers, AC's upstairs, putting on his two piece black suit, white shirt, blue tie and black Stacy Adams when his phone rings. Ring-Ring. Yeah this is AC, whose speaking? Yo bro., your ride is here! Thanks Manny, coming down in a few. Alright bro.! He walks over to his dresser, picks up the Cool Water cologne, splashes some on, grabs his keys and head downstairs to the limo. Manny is standing in the middle of the lobby when he exits the elevator. Oh shit, look at my boy! What's up fool, you GQ today huh? Hey, I have to make a good first impression on these new girls. Yeah, you better be careful, you know Sabrina works at that club too! Manny, shut up fool, I aint worried about that shit. Yo, I look good though right! Yeah, you clean brother, you clean. Alright Capo, let me go handle this business.

He walks outside to the club Limo; the driver was leaning against the back door smoking a cigarette when AC came out. Hi Mr. Cooper, looking sharp this evening Sir. Thanks man. The driver opens the back door, let's him, gets into his driver's seat and starts the limo. Are you ready to go Sir? Yep, let's do it. OK! He pulls off the Towers lot and heads South up the strip towards the airport. Knock-Knock. AC taps on the driver's window. Turn on the radio man. No problem Sir. He turns on the CD player, 2pac's; Run the streetz is playing. "You can run the streetz with your thugs" "I'll be waitin for you... Until you get through... I'll be waitin". See my man, that's what I'm talking about, now this is some good music. He starts to sing along. "Now peep it... Here go the secret on how to keep a playa" "Some love makin and home cookin... I'll see ya later". Yo bro., step on it, we don't have much time. We will be there in just 5 more minutes Sir.

You can make it in 2! Speed this thing up! The driver steps on the gas and speeds pass the slower traffic, cutting in and out of the lanes down the busy highway. He swings a right off Tropicana and pulls into the Airport terminal lane for arriving flights. Hey man, slow down at baggage claim B gate. The driver slows up and pulls over in front of baggage claim sliding doors. Cool, park right here. AC jumps out of the Limo and head inside to meet Sam, Smiley and the ladies. The airport is swarming with people coming and going for the Holidays, all the baggage carousels are surrounded by travelers, everyone stood there impatiently after their long flights waiting for their luggage to appear on the belt. Bleep! Bleep! A red siren flashes and sounds to alarm everyone that the bags were being loaded. AC approaches the impatient crowd to search for Smiley and Sam, but they are nowhere in sight, he walks over by the escalator to see if he could spot them coming down from their gate.

Hey, AC my friend! My friend! AC! He hears his name, turns around and there was Sam and Smiley standing over by the service desk with three tall beautiful blondes. Smiley! Sam! Fellas, I was looking all over for you! Yeah, we had to come get these bags from customer service, we caught a later flight and the ladies bags came on our original flight which landed 30 minutes before we did. OK cool, so what time are you guys headed to Thailand? Man, we have like an hour and a half before we take off, never mind that my friend we are fine. Sam waves to the three blondes for them to come over. Come here ladies; meet our American friend, AC. The ladies walked over to Sam and AC. My friend, this is Ilona, Rhonda and Vicky from Germany. Hi ladies, how did you guys enjoy your flight? Oh was very long! Ha-ha-ha. I bet it was Ilona; your English is pretty good, where did you learn to speak? I was exchange student in U.S.A for one year. Are you guys sisters; I see you all are dressed alike; I can't help but to see the resemblance. Ha-ha-ha. No we're not; we all just wore blue jeans, black top and black shoes, because it was more comfortable to travel. I see and you are Rhonda right? Yes that is right. Well, are you ladies ready to go? Yeah, very ready, I'm ready for some food. You hungry Vicky? Yes, I want an American burger and some beer. Ha-ha-ha. OK, let's get you guy's bags loaded in the Limo and we can go get something to eat. Hold on my friend, we will help you with the bags. Smiley said to Coop. Cool, the Limo is just right outside this door.

AC, Sam and Smiley pick up the bags and head outside to the limo, the driver see them coming, pops the trunk then runs to help with the bags. Hey, we got the bags man, go ahead and get the ladies in the limo. Yes Sir! The driver meets the girls at the curb. Here you go my friend, this is last one. Thanks Smiley! AC puts the last of the luggage in the trunk, closes it and walks over to Sam and Smiley. Thanks for the help guys; you better head back to your gate before it's too late. Well my friend, we will see you next month with some more girls, have a Happy

Holiday. Hey thanks bro., same to you. AC and the guys shake hands before they enter the airport and head back to their gate.

   The driver is standing there with the door open waiting for him, he walks to the limo. Hey my man, stop by In and Out before we head to Summerlin, so I can get these ladies some burgers. Yes Sir, as you wish. AC joins the women in the back of the limo; the driver walks around back to make sure that the trunk was closed then proceed to the driver's seat.

   Ring-Ring. Damn, whose this calling me now? He answers his mobile. Hello! Hey daddy! Hey Brina, what's up baby? Did you hear the news? No, what news? Bobby got a call from the cops earlier. Oh yeah, about what? Somebody robbed the video store and killed the old man. What the fuck! Yep! Where was Loon and Denna? I don't know, the cops say he was the only employee there. Damn, that's fucked up! Let me call you back baby! He hangs up his phone then calls Loon. Ring-Ring. Yo, who this! Loon! Yo, what up Coop? Did you hear about Keiser? No, what about him, is he tripping again? No fool, someone robbed the store today and killed him! Damn, he had that shit coming though AC. Whatever fool; where your ass at? I'm in Lake Tahoe. Tahoe! With who Denna? Yep! Man, when yall coming back, you fools need to be at that store tomorrow. Yeah, we will partner, don't worry. Alright nigga, tell Denna I said what's up. OK bro., later. Knock-Knock. AC taps on the driver's window. Hey, change of plans bro.; go straight to the Mansion, some important business just came up. As you wish Sir. Ladies we're going straight to the Mansion where you will be living, the house mom will make sure you have everything you need to make you guys feel comfortable as possible. I promise I will take all of you out for burgers and beer one night after work. So, you're not staying at the house with us? No, I wish I was! He smiles at Ilona. That would be nice, want it! Awww, you promise you will make up? I promise Ilona. The driver roles up his divider window, makes a u turn and heads towards the mansion to drop off the ladies.

   Bobby just arrived at the video store and sees the officers there at the scene of the crime. Hello Sir, are you Mr. Delgato? Yes Mam! Hi Sir, I'm Detective Casey and this is my partner Briggs. She reaches out and shakes his hand. So my friend is dead? Yes, I'm afraid so Sir. Damn, what happened, did you catch the person responsible? It looks to be an armed robbery but we still have some things we need to check out first before we make our final decision, we do have a lead on a suspect that we are currently working. Bobby and the detectives walk inside the building, Bobby sees the bloody mess over by the counter. Do you have any more questions for us Sir? No, just call me when you find out something. Yes Sir, I will call you myself. Thanks Casey, I appreciate that. We noticed a camera above the door but we didn't see a recorder, do you know where the VCR is? Oh, that thing doesn't work, it stopped years ago. Really, that's not good. I've been meaning to change it. You might want to do that, it would have helped us out tremendously, anyway Mr. Delgato, we're going to head back to the precinct and follow up on these leads. Once again, sorry for your lost, here's my card if you need to call me. OK, thanks guys.

   The Detectives leave the premises and head to the station; he pulls his phone out to call his Vinny. Ring-Ring. Hello! Vinny! What's up bro.! Is it bad? Yeah, they killed him. Damn! You need me to do anything? Yeah, send Sil and a crew over to clean up this blood and shit so we can open tomorrow, I'm going to lock up and go grab a drink or two over at Dante's to calm my nerves. OK brother, I will take care of it. Thanks, I will call you later Vin. Click! Bobby hangs up the phone then locks the front door; he goes to the back to check the dressing room and private booth area. The emergency door alarm is still sounding, he takes his key and turns the lock to the left to secure the door and silence the alarm. No one was in the dressing room or peep show booths, Bobby turned off the lights and double checked the door to make sure it was locked. After clearing the back, he went up front to close out the register and get things ready for the next day; he finished at the register, turned off the lights and put the closed sign in the window. To him it felt strange, he had just lost a longtime friend and employee, the store hasn't been closed since they opened several years ago, it was always 24 hours of business in and out the doors nonstop, which was easy to do in the city that never slept. It was no doubt that tonight would be a hard pill to swallow for this mobster. As the night fell over the city, the neon lights again illuminated the skyline, the taillights of his car blended in with the busy traffic as he drove up the strip.

Man, it feels good out here today. Hell yeah Coop, this is that football weather. It's a warm 72 degree December day over at the Towers, Will and AC are upstairs, sitting outside on his balcony, smoking on a blunt and watching the tourist and locals on the strip below. So will that thing with Keiser effect our operation and the hit we got planned next week? No, it actually made things easier for us. Oh yeah, why you say that? Shit, that's less people we have to knock off next week. I dig it. Are you really ready for this brother? Hell yeah, I've been waiting for this a long time. Yeah, me too nigga, you know we can't play no games with these fools when we take over. Will, you know I aint cutting no corners nigga, we knocking off any motherfuckers that wasn't down with us from the start. That's what I'm talking about brother! He gives AC a pound. I want you to run Dolls, I'm putting Duck over the whore house, Nina can run Angels, Denna and Loon are going to keep the Video store for now. That's cool, what about Manny? Oh, that fool is going to be Capo. Yeah, he's going to like that, did you tell him already? Yep, we spoke on it a few days ago. That's what's up. Man, this weed is making me hungry as hell, what you got to eat in this bitch? Ha-ha-ha. AC laughs. It's some ham and cheese in the fridge. Hell yeah, I'm about to make me two of them fuckers, you want one bro.? Yeah, let me get one too.

Will gets up, goes inside to make the sandwiches, AC leans over the rail of the balcony, looks down and takes a pull off the blunt. Hey Will, turn on the radio dog! Alright man, I got you! Play that Outkast Cd bro., it's in the deck number 3, play track 6, that Elevators. Will turns on the CD player, selects number 3 then track 6. "One for the money yes uhh two for the show" "A couple of years ago on Headland and Delowe" "Was the start of something good" Yeah Me and You, your momma and your cousin too. AC starts to sing out loud over the balcony as he took a few pulls off the blunt.

Hey nigga, put some mayo on my sandwich! Nigga, you aint got no damn Mayo! Ha-ha-ha. Damn! My bad bro., I forgot about that. It's all good. Hey Will, you know what time that Notre Dame vs. Michigan game comes on? I think at 4pm. What time is it? It's 2:30 right now. Why, what's crackin? Loon and Duck are supposed to be coming over to watch it on the big screen. Shit, that's what's poppin, call them fools and tell them to pick up a case of beer. Man you late, we already got that taken care of partner, just chill. OK, my bad AC, you the man. Will walks out on the balcony with the sandwiches. Here you go man. Thanks bro.! Damn, this hit the spot playa. He starts chopping down the ham sandwich. Knock-Knock. That must be them fools now; come in! Hey daddy! Hey Will! What's up Sabrina? Hey baby, what you doing here? My girl gave me some chronic at work last night, I knew you were almost out so I brought you some. See, that's why I like you girl, come over here and give daddy a kiss. Ha-ha-ha. You know I got your back daddy. She walks over to give AC a kiss.

Oh Will; my girl Poison told me to give you her number, she wants to hook up. Is that right? Yep! Man I heard that chic was crazy though. Dude, I aint worried about no skirt doing no crazy shit to me, I will Donkey Kong that hoe if she starts tripping. Ha-ha-ha. Nigga you stupid! She aint crazy Will; my girl is cool. Alright, call her, tell her to come over and kick it with us today then. When, right now? Yep, right now! OK hold on. Isn't she from Rio or something like that baby? Yeah Brazil! Sabrina picks up the cordless phone to call her. Ring-Ring-Ring. Hello! Hey girl, this is Megan, what you doing? Hey girl, I'm about to do a line real quick and get in the tub. That's what's up. What you doing? Shit, I just got to AC's; we're about to fire up the hot box and watch the game. Damn, that sounds good. Will's here, I told him what you said. For real, what did he say? That's why I'm calling, he told me to invite you over. Whatever, stop playing bitch! I'm serious! Well, where does AC live? In the Towers, 44th floor. OK, I'm coming as soon as I get done washing up. Alright baby, when you get here, knock on the door that says Cooper. OK honey, see you in a few. Bye girl. She will be here in a few Will. Cool, that's what's poppin.

Knock-Knock. Come in! Yo-Yo. What's crackin folks! Loon! Duck! What's up playas? Notre Dame is about to get in yalls ass! That's what's up! You crazy, you want to bet on that Loon? What you got Coop? Shit, $100, straight up! I'll take that action. Will, Duck, yall want some? Hell yeah, fool let me get $100 on them Wolverines, Irish aint getting nothing today bruh! Alright Will, I'll take your money too! Duck you don't want none of this? I'm going for the Irish too. So put in with me, let's make the pot $200! That's what's up, count me in. Yeah my nigga, let's take these fools money. I'm glad I got you two fools in the room at the same time, now tell me what the fuck happened out there at the new housing development, was that our guy they found? Hell nah brother! Will, why you aint tell this fool? Man, I forgot all about that after we found out it wasn't our guy. So you trying to say somebody else put a body out there too? All I know is that isn't the dude we put out there Coop, the damn house we put him under is already finished. I think it might be some homeless guy or something that was sleeping out there; I don't even know and don't give a damn! Duck, throw me one of those beers playa! He pulls a brew from the box and tosses it to Loon, then gives one to Will and AC as well. Hey Coop, I'm putting this case in the fridge! Alright, you good playa, go ahead.

Daddy I'm hungry, you guys want to order some pizza? Hell yeah baby, that's a good idea. Cool, what toppings do you guys want? It doesn't matter baby, just make sure you order like 4 pizzas and get about 24 hot wings too. OK! Hey Brina, order some girls while you at it! Ha-ha-ha. Loon; shut your crazy ass up. Shit, I'm serious Will; nobody wants to look at a bunch of knuckle heads all day. Oh, I'm good pimp; I got me a skirt coming over. Oh yeah, who? This chic from the club, one of Sabrina's friends. Damn, it's like that, you and AC got some girls but me and Duck gone be left holding our dicks and shit! Fuck that playa, it aint even going down like that today. Sabrina! Sabrina! Yeah, what's up Loon? Don't you have two more friends you can call for me and Duck? Hold on, let me order this food real quick and I will check with some of them. Cool, good looking out! AC, that's a down bitch you got there playa! Yeah nigga, whatever, turn the game on already. Damn, what time does Manny get off; it doesn't feel right with him not being here. I think he gets off at 5, he's coming up then. Cool, that's what's poppin. OK guys, the food will be here in 35 minutes. Great! Thanks baby! Yo Brina, what's up with the chics? I don't know Loon, maybe I can get Malibu and Asia to come. Well, how do they look Brina? You'll like them Duck, Asia is Asian of course and Malibu is this pretty light skin chic with blonde hair. Hell yeah, I like Asians, Loon can have the redbone. Hey, I love red bones pimp, you aint said nothing but a thing, go ahead, call them Bri! OK, give me a sec; I have to use the bathroom.

Yo Will. Yeah AC what's up? When you and Loon went out to the housing development the other day, did you guys noticed if they were almost done or not? Man, their no way near being finished, why you ask? We have three more deliveries to make next week. Oh yeah, when next week? The night of the 23rd. Do you want us to wrap them the same way? Nah Loon, we need three fresh boxes this time but all under their own separate tree. How big should the boxes be? Their some pretty big gifts, so 6 will work fine. So that's 3 gifts in size 6 boxes all under different trees? Yep, that's it Will. OK, we will take care of it. Cool, I will be delivering the gifts with you next week. Alright, let's make it happen then. Hey Loon! Yeah, what's poppin Brina? Asia says she has to pick up Malibu and they will be here in an hour or so. Hell yeah Bri, you're the shit, no matter what AC says about you! What? What did you say about me daddy? Girl don't pay Loon no mind! Ha-ha-ha. I was just fucking with you Sabrina. The game is about to start, the guys are all sitting on the couch and sofa around the TV, Sabrina is sitting on the floor with her back, against the sofa and between AC's legs. Will pulls out 5 twenty dollar bills and smacks them on the coffee table. Bam! Oh yeah, that's how you want to do it! AC takes a $100 bill and smacks it on the table also. Bam! Loon and Duck throw eight twenty dollar bills on the table with the other money. Now, let's see these Irish get that ass spanked! Loon, you're about to lose your money! What? I know you don't want none Brina! Nah, my man got you! OK! Yall tag teaming a nigga! Ha-ha-ha. That's cool!

Knock-Knock. Come in! Hey everybody! Damn! Duck said out loud. Who are you? Man chill, that's Poison from the club. Hey baby, come on in and join us. Hey girl! Hey Megan! Dude, I need to come hang out at the club if yall doing it like that. Poison walks in wearing tight Ck jeans, red 6 inch stiletto's and a red fitted body top with no bra. Hey Will. What's up Poison? You're looking sexy as hell right now. Thank you! Come over here, have a seat on the couch beside me. Yo Sabrina, I hope Malibu and Asia is as sexy as your girl over there. Loon; all my bitches are sexy kid, don't even go there. What, you doing it like that, I aint mad at cha baby girl. Loon looks over at her then gives a smile and a head nod. Alright, let's go baby the game is about to start, yall in trouble boy; we're Michigan too! Let's Go Blue! That doesn't mean nothing AC, we gone spank that ass at home. Duck give it a rest playboy, yall aint ready. Ring-Ring. I think your phones ringing baby.

Ring-Ring. Can you hand me my purse off the table daddy. Sure. Ring-Ring. AC reaches over and grabs her purse off the end table. Ring-Ring-Ring. Hello! Hey bitch, this is Malibu, we're parking now, what floor are you on? We're on the 44th floor, come to the door that says Mr. Cooper. OK, we'll be up in a minute, hope yall got some blow, I only have a little bit. I don't think so baby, but we can get some, no problem. Good, because I'm going to need it. Hey, who was that baby? That was Malibu, she's downstairs, she wanted to know if we had some blow, her and Asia are parking now. Damn, I didn't know she was a cake head! Daddy, that girl was on ex last month, now it's coke, shit, she changes drugs more than she change underwear. Ha-ha-ha. Baby you crazy.

Knock-Knock. Come in! Asia and Malibu both walk in wearing black stilettos and black fitted dresses. Hello everyone are we in time for the party? Hey ladies! Hey Megan! What's up Poison! Bitch, what are you doing here, look at you, all sexy in your jeans, I love those red shoes girl. Thank you Malibu!

Hey ladies I'm Duck and this is Loon. Hi fellas. Hey AC! Hey Will! Hey girls. Loon; gets two chairs from the kitchen table and bring them in the living room area. Asia sits on the couch with Will, Poison and Duck. Malibu and Loon take a seat in the two kitchen chairs. So who's winning? Nobody scored yet but Notre Dame has the ball in the red zone. Whooo! Go Irish! What; are you a fan Asia? Hell yeah, my dad went to Notre Dame. What? Get the fuck out of here! That's what's up! Did you hear that AC? What Duck? Asia's dad went to Notre Dame. So what, he can watch his alma mater get smashed too. Ha-ha-ha. Whatever! Fuck you Coop! Ha-ha-ha. Don't get mad Duck! Here baby, role this blunt for me. He hands the cigar to her. Sure, let me hold it daddy.

Sniff-Sniff. Girl, what you over here sniffling for, you got a cold or something? Shit naw, it's this damn nose candy habit I got! Excuse me, I'll be right back. Malibu gets up, grabs her purse and goes to the bathroom. Yo Sabrina, why you hook me up with a powder head yo? Man, I didn't know she had it that bad. Hell, it's all good though, at least she's finer than a motherfucker. Ha-ha-ha. You a trip Loon. Oh yeah! Oh yeah! Touchdown! Damn! Yeah baby! Let's go Irish! Get some Coop! Yeah! Asia and Duck are standing up clapping and yelling. It's OK daddy; we'll get them back, here light your blunt. Thanks baby. Coop takes the blunt, lights it up, takes a long pull then says to Brina in a low voice with his lungs full of chronic. Damn, this is some good bud baby. The bathroom door opens, Malibu walks out looking fresh and smelling like Ck one. Hey, what did I miss, I heard you guys yelling. The Irish scored! Oh, is that it, screw the Irish! Let's Go Blue!

Knock-Knock. Damn, who is it now? Baby, it must be the pizza. Oh, I forgot about that! Who is it? It's Dante's delivery! Come in! The delivery guy opens the door with four pizzas and a box of hot wings in his red thermal bag. Hey, how are you guys doing, I have four extra-large combo pizza's and a box of hot wings. Yep, that sounds about right. Your total is $32.88. Here, just put it on the table. Sabrina says to him as she gets up to get her purse. OK Mam, no problem. She walks over to the table and hands him two twenty dollar bills. Here you go man, keep the change. Thanks Mam, you guys have a good day. Baby, do you have any paper plates? Yeah, look under the cabinet by the sink. OK thanks. Sabrina gets the plates and sits them on the table by the wings and pizza. Alright guys, eat up! AC throws Loon a Philly. Here bruh, roll that smoke. I got you player, hold on. You smoke Malibu? Yep, I do that too. Awww man! This fool threw a damn pick! Oh shit! He's gone baby! He's Gone! Yall aint catching him! Yeah fool! Yeah! Touchdown! Loon jumps up and yells. Fuck! AC taunts him. Yeah, Go Irish! That's, 14 to 0 playa! You fools about to lose that money! Shut up Duck! It aint over yet. Don't get mad know Will! I ain't mad bruh, we got two quarters left, let me hit that blunt.

AC hands him the chronic then heads over to the table to get a few wings and a slice of pizza, Loon gives the Philly to Malibu, she splits it and clears out the tobacco as he prepares the weed. Asia, Poison and Sabrina go over to the table to fix a plate. Man, this is some bomb ass weed. Duck says in a low voice after blowing out some smoke. Run boy! Run dammit! Run! Fuck yeah! Touchdown nigga! That fool just ran for 45 yards on yall ass! Get some! Yeah Go Blue! 14-7 now motherfucker! It aint over! Yeah don't get too happy AC! Don't hate Loon, we coming for that ass baby! Whooo! Yeah, Wolverines baby! Girl, give me that blunt! Awww, are you mad at me baby? Naw, I don't care if you like the Wolverines Malibu, yall still suck. Ha-ha-ha. You are mad! Give me that blunt girl, let me roll this smoke. He tried to take the leaf from her hand and missed. My bad baby, here you go. She hands him the blunt, he sprinkles in the weed, rolls it up, licks it then run the lighter across it to dry and seal it.

Now, this is a tight blunt right here nigga. Here you go Malibu, hit that shit! Damn, I'm already high off this blow man, how high are you trying to get me?

Fuck it, don't worry about it, give it back then. Wait, let me hit it first! Light it up then girl! Malibu puts the blunt up to her lips, her mind was saying not to but the familiar feeling of peer pressure had took its toll over her once again as it did so many times before. Loon reached over, lit it for her, she inhaled, held it in for a second and released the smoke. Malibu's eyes became glassy as her heart sped up to an alarming rate. She takes another pull off the chronic to enhance her already cocaine induced high, then slowly passed it over to Loon. Her glassy eyes are now half closed, her arms crossed as she leaned back in the chair and falls into a daze. Damn bitch, you alright over here? Hey Malibu! She slowly turns her head to look at him, smiles then nods her head to say yeah. Loon inhales the chronic, holds it in then blows the smoke in her face. You high as a motherfucker right now girl, aint you?

She looks at him and just smiles. Yo Duck, you wanna hit this, I'm about to take this chic in the room. Yeah, Asia hand me that blunt will you? Sure. She reaches over and takes the spliff from Loon; he lifts Malibu to her feet. Hey fool, what you doing? I'm about to take her in the room so she can lay down, this bitch is too high AC. Alright hold on; Sabrina go put a blanket across the bed please, I don't want that bitch fucking up my comforter. OK daddy, I'll get it for you. She runs in the room to put a sheet over the comforter as Loon stood in the doorway holding Malibu in his arms. Alright, that should do it; you can lay her down now Loon. Come on girl; let's get you in the bed before you pass out. He picks her up and walks over to the bed. Damn Asia, why is she so fucked up? Girl, Malibu does her own thing; I don't have anything to do with it. Every time I try to stop her or at least slow her ass down, she starts tripping, I don't even try no more. Shit, I hear that, let that hoe handle her own problems.

Yo Loon, get your ass in here! It's last quarter with 45 seconds left, the score is 14-10 and they got the ball! Damn, what yard line are they on Duck? He yells out from the room. The 12 Nigga, they're in the red zone! Yeah, Let's Go Blue! Whoooo! Let's go Wolverines! Loon runs in the front room and takes his seat. Come on baby, we need this first down! Will yells out. Michigan's QB takes the long snap, then rolls left, the right tight end cuts across the field in a post route. Number 18 runs a fade route down the right sideline, the running back shoots up the middle and stops on the five. The tight end runs in the end zone then looks over his left shoulder. Bam! The ball hits him right between the numbers! He clinches it and falls down in the end zone. Damn! Damn! Motherfucker! Yeah baby! Yeah! Go Blue! Give up that cash baby! AC and Will pick up the cash from the table. Man that's some bullshit! Duck screams. The Wolverines set up for the field goal. Man, turn that shit off the games over now. Awwww. Are you mad Loon? Leave me alone Sabrina, that shit aint funny.

AC, I will holler at you later man, I'm going downstairs to the bar. Hold up L, I'm coming too. What's up Asia, you coming? Sure Duck. Wait a damn minute boys, we might as well come with you guys and spend some of this money we just won! Ha-ha-ha. Whatever Will! Hey! You know its all love nigga! Daddy, what about Malibu? Just let her rest for a bit, we can come back and get her later. Come on Poison; let's go get some Rum shots baby. She gets up and joins Will and the others as they gather to go downstairs. The place is now quiet and all you could hear was Malibu in the room snoring as AC locked the door behind them. The group entered the elevator and went down to the lobby floor. Tourist and locals crowded the restaurant and bar area, cigar smoke, fresh bread and baked chicken filled the air as the live band entertained the patrons while playing the latest hits and crowd favorites. AC, Sabrina, Will and the others disappeared in the crowd as they entered the lounge to hear some good music and enjoy the spirits, just a little taste of what the Towers had to offer to their patrons and guest of Sin City.

Good Morning Las Vegas, this is your AM jock Shy C checking in baby, it's two days before Christmas and we're scheduled for good weather everyday this Holiday week. I'm sending a warm welcome out to everyone visiting Las Vegas this Holiday season, we're glad to have you and I wish you all a Merry Christmas! AC is lying in bed looking up at the ceiling, getting upset because his ex-wife want let him see or talk to his kids this Christmas when the phone rings. Ring-Ring-Ring. Hello! Hey daddy! Hey baby. Are you up yet daddy? Yeah, kind of. Well get up, you know you have to be at the club early today. OK, I'm getting up now. Good, I will see you later at work, me and my mom are going to pick up some things for dinner right now. Alright Sabrina, see you later baby. Bye Daddy! He gets up from bed, walks over to the dresser and looks at himself in the mirror, he could see the fire burning in his eyes and feel his heart turn ice cold whenever he thought about losing his family. What the others didn't know, it was this very thing that made him a cold hearted criminal; after all, he had nothing else to live for. AC picked up the cordless phone and dials a number. Ring-Ring-Ring. Hello! Hector, what's crackin, this is AC. Hey amigo! What's up, you got your folks ready? We all set homes, just give me the call. Alright bro., I will hit you up in a few hours. Cool, later homes. He hangs up then dials another number.

Ring-Ring-Ring. Yo what up! Hey Will! What's up Coop? Did you get those three presents ready? Yep, everything is a go. Cool, that's what's up playa, see you at the club. Alright partner, later! He hangs up the phone then makes another call. Ring-Ring-Ring. Hello! Loon, what's poppin playa? What up Coop? Yo, tonight is the night, you and Duck be ready to go! Alright boss, we will be waiting on that call. Cool, I will holler at you later. AC hangs up the phone then go makes his bed, pulls out some work clothes and placed them on the chair, he walks into the bathroom, picks up the clippers to trim his beard and shave his head. It's going on 11am and he's running out of time, Cooper runs the water from the sink over his toothbrush then squeezes on some toothpaste, brushes his teeth then rinses his mouth. He reaches in the tub, turns on the shower, takes off his boxers and jumps in to take a quick 5 minute shower.

Five minutes pass, he steps out dripping wet onto the bathroom rug, pulls his towel from the rack, dries off and slips on some fresh under clothes and socks. The mirror was still fogged up in the bathroom so he went to use the one over his room dresser. He splashed on some Cool Water cologne, put on his work clothes; then the phone rings. Ring-Ring-Ring. Hello! Yo brother, what you doing, it's like 11:30! I'm coming down now Manny. Hurry your ass up, this is the big day! I'm coming, I'm coming. What you driving? Shit, pull the Rover. OK, I'm on it, hurry up; get your ass down here! Did you call Hector and the fellas yet? Yep, everybody is in play. Cool, see you in a minute. Click! They hang up. The adrenalin was running through his body as he stepped over to check himself in the mirror one last time. Beads of sweat begin to roll off his head and down the side of his face. He stood there for a second and stared at himself in the mirror, A calm peace came over him as he sucked it all in, that familiar feeling of going to war, hunting your prey and going in for the kill had overcame him. In his mind, he flashed back to the Desert where they killed enemies every day, with no hesitation, just an M-16 and the will to survive.

AC slid his black Versace shades over that cold death stare and headed downstairs to complete his six month long mission. The team was all in place, this was the moment they were planning for the past several months, it was about to go down. He locked his door behind him, got on the elevator and headed downstairs, 44 floors later the elevator doors opened and he walked out focused with a confident swagger about him. The handle of his 380 in the small of his back, stuck out above his belt, Manny met him at the exit, pulled him close and spoke in a soft voice... Brother, whatever you do, don't lose focus, today is the first day of the rest of our lives, see the enemy, attack the enemy; terminate the enemy. Death before Dishonor brother, remember we got your back. I got it Capo, wait for my call, I will hit you as soon as phase 1 is done, call the twins, tell them to hold their positions and wait for further instructions. Roger that! AC heads out to the valet, gets in the Rover, pulls onto the strip and takes a short cut by cutting through the casino parking lots to get onto Industrial Boulevard. He drove a few miles down the boulevard not paying attention to any stop lights or pedestrians. Beep! Beep! A large garbage truck blew its horn at him as he nearly hit them head on, when he ran a red light, the sound of the horn had awaken him from his daydream. He got his self together and safely made it the next two blocks down to the club parking lot.

Over at Dolls, the day shift crew was just arriving, Vinny and Bobby had just unlocked the doors, everyone followed them in to prepare the club for its first shift. AC is the last one to enter; he goes over to the bar and picks up the phone to call Hector. Ring-Ring-Ring. Hello! Hector, it's time to get in place. Alright homes, we will be posted in a few minutes. Cool, make sure you guys can see the doors from where you park; I don't know what the brothers are driving today. We got it covered amigo, just relax and let the homies take it from here. Say no more. Click! They hang up. AC begins to inventory and stock the bar. Hey Dillinger, I got something for you. Vinny approaches the bar and slides a white envelop across the counter. Here you go brother; you're doing a good job, keep it up and have a Happy Holiday. Thanks Vin! Yeah, your welcome, that's just a little something from me and Bobby to show our appreciation. Coop, picks up the envelope; opens it and find 15 crisp $100 bills. Wow, man I really appreciate it! He reaches over the bar and shakes Vinny's hand. Would you tell Bobby I said thanks also. Sure thing pal. Vinny turns and walks away. Remy, Poison, Malibu and Dylan enter the club to start their shift. Hey AC! Hey ladies. Will comes in shortly after the ladies with two cups of coffee in hand. Good morning brother, here's some coffee for you playa. Thanks bro... Yeah no problem, so are we a go for today? Yep, it's going down. Cool, it's about fucking time, I'm tired of this bouncing shit, time to get that real paper, you dig! They give each other a pound. Damn real, where's red, she aint working today? Yeah, she's working mid shift tonight. Oh, that's what's up. Alright pimp, let me go clock in for the last time. I hear that! Will leaves the bar and heads to the office.

Max, Honey, Kiwi, Pebbles and Megan entered the club with only a few minutes left to get dressed and ready. Megan runs over to the bar. Hey Daddy! She leans over the counter and gives him a kiss on the lips. Muah! Hey baby, how's your Mom? She's good, just a little stressed, trying to get everything ready for dinner tonight. You guys must have a lot of people coming over. Yep! She turns and runs to the dressing room. Then yells out. I will be right back, got to get dressed! He nods his head at her as she runs away. Bobby and Vinny exit the office and approach the bar. AC, come here for a minute brother. They stood waiting for him at the end of the bar by the waitress section.

He walks over, stands there and looks at the brothers as he waited for instructions. Yeah, what's up Boss man? Me and Vin are going out to run a few errands, I need you and Will to hold things down until we get back, can you guys handle that? Sure man, go ahead, we got it, no problem. Cool, we will back in a few. Bobby pats him on the back, then he and Vinny head outside to the parking lot. It's another nice warm December day; the Sun is shining bright over Sin City. The reflection off a chrome side mirror, attached to a 1962 white Impala, parked across the street, blinded them as they approached their money green, 1996 Cadillac Seville. Fuck! Where is my shades; that beam of light could blind Jesus! Vinny opened the driver's side door as Bobby entered the passenger's side. Bobby took a pair of shades off the dash and handed them to his brother. Here man, put these on, with your blind ass. Ha-ha-ha. I can see better than you! Yeah, that may be so but that Sun is too bright to be driving without any shades on. Yeah, I guess you're right. Vinny slips the shades on, starts the car and pulls off the lot; he takes Industrial Boulevard down to the over pass and make a right turn onto Charleston. The Impala had pulled off behind them and was now about three cars back in their rear view.

The traffic down Charleston had begun to slow up during the lunch rush as patrons doing their last minute Christmas shopping added to this already normally congested traffic jam. Vinny had come to a red light and the white Impala had fallen further than 4 cars back as they tried to keep up with the brothers. Yo Chino, don't lose that Cadi homes! Calm down, I see them amigo, just chill out homes! The light turned green, Vinny drove two blocks down and made a right into an Albertson's Shopping Center. Hey, slow down homes, they turned right there, slow down, and get over in the right lane homes! Hector yelled at him. Vinny and Bobby had pulled in a parking space, turned off the car and walked up to the plaza beside the grocery store.

Chino had just turned onto the lot. Aye, that's them right there Hector. Yeah, I see them, hurry up and park homes. He drove pass a few cars before he finally found an empty space. Stop homes! Park here! OK, OK! He parked the Impala. Get your guns ready. Hector said to Chino and to Poncho who was sitting in the back seat. The parking lot was full of cars and patrons, Clothing stores, Shoe stores, A Dagwood's sandwich shop and a Vegas Bank and Trust surrounded the Albertson's, in this busy shopping center. Hector and the boys cock their nines. Click! Click! They see the brothers walking up to the double doors beside the grocery store. Alright homes, let's do these fools and get the fuck out of here, put on your gloves and ski mask, It's time to get paid homes! Vinny and Bobby walk into the building talking and laughing with each other. Hey Bobby, did I tell you, I fucked Max the other day. Man you crazy, why you fuck that loony ass bitch? Now, she's going to want special treatment and shit like that. Yeah, I got a special for her ass alright! The brothers approach the long line of customers. Damn Vinny, I knew this place would be pack. Hey, what are you gonna do, this shit has to be done. We're going to be here for a few minutes, looks like.

Hector, Chino and Poncho hide their guns in their black Ben Davis pants; pulls their black shirts down over the grip, slips on their black gloves and pulls down their black ski mask. The boys jumped out the Impala and started running, all you could see was a blur of their black Chuck Taylors, as they ran across the lot and into the building, where the brothers were standing in line. One long, grey marble, counter top ran across the back of the wall. Several employees stood behind it, serving their patrons patiently as the next person stood eagerly awaiting their turn. Green marble tile covered the floors, two large oak desk sat empty in the north corner, the double glass doors at the entrance swung open. Hector and the fellas ran in, Chino guarded the door, Poncho ran to the counter, Hector stood in the middle of the floor and started shouting. Alright motherfucker's, yall know what this is! Get your asses on the floor! Now Fuckers! Get down and shut up! Face on the ground, hands behind your heads! Come on! Do it! Everybody down! If anybody even breathes hard; were clapping your punk ass! Tellers; clean out those fucking drawers and put all the money in the bag! No small bills either Bitch! Poncho, held his nine in the right hand and the bag in the other. Come on, fill it bitch! Let's go Bitch! The teller in a panic started emptying the cash from the drawers and putting it in the bag, Hector looks on the floor for Vinny and Bobby.

Hey! Hey! Yeah, you two grease ball fuckers! Get up! The brothers stand to their feet. Look man, we don't want any trouble. Shut the fuck up! Did I tell you to speak fucker! Vinny stands there quiet, Bobby is standing beside him. Hey, give me that Rolex grease ball! Hector takes the watch off Bobby's wrist. Oh shit, you got one too, huh fucker? Come on, give it up! Vinny takes off his watch and hands it over. Yo! Hurry up Bitch, clear out those damn cash registers! Yo homes, did you get all of it! Got it homes! Cool, let's roll! Poncho wraps up the bag and head for the door as Hector is standing there with Bobby and Vinny at gun point. POW! He shoots Bobby in the head, point blank range, his body falls face first on the cold tiled floor. No! No! Vinny falls to the floor crying over his brother. POW! Hector shoots Vinny point blank, in the back of the head, he falls down and lands on his brother's back, the blood from them both started to slowly ooze over the tile and between the cracks. Chino opens the door so Poncho and Hector can run out, then he runs behind them across the lot and jumps in the Impala, they speed off the lot. Skkkeeeerrrrrrt! The Impala spins off up the street. Vroom-Vroom. The dual exhaust sounds off as they cut in and out of traffic leaving the scene of the crime.

They get to the light, bust a U turn and cut through the Palace Station parking lot, then on to the side street behind the casino. Aye, you straight smoked those fools' homes! Fuck em, that's what we got paid to do! Poncho, count that loot homie! Poncho dumps the money on the back seat and starts counting; Chino slows the Impala down to the speed limit as they approached the Red and Yellow warehouse on Industrial where they did most of their business. Ruff! Ruff! Ruff! The dogs bark as the gates open, the Impala rolls on the lot secured behind the tall fence and vicious canines, Hector gets out of the car and so does Chino. Damn Punta, you aint done counting that money yet! Poncho is still in the back seat, separating the money by 20's 50's and 100's. Hold on homes, I'm almost done! Let's see, there's like 10 stacks here and I got 5 g's in each stack, so we got 50 g's Homes! Hell yeah! That's how you handle business gentlemen; we just made $150,000.00 in 2 minutes! Who the fuck, says crime don't pay! Homes, I said 50, what do you mean 150? Poncho, the hit pays $100,000.00 by itself, not to mention we just got $50,000.00 from the bank. Oh, hell yeah! Poncho starts dancing and counting the money while he was still sitting in the car.

Hector walks in the garage and gets the phone to call AC. Ring-Ring-Ring. Hello! Homes! Hector, what's the word brother? It's done homes. Cool. AC says in a calm voice and hangs up the phone. Hey Will! What up man? Phase 1 is done bro., go ahead and make your move, I'm going to call Nina and have her put her end in motion. Alright Coop, got it. AC picks up the bar phone and calls Nina. Ring-Ring. Hello, thanks for calling Angel's Escorts, who would you like to book today? Hey Nina; its AC. Hey bro., what's up? Phase 1 is done. Cool, what's next? Tell Paula that the Bosses called and scheduled a mandatory meeting in the next two hours, have her call the ranch too and have the house mom and bartender ready to attend, I will be sending a limo to pick all of them up. Alright bro. got it. They hang up.

Paula was sitting in the chair watching TV and overheard Nina on the phone. Who was that sweetie? Oh that was Vinny from the club, he told me to tell you that there's a mandatory meeting in two hours for all staff, he said to make sure that the staff at the ranch was ready too. Their sending a limo to pick you guys up in a few hours. Thanks sweetie, I'll call the ranch from my cell phone. I hope no one is in trouble Paula! No sweetie, they probably want to take us out for Christmas dinner and give us a bonus for a good year, I remember a few years ago when they surprised us the same way. Wow, that would be really nice of them. Yeah, Vinny and Bobby can be assholes sometimes but they do know how to take care of their own, I'll be right back Nina. I'm going down the hall to make some copies of these applications, I'll just call the ranch while I'm walking down there, don't want to tie up the business phones. I will be back in a bit, sweetie. OK Paula.

Nina picks of the phone and calls Duck. Ring-Ring-Ring. Hello! Hey Duck! Who's this? Nina dummy! What's up? AC just called, phase 2 is in play, call Loon and have him stand by. AC will be sending a limo to pick you guys up. Alright sis, Roger that! She hangs up the phone then calls AC back. Ring-Ring. Hello! We're all set poppy. Cool, I'm sending the Limo now. Alright, later poppy. AC walks from behind the bar and heads outside to the Club parking lot, he approaches the Limo driver. Hey my man, come here a second. The driver walks over. Yes Sir! I need for you to work over at Angel's, your switching with a guy name Duck; he will be standing outside with the other limo drivers. Once you get there, tell him your his replacement, he drives the stretch Navigator, we have a request for it tonight. Can you do that young man? Yes Sir! Well, what are you waiting on, make it happen already!

The driver jumps in the limo and heads over to Angel's. AC picks up his cell phone to call Duck. Ring- Ring. Yeah, hello! Bro., it's Coop. Hey bro., I got the message. Cool, listen and listen good, I'm sending a Limo over to you as we speak, when it gets there have the driver take your spot. OK, got it covered, is there anything else? Yes, once you guys switch, I need for you to take a trip out to the ranch, pick up that bartender and Nancy the House Mom. Can you do that? Yeah, I know how to get there. Good! Right after you pick them up, head back to town, come scoop me and Loon up from the club, it shouldn't take any longer than 2 hours to do all of that. Are you sure you can handle it? Coop, stop tripping, I got you. Cool, call me when you're on the way to the club. Got it, see you later bro.! Alright man, don't fuck this up! Bye man! Duck hangs up the phone and takes the keys for the Navi off the rack and place them in his pocket.

20 minutes later on the other side of town, a patron was pulling onto the Dolls parking lot. The driver was parking alongside the building when a big grey cadi sped past him and parked in his place, the door of the cadi opened and out stepped Loon. He reached in the car, picked up his chrome 357 from under the seat, placed it in the shoulder harness that was strapped across his back under his jacket. Manny exited the cadi from the passenger's side and reached in the back seat to get his jacket. He stood by the car, using the window as a mirror, trying to make sure his jacket was covering the nine he had strapped in his shoulder harness. Come on Capo; let's get a drink before we go handle this business! Loon yelled out to Manny as he walked in the club. I coming dawg, hold your horses, order me a Crown and coke when you get in. Yeah, yeah, hurry your ass up!

Loon enters the club, Manny isn't far behind. What's up Mr. Cooper! What's up Loon? I'm ready to put in work nigga, let's do this shit. Yeah, we will, in a few. What's up Manny? Hey AC, you alright, you ready? Born ready, playa, what you knuckle heads want to drink? Shit, let me get some of that goose! Manny, how about you? Let me get a crown and coke man. Alright, one goose and one crown coming right up. So, what time are we heading out man? As soon as Duck gets here bro... How long is that going to be Coop? Anytime now Loon, here's your drinks fellas. He places the Crown and the Goose on the bar. Thanks bro.! Hey Rookie, what's going on over here? Hey Red, just serving a few drinks to the guys over here. Has it been this slow all day? Yep! Damn, this is some bullshit. Well, it's all yours now baby, my shift is over. Ha-ha-ha. Whatever man! AC walks from behind the bar. See you tomorrow Deb! OK babe! Loon and Manny pick up their drinks and take them to the head. Hey Will, I'll call you later man and let you know about that thing. OK Coop, you guys be safe, don't get in any trouble. Manny, Loon and AC head outside to wait for Duck.

It's around 4:15 PM, the parking lot is almost empty with the exception of 5 cars, Manny pulls a blunt from his top jacket pocket, lights it, takes a few pulls then passes it to Loon. Did you guys make the gifts 6 deep this time or 4? Boss stop worrying, we took care of it, I promise. Loon said in a low voice as he held in the chronic smoke then exhaled. Yeah, that's what yall said last time. We got it covered Coop, we took care of it! He looks at Loon and shakes his head. Chill out, AC, damn brother. Yeah man, be cool, that body they found the other day wasn't even our guy! Don't tell me to chill Manny! I'm trying to cover our asses! Loon; that wasn't our guy but Will told me you guys only went 4 deep, remember! So yeah, yall fucked it up, we're just lucky they didn't find our guy! I'm sorry man, damn, you about to fuck up my high! Here, take a hit off this here, calm your nerves fool! He hands AC the blunt. Ha-ha-ha-ha. Yall are too damn funny. Fuck you Manny! Don't get mad at me Coop because yall loco. AC gets the blunt, takes a long drag, holds it in, looks at the blunt, exhales then takes another drag.

Beep! Beep! Beep! Several cars driving down industrial blow their horns at the Limo as it came across two lanes cutting off oncoming traffic. Shit, look at that fool, I don't know why you got his ass driving the Limo anyway. Ha-ha-ha-ha. That fool probably high! Manny, your ass drive high all the time, I know you're not laughing at nobody. Yeah but I can drive safe when I'm high, Duck can't drive when his ass is sober, let alone high! Ha-ha-ha-ha. All three guys laugh as Duck pulls the Limo in front of the club. He comes to a complete stop and rolls down his window. Hey what you fools laughing at, I had my signal on, It's not my fault they didn't want to let me get over. Fuck em! Whatever man, unlock the damn door so we can get in already! It's unlocked AC; try it again. The doors come open as if someone had pushed it. Here you go guys, that door gave me a hard time earlier too. Thanks man. You're welcome. Loon, AC and Manny join Nancy and the Bartender in back. What's up guys, I'm AC, this is Loon and that guy at the end is Manny. Hi fellas, we work at the ranch. Yeah don't bother, we already know who you are, you're the House mom and you're the bartender, right? Yep, you got us red handed.

Hey bartender, want you pour us some champagne. Sure! Duck looks back over the seat. Alright guys, are we ready to go? Yep, go by Angel's and pick up Paula, then we're headed to the meeting. You got it AC. The bartender pops a bottle of Moet, everyone grabs a glass from the rack, he tops off all four glasses and kept his in the bottle. Ummm-ummmm! Manny clears his throat. I propose a toast! Everyone holds up their glass, the bartender held up his bottle. I like to wish you all a Happy Holiday! They all say. Happy Holidays! Then downs the champagne. Duck slowly makes a right turn onto Industrial Boulevard. Damn, we need another drink, what else is over there bartender? Hmmm. Let's see Loon, well there's another bottle of Moet, some Crown and a bottle of Martel. What do you think fellas, shall we pop another bottle of Moet or the Martel. Pop that other bottle of Moet man, we can open that Martel after the meeting. Good idea AC! You heard the man bartender, pop that Mo! Alright, let's do it.

He picks up the champagne, points it towards the sun roof, pops the cork then refills everyone's glasses. So bartender, how many of them girls you slept with already, out at the ranch. Ha-ha-ha. He laughs, then looks at Manny and smile. None of them, actually. What, I know that's a lie, all that damn pussy out there and you aint tap none of it? Nope, none of it. Dude, you must be gay or some shit, aint no way! Well actually, I am Loon. Am what? I'm Gay. Ha-ha-ha. Stop playing. No, I'm serious. Well aint this a bitch! No wonder they let you work out there, you think you got a pussy too! Ha-ha-ha-ha. They all laugh. Shut up AC, you crazy as hell. Man, I aint crazy, this fool is crazy, for being gay around all that pussy.

Ha-ha-ha-ha. Loon falls on the floor laughing. Hey Nancy, why you over there so quiet? I'm just relaxing young man, enjoying the day. Is that right. Yes Sir, sometimes you have to sit back, breath, take it all in and stop to smell the Roses as they say, you never know when it's your last breath. Well, I sure will drink to that! Manny, holds up his glass. Here's to stopping to smell the roses! Cheers everyone! Yeah cheers, I still can't believe this fool is gay, all that pussy walking around. AC says to Manny, then shakes his head at the situation. Well, he's going to wish he had of fuck them hoes, because he's about to take a dirt nap. Manny said to AC in a low voice. Ha-ha-ha. Now, I'll drink to that amigo! AC lifts his glass and toast Manny. The limo slowed down and came to a complete stop. Yo AC, we're here! Oh shit, my bad man, hold tight, let me call Nina. He picks up the car phone. Ring-Ring-Ring. Hi, thanks for calling Angel's, how can I help you today? Nina, it's AC, we're out front. Oh OK, I will tell Paula. Thanks sis!

Hey Paula. Yes sweetie! That was the limo driver, he's out front. It's about time! Paula stands up, straightens her dress, fix her hair and head towards the door. Alright sweetie, I will see you when I get back. OK, bye Paula. She exits into the long narrow, moldy hallway then heads outside to the limo. AC opens the back door to let her in. Hi, everybody. Hey Paula, I don't believe we've met, I'm AC, this is Loon and that's our partner Manny, we're all new to the company. Nice to meet you gentlemen. Thank you Paula, we've heard so much about you. Well sweetie, only believe half of what they told you and most of that isn't true. Ha-ha-ha-ha. Just kidding. Paula, what are you drinking darling? Why you already know the answer to that, my favorite bartender! Yes Mam, one Crown and cranberry coming right up.

We'll hello there Nancy, what are you sipping on over there? Oh, it's just some champagne baby. Guys be careful, this little lady over here is the meanest house mom in Nevada, she doesn't take any shit from those hoes! Ha-ha-ha. I'm a sweet old lady. Yeah, to let you tell it. Paula smiles and pats Nancy on the knee. The limo turns left on Sahara, drives down a few miles, go over the bridge, then make a right on to interstate 15. Everyone is in the back of the limo, laughing, conversing and enjoying the spirits on this calm Holiday evening. Loon taps on the divider to get Duck's attention. Tap-Tap. Yeah, what's up man? Can you put on some music, please Sir? Yes Sir, coming right up. The radio comes on and Coolio's; Gangsta's Paradise was playing." As I walk through the Valley of the shadow of death" "I take a look at my life and realize there's not much left". Yeah boy, Coolio killed this shit! Hell yeah Loon, this is his best track yet. LV is blowin that chorus too boy. Tell em Manny, this is the shit right here. Everybody is in the back of the Limo, boppin and singing along with the radio. "Been spendin most their lives, Livin in the gangsta's paradise" "Keep spendin most our lives, Livin in the gangsta's paradise".

The Sun had set over the desert as they traveled over the I-15 interstate, leaving the neon skyline in their rear view as they left the city of Sin, heading towards the suburbs. Five minutes, outside the city, they arrived at a newly developed housing community, construction workers and City officials had already left for today. Duck entered the development and drove pass the first three rows of completed homes. He approached the last row of construction and drove all the way down to the end, where the building crew kept the blue 24 foot long construction clean up dumpster. The limo slowed down as it drove off the paved road and onto the desert gravel, then rolled to a complete stop, right beside the dumpster. Duck roles down the divider window. AC, this is it brother. Cool bro.! AC looks over at Loon and Manny, reaches under his jacket and pulls out his gun, Manny and Loon follows suit. Coop points his gun at the bartender, Manny points his at Nancy and Loon points his at Paula. Alright people, this is the end of the road for you. Hey, what are you guys doing, this is a joke right! I'm afraid not, bitch! Now shut up and get the fuck out of the car! Loon shoves his gun in Paula's chest and forces her to open the door. Oh my god, please don't kill me, please! AC puts his gun up side the bartenders head. Dude, shut your faggot ass up and get the fuck out! Hey, can I finish my drink first, before you kill me, I'm old as hell anyway, I've been ready to leave this damn earth! Hell no, get your ass out! Manny puts his gun in Nancy's back and forces her out the limo with the others.

A cool wind is blowing across the dark Mojave' Desert as the sand formed small whirl winds that dusted across its plane. All three of the victims are standing outside in front of the Limo at gun point, AC yells out to Duck. Duck, turn on the headlights! The lights come on and about 8 feet in the distance you could see a mound of red dirt. OK Manny, lead the way! Manny shoves his victim in the back. Alright, start walking and shut the fuck up. Loon has his gun shoved in Paula's neck as he forces her to follow Manny and Nancy. AC shoves his gun in his victim's ear. Let's go, sweet pants, kick rocks! As they approach the mound of dirt he could see Loon, Manny and the victims stop, both victims fall to their knees and started to pray. Lord, please! Hey shut up, pray to yourself, we don't wanna hear that shit.

AC and the bartender approach the others, as Manny stands there yelling at the victims, telling them to be quiet. Loon, what the fuck is this? Where's the three holes! Man, its 6 feet deep and 18 feet wide, we can put all these motherfuckers in this bitch, with no problem. POW! Loon shoots Paula in the back of the head and she falls, face first down in the hole. Come on man; kill them fools so we can go! It's getting cold out here in this damn desert! Loon shouts and heads back to the limo. POW! Manny shoots the old lady in the back of the head and kicks her down in the grave. Hey man, please don't kill me, I want tell anybody, anything! Shut up fool, turn around; get on your knees! Man, wait; please! AC is standing there with his gun pointed to the bartender's temple. Man I swear!

POW! The bartender body collapses and falls to the ground, AC kicks the corpse and it rolls down in the grave with the others.

Hey Duck, go get that cement truck from over there. Duck leaves the limo, jumps in the truck and drives it over to the grave. Beep-Beep. The truck sounds as it backs closer to the hole. Alright, that's good right there! Coop stops him, turns the cement shoot over the hole and releases the lever to pour in the cement mix. Beep-Beep. The truck sounds, as Manny stands there watching AC pour concrete in the hole. Hey Capo, go get the bull Dozier! He goes over by the dumpster, climbs up in the Dozier, starts it and drives over to the grave. AC turns off the cement shoot after the mix got about 3 feet deep and covered the bodies. OK Duck, you can take it back over now. He puts the truck in drive, takes it back over to its original location, parks it, turns it off and walks over to the grave. Manny is pushing the pile of dirt back in the hole over the cement with the bull Dozier. AC and Duck stand there watching him as the hole starts to fill up with the red dirt, Loon steps out of the Limo and yells out to the others. Hey man, yall fools aint done yet! Manny lifts the bull Dozier shovel up, drops it, to pack the dirt down. He then drives back and forth over it to make sure it was level and that it blended in with the surrounding area. Shut up Loon and light up that spliff playa, we're almost done. Shit, you aint said nothing but a word Boss!

Manny pulls the Dozier back over in front of the dumpster, parks it and turns it off, jumps down and walks with AC and Duck back to the limo. Loon is standing there with the door open and music blasted. Tupac's; No More Pain is bumping through the speakers. "My adversaries cry like hoes, fully eradicate my foes" "My lyrics explode on contact, Gamin you hoes" " Who else but Momma's only son, Fuck the phony niggaz I'm the one". Loon takes a pull off the blunt, holds it in, exhales, then speaks in a calm voice. So this is the start of it all, right here fellas, now we can take over Sin City. He passes the blunt to Coop. AC takes a pull and passes it over to Manny. We have a few more moves to make, so everyone knows that its official then it's on and crackin. Man, these fools aint ready for us Coop, we aint taking no fucking prisoners around this motherfucker. Manny passes the blunt to Duck. Hey, what's up with Hector and his crew Coop? Their down with us Capo, we're running the money and they got the streets covered, we don't have to get our hands dirty.

Duck passes the blunt back to Loon and heads to the driver's seat. Let's get the fuck out of here fellas. They get in the back of the limo, the music is still bumping. " I came to bring the pain, hard core to your brain" " Let's go inside my astral plane" " I came to bring the pain, hard core to your brain" " Let's go inside my astral plane". The Limo cruises through the unfinished development; pass the first three completed rows of houses and exits out onto interstate 15, headed back towards the city. The night is clear, sky full of stars as they speed back towards the strip of green, red, blue and yellow neon lights that made Las Vegas Boulevard. The closer they got, the colors turned to buildings, castles and pyramids, a desert wonderland, surrounded by miles and miles of traffic and people from all walks of life. The limo pulls off onto the Tropicana exit and makes a right towards Industrial Boulevard, Duck cuts in and out of traffic then gets lost in the Holiday rush as they head back to Club Dolls.

It's the next evening, a warm Christmas Eve over at Club 662, BMW's, Rovers, Benz's, Jaguars, Hummers and Limo's crowd the VIP parking spaces in front of the club's entrance. Several security guards and Valet's stood outside patrolling the lot and parking the dozens of cars that we're coming in by the minute. Ladies we're walking down the red carpet entrance, in groups of three and four. Rose had just pulled up in her yellow stretched Hummer, the Valet ran over to open the back door, she stepped out, dressed in black knee high Gucci boots, with a 5 inch steel heel, black Gucci dress and a Grey and Black Chinchilla, fur coat. One of the security guards, who was dressed in a black suit and tie, escorted her inside to the annual company Christmas party.

The wait staff from Dolls had just walked up and entered the club in one big group, which included 5 ladies and 4 guys. Brass poles and red velvet rope surrounded the red carpet and walk way of the Blue, Grey and Red brick building. Outside speakers, built in the upper corners of the building, blasted the music that was being played, on the inside of the club. A black Range Rover, pulled up to the front, the valet opens the driver's door. Dupree along with three members of his crew step out, dressed in black slacks, dress shoes and Versace shirts, they walked down the red carpet and entered the party as the valet parked the Rover. Snoop Doggs; Gin and Juice, bumped over the speakers outside as cars continued to pull up. "With so much drama in the L.B.C." "It's kinda hard being the Snoop D-O- double-G" " But I, Somehow, Some way" " Keep coming up with funky ass shit like every single day". A white Tahoe pulls up to the valet, Fat Boy along with a tall black female, dressed in a sky blue Coogi dress and matching heels, gets out of the passenger side as the valet opens her door. The other valet, opens Fat Boy's door, he steps out wearing blue jeans, white Bally's and a white Coogi sweater. He makes his way over to the red carpet; where his date is standing and waiting for him, he grabs his date by the arm, escorts her down the red carpet and into the party.

A black shiny, stretch Navigator, pulls up, the valet opens the door, out steps Max, Dylan, Remy, Malibu, Asia, Kiwi, Poison and Deb. Hello ladies! Hi handsome! Deb said to the valet. Right this way ladies! The security guy says to the girls as he led them down the red carpet and into the club. Vroom-Vroom. A black 1500 Ninja pulls up to the valet, the rider steps off and hands his helmet to the valet. He takes his hand, rubs his silky black hair back, straightens his black tie and red Louis Vuitton jacket, then gives a high five to the security guard. What's up Sil, how you doing? Hey, I'm doing alright Paco, considering. Yeah, I'm sorry to hear about Vinny and Bobby man. He says to Sil as he's brushing off his jeans and checking his red Louis shoes for scuffs. Hey man, what are you going to do, shit happens. Yep! Well, be safe man, I'm going to check out this party. OK Paco, later. He walks down the red carpet and enters the club.

Vroom-Vroom-Vroom. The engine revs, as a silver; drop top Corvette, pulls up to the front of the club. The valet walks over to open the driver's door, out steps Diego; he wore Blue framed D&G glasses, black slacks, blue long sleeve D&G shirt and blue leather boots, with a solid gold heel. Diego reached in his front pocket, pulled out a knot of money, peeled off two one hundred dollar bills, handed them to the valet and says to him, with his deep Latin accent. Here you go my friend, move one of those damn cars from up front, put my shit there, can you make that happen? Yes Sir! I got you! Diego pats the valet on the back, walks down the red carpet and enters the club. The music continues to play on the outside speakers, WU-Tang's; C.R.E.A.M. is blasting through the parking lot. " Cash Rules everything around me" " Cream get the money" " Dollar, dollar bill yall" "I grew up on the crime side, the New York Times side" " Stayin alive was no jive" " At second hands, Moms bounced on ol man" " So we moved to Shaolin land". A black hummer pulled up to the valet, parks, then Steel and Jesse jumps out, dressed in all black dickie suits, white air forces and black NY fitted caps. Yeah nigga, yall bumpin that good shit right there son! Steel shouts as he walks to the red carpet. Cash rules everything around me, cream get the money! Yeah nigga, that's my joint! New York, in the fucking building! Jess, hurry your ass up nigga; let's go get some of these bitches! Jess walks over to the red carpet, then he and Steel go join the party.

A black Limo Town car, cruises up to the valet, he walks over and opens the back door. AC and Manny step out dressed in black Versace suits, Coop wore a black silk shirt, no tie, Manny sported a red silk shirt, no tie, both fellas had on black Versace dress shoes, black shades and each wore a diamond studded gold pinky ring. Denna, Sabrina and Nina step out next, wearing Red Prada dresses and black Prada shoes with 5 inch gold heels. Loon, Will and Duck get out last, dressed in black Louis Vuitton suits, with white Louis V shoes, white silk shirts, no ties and they each wore diamond studded white gold pinky rings. They join the others on the red carpet and enter the annual Christmas party to go meet their new friends and allies. Two gentlemen in black suits open the doors and escorted the crew through the crowded, chronic smoke filled club.

The dance floor was packed, elbow to elbow, then everyone seem to paused, stopped doing what they we're doing and stood there admiring AC, the new Boss and his crew. The crowd on the dance floor seem to part like the red sea as AC, Manny, Will, Loon, Duck, Denna, Nina and Sabrina made their way across the dance floor to the stage, that over looked the entire club. Red velvet rope surrounded the stage and a 16 foot long table that was draped with a cocaine white, table cloth. Eight Red Velvet, King size chairs, trimmed in Gold, sat behind the table that held 2 bottles of Dom P, 4 bottles of Moet and 2 bottles of Cristal in 8 shiny Gold and Diamond, Champagne buckets. AC and Manny took their seats in the largest two chairs that sat in the middle of the eight. Will, Loon and Sabrina sat to the left of AC while Duck, Denna and Nina sat to the right of Manny. Alongside the left wall of the dance floor, a Gold velvet rope, sectioned off a large VIP section that seated Diego, Dupree and his crew, along with Paco and fat Boy. On the other side of the floor, white leather couches lined the wall behind Red velvet rope; that sectioned off this VIP area. Rose, Steel and his crew along with Hector, Poncho and Chino occupied this section.

The others, that were there celebrating the annual company party, had no idea that they were surrounded by the crews that ran the underworld of Sin City. These ruthless individuals, had no intentions on loosing at this life of crime and would kill you before they let that happened. Diego poured himself a glass of champagne, looked over at the stage and made eye contact with AC. Coop noticed the ruby eye blinging under the flashing lights and looked his way. The two made eye contact, Diego raised his glass in a gesture to toast, AC poured himself a glass, stood up and honored the gesture. They both nod their heads and sip from their glasses, then went on about their business. AC leaned over and whispered to his Capo. Yo, go down there and let all the Drug Bosses know, we are taking Vinny and Bobby's place and that things will remain the same as they always was. He reaches in his inside jacket pocket and pulls out a white envelope. Capo, another thing too, give this envelop to Hector and tell him thanks for doing a great job. AC pats his Capo on the shoulder; Manny gets up, excuses himself from the table, walks down to the VIP and approaches Hector.

How you doing amigo? I'm good homes, what's happening. He shakes Hector's hand, pulls him in close, reaches in his inside jacket pocket, pulls out the envelop and hands it to him. Boss says, thanks for doing a great job and we will be in contact regarding some more business later. Thanks homes. He takes the envelope, puts it in his pocket, looks across the room at AC and gives him a head nod; Coop nods back. Manny pats Hector on the back then walks over to Rose and Steel, wraps his arms around both of them and escorts the two over to an empty couch. They sit down, Manny takes a bottle of open Moet from the table, pours two glasses, gives each of them one and begins to talk.

Listen up guys, because of recent events, we wanted to let you know, our crew will be running things from now on and things will remain the same. Diego will still be the only supplier; your taxes will be due the same time every week as usual no fuck ups, no second chances, do you guys understand? Sure, that's no problem pimp. How about you Rose? Yeah, I'm good Daddy; just make sure you keep my product coming. Ha-ha-ha. You don't have to worry about that sugar. Cool, then I'm alright, what's your name, are you the new Boss? I'm Manny and no I'm not the Boss but I am the Capo. Manny turns around and points at the stage. You see that bald head black guy, sitting up there on the stage in the big chair. Yeah, that's AC right? Yes it is, he's the new Boss! Wow, get the fuck out of here; the bartender got more balls than I thought he had. Hey Capo, you guys are alright with me, tell AC I said good job, we've met already, tell him I said to call me. I sure will Mam. Manny gets up, shakes both their hands and head across the dance floor to the other VIP section.

The bouncer sees Manny cutting across the floor, runs over to clear the way, pushing people aside as he cleared a walk way to the VIP section. Manny approaches the Gold roped off section, the guard lifts the rope, he walks over to Diego and introduces himself. Hey amigo, I'm Manny, AC's Capo, I've heard a lot about you, it's a pleasure to finally meet, we're looking forward to doing business with you. Nice to meet you too my friend, the pleasure is all mines. Manny looks at him, nods his head and walks over to the section where Dupree and his crew are sitting. He looks over to the other section, calls Fat Boy and Paco over. Yo Pree, can you ask your people to give us a minute? Yeah pimp, no problem. Hey fellas, we're about to talk business; excuse yourselves. The guys get up and leave the area; Fat Boy and Paco take a seat beside Dupree on the couch.

Alright fellas, here's the deal, as you know, Vinny and Bobby are no longer with us. The new Boss AC; will be running things from now on, we want to assure you that nothing is going to change, Diego will still be the only supplier, taxes will remain the same and will be due on time as usual or pay the penalties. One thing you should know, when it comes to money, the new Boss doesn't fuck around! He will erase your ass, replace you and ask questions later, can yall dig that? You don't have to worry about that shit from my side pimp, Dupree handles his business playa; believe that. Cool, let's keep it that way! Fat Boy, Paco, are we clear? Yeah man, I'm good. Fat Boy, how about you? Dude, aint no problems gone come from this end. Cool, if you guys have any questions, or concerns, make sure you talk to me first. I'm the new Capo, I will make sure everything is on the up and up, if it gets to the Boss, it will be too late for any reasoning, fuck talking! He stands up and looks at all three of them. Got that! We got it! All three gentlemen say at the same time. Good, enjoy the rest of your evening fellas, remember; call me if you come across anything you can't handle. Manny and the fellas stand up, he shakes all of their hands then heads back to his seat on the stage.

Manny follows the bouncer through the overcrowded dance floor, to the stage, walks behind the others and take his seat beside AC. Coop stands up, gets the Dj's attention, then signals for him to cut the music; the room is now silent. Hi everyone, I'm glad that you all could join us tonight for the annual Christmas party. I know all of you don't know or haven't had the chance to meet me yet, allow me to introduce myself. My name is AC, I started working for the company a few months ago, right now, I want to take time to have a moment of silence for our deceased bosses Vinny and Bobby Delgato; the two will be truly missed. They were like father figures to all of us and taught us all that you always take care of your own. Me and my friend Manny here, will be taking over all operations within the company, our other crew members up here by my side, will be running the company's other interest. I look forward to working with and meeting each and every one of you. Now that I got that out of the way, let's have a moment of silence for our beloved bosses.

The entire club goes silent for 60 seconds then AC points at the Dj to get the party started again. Alright people, this is your boy! Dj Skillz! We got 30 minutes left before the party ends, so get your drink on, mack on, smoke on and whatever else you have to get on, before it's time to get the hell on! Shout out to the new Boss, AC, we see you Big Dog! Yeah people, let's bring it back! "With so much trouble in the L.B.C." "It's kinda hard being Snoop D-O-double-G" " But I, Somehow some way, keep coming up with funky ass shit like each and every day." Yeah, let's hear it!

The crowd sings. "Rollin down the street smoking indo, sipping on gin and juice! Laaaiiiddd Back!" AC, Manny and the crew get up and head outside through the back door that was to the right of the stage. Once outside, Will starts looking for the driver, he spots him, up front, smoking on a cigarette and talking to the valet. Will leaves the others by the back entrance and walks over to the driver. Hey bro., go get the Limo; let's get the fuck out of here, its Christmas Eve and we got shit to do with our families tomorrow. Yes sir! The driver throws down his cigarette, steps on it, then runs over to get the limo. He pulls to the rear of the club, parks the limo, then runs to the back to open the door, the crew steps inside the limo. The driver closes the door and walks around to get in the driver's seat. He then cruises off the lot and turns right on to Flamingo Boulevard, as he got further and further away the red tail lights got smaller and smaller as the limo disappeared into the night among the holiday traffic.

Ring-Ring-Ring. Hello! Yo, Boss man, what's poppin? Not much, what's up Loon? Aint shit, what's the move tonight for New Year's Eve, are we still coming over to your place? Yep, as far as I know. OK, that's cool my nigga, I think me and Denna are going to tell the rest of the crew about us tonight. Oh yeah, are you sure about that? Man, they're going to find out sooner or later! Yeah, I guess you're right. Alright Boss man, I will see you later I guess. What do you want me to bring? Want you make some of that homemade salsa, like you did last time. Cool, I got you bro... Thanks man, holler at you later. Sabrina walks in the front room with her purse over her shoulder and keys in hand. Hey daddy, I will be back later tonight, I have to take my little cousin to the movies and we're getting some pizza after. OK baby, I will see you tonight. Do you need me to pick up anything for the party while I'm out? Yeah, get some red wine, maybe two bottles. OK daddy, I can do that. Thanks. Muah! He gives Sabrina a kiss before she walks out the door. Bye daddy. Later baby. He picks up the cordless phone and makes a call.

Ring-Ring. Hola! Capo! Yo, what's up Don Dada! Chillin, what time you and Sophie coming through tonight? Shit, probably around 9ish. 9ish, fool what the hell is 9ish! Man, like 9:30 or 9:40, you know what I'm saying. Man, you crazy, just say that then, talking about some damn 9ish! You smoke too much damn chronic, it got you making up words and shit. Ha-ha-ha. Fuck you AC! You know I'm right! Man, we'll see you later and tell Sabrina to bring some of that bomb ass chronic. Hell naw, that's what's wrong with your ass now. Dude, stop fucking around man, I need that smoke. Ha-ha-ha. OK man, I got you. Alright, later fool. Knock-Knock-Knock. Yeah, who is it? It's Will man! Hold on bruh, I'm coming. He walks over to unlock the door. What's up Will, hey Poison, how are you lady? Hey AC, I'm doing fine. That's good, come in guys. Will, you can put your coats in that front closet. Alright, where do you want these wings? Oh put them on the counter. Will walks over to the kitchen and placed the hot wing platter on the counter beside the chips and Hennessy.

Hey AC, where's my girl at man? Oh she had to take her cousin to the movies earlier, she should be back shortly. OK that's cool, do you have any blunts, I got some chronic. Yeah, look in that kitchen drawer, right beside the stove. Sweet, go get them for me baby. OK! Poison runs in the kitchen to find the blunts. So, is everything good with you Coop? Yeah, I'm good Will, why you ask that? I know you brother and right now, it looks like you have something on your mind. Yeah, something is bugging me but I can't put my finger on it yet, just got a funny feeling, know what I'm saying? Yep, I hate that! Well, let me know if you need anything, I always got your back brother. Thanks dub, I appreciate that bro.! No problem man, you want a drink, I'm about to fix me some of that Hen and coke. Yeah, let me get one too. Cool. Will walks over to the kitchen to fix the drinks. Knock-Knock. It's open, come in! Sophia and Manny walks in the door. Damn, is it 9ish! Ha-ha-ha! Shut up AC! Just kidding Capo! He walks over to greet them. Hey Sophie, how are you baby? AC gives her a hug then a kiss on the cheek. I'm great Cooper, how are you this New Year's eve? I'm doing better than ever; here, let me take that coat for you. Oh thank you! Sure, it's no problem, come in, get comfortable, that young lady over there is Poison, Will's friend. OK! Hello everyone! Hi Sophie! Hi Will!

Poison walks out of the kitchen and in to the den. Hi, how are you, they call me Poison but my real name is Tonya, you may call me either one. Nice to meet you Tonya! It's nice to meet you too Sophie! The two ladies go have a seat on the couch and turn on the TV; Manny walks over to the table. Hey Will, what you doing in there playa? Shit, fixing some drinks, you want one too partner? Hell yeah! Say no more, got you covered. Hey Coop! Yeah Manny, what's up? I heard Hector and the crew; made an extra 50 stacks on that hit the other day. Oh yeah, is that right? Yep, they robbed the bank and hit the targets at the same time. Damn, now that's what I call a smart gangster! Ha-ha-ha-ha. That's why we got those fools on our team, I fucking love it! I invited him over to hang out with the crew, this way; we all can get to know him a little better. Cool, that was a good idea; after all we're going to be making plenty of moves together. Will says as he's walking over to the den to deliver the drinks. Here you go guys, Hen and coke on ice. Thanks Will. Don't mention it. Sophie and Poison are on the couch getting ready to light the blunt when someone else knocks on the door.

Knock-Knock. Damn, let me put this up! You cool Poison, light that shit up baby. It's open, come in. Nina, Hector, Chino and Selena, Hector's girlfriend walks in. Homes, what's up? Hector, what's crackin homie! Nina, what's up sis, who's this young lady with you Hector? Oh, this is my girl, Selena, Selena, this is my homie AC. Hi AC. Hello Ms. Selena, nice to meet you, welcome to my home and please, make yourself comfortable. The two ladies over there are Sophie and Poison; you can join them if you want. OK, thank you! Nina, what's up sis, how are you? I'm good poppy. She gives him a hug. Hey Manny! Will! Sophie, how are you doing girl? Hey Nina, come over and hit this blunt with us. Cool, let me hang this jacket up. Here, let me have it sis, I'll get it for you. Thanks bro.! AC, this is my right hand man, Chino. What's up Chino, make yourself comfortable dog, this is Will and that's Manny, two members from our crew.

Hey homies, what's crackin? It's all good pimp, you want a drink? Fuck yeah homes. Cool, we got some Hen and coke over on the counter and there's some beer in the fridge. Thanks homes. He heads in the kitchen. Yo Chino, bring me a brew too. Alright Hector, I got you homes. I heard you came off on the hit Hector. Shit, I seen an opportunity to make some more loot and took advantage of it homes. AC puts his hand on Hector's right shoulder. Hey, that was some clever shit my nigga, we applaud you on that move. Yeah, that was a gangsta ass move, right there my man. Thanks Will. No, thank you for taking them fools out! I was just doing my job homes. Manny pulls a blunt from his top shirt pocket, lights it, takes a pull then says. So tell me home boy, did they beg for their lives? Man, those two fools were crying like some little bitches! I put them out of their misery and popped them in the back of the head; one shot homes! Hell yeah, that's how you do it brother, now we can get this money! Manny takes another pull off the spliff then passes it to Hector.

Man, it's crazy as hell out there tonight, we had to park two streets back and walk to this bitch homes. Yeah Chino, they closed off the entire strip at 9pm, it's so many people down there; it's crazy! You think it's crazy now; wait until 11pm. Knock-Knock. Come in, it's open! Duck and Asia walk in. Duck, what's up dawg? Hey Boss man, what's crackin? About to get this thing started player, that's what it is. Come in and join the party; make yourself comfortable. Hey everybody, Happy New Year, you all know Asia right? Yep, hey girl, come over and smoke this chronic with us. Here baby! Asia hands Duck her coat. Oh Duck, you can just hang it up in that closet behind you.

Cool! He turns around and puts both their jackets in the closet; Asia makes her way over to the couch to join the ladies. Here you go girl. Poison passes her the blunt. What's up Fellas! Manny, Will, Hector and Chino hold up their drinks as to toast him. What's up Man! The front door comes open. What's up motherfuckers, Loon and Denna is in the house, where's the smoke at! Denna takes off her coat and hands it to Loon. Here, take care of that poppy.

AC, where's my girl? She will be here in a few. Call her, tell her to bring some wine, I forgot to stop on the way here. I already told her to get some sis. OK cool, Loon has that salsa over there too. Thanks! Hey L, bring me that salsa man, so I can dig into these chips. Hold on playa; let me put these jackets up. Coop walks over to him and takes the salsa. Man, give me that shit, you moving too slow! Ha-ha-ha. Damn nigga, I said I was coming. He stands there holding his arms out and laughing at him. What's up fellas! What up man! All the guys yell out. Hey Loon, this is Hector and his partner Chino. Oh yeah, is this Denna cuz Hector? Yep! My nigga, what's poppin, good job on that hit playa! Thanks bro.! Yeah, no problem, you did that, welcome to the team. Coop, where's your bitch at? She will be here in a few Loon and you don't have to call her a bitch. Man whatever; you can call my girl a bitch and I want get mad. I aint mad bro., just respect my shit. Alright you're right, my bad Boss. Loon walks over to him and shakes his hand. You know I'm just fucking with you, right bro.! It's all good man, we cool.

Manny and AC walk out on the balcony to take a look at the New Year's Eve crowd and events that were taking place down below on the strip. Look at all this money down there bruh, people traveled from all over to be here tonight. All the damn hotels are sold out and you know they jacked the prices up by 50%. How much loot do you think we would get tonight Boss, if we crewed up, then went down there and started jacking fools? I'm sure we would come up Capo, hell, aint even that many police down there either. That's what I'm saying, we crew up with Hector's people, get the gats and go get paid, fuck a party! You serious, huh Capo? Hell yeah Boss! Money over Bitches all day, every day! Remember! Let me think on it playa. Hmmmm. Give them fools some time to get wasted and we hit em off guard. See, that's why you're the Boss, let's get this money!

Will and Loon walk out on the balcony to join them. What you fools out here talking about? Shit, we were looking down at all those people and started thinking. We can hit a big lick tonight if we crewed up, went down there and started jacking them fools after they got all liquored up. Will leans back against the rail and looks down at the crowd over his right shoulder. Manny, that would be a good lick. Loon walks over to the rail and looks down. Hmmm. Do you think we could crew up in time? Coop steps away from the rail, Loon hands him the blunt. Here you go dawg. He takes it, takes a pull and leans back up against the sliding glass doors. Manny, Loon and Will stand across from him leaning against the rail facing him and waiting for a response. AC takes another drag off the spliff, looks at the fellas and exhales the smoke. Ring-Ring-Ring. AC, your phone is ringing! Denna shouts.

Ring-Ring. Hey, bring me the cordless sis! Ring-Ring. Denna walks to the door and hands him the phone. Ring-Ring-Ring. Hello! What's up nigga! I got your Bitch! What! Who the fuck is this! Shut up nigga and listen! Ummmm-Ummmm. Suck it bitch! No! Stop! You hear that nigga! That's your Bitch, sucking my dick! Man fuck you, I aint got no time for games! Games! Here Bitch! Say something to your punk ass nigga! Daddy! Daddy! Sabrina! Yeah, now you get the picture nigga! Manny and the fellas shout out. Coop, who the fuck is that! He ignores them. Don't you fucking hurt her! Nigga, fuck this bitch! You got 24 hours to come up with 5 million dollars or this stinking hoe is dead son! What! Shut up nigga! 24 hours son! Have my fucking loot when I call your ass tomorrow! Hey man! Hey! No one answers, AC stands there with the phone to his ear then a dial tone comes on. Click!

In MADE II, the new crime family of Las Vegas; begin their reign over Sin City, more sex, more drugs and more violence, occur on their rise to the top. The fall of one family and rise of another comes with a huge price; will they all survive this tale of Organized Crime? What will become of Sabrina? Who kidnapped her? Can AC hold the reigns over the Devils playground? All of these questions and more; will be answered in the release of MADE II, Rise of A Family.........

PRINTHOUSE BOOKS

ATLANTA, GA

www.Printhousebooks.com

VIP INK Publishing Group, Incorporated.

Photo by Paul Lawson.

ANT BANK$ writes from his soul, built from experiencing time in the military, the streets of Vegas, the Adult industry and several other ventures that he rather not discuss. Together they all combine to make for an intriguing, innovative and prolific writer. As a reader of his work, you will never get bored or lose interest in his ability to capture you in an unforgettable tale. Thanks again for reading MADE: Sex, Drugs and Murder, The Recipe for Success. Be on the lookout for more titles from ANT BANK$ and the PrintHouse Books imprint.

149